W9-ABA-654

THE DARK DESCENT
edited by David G. Hartwell

The Color of Evil
The Medusa in the Shield
A Fabulous Formless Darkness

THE COLOR OF EVIL

The Dark Descent
Vol. 1
edited by David G. Hartwell

TOR
HORROR

A TOM DOHERTY ASSOCIATES BOOK
NEW YORK

This is a work of fiction. All the characters and events portrayed in this book are fictitious, and any resemblance to real people or events is purely coincidental.

THE COLOR OF EVIL

Copyright © 1987 by David G. Hartwell

This book first appeared as part of the Tor hardcover, THE DARK DESCENT.

A Tor Book
Published by Tom Doherty Associates, Inc.
49 West 24th Street
New York, N.Y. 10010

ISBN: 0-812-51898-5

First printing: September 1991

Printed in the United States of America

0 9 8 7 6 5 4 3 2 1

DEDICATION

To Tom Doherty and Harriet P. McDougal and the Tor Books Horror imprint, and especially Melissa Ann Singer, editor, for support and patience.

To Kathryn Cramer and Peter D. Pautz for their hard work and enthusiasm, as well as provocative discussion.

To Patricia W. Hartwell for letting the books pile up and the piles of paper fall over throughout the house and still loving me.

ACKNOWLEDGMENTS

This anthology grew out of three years of weekly discussions with Peter D. Pautz and Kathryn Cramer on the nature and virtues of horror literature, and its evolution. Peter's knowledge of the contemporary field and Kathryn's theoretical bent were seminal in the genesis of my own thoughts on what horror literature is and has become. Jack Sullivan, Kirby McCauley and Peter Straub were particularly helpful in discussing aspects of horror, and Samuel R. Delany contributed valuable insights, as well as the title for Part III. And I owe an incalculable debt to the great anthologists—from M. R. James and Dashiell Hammett, Elizabeth Bowen, Dorothy Sayers through Wise and Fraser, Boris Karloff and August Derleth to Kirby McCauley, Ramsey Campbell and Jack Sullivan—whose research and scholarship and taste guided my reading over the decades. Robert Hadji and Jessica Salmonson gave valuable support in late-night convention discussions, and the World Fantasy Convention provided an annual environment for advancing ideas in the context of the fine working writers and experts who make horror literature a vigorous and growing form in our time. Finally, my sincere thanks to Stephen King for *Danse Macabre*.

Copyright Acknowledgments

CONTENTS

INTRODUCTION TO THE DARK DESCENT

To taste the full flavor of these stories you must bring an orderly mind to them, you must have a reasonable amount of confidence, if not in what used to be called the laws of nature, at least in the currently suspected habits of nature. . . . To the truly superstitious the "weird" has only its Scotch meaning: "Something which actually takes place."

—Dashiell Hammett, *Creeps by Night*

The appeal of the spectrally macabre is generally narrow because it demands from the reader a certain degree of imagination and a capacity for detachment from everyday life. Relatively few are free enough from the spell of daily routine to respond. . . .

—H. P. Lovecraft, *Supernatural Horror in Literature*

I

O n a July Sunday morning, I was moderating a panel discussion at Necon, a small New England convention devoted to dark fantasy. The panelists included Alan Ryan, Whitley Strieber, Peter Straub, Charles L. Grant and, I believe, Les Daniels, all of them horror novelists. The theme of the discussion was literary influences, with each participant naming the horror writers he felt significant in the genesis of his career. As the minutes rolled by and the litany of names, Poe and Bradbury and Leiber and Lovecraft and Kafka and others, was uttered, I realized that except for a ritual bow to Stephen King, every single influential writer

1

named had been a short story writer. So I interrupted the panel and asked them all to spend the last few minutes commenting on my observation. What they said amounted to this: the good stuff is pretty much all short fiction.

After a few months of thought, I spent a late Halloween night with Peter Straub at the World Fantasy Convention, getting his response to my developing ideas on the recent evolution of horror from a short story to a novel genre. My belief that the long-form horror story is avant-garde and experimental, an unsolved aesthetic problem being attacked with energy and determination by Straub and King and others in our time, solidified as a result of that conversation.

But it seemed to me too early to generalize as to the nature of the new horror novel form. What, then, I asked myself, has happened to the short story? The horror story has certainly not up and vanished after 160 years of development and popularity; far from it. As an administrator of the annual World Fantasy Awards since 1975, I was aware of significant growth in short fiction in the past decade. And so the idea of this book was conceived, to conclude the era of the dominance of short-form horror with a definitive anthology that attempts to represent the entire evolution of the form to date and to describe and point out the boundaries of horror as it has been redefined in our contemporary field. For it seemed apparent to me that the conventional approach to horror codified by the great anthologies of the 1940s is obsolete, was indeed becoming obsolete as those books were published, and has persisted to the detriment of a clearer understanding of the literature to the present. It has persisted to the point where fans of horror fiction most often restrict their reading to books and stories given the imprimatur of a horror category label, thus missing some of the finest pleasures of this century in that fictional mode. I have gathered as many as could be confined within one huge volume here in *The Dark Descent*, with the intent of clearing the air and broadening future considerations of horror.

Fear has its own aesthetic—as Le Fanu, Henry James, Montagu James and Walter de la Mare have repeatedly shown—and also its own propriety. A story dealing in fear ought, ideally, to be kept at a certain pitch. And that austere other world, the world of the ghost, should inspire, when it impacts on our own, not so much revulsion or shock as a sort of awe.

—Elizabeth Bowen, *The Second Ghost Book*

The one test of the really weird is simply this—whether or not there be excited in the reader a profound sense of dread, and of contact with unknown spheres and powers.

—H. P. Lovecraft, *Supernatural Horror in Literature*

II The Evolution of Horror Fiction

For more than 150 years horror fiction has been a vital component of English and American literature, invented with the short story form itself and contributing intimately to the evolution of the short story. Until the last decade, the dominant literary form of horror fiction was the short story and novella. This is simply no longer the case. Shortly after the beginning of the 1970s, within a very few years, the novel form assumed the position of leadership. First came a scattering of exceptionally popular novels—*Rosemary's Baby, The Other, The Exorcist, The Mephisto Waltz*, with attendant film successes—then, in 1973, the deluge, with Stephen King on the crest of the wave, altering the nature of horror fiction for the foreseeable future and sweeping along with it all the living generations of short fiction writers. Very few writers of horror fiction, young or old, resisted the commercial or aesthetic temptation to expand into the novel form, leading to the creation of some of the best horror novels of all time as well as a large amount of popular trash rushed into print. The models for these works were the previous bestsellers, popular films and the short fiction masterpieces of previous decades.

When the tide ebbed in the 1980s, much of the trash was left dead in the backlists of paperback publishers, but the horror novel had become firmly established. This is significant from a number of perspectives. Rapid evolution and experimentation were encouraged. All kinds of horror literature benefited from the incorporation of every conceivable element of horrific effect and technique from other literature and film and video and comics.

The most useful and provocative view we can take on the horror novel in recent years is that it constitutes an avant-garde and experimental literary form which attempts to translate the horrific effects previously thought to be the nearly exclusive domain of the short forms into newly conceived long forms that maintain the proper atmosphere and effects. Certainly isolated examples of more or less successful novel-length horror fiction exist, from *Frankenstein* and *Dracula* to *The Haunting of Hill House*, but they are comparatively infrequent next to the constant, rich proliferation and development of horror in shorter forms in every decade from Poe to the present. The horror novels of the past do not in aggregate form a body of traditional literature and technique from which the present novels spring and upon which they depend.

It is evident both from the recent novels themselves and from the public statements of many of the writers that Stephen King, Peter Straub and Ramsey Campbell, and a number of other leading novelists, have been discussing among themselves—and trying to solve in their works—the perceived problems of developing the horror novel into a sophisticated and effective form. In so doing, they have highlighted the desirability of a volume such as *The Dark Descent*, which represents the context from which the literature springs and attempts to elucidate the whole surround of horror today.

Horror novels grow to a very large extent out of the varied

and highly evolved novellas and short stories exemplified in this book. Our perceptions of the nature of horror literature have been changing and evolving rapidly in recent decades, to the point where a compilation of the horror story, organized according to new principles, is needed to manifest the broadened nature of the literature.

Before proceeding in the next section to begin an anatomy of horror, it is interesting to note that there has been a renewed fashion for horror in every decade since the First World War, but this is the first such "revival" that has produced numerous novels.

There was a general increase in horror, particularly the ghost story, in the 1920s under the influence of M. R. James, both a prominent writer and anthologist, and such masters as Algernon Blackwood, Walter de la Mare, Edith Wharton and others. At that time the great horror magazine, *Weird Tales*, was founded in the U.S. In the 1930s, the dark fantasy story or weird tale became prominent, influenced by the magazine mentioned above, the growth of the H. P. Lovecraft circle of writers, and a proliferation of anthologies, either in series or as huge compendiums celebrating the first century of horror fiction. After the films and books of the 1930s, the early 1940s produced the finest "great works" collections, epitomized by *And the Darkness Falls*, edited by Boris Karloff, and *Great Tales of Terror and the Supernatural*, edited by Herbert Wise and Phyllis Fraser; and Arkham House, the great specialty publisher devoted to this day to bringing into print collections by great horror authors, was founded by writer Donald Wandrei to print the collected works of H. P. Lovecraft. After the war came the science fiction horrors of the 1950s, in all those monster films and in the works of Richard Matheson, Jack Finney, Theodore Sturgeon and Ray Bradbury. In the early sixties we had the craze for "junk food" paperback horror anthologies and collections, under the advent of the midnight horror movie boom on TV. But as we remarked above, short fiction always remained at the forefront. Even the novelists were famous for their short stories.

A lot has changed.

Atmosphere is the all-important thing, for the final criterion of authenticity is not the dovetailing of a plot but the creation of a given sensation.

—H. P. Lovecraft, *Supernatural Horror in Literature*

Much as we ask for it, the *frisson* of horror, among the many oddities of our emotional life, is one of the oddest. For one thing, it is usually a response to something that is not there. Under normal circumstances, that is, it attends only such things as nightmares, phobias and literature. In that respect it is unlike terror, which is extreme and sudden fear in the face of a material threat. . . . The terror can be dissipated by a round of buckshot. Horror, on the other hand, is fascinated dread in the presence of an immaterial cause. The frights of nightmares cannot be dissipated by a round of buckshot; to flee them is to run into them at every turn.

—Sigmund Freud, *The Uncanny*

III   What It Is

Sigmund Freud remarked that we immediately recognize scenes that are supposed to provoke horror, ''even if they actually provoke titters.'' It seems to me, however, that horror fiction has usually been linked to or categorized by manifest signs in texts, and this has caused more than a little confusion among commentators over the years. Names such

as weird tales, gothic tales, terror tales, ghost stories, supernatural tales, macabre stories—all clustered around the principle of a real or implied or fake intrusion of the supernatural
into the natural world, an intrusion which arouses fear—have
been used as appellations for the whole body of literature,
sometimes interchangeably by the same writer. So often, and
in so many of the best works, has the intrusion been a ghost,
that nearly half the time you will find "horror story" and
"ghost story" used interchangeably. And this is so in spite
of the acknowledged fact that supernatural horror in literature
embodies many manifestations (from demons to vampires to
werewolves to pagan gods and more) and, further, that ghosts
are recognizably not supposed to horrify in a fair number of
ghost stories.

J. A. Cuddon, a thorough scholar, has traced the early
connections between ghost and horror stories from the 1820s
to the 1870s, viewing them as originally separable: "The
growth of the ghost story and the horror story in this mid-
century period tended to coalesce; indeed, it is difficult to
establish objective criteria by which to distinguish between
the two. A taxonomical approach invariably begins to break
down at an early stage. . . . On balance, it is probable that a
ghost story will contain an element of horror." Jack Sullivan,
another distinguished scholar and anthologist, sums up the
problems of definition and terminology thusly: "We find ourselves in a tangled morass of definitions and permutations
that grows as relentlessly as the fungus in the House of
Usher." Sullivan chooses "ghost story" as generic, presumably to have one leg to stand on facing in each direction.

We choose "horror" as our term, both in accordance with
the usage of the marketplace (Tor Books has a Tor Horror
line; horror is a label for the marketing category under which
novels and collections appear), and because it points toward
a transaction between the reader and the text that is the es-
sence of the experience of reading horror fiction, and not anything contained within that text (such as a ghost, literal or
implied). And moreover, H. P. Lovecraft, the theoretician

and critic who most carefully described the literature in his *Supernatural Horror in Literature*, who was certainly the most important American writer of horror fiction in the first half of this century, has to the best of my memory not a single conventional ghost story in the corpus of his works.

It is Lovecraft's essay that provides the keystone upon which any architecture of horror must be built: atmosphere. And it seems to me that Freud is in accord. What this means is that you can experience true horror in, potentially, any work of fiction, be it a western, a contemporary gothic, science fiction, mystery, whatever category of content the writer may choose. A work may be a horror story (and indeed included in this anthology) no matter what, as long as the atmosphere allows. This means that horror is set free from the supernatural, that it is unnecessary for the story to contain any overt or implied device or manifestation whatsoever. The emotional transaction is paramount and definitive, and we recognize its presence even when it doesn't work as it is supposed to.

> To them [people who don't read horror] it is a kind of pornography, inducing horripilation instead of erection. And the reader who appears to relish such sensations— why he's an emotional masochist, the slave of an unholy drug, a decadent psychotic beast.

—David Aylward, *Revenge of the Past*

First, the longing for mystic experience which seems always to manifest itself in periods of social confusion, when political progress is blocked: as soon as we feel that our own world has failed us, we try to find evidence for another world; second, the instinct to inoculate ourselves against panic at the real horrors loose on the earth . . . by injections of imagery horror, which soothe us with the momentary illusion that the forces of madness and murder may be tamed and compelled to provide us with a mere dramatic entertainment.

—Edmund Wilson, *A Literary Chronicle*

I used to read horror when I was depressed to jump-start my emotions—but it only gave me temporary relief.

—Kathryn Cramer (personal correspondence)

It proves that the tale of horror and/or the supernatural *is* serious, *is* important, *is* necessary . . . not only to those human beings who read to think, but to those who read to feel; the volume may even go a certain distance toward proving the idea that, as this mad century races toward its conclusion—a conclusion which seems ever more ominous and ever more absurd—it may be the most important and useful form of fiction which the moral writer may command.

—Stephen King, Introduction to *The Arbor House Treasury of Horror and the Supernatural*

IV The Death of Horror

The death of the novel and the death of the short story are literary topics we joke about, so it should come as no particular surprise that a recent, and otherwise excellent, collection of essays on supernatural fiction in America from 1820–1920 states that supernatural fiction died around 1920 (''dematerialized''), to be replaced by psychoanalysis, which took over its function. Now it seems to me surprising to maintain that fiction that embodies psychological truth in metaphor is replaceable by science—it sounds rather too much like replacing painting with photography. Yet this is only a recent example of the obituary approach, an effective gambit when dealing with material you wish to exterminate, and often used by self-appointed arbiters of taste.

Let's resurrect the great Modernist critic, Edmund Wilson, for a few minutes. Wilson wrote an essay on horror in the early 1940s that challenged the whole canon of significant works established by the anthologists of the 1930s and '40s, from Dorothy Sayers and M. R. James and Hugh Walpole and Marjorie Bowen to Wise and Fraser, and Karloff. Wilson proposed his own list of masterpieces, from Poe and Gogol ("the greatest master") and Melville and Turgenev through Hardy, Stevenson, Kipling, Conrad's *The Heart of Darkness* and Henry James' *The Turn of the Screw* to Walter de la Mare and, ultimately, Kafka ("he went straight for the morbidities of the psyche"). He, Wilson, seems to be reaching toward a redefinition of horror literature, but unfortunately his essay vibrates with the discomfort of the humanist and rationalist confronting the supernatural. He rejects nearly every classic story in the horror canon and every single writer principally known for work in the field, reserving particular antipathy for H. P. Lovecraft, the anti-Modernist (to whom he devoted a whole separate essay of demolition).

Wilson's comments on Kafka are instructive. Kafka's "visions of moral horror" are "narratives that compel our attention, and fantasies that generate more shudders than the whole of Algernon Blackwood or M. R. James combined." Kafka's characters "have turned into the enchanted denizens of a world in which, prosaic though it is, we can find no firm foothold in reality and in which we can never even be certain whether souls are being saved or damned . . . he went straight for the morbidities of the psyche with none of the puppetry of specters and devils that earlier writers still carried with them." Wilson's view of the evolution of horror is implicit in these comments. He sees the literature as evolving in a linear fashion into fantasies of the psyche removed entirely from supernatural trappings. Any audience interested in these trappings is regressive. He sees no value to a modern reader in obsolete fiction.

Since Wilson's presupposition is that the evolution of horror ended with Kafka, his theory of horror reading among his contemporaries—that they are indulging in a "revived" taste for an obsolete form—allows him to start from the premise that the ghost story is dead, that it died with the advent of the electric light, and to conclude immediately that contemporary versions are doomed attempts to revive the corpse of the form. Sound familiar? It's the familiar "death of literature" obituary approach. Well, back to the grave, Edmund. You're dead, and horror literature is alive and well, happily evolving and diversifying.

But Wilson's approach to the horror canon was and remains generally stimulating. For it appears that as horror has evolved in this century it has grown significantly in the areas of "the morbidities of the psyche" and fantasies of "a world in which, prosaic though it is, we can find no firm foothold in reality."

> In order to achieve the fantastic, it is neither necessary nor sufficient to portray extraordinary things. The strangest event will enter into the order of the universe if it is alone in a world governed by laws. . . . You cannot impose limits on the fantastic; either it does not exist at all, or else it extends throughout the universe. It is an entire world in which things manifest a captive, tormented thought, a thought both whimsical and enchained, that gnaws away from below at the mechanism's links without ever managing to express itself. In this world, matter is never entirely matter, since it offers only a constantly frustrated attempt at determinism, and mind is never completely mind, because it has fallen into slavery and has been impregnated and dulled by matter. All is woe. Things suffer and tend towards inertia, without ever attaining it; the debased, enslaved mind unsuccessfully strives toward consciousness and freedom.

> —Jean-Paul Sartre, *AMINADAB or The Fantastic Considered as a Language*

V   The Three Streams

We return to the life and state of horror fiction in the present. Contemporary horror fiction occurs in three streams, in three principal modes or clusters of emphasis: 1. moral allegorical 2. psychological metaphor 3. fantastic. The stories in this anthology are separated according to these categories. These modes are not mutually exclusive, but usually a matter of emphasis along a spectrum from the overtly moral at one extreme to the nearly totally ambiguous at the other, with human psychology always a significant factor but only sometimes the principal focus. Perhaps we might usefully imagine them as three currents in the same ocean.

Stories that cluster at the first pole are characteristically supernatural fiction, most usually about the intrusion of supernatural evil into consensus reality, most often about the horrid and colorful special effects of evil. These are the stories of children possessed by demons, of hauntings by evil ghosts from the past (most ghost stories), stories of bad places (where evil persists from past times), of witchcraft and satanism. In our day they are often written and read by lapsed Christians, who have lost their firm belief in good but still have a discomforting belief in evil. Stories in this stream imply or state the Manichean universe that is so difficult to perceive in everyday life, wherein evil is so evident, horror so common that we are left with our sensitivities partly or fully deadened to it in our post-Holocaust, post-Vietnam, six-o'clock news era. A strong extra-literary appeal of such fiction, it seems to me, is to jump-start the readers' deadened emotional sensitivities.

And the moral allegory has its significant extra-literary appeal in itself to that large audience that desires the attribution of a moral calculus (usually teleological) deriving from ultimate and metaphysical forms of good and evil behind events in an everyday reality. Ginjer Buchanan says that "all the best horror is written by lapsed Catholics."

In speaking of stories and novels in this first stream, we are speaking of the most popular form of horror fiction today, the commercial bestseller lineage of *Rosemary's Baby* and *The Exorcist*, and a majority of the works of Stephen King. These stories are taken to the heart of the commercial-category audience that is characteristically style-deaf (regardless of the excellence of some of the works), the audience that requires repeated doses of such fiction for its emotional effect to persist. This stream is the center of category horror publishing.

The second group of horror stories, stories of aberrant human psychology embodied metaphorically, may be either purely supernatural, such as *Dracula*, or purely psychological, such as Robert Bloch's *Psycho*. What characterizes them as a group is the monster at the center, from the monster of Frankenstein, to Carmilla, to the chain-saw murderer—an overtly abnormal human or creature, from whose acts and on account of whose being the horror arises. D. H. Lawrence's little boy, Faulkner's Emily, and, more subtly, the New Yorker of Henry James' "The Jolly Corner" show the extent to which this stream interpenetrates and blends with the mainstream of psychological fiction in this century. Both Lovecraft and Edmund Wilson, from differing perspectives, see Joseph Conrad's *The Heart of Darkness* as essentially horror fiction. There has been strong resistance on the part of critics, from Wilson to the present, to admitting nonsupernatural psychological horror into consideration of the field, allowing many to declare the field a dead issue for contemporary literature, of antiquarian interest only since the 1930s. This trend was probably aided by the superficial examination of the antiquarianism of both M. R. James and H. P. Lovecraft.

But by 1939 an extremely significant transition is apparent, particularly in the U.S. *Weird Tales* and the Lovecraft circle of writers, as well as the popular films, had made horror a vigorous part of popular culture, had built a large audience among the generally nonliterary readership for pulp fiction, a "lower-class" audience. And in 1939 John W. Campbell, the famous science fiction editor, founded the revolutionary pulp fantasy magazine, *Unknown*. From 1923 to 1939, the leading source of horror and supernatural fiction in the English language was *Weird Tales*, publishing all traditional styles but tending toward the florid and antiquarian. *Unknown* was an aesthetic break with traditional horror fiction. Campbell demanded stories with contemporary, particularly urban, settings, told in clear, unornamented prose style. *Unknown* featured stories by all the young science fiction writers whose work was changing that genre in Campbell's *Astounding*. Alfred Bester, Eric Frank Russell, Robert A. Heinlein, A. E. Van Vogt, L. Ron Hubbard and others, particularly such fantasists as Theodore Sturgeon, Jane Rice, Anthony Boucher, Fredric Brown and Fritz Leiber.

The stories tended to focus equally on the supernatural and the psychological. Psychology was often quite overtly the underpinning for horror, as in, for example, Hubbard's "He Didn't Like Cats," in which there is an extended discussion between the two supporting characters as to whether the central character's problem is supernatural or psychological . . . and we never know, for either way he's doomed. *Unknown* broke the dominance of *Weird Tales* and influenced such significant young talents as Ray Bradbury and Shirley Jackson. The magazine encouraged the genrification of certain types of psychological fiction and, at the same time, crossbred a good bit of horror into the growing science fiction field. This reinforced a cultural trend apparent in the monster and mad scientist films of the 1930s, giving us the enormous spawn of SF/horror films of the 1950s and beyond.

It is interesting to note that as our perceptions of horror fiction and what the term includes change over the decades, differing works seem to fall naturally into or out of the category. The possibilities of psychological horror seem in the end to blur distinctions, and there is no question that horror is becoming ever more inclusive.

Stories of the third stream have at their center ambiguity as to the nature of reality, and it is this very ambiguity that

generates the horrific effects. Often there is an overtly supernatural (or certainly abnormal) occurrence, but we know of
it only by allusion. Often, essential elements are left unde-
scribed so that, for instance, we do not know whether there
was really a ghost or not. But the difference is not merely
supernatural versus psychological explanation: third stream
stories lack any explanation that makes sense in everyday
reality—we don't know, and that doubt disturbs us, horrifies
us. This is the fiction to which Sartre's analysis alludes, the
fantastic. At its extreme, from Kafka to the present, it blends
indistinguishably with magic realism, the surreal, the absurd,
all the fictions that confront reality through paradoxical distance. It is the fiction of radical doubt. Thomas M. Disch
once remarked that Poe can profitably be considered as a
contemporary of Kierkegaard, and it is evident that this
stream develops from the beginnings of horror fiction in the
short story. In the contemporary field it is a major current.

Third stream stories tend to cross all category lines but
usually they do not use the conventional supernatural as a
distancing device. While most horror fiction declares itself at
some point as violating the laws of nature, the fantastic worlds
of third stream fiction use as a principal device what Sartre
has called the language of the fantastic.

At the end of a horror story, the reader is left with a new
perception of the nature of reality. In the moral allegory
strain, the point seems to be that this is what reality was and
has been all along (i.e., literally a world in which supernatural forces are at work) only you couldn't or wouldn't recognize it. Psychological metaphor stories basically use the
intrusion of abnormality to release repressed or unarticulated
psychological states. In her book, *Powers of Horror*, critic
Julia Kristeva says that horror deals with material just on the
edge of repression but not entirely repressed and inaccessi-
ble. Stories from our second stream use the heightening effect
of the monstrously abnormal to achieve this release. Third
stream stories maintain the pretense of everyday reality only
to annihilate it, leaving us with another world entirely, one

in which we are disturbingly imprisoned. It is in perceiving the changed reality and its nature that the pleasure and illumination of third stream stories lies, that raises this part of horror fiction above the literary level of most of its generic relations. So the transaction between the reader and the text that identifies all horror fiction is to an extent modified in third stream stories (there is rarely, if ever, any terror), making them more difficult to classify and identify than even the borderline cases in the psychological category. Gene Wolfe's "Seven American Nights" is, in my opinion, a story on the borderline of third stream, deeply disturbing but not conventionally horrifying. The mass horror audience is not much taken with third stream stories, regardless of craft or literary merit, because they modify the emotional jolt.

> Although the manifest images of horror fiction are legion, their latent meanings are few. Readers and writers of horror fiction, like those of all the popular genres, seem under a compulsion to repeat. Certainly the needs satisfied by horror fiction are recurrent and ineradicable.
>
> —George Stade, *The New York Times*,
>   Oct. 27, 1985

> I recognize terror as the finest emotion and so I will try to terrorize the reader. But if I find that I cannot terrify, I will try to horrify, and if I find that I cannot horrify, I'll go for the gross-out.
>
> —Stephen King, *Danse Macabre*

VI The Dark Descent

The descent of horror fiction from its origins in the nineteenth century to the many and sophisticated forms of the contemporary field has taken place in shorter stories. Now that the novel has taken over, the major writers are unlikely to devote their principal efforts to short fiction. So we have reached a point in the evolution of this literary mode at which we can take stock of its achievements in short fiction and assess its qualities and contributions to all of literature. The stories assembled in this book are divided according to the three streams we have identified, both to provide extended examples and to provoke further discussion. The short story is vigorously alive in horror today, in magazines, anthologies, and collections. Let it, for a moment, occupy the center of your attention. The best short fiction in modern horror is the equal of the best of all times and places.

Stephen King

THE REACH

Stephen King is the single most popular writer of horror fiction since Charles Dickens; one of the most popular writers of fiction in the English language today. He is a pop culture phenomenon, the king of horror just as Elvis Presley was the king of rock and roll. He has millions of fans. He has written the best book on contemporary horror, *Danse Macabre*, full of enthusiasm for the horrific effects of radio, film, television, comics, and stories, and best of all sympathetic and illuminating comments on the works of living writers, with extensive comments from the writers themselves often provided. King's eclectic taste and willingness to respond to a variety of styles and approaches points out rich pathways for broadening our conceptions of the nature of horror stories and their virtues. And then there are the stories and novels: *Salem's Lot* and *Carrie*, *The Shining* and *The Stand*, *Night Shift* and *Skeleton Crew* and more each year. King by precept and example is the greatest force for change in horror literature in our time, unfettered by category boundaries. Whatever he writes is mainstream fiction. His example has drawn nearly every short fiction writer of the past decade into attempting the novel form, creating a publishing boom and a fertile chaos of creativity that has outlasted the boom. "The Reach," originally published as "Do the Dead Sing," is often considered his best short story. It is a work of unusual subtlety and sentiment, a ghost story of love and death, a virtuoso performance in which the horror is distanced but underpins the whole. It represents the theme of the first section of this book, embodying King's feeling that horror fiction "may be the most important and useful form of fiction which the moral writer may command."

"The Reach was wider in those days," Stella Flanders told her great-grandchildren in the last summer of her life, the summer before she began to see ghosts. The children looked at her with wide, silent eyes, and her son, Alden, turned from his seat on the porch where he was whittling. It was Sunday, and Alden wouldn't take his boat out on Sundays no matter how high the price of lobster was.

"What do you mean, Gram?" Tommy asked, but the old woman did not answer. She only sat in her rocker by the cold stove, her slippers bumping placidly on the floor.

Tommy asked his mother: "What does she mean?"

Lois only shook her head, smiled, and sent them out with pots to pick berries.

Stella thought: She's forgot. Or did she ever know?

The Reach had been wider in those days. If anyone knew it was so, that person was Stella Flanders. She had been born in 1884, she was the oldest resident of Goat Island, and she had never once in her life been to the mainland.

Do you love? This question had begun to plague her, and she did not even know what it meant.

Fall set in, a cold fall without the necessary rain to bring a really fine color to the trees, either on Goat or on Raccoon Head across the Reach. The wind blew long, cold notes that fall, and Stella felt each note resonate in her heart.

On November 19, when the first flurries came swirling down out of a sky the color of white chrome, Stella celebrated her birthday. Most of the village turned out. Hattie

Stoddard came, whose mother had died of pleurisy in 1954 and whose father had been lost with the *Dancer* in 1941. Richard and Mary Dodge came, Richard moving slowly up the path on his cane, his arthritis riding him like an invisible passenger. Sarah Havelock came, of course; Sarah's mother Annabelle had been Stella's best friend. They had gone to the island school together, grades one to eight, and Annabelle had married Tommy Frane, who had pulled her hair in the fifth grade and made her cry, just as Stella had married Bill Flanders, who had once knocked all of her schoolbooks out of her arms and into the mud (but she had managed not to cry). Now both Annabelle and Tommy were gone and Sarah was the only one of their seven children still on the island. *Her* husband, George Havelock, who had been known to everyone as Big George, had died a nasty death over on the mainland in 1967, the year there was no fishing. An ax had slipped in Big George's hand, there had been blood—too much of it!—and an island funeral three days later. And when Sarah came in to Stella's party and cried, "Happy birthday, Gram!" Stella hugged her tight and closed her eyes

(do you do you love?)

but she did not cry.

There was a tremendous birthday cake. Hattie had made it with her best friend, Vera Spruce. The assembled company bellowed out "Happy Birthday to You" in a combined voice that was loud enough to drown out the wind . . . for a little while, anyway. Even Alden sang, who in the normal course of events would sing only "Onward, Christian Soldiers" and the doxology in church and would mouth the words of all the rest with his head hunched and his big old jug ears just as red as tomatoes. There were ninety-five candles on Stella's cake, and even over the singing she heard the wind, although her hearing was not what it once had been.

She thought the wind was calling her name.

"I was not the only one," she would have told Lois's children if she could. *"In my day there were many that lived and*

died on the island. There was no mail boat in those days;
Bull Symes used to bring the mail when there was mail. There
was no ferry, either. If you had business on the Head, your
man took you in the lobster boat. So far as I know, there
wasn't a flushing toilet on the island until 1946. '*Twas Bull's*
boy Harold that put in the first one the year after the heart
attack carried Bull off while he was out dragging traps. I
remember seeing them bring Bull home. I remember that they
brought him up wrapped in a tarpaulin, and how one of his
green boots poked out. I remember . . .''

And they would say: ''What, Gram? What do you remember?''

How would she answer them? Was there more?

On the first day of winter, a month or so after the birthday
party, Stella opened the back door to get stovewood and discovered a dead sparrow on the back stoop. She bent down
carefully, picked it up by one foot, and looked at it.

''Frozen,'' she announced, and something inside her spoke
another word. It had been forty years since she had seen a
frozen bird—1938. The year the Reach had frozen.

Shuddering, pulling her coat closer, she threw the dead
sparrow in the old rusty incinerator as she went by it. The
day was cold. The sky was a clear, deep blue. On the night
of her birthday four inches of snow had fallen, had melted,
and no more had come since then. ''Got to come soon,''
Larry McKeen down at the Goat Island Store said sagely, as
if daring winter to stay away.

Stella got to the woodpile, picked herself an armload and
carried it back to the house. Her shadow, crisp and clean,
followed her.

As she reached the back door, where the sparrow had
fallen, Bill spoke to her—but the cancer had taken Bill twelve
years before. ''Stella,'' Bill said, and she saw his shadow fall
beside her, longer but just as clear-cut, the shadow-bill of his
shadow-cap twisted jauntily off to one side just as he had

always worn it. Stella felt a scream lodged in her throat. It was too large to touch her lips.

"Stella," he said again, "when you comin across to the mainland? We'll get Norm Jolley's old Ford and go down to Bean's in Freeport just for a lark. What do you say?"

She wheeled, almost dropping her wood, and there was no one there. Just the dooryard sloping down to the hill, then the wild white grass, and beyond all, at the edge of everything, clear-cut and somehow magnified, the Reach . . . and the mainland beyond it.

"Gram, what's the Reach?" Lona might have asked . . . although she never had. And she would have given them the answer any fisherman knew by rote: a Reach is a body of water between two bodies of land, a body of water which is open at either end. The old lobsterman's joke went like this: know how to read y'compass when the fog comes, boys; between Jonesport and London there's a mighty long Reach.

"Reach is the water between the island and the mainland," she might have amplified, giving them molasses cookies and hot tea laced with sugar. "I know that much. I know it as well as my husband's name . . . and how he used to wear his hat."

"Gram?" Lona would say. "How come you never been across the Reach?"

"Honey," she would say, "I never saw any reason to go."

In January, two months after the birthday party, the Reach froze for the first time since 1938. The radio warned islanders and mainlanders alike not to trust the ice, but Stewie McClelland and Russell Bowie took Stewie's Bombardier Skiddoo out anyway after a long afternoon spent drinking Apple Zapple wine, and sure enough, the skiddoo went into the Reach. Stewie managed to crawl out (although he lost one foot to frostbite). The Reach took Russell Bowie and carried him away.

* * *

That January 25 there was a memorial service for Russell. Stella went on her son Alden's arm, and he mouthed the words to the hymns and boomed out the doxology in his great tuneless voice before the benediction. Stella sat afterward with Sarah Havelock and Hattie Stoddard and Vera Spruce in the glow of the wood fire in the town-hall basement. A going-away party for Russell was being held, complete with Za-Rex punch and nice little cream-cheese sandwiches cut into triangles. The men, of course, kept wandering out back for a nip of something a bit stronger than Za-Rex. Russell Bowie's new widow sat red-eyed and stunned beside Ewell Mc-Cracken, the minister. She was seven months big with child—it would be her fifth—and Stella, half-dozing in the heat of the woodstove, thought: *She'll be crossing the Reach soon enough, I guess. She'll move to Freeport or Lewiston and go for a waitress, I guess.*

She looked around at Vera and Hattie, to see what the discussion was.

"No, I didn't hear," Hattie said. "What *did* Freddy say?"

They were talking about Freddy Dinsmore, the oldest man on the island (two years younger'n me, though, Stella thought with some satisfaction), who had sold out his store to Larry McKeen in 1960 and now lived on his retirement.

"Said he'd never seen such a winter," Vera said, taking out her knitting. "He says it is going to make people sick."

Sarah Havelock looked at Stella, and asked if Stella had ever seen such a winter. There had been no snow since that first little bit; the ground lay crisp and bare and brown. The day before, Stella had walked thirty paces into the back field, holding her right hand level at the height of her thigh, and the grass there had snapped in a neat row with a sound like breaking glass.

"No," Stella said. "The Reach froze in '38, but there was snow that year. Do you remember Bull Symes, Hattie?"

Hattie laughed. "I think I still have the black-and-blue he gave me on my sit-upon at the New Year Eve's party in '53. He pinched me *that* hard. What about him?"

"Bull and my own man walked across to the mainland that year," Stella said. "That February of 1938. Strapped on snowshoes, walked across to Dorrit's Tavern on the Head, had them each a shot of whiskey, and walked back. They asked me to come along. They were like two little boys off to the sliding with a toboggan between them."

They were looking at her, touched by the wonder of it. Even Vera was looking at her wide-eyed, and Vera had surely heard the tale before. If you believed the stories, Bull and Vera had once played some house together, although it was hard, looking at Vera now, to believe she had ever been so young.

"And you didn't go?" Sarah asked, perhaps seeing the reach of the Reach in her mind's eye, so white it was almost blue in the heatless winter sunshine, the sparkle of the snow crystals, the mainland drawing closer, walking across, yes, walking across the ocean just like Jesus-out-of-the-boat, leaving the island for the one and only time in your life on *foot*—

"No," Stella said. Suddenly she wished she had brought her own knitting. "I didn't go with them."

"Why *not*?" Hattie asked, almost indignantly.

"It was washday," Stella almost snapped, and then Missy Bowie, Russell's widow, broke into loud, braying sobs. Stella looked over and there sat Bill Flanders in his red-and-black-checked jacket, hat cocked to one side, smoking a Herbert Tareyton with another tucked behind his ear for later. She felt her heart leap into her chest and choke between beats.

She made noise, but just then a knot popped like a rifle shot in the stove, and neither of the other ladies heard.

"Poor *thing*," Sarah nearly cooed.

"Well shut of that good-for-nothing," Hattie grunted. She searched for the grim depth of the truth concerning the departed Russell Bowie and found it: "Little more than a tramp for pay, that man. She's well out of *that* two-hoss trace."

Stella barely heard these things. There sat Bill, close enough to the Reverend McCracken to have tweaked his nose if he so had a mind; he looked no more than forty, his eyes barely marked by the crow's-feet that had later sunk so deep, wearing his flannel pants and his gum-rubber boots with the gray wool socks folded neatly down over the tops.

"We're waitin on you, Stel," he said. "You come on across and see the mainland. You won't need no snowshoes this year."

There he sat in the town-hall basement, big as Billy-be-damned, and then another knot exploded in the stove and he was gone. And the Reverend McCracken went on comforting Missy Bowie as if nothing had happened.

That night Vera called up Annie Phillips on the phone, and in the course of the conversation mentioned to Annie that Stella Flanders didn't look well, not at all well.

"Alden would have a scratch of a job getting her off-island if she took sick," Annie said. Annie liked Alden because her own son Toby had told her Alden would take nothing stronger than beer. Annie was strictly temperance, herself.

"Wouldn't get her off 'tall unless she was in a coma," Vera said, pronouncing the word in the downeast fashion: *comer*. "When Stella says 'Frog,' Alden jumps. Alden ain't but half-bright, you know. Stella pretty much runs him."

"Oh, ayuh?" Annie said.

Just then there was a metallic crackling sound on the line. Vera could hear Annie Phillips for a moment longer—not the words, just the sound of her voice going on behind the crackling—and then there was nothing. The wind had gusted up high and the phone lines had gone down, maybe into Godlin's Pond or maybe down by Borrow's Cove, where they went into the Reach sheathed in rubber. It was possible that they had gone down on the other side, on the Head . . . and some might even have said (only half-joking) that Russell Bowie had reached up a cold hand to snap the cable, just for the hell of it.

Not 700 feet away Stella Flanders lay under her puzzle-quilt and listened to the dubious music of Alden's snores in the other room. She listened to Alden so she wouldn't have to listen to the wind . . . but she heard the wind anyway, oh yes, coming across the frozen expanse of the Reach, a mile and a half of water that was now overplated with ice, ice with lobsters down below, and groupers, and perhaps the twisting, dancing body of Russell Bowie, who used to come each April with his old Rogers rototiller and turn her garden.

Who'll turn the earth this April? she wondered as she lay cold and curled under her puzzle-quilt. And as a dream in a dream, her voice answered her voice: *Do you love?* The wind gusted, rattling the storm window. It seemed that the storm window was talking to her, but she turned her face away from its words. And did not cry.

"But Gram," Lona would press (she never gave up, not that one, she was like her mom, and her grandmother before her), "you still haven't told why you never went across."

"Why, child, I have always had everything I wanted right here on Goat."

"But it's so small. We live in Portland. There's buses, Gram!"

"I see enough of what goes on in cities on the TV. I guess I'll stay where I am."

Hal was younger, but somehow more intuitive; he would not press her as his sister might, but his question would go closer to the heart of things: "You never wanted to go across, Gram? Never?"

And she would lean toward him, and take his small hands, and tell him how her mother and father had come to the island shortly after they were married, and how Bull Symes's grandfather had taken Stella's father as a 'prentice on his boat. She would tell him how her mother had conceived four times but one of her babies had miscarried and another had died a week after birth—she would have left the island if they could have saved it at the mainland hospital, but of course it was over before that was even thought of.

She would tell them that Bill had delivered Jane, their grandmother, but not that when it was over he had gone into

*the bathroom and first puked and then wept like a hysterical
woman who had her monthlies p'ticularly bad. Jane, of
course, had left the island at fourteen to go to high school;
girls didn't get married at fourteen anymore, and when Stella
saw her go off in the boat with Bradley Maxwell, whose job
it had been to ferry the kids back and forth that month, she
knew in her heart that Jane was gone for good, although she
would come back for a while. She would tell them that Alden
had come along ten years later, after they had given up, and
as if to make up for his tardiness, here was Alden still, a
lifelong bachelor, and in some ways Stella was grateful for
that because Alden was not terribly bright and there are plenty
of women willing to take advantage of a man with a slow
brain and a good heart (although she would not tell the children that last, either).*

She would say: "Louis and Margaret Godlin begat Stella
Godlin, who became Stella Flanders; Bill and Stella Flanders
begat Jane and Alden Flanders and Jane Flanders became
Jane Wakefield; Richard and Jane Wakefield begat Lois Wakefield, who became Lois Perrault; David and Lois Perrault
begat Lona and Hal. Those are your names, children: you
are Godlin-Flanders-Wakefield-Perrault. Your blood is in the
stones of this island, and I stay here because the mainland
is too far to reach. Yes, I love; I have loved, anyway, or at
least tried to love, but memory is so wide and so deep, and
I cannot cross. Godlin-Flanders-Wakefield-Perrault . . ."

That was the coldest February since the National Weather
Service began keeping records, and by the middle of the
month the ice covering the Reach was safe. Snowmobiles
buzzed and whined and sometimes turned over when they
climbed the ice-heaves wrong. Children tried to skate, found
the ice too bumpy to be any fun, and went back to Godlin's
Pond on the far side of the hill, but not before little Justin
McCracken, the minister's son, caught his skate in a fissure
and broke his ankle. They took him over to the hospital on

the mainland where a doctor who owned a Corvette told him, "Son, it's going to be as good as new."

Freddy Dinsmore died very suddenly just three days after Justin McCracken broke his ankle. He caught the flu late in January, would not have the doctor, told everyone it was "Just a cold from goin out to get the mail without m'scarf," took to his bed, and died before anyone could take him across to the mainland and hook him up to all those machines they have waiting for guys like Freddy. His son George, a tosspot of the first water even at the advanced age (for tosspots, anyway) of sixty-eight, found Freddy with a copy of the *Bangor Daily News* in one hand and his Remington, unloaded, near the other. Apparently he had been thinking of cleaning it just before he died. George Dinsmore went on a three-week toot, said toot financed by someone who knew that George would have his old dad's insurance money coming. Hattie Stoddard went around telling anyone who would listen that old George Dinsmore was a sin and a disgrace, no better than a tramp for pay.

There was a lot of flu around. The school closed for two weeks that February instead of the usual one because so many pupils were out sick. "No snow breeds germs," Sarah Havelock said.

Near the end of the month, just as people were beginning to look forward to the false comfort of March, Alden Flanders caught the flu himself. He walked around with it for nearly a week and then took to his bed with a fever of a hundred and one. Like Freddy, he refused to have the doctor, and Stella stewed and fretted and worried. Alden was not as old as Freddy, but that May he would turn sixty.

The snow came at last. Six inches on Valentine's Day, another six on the twentieth, and a foot in a good old norther on the leap, February 29. The snow lay white and strange between the cove and the mainland, like a sheep's meadow where there had been only gray and surging water at this time of year since time out of mind. Several people walked across to the mainland and back. No snowshoes were necessary this year because the snow had frozen to a firm, glittery crust. They might take a knock of whiskey, too, Stella thought, but they would not take it at Dorrit's. Dorrit's had burned down in 1958.

And she saw Bill all four times. Once he told her: "Y'ought to come soon, Stella. We'll go steppin. What do you say?"

She could say nothing. Her fist was crammed deep into her mouth.

"Everything I ever wanted or needed was here," she would tell them. "We had the radio and now we have the television, and that's all I want of the world beyond the Reach. I had my garden year in and year out. And lobster? Why, we always used to have a pot of lobster stew on the back of the stove and we used to take it off and put it behind the door in the pantry when the minister came calling so he wouldn't see we were eating 'poor man's soup.'

"I have seen good weather and bad, and if there were times when I wondered what it might be like to actually be in the Sears store instead of ordering from the catalogue, or to go into one of those Shaw's markets I see on TV instead of buying at the store here or sending Alden across for something special like a Christmas capon or an Easter ham . . . or if I ever wanted, just once, to stand on Congress Street in Portland and watch all the people in their cars and on the sidewalks, more people in a single look than there are on the whole island these days . . . if I ever wanted those things, then I wanted this more. I am not strange. I am not peculiar, or even very eccentric for a woman of my years. My mother sometimes used to say, 'All the difference in the world is between work and want,' and I believe that to my very soul. I believe it is better to plow deep than wide.

"This is my place, and I love it."

One day in middle March, with the sky as white and lowering as a loss of memory, Stella Flanders sat in her kitchen for the last time, laced up her boots over her skinny calves for the last time, and wrapped her bright red woolen scarf (a Christmas present from Hattie three Christmases past) around her neck for the last time. She wore a suit of Alden's long underwear under her dress. The waist of the drawers came up to just below the limp vestiges of her breasts, the shirt almost down to her knees.

Outside, the wind was picking up again, and the radio said there would be snow by afternoon. She put on her coat and her gloves. After a moment of debate, she put a pair of Alden's gloves on over her own. Alden had recovered from the flu, and this morning he and Harley Blood were over rehanging a storm door for Missy Bowie, who had had a girl. Stella had seen it, and the unfortunate little mite looked just like her father.

She stood at the window for a moment, looking out at the Reach, and Bill was there as she had suspected he might be, standing about halfway between the island and the Head, standing on the Reach just like Jesus-out-of-the-boat, beckoning to her, seeming to tell her by the gesture that the time was late if she ever intended to step a foot on the mainland in this life.

"If it's what you want, Bill," she fretted in the silence. "God knows I don't."

But the wind spoke other words. She did want to. She wanted to have this adventure. It had been a painful winter for her—the arthritis which came and went irregularly was back with a vengeance, flaring the joints of her fingers and knees with red fire and blue ice. One of her eyes had gotten dim and blurry (and just the other day Sarah had mentioned—with some unease—that the fire-spot that had been there since Stella was sixty or so now seemed to be growing by leaps and bounds). Worst of all, the deep, griping pain in her stomach had returned, and two mornings before she had gotten up at five o'clock, worked her way along the exquisitely cold floor into the bathroom, and had spat a great wad of bright red blood into the toilet bowl. This morning there had been some more of it, foul-tasting stuff, coppery and shuddersome.

The stomach pain had come and gone over the last five years, sometimes better, sometimes worse, and she had known almost from the beginning that it must be cancer. It had taken her mother and father and her mother's father as well. None of them had lived past seventy, and so she supposed she had beat the tables those insurance fellows kept by a carpenter's yard.

"You eat like a horse," Alden told her, grinning, not long after the pains had begun and she had first observed the blood in her morning stool. "Don't you know that old fogies like you are supposed to be peckish?"

"Get on or I'll swat ye!" Stella had answered, raising a hand to her gray-haired son, who ducked, mock-cringed, and cried: "Don't, Ma! I take it back!"

Yes, she had eaten hearty, not because she wanted to, but because she believed (as many of her generation did), that if you fed the cancer it would leave you alone. And perhaps it worked, at least for a while; the blood in her stools came and went, and there were long periods when it wasn't there at all. Alden got used to her taking second helpings (and thirds, when the pain was particularly bad), but she never gained a pound.

Now it seemed the cancer had finally gotten around to what the froggies called the *pièce de résistance*.

She started out the door and saw Alden's hat, the one with the fur-lined ear flaps, hanging on one of the pegs in the entry. She put it on—the bill came all the way down to her shaggy salt-and-pepper eyebrows—and then looked around one last time to see if she had forgotten anything. The stove was low, and Alden had left the draw open too much again—she told him and told him, but that was one thing he was just never going to get straight.

"Alden, you'll burn an extra quarter-cord a winter when I'm gone," she muttered, and opened the stove. She looked in and a tight, dismayed gasp escaped her. She slammed the door shut and adjusted the draw with trembling fingers. For a moment—just a moment—she had seen her old friend Annabelle Frane in the coals. It was her face to the life, even down to the mole on her cheek.

And had Annabelle winked at her?

She thought of leaving Alden a note to explain where she had gone, but she thought perhaps Alden would understand, in his own slow way.

Still writing notes in her head—*Since the first day of winter I have been seeing your father and he says dying isn't so bad; at least I think that's it*—Stella stepped out into the white day.

The wind shook her and she had to reset Alden's cap on her head before the wind could steal it for a joke and cartwheel it away. The cold seemed to find every chink in her clothing and twist into her; damp March cold with wet snow on its mind.

She set off down the hill toward the cove, being careful to walk on the cinders and clinkers that George Dinsmore had spread. Once George had gotten a job driving plow for the town of Raccoon Head, but during the big blow of '77 he had gotten smashed on rye whiskey and had driven the plow smack through not one, not two, but three power poles. There had been no lights over the Head for five days. Stella remembered now how strange it had been, looking across the Reach and seeing only blackness. A body got used to seeing that brave little nestle of lights. Now George worked on the island, and since there was no plow, he didn't get into much hurt.

As she passed Russell Bowie's house, she saw Missy, pale as milk, looking out at her. Stella waved. Missy waved back.

She would tell them this:

"On the island we always watched out for our own. When Gerd Henreid broke the blood vessel in his chest that time, we had covered-dish suppers one whole summer to pay for his operation in Boston—and Gerd came back alive, thank God. When George Dinsmore ran down those power poles and the Hydro slapped a lien on his home, it was seen to that the Hydro had their money and George had enough of a job

to keep him in cigarettes and booze . . . why not? He was
good for nothing else when his workday was done, although
when he was on the clock he would work like a dray-horse.
That one time he got into trouble was because it was at night,
and night was always George's drinking time. His father kept
him fed, at least. Now Missy Bowie's alone with another baby.
Maybe she'll stay here and take her welfare and ADC money
here, and most likely it won't be enough, but she'll get the
help she needs. Probably she'll go, but if she stays she'll not
starve . . . and listen, Lona and Hal: if she stays, she may
be able to keep something of this small world with the little
Reach on one side and the big Reach on the other, something
it would be too easy to lose hustling hash in Lewiston or
donuts in Portland or drinks at the Nashville North in Bangor.
And I am old enough not to beat around the bush about what
that something might be: a way of being and a way of living—
a feeling."

They had watched out for their own in other ways as well,
but she could not tell them that. The children would not understand, nor would Lois and David, although Jane had
known the truth. There was Norman and Ettie Wilson's baby
that was born a mongoloid, its poor dear little feet turned in,
its bald skull lumpy and cratered, its fingers webbed together
as if it had dreamed too long and too deep while swimming
that interior Reach; Reverend McCracken had come and bap-
tized the baby, and a day later Mary Dodge came, who even
at that time had midwived over a hundred babies, and Norman took Ettie down the hill to see Frank Child's new boat
and although she could barely walk, Ettie went with no complaint, although she had stopped in the door to look back at
Mary Dodge, who was sitting calmly by the idiot baby's crib
and knitting. Mary had looked up at her and when their eyes
met, Ettie burst into tears. "Come on," Norman had said,
upset. "Come on, Ettie, come on." And when they came
back an hour later the baby was dead, one of those crib-
deaths, wasn't it merciful he didn't suffer. And many years
before that, before the war, during the Depression, three little

girls had been molested coming home from school, not badly molested, at least not where you could see the scar of the hurt, and they all told about a man who offered to show them a deck of cards he had with a different kind of dog on each one. He would show them this wonderful deck of cards, the man said, if the little girls would come into the bushes with him, and once in the bushes this man said, "But you have to touch this first." One of the little girls was Gert Symes, who would go on to be voted Maine's Teacher of the Year in 1978, for her work at Brunswick High. And Gert, then only five years old, told her father that the man had some fingers gone on one hand. One of the other little girls agreed that this was so. The third remembered nothing. Stella remembered Alden going out one thundery day that summer without telling her where he was going, although she asked. Watching from the window, she had seen Alden meet Bull Symes at the bottom of the path, and then Freddy Dinsmore had joined them and down at the cove she saw her own husband, whom she had sent out that morning just as usual, with his dinner pail under his arm. More men joined them, and when they finally moved off she counted just one under a dozen. The Reverend Mc-Cracken's predecessor had been among them. And that evening a fellow named Daniels was found at the foot of Slyder's Point, where the rocks poke out of the surf like the fangs of a dragon that drowned with its mouth open. This Daniels was a fellow Big George Havelock had hired to help him put new sills under his house and a new engine in his Model A truck. From New Hampshire he was, and he was a sweet-talker who had found other odd jobs to do when the work at the Havelocks' was done . . . and in church, he could carry a tune! Apparently, they said, Daniels had been walking up on top of Slyder's Point and had slipped, tumbling all the way to the bottom. His neck was broken and his head was bashed in. As he had no people that anyone knew of, he was buried on the island, and the Reverend McCracken's predecessor gave the graveyard eulogy, saying as how this Daniels had been a hard worker and a good help even though he was two fingers shy on his right hand. Then he read the benediction and the graveside group had gone back to the town-hall basement where they drank Za-Rex punch and ate cream-cheese sandwiches, and Stella never asked her men where they had gone on the day Daniels fell from the top of Slyder's Point.

"Children," she would tell them, "we always watched out for our own. We had to, for the Reach was wider in those days and when the wind roared and the surf pounded and the dark came early, why, we felt very small—no more than dust motes in the mind of God. So it was natural for us to join hands, one with the other.

"We joined hands, children, and if there were times when we wondered what it was all for, or if there was any such a thing as love at all, it was only because we had heard the wind and the waters on long winter nights, and we were afraid.

"No, I've never felt I needed to leave the island. My life was here. The Reach was wider in those days."

Stella reached the cove. She looked right and left, the wind blowing her dress out behind her like a flag. If anyone had been there she would have walked further down and taken her chance on the tumbled rocks, although they were glazed with ice. But no one was there and she walked out along the pier, past the old Symes boathouse. She reached the end and stood there for a moment, head held up, the wind blowing past the padded flaps of Alden's hat in a muffled flood.

Bill was out there, beckoning. Beyond him, beyond the Reach, she could see the Congo Church over there on the Head, its spire almost invisible against the white sky.

Grunting, she sat down on the end of the pier and then stepped onto the snow crust below. Her boots sank a little; not much. She set Alden's cap again—how the wind wanted to tear it off!—and began to walk toward Bill. She thought once that she would look back, but she did not. She didn't believe her heart could stand that.

She walked, her boots crunching into the crust, and listened to the faint thud and give of the ice. There was Bill, further back now but still beckoning. She coughed, spat blood onto the white snow that covered the ice. Now the Reach spread wide on either side and she could, for the first time in her life, read the "Stanton's Bait and Boat" sign over there without Alden's binoculars. She could see the cars passing to and fro and on the Head's main street and thought with real wonder: *They can go as far as they want . . . Portland . . . Boston . . . New York City. Imagine!* And she could almost do it, could almost imagine a road that simply rolled on and on, the boundaries of the world knocked wide.

A snowflake skirled past her eyes. Another. A third. Soon it was snowing lightly and she walked through a pleasant world of shifting bright white; she saw Raccoon Head through a gauzy curtain that sometimes almost cleared. She reached up to set Alden's cap again and snow puffed off the bill into her eyes. The wind twisted fresh snow up in filmy shapes, and in one of them she saw Carl Abersham, who had gone down with Hattie Stoddard's husband on the *Dancer*.

Soon, however, the brightness began to dull as the snow came harder. The Head's main street dimmed, dimmed, and at last was gone. For a time longer she could make out the cross atop the church, and then that faded out too, like a false dream. Last to go was that bright yellow-and-black sign reading "Stanton's Bait and Boat," where you could also get engine oil, flypaper, Italian sandwiches, and Budweiser to go.

Then Stella walked in a world that was totally without color, a gray-white dream of snow. *Just like Jesus-out-of-the-boat,* she thought, and at last she looked back but now the island was gone, too. She could see her tracks going back, losing definition until only the faint half-circles of her heels could be seen . . . and then nothing. Nothing at all.

She thought: *It's a whiteout. You got to be careful, Stella, or you'll never get to the mainland. You'll just walk around in a big circle until you're worn out and then you'll freeze to death out here.*

She remembered Bill telling her once that when you were lost in the woods, you had to pretend that the leg which was on the same side of your body as your smart hand was lame. Otherwise that smart leg would begin to lead you and you'd walk in a circle and not even realize it until you came around to your backtrail again. Stella didn't believe she could afford to have that happen to her. Snow today, tonight, and tomorrow, the radio had said, and in a whiteout such as this, she would not even know if she came around to her backtrail, for the wind and the fresh snow would erase it long before she could return to it.

Her hands were leaving her in spite of the two pairs of gloves she wore, and her feet had been gone for some time. In a way, this was almost a relief. The numbness at least shut the mouth of her clamoring arthritis.

Stella began to limp now, making her left leg work harder. The arthritis in her knees had not gone to sleep, and soon they were screaming at her. Her white hair flew out behind her. Her lips had drawn back from her teeth (she still had her own, all save four) and she looked straight ahead, waiting for that yellow-and-black sign to materialize out of the flying whiteness.

It did not happen.

Sometime later, she noticed that the day's bright whiteness had begun to dull to a more uniform gray. The snow fell heavier and thicker than ever. Her feet were still planted on the crust but now she was walking through five inches of fresh snow. She looked at her watch, but it had stopped. Stella realized she must have forgotten to wind it that morning for the first time in twenty or thirty years. Or had it just stopped for good? It had been her mother's and she had sent it with Alden twice to the Head, where Mr. Dostie had first marveled over it and then cleaned it. Her watch, at least, had been to the mainland.

She fell down for the first time some fifteen minutes after she began to notice the day's growing grayness. For a moment she remained on her hands and knees, thinking it would be so easy just to stay here, to curl up and listen to the wind, and then the determination that had brought her through so much reasserted itself and she got up, grimacing. She stood in the wind, looking straight ahead, willing her eyes to see . . . but they saw nothing.

Be dark soon.

Well, she had gone wrong. She had slipped off to one side or the other. Otherwise she would have reached the mainland by now. Yet she didn't believe she had gone so far wrong that she was walking parallel to the mainland or even back in the direction of Goat. An interior navigator in her head whispered that she had overcompensated and slipped off to the left. She believed she was still approaching the mainland but was now on a costly diagonal.

That navigator wanted her to turn right, but she would not do that. Instead, she moved straight on again, but stopped the artificial limp. A spasm of coughing shook her, and she spat bright red into the snow.

Ten minutes later (the gray was now deep indeed, and she found herself in the weird twilight of a heavy snowstorm) she fell again, tried to get up, failed at first, and finally managed to gain her feet. She stood swaying in the snow, barely able to remain upright in the wind, waves of faintness rushing through her head, making her feel alternately heavy and light.

Perhaps not all the roaring she heard in her ears was the wind, but it surely was the wind that finally succeeded in prying Alden's hat from her head. She made a grab for it, but the wind danced it easily out of her reach and she saw it only for a moment, flipping gaily over and over into the darkening gray, a bright spot of orange. It struck the snow, rolled, rose again, was gone. Now her hair flew around her head freely.

"It's all right, Stella," Bill said. "You can wear mine."

She gasped and looked around in the white. Her gloved hands had gone instinctively to her bosom, and she felt sharp fingernails scratch at her heart.

She saw nothing but shifting membranes of snow—and

then, moving out of that evening's gray throat, the wind screaming through it like the voice of a devil in a snowy tunnel, came her husband. He was at first only moving colors in the snow: red, black, dark green, lighter green; then these colors resolved themselves into a flannel jacket with a flapping collar, flannel pants, and green boots. He was holding his hat out to her in a gesture that appeared almost absurdly courtly, and his face was Bill's face, unmarked by the cancer that had taken him (had that been all she was afraid of? that a wasted shadow of her husband would come to her, a scrawny concentration-camp figure with the skin pulled taut and shiny over the cheekbones and the eyes sunken deep in the sockets?) and she felt a surge of relief.

"Bill? Is that really you?"

"Course."

"Bill," she said again, and took a glad step toward him. Her legs betrayed her and she thought she would fall, fall right through him—he was, after all, a ghost—but he caught her in arms as strong and as competent as those that had carried her over the threshold of the house that she had shared only with Alden in these latter years. He supported her, and a moment later she felt the cap pulled firmly onto her head.

"Is it really you?" she asked again, looking up into his face, at the crow's-feet around his eyes which hadn't sunk deep yet, at the spill of snow on the shoulders of his checked hunting jacket, at his lively brown hair.

"It's me," he said. "It's all of us."

He half-turned with her and she saw the others coming out of the snow that the wind drove across the Reach in the gathering darkness. A cry, half joy, half fear, came from her mouth as she saw Madeline Stoddard, Hattie's mother, in a blue dress that swung in the wind like a bell, and holding her hand was Hattie's dad, not a mouldering skeleton somewhere on the bottom with the *Dancer*, but whole and young. And there, behind those two—

"Annabelle!" she cried. "Annabelle Frane, is it you?"

It *was* Annabelle; even in this snowy gloom Stella recognized the yellow dress Annabelle had worn to Stella's own wedding, and as she struggled toward her dead friend, holding Bill's arm, she thought that she could smell roses.

"*Annabelle!*"

"We're almost there now, dear," Annabelle said, taking her other arm. The yellow dress, which had been considered Daring in its day (but, to Annabelle's credit and to everyone else's relief, not quite a Scandal), left her shoulders bare, but Annabelle did not seem to feel the cold. Her hair, a soft, dark auburn, blew long in the wind. "Only a little further."

She took Stella's other arm and they moved forward again. Other figures came out of the snowy night (for it *was* night now). Stella recognized many of them, but not all. Tommy Frane had joined Annabelle; Big George Havelock, who had died a dog's death in the woods, walked behind Bill; there was the fellow who had kept the lighthouse on the Head for most of twenty years and who used to come over to the island during the cribbage tournament Freddy Dinsmore held every February—Stella could almost but not quite remember his name. And there was Freddy himself! Walking off to one side of Freddy, by himself and looking bewildered, was Russell Bowie.

"Look, Stella," Bill said, and she saw black rising out of the gloom like the splintered prows of many ships. It was not ships, it was split and fissured rock. They had reached the Head. They had crossed the Reach.

She heard voices, but was not sure they actually spoke:

Take my hand, Stella—

(do you)

Take my hand, Bill—

(oh do you do you)

Annabelle . . . Freddy . . . Russell . . . John . . . Ettie . . . Frank . . . take my hand, take my hand . . . my hand . . .

(do you love)

"Will you take my hand, Stella?" a new voice asked.

She looked around and there was Bull Symes. He was

smiling kindly at her and yet she felt a kind of terror in her at what was in his eyes and for a moment she drew away, clutching Bill's hand on her other side the tighter.

"Is it—"

"Time?" Bull asked. "Oh, ayuh, Stella, I guess so. But it don't hurt. At least, I never heard so. All that's before."

She burst into tears suddenly—all the tears she had never wept—and put her hand in Bull's hand. "Yes," she said, "yes I will, yes I did, yes I do."

They stood in a circle in the storm, the dead of Goat Island, and the wind screamed around them, driving its packet of snow, and some kind of song burst from her. It went up into the wind and the wind carried it away. They all sang then, as children will sing in their high, sweet voices as a summer evening draws down to summer night. They sang, and Stella felt herself going to them and with them, finally across the Reach. There was a bit of pain, but not much; losing her maidenhead had been worse. They stood in a circle in the night. The snow blew around them and they sang. They sang, and—

—and Alden could not tell David and Lois, but in the summer after Stella died, when the children came out for their annual two weeks, he told Lona and Hal. He told them that during the great storms of winter the wind seems to sing with almost human voices, and that sometimes it seemed to him he could almost make out th words: "Praise God from whom all blessings flow/Praise Him, ye creatures here below . . ."

But he did not tell them (imagine slow, unimaginative Alden Flanders saying such things aloud, even to the children!) that sometimes he would hear that sound and feel cold even by the stove; that he would put his whittling aside, or the trap he had meant to mend, thinking that the wind sang in all the voices of those who were dead and gone . . . that they stood somewhere out on the Reach and sang as children do. He seemed to hear their voices and on these nights he sometimes slept and dreamed that he was singing the doxology, unseen and unheard, at his own funeral.

There are things that can never be told, and there are things, not exactly secret, that are not discussed. They had found Stella frozen to death on the mainland a day after the storm had blown itself out. She was sitting on a natural chair of rock about one hundred yards south of the Raccoon Head town limits, frozen just as neat as you please. The doctor who owned the Corvette said that he was frankly amazed. It would have been a walk of over four miles, and the autopsy required by law in the case of an unattended, unusual death had shown an advanced cancerous condition—in truth, the old woman had been riddled with it. Was Alden to tell David and Lois that the cap on her head had not been his? Larry McKeen had recognized that cap. So had John Bensohn. He had seen it in their eyes, and he supposed they had seen it in his. He had not lived long enough to forget his dead father's cap, the look of its bill or the places where the visor had been broken.

"These are things made for thinking on slowly," he would have told the children if he had known how. "Things to be thought on at length, while the hands do their work and the coffee sits in a solid china mug nearby. They are questions of Reach, maybe: do the dead sing? And do they love the living?

On the nights after Lona and Hal had gone back with their parents to the mainland in Al Curry's boat, the children standing astern and waving good-bye, Alden considered that question, and others, and the matter of his father's cap.

Do the dead sing? Do they love?

On those long nights alone, with his mother Stella Flanders at long last in her grave, it often seemed to Alden that they did both.

John Collier

EVENING PRIMROSE

John Collier's characteristic stories of satirical horror (a small but distinguished tradition including certain works of Saki and Avram Davidson) have fallen out of print in recent years. "Evening Primrose" is a particularly vivid example of the subversive little moral tale, so psychologically acute that it leaves us more than a bit uncomfortable about what goes on at night in the most ordinary and seductive of middle-class environments: the department store, the abode of grotesques, human and otherwise.

In a pad of Highlife Bond, bought by
Miss Sadie Brodribb at Bracey's for 25¢

MARCH 21

Today I made my decision. I would turn my back for good and all upon the *bourgeois* world that hates a poet. I would leave, get out, break away—

And I have done it. I am free! Free as the mote that dances in the sunbeam! Free as a house-fly crossing first-class in the largest of luxury liners! Free as my verse! Free as the food I shall eat, the paper I write upon, the lamb's-wool-lined softly slithering slippers I shall wear.

This morning I had not so much as a car-fare. Now I am

here, on velvet. You are itching to learn of this haven; you would like to organize trips here, spoil it, send your relations-in-law, perhaps even come yourself. After all, this journal will hardly fall into your hands till I am dead. I'll tell you.

I am at Bracey's Giant Emporium, as happy as a mouse in the middle of an immense cheese, and the world shall know me no more.

Merrily, merrily shall I live now, secure behind a towering pile of carpets, in a corner-nook which I propose to line with eiderdowns, angora vestments, and the Cleopatrean tops in pillows. I shall be cosy.

I nipped into this sanctuary late this afternoon, and soon heard the dying footfalls of closing time. From now on, my only effort will be to dodge the night-watchman. Poets can dodge.

I have already made my first mouse-like exploration. I tiptoed as far as the stationery department, and, timid, darted back with only these writing materials, the poet's first need. Now I shall lay them aside, and seek other necessities: food, wine, the soft furniture of my couch, and a natty smoking-jacket. This place stimulates me. I shall write here.

DAWN, NEXT DAY

I suppose no one in the world was ever more astonished and overwhelmed than I have been tonight. It is unbelievable. Yet I believe it. How interesting life is when things get like that!

I crept out, as I said I would, and found the great shop in mingled light and gloom. The central well was half illuminated; the circling galleries towered in a pansy Piranesi of toppling light and shade. The spidery stairways and flying bridges had passed from purpose into fantasy. Silks and velvets glimmered like ghosts, a hundred pantie-clad models offered simpers and embraces to the desert air. Rings, clips, and bracelets glittered frostily in a desolate absence of Honey and Daddy.

Creeping along the transverse aisles, which were in deeper darkness, I felt like a wandering thought in the dreaming brain of a chorus girl down on her luck. Only, of course, their brains are not as big as Bracey's Giant Emporium. And there was no man there.

None, that is, except the night-watchman. I had forgotten him. As I crossed an open space on the mezzanine floor, hugging the lee of a display of sultry shawls, I became aware of a regular thudding, which might almost have been that of my own heart. Suddenly it burst upon me that it came from outside. It was footsteps, and they were only a few paces away. Quick as a flash I seized a flamboyant mantilla, whirled it about me and stood with one arm outflung, like a Carmen petrified in a gesture of disdain.

I was successful. He passed me, jingling his little machine on its chain, humming his little tune, his eyes scaled with refractions of the blaring day. "Go, worldling!" I whispered, and permitted myself a soundless laugh.

It froze on my lips. My heart faltered. A new fear seized me.

I was afraid to move. I was afraid to look around. I felt I was being watched by something that could see right through me. This was a very different feeling from the ordinary emergency caused by the very ordinary night-watchman. My conscious impulse was the obvious one: to glance behind me. But my eyes knew better. I remained absolutely petrified, staring straight ahead.

My eyes were trying to tell me something that my brain refused to believe. They made their point. I was looking straight into another pair of eyes, human eyes, but large, flat, luminous. I have seen such eyes among the nocturnal creatures, which creep out under the artificial blue moonlight in the zoo.

The owner was only a dozen feet away from me. The watchman had passed between us, nearer him than me. Yet he had not seen him. I must have been looking straight at him for several minutes at a stretch. I had not seen him either.

He was half reclining against a low dais where, on a floor of russet leaves, and flanked by billows of glowing homespun, the fresh-faced waxen girls modeled spectator sports suits in herringbones, checks, and plaids. He leaned against the skirt of one of these Dianas; its folds concealed perhaps his ear, his shoulder, and a little of his right side. He, himself, was clad in dim but large patterned Shetland tweeds of the latest cut, suède shoes, a shirt of a rather broad *motif* in olive, pink, and grey. He was as pale as a creature found under a stone. His long thin arms ended in hands that hung floatingly, more like trailing, transparent fins, or wisps of chiffon, than ordinary hands.

He spoke. His voice was not a voice; it was a mere whistling under the tongue. "Not bad, for a beginner!"

I grasped that he was complimenting me, rather satirically, on my own, more amateurish, feat of camouflage. I stuttered. I said, "I'm sorry. I didn't know anyone else lived here." I noticed, even as I spoke, that I was imitating his own whistling sibilant utterance.

"Oh, yes," he said. "*We* live here. It's delightful."

"We?"

"Yes, all of us. Look!"

We were near the edge of the first gallery. He swept his long hand round, indicating the whole well of the shop. I looked. I saw nothing. I could hear nothing, except the watchman's thudding step receding infinitely far along some basement aisle.

"Don't you see?"

You know the sensation one has, peering into the half-light of a vivarium? One sees bark, pebbles, a few leaves, nothing more. And then, suddenly, a stone breathes—it is a toad; there is a chameleon, another, a coiled adder, a mantis among the leaves. The whole case seems crepitant with life. Perhaps the whole world is. One glances at one's sleeve, one's feet.

So it was with the shop. I looked, and it was empty. I

looked, and there was an old lady, clambering out from behind the monstrous clock. There were three girls, elderly
ingénues, incredibly emaciated, simpering at the entrance of
the perfumery. Their hair was a fine floss, pale as gossamer.
Equally brittle and colourless was a man with the appearance
of a colonel of southern extraction, who stood regarding me
while he caressed mustachios that would have done credit to
a crystal shrimp. A chintzy woman, possibly of literary tastes,
swam forward from the curtains and drapes.

They came thick about me, fluttering, whistling, like a
waving of gauze in the wind. Their eyes were wide and flatly
bright. I saw there was no colour to the iris.

"How raw he looks!"

"A detective! Send for the Dark Men!"

"I'm not a detective. I am a poet. I have renounced the
world."

"He is a poet. He has come over to us. Mr. Roscoe found
him."

"He admires us."

"He must meet Mrs. Vanderpant."

I was taken to meet Mrs. Vanderpant. She proved to be
the Grand Old Lady of the store, almost entirely transparent.

"So you are a poet, Mr. Snell? You will find inspiration
here. I am quite the oldest inhabitant. Three mergers and a
complete rebuilding, but they didn't get rid of me!"

"Tell how you went out by daylight, dear Mrs. Vanderpant, and nearly got bought for Whistler's *Mother*."

"That was in pre-war days. I was more robust then. But
at the cash desk they suddenly remembered there was no
frame. And when they came back to look at me—"

"—She was gone."

Their laughter was like the stridulation of the ghosts of
grasshoppers.

"Where is Ella? Where is my broth?"

"She is bringing it, Mrs. Vanderpant. It will come."

"Tiresome little creature! She is our foundling, Mr. Snell.
She is not quite our sort."

"Is that so, Mrs. Vanderpant? Dear, dear!"

"I lived alone here, Mr. Snell, for many years. I took refuge here in the terrible times in the eighties. I was a young girl then, a beauty, people were kind enough to say, but poor Papa lost his money. Bracey's meant a lot to a young girl, in the New York of those days, Mr. Snell. It seemed to me terrible that I should not be able to come here in the ordinary way. So I came here for good. I was quite alarmed when others began to come in, after the crash of 1907. But it was the dear Judge, the Colonel, Mrs. Bilbee—"

I bowed. I was being introduced.

"Mrs. Bilbee writes plays. *And* of a very old Philadelphia family. You will find us quite *nice* here, Mr. Snell."

"I feel it a great privilege, Mrs. Vanderpant."

"And of course, all our dear *young* people came in '29. *Their* poor papas jumped from skyscrapers."

I did a great deal of bowing and whistling. The introductions took a long time. Who would have thought so many people lived in Bracey's?

"And here at last is Ella with my broth."

It was then I noticed that the young people were not so young after all, in spite of their smiles, their little ways, their *ingénue* dress. Ella was in her teens. Clad only in something from the shop-soiled counter, she nevertheless had the appearance of a living flower in a French cemetery, or a mermaid among polyps.

"Come, you stupid thing!"

"Mrs. Vanderpant is waiting."

Her pallor was not like theirs; not like the pallor of something that glistens or scuttles when you turn over a stone. Hers was that of a pearl.

Ella! Pearl of this remotest, most fantastic cave! Little mermaid, brushed over, pressed down by objects of a deadlier white—tentacles—! I can write no more.

MARCH 28

Well, I am rapidly becoming used to my new and half-lit world, to my strange company. I am learning the intricate laws of silence and camouflage which dominate the apparently casual strollings and gatherings of the midnight clan. How they detest the night-watchman, whose existence imposes these laws on their idle festivals!

"Odious, vulgar creature! He reeks of the coarse sun!"

Actually, he is quite a personable young man, very young for a night-watchman, so young that I think he must have been wounded in the war. But they would like to tear him to pieces.

They are very pleasant to me, though. They are pleased that a poet should have come among them. Yet I cannot like them entirely. My blood is a little chilled by the uncanny ease with which even the old ladies can clamber spider-like from balcony to balcony. Or is it because they are unkind to Ella?

Yesterday we had a bridge party. Tonight, Mrs. Bilbee's little play, *Love in Shadowland*, is going to be presented. Would you believe it?—another colony, from Wanamaker's, is coming over *en masse* to attend. Apparently people live in all the great stores. This visit is considered a great honour, for there is an intense snobbery in these creatures. They speak with horror of a social outcast who left a high-class Madison Avenue establishment, and now leads a wallowing, beachcomberish life in a delicatessen. And they relate with tragic emotion the story of the man in Altman's, who conceived such a passion for a model plaid dressing jacket that he emerged and wrested it from the hands of a purchaser. It seems that all the Altman colony, dreading an investigation, were forced to remove beyond the social pale, into a five-and-dime. Well, I must get ready to attend the play.

APRIL 14

I have found an opportunity to speak to Ella. I dared not before; here one has a sense always of pale eyes secretly watching. But last night, at the play, I developed a fit of hiccups. I was somewhat sternly told to go and secrete myself in the basement, among the garbage cans, where the watchman never comes.

There, in the rat-haunted darkness, I heard a stifled sob. "What's that? Is it you? Is it Ella? What ails you, child? Why do you cry?"

"They wouldn't even let me see the play."

"Is that all? Let me console you."

"I am so unhappy."

She told me her tragic little story. What do you think? When she was a child, a little tiny child of only six, she strayed away and fell asleep behind a counter, while her mother tried on a new hat. When she woke, the store was in darkness.

"And I cried, and they all came around, and took hold of me. 'She will tell, if we let her go,' they said. Some said, 'Call in the Dark Men.' 'Let her stay here,' said Mrs. Vanderpant. 'She will make me a nice little maid.' "

"Who are these Dark Men, Ella? They spoke of them when I came here."

"Don't you know? Oh, it's horrible! It's horrible!"

"Tell me, Ella. Let us share it."

She trembled. "You know the morticians, 'Journey's End,' who go to houses when people die?"

"Yes, Ella."

"Well, in that shop, just like here, and at Gimbel's, and at Bloomingdale's, there are people living, people like these."

"How disgusting! But what can they live upon, Ella, in a funeral home?"

"Don't ask me! Dead people are sent there, to be embalmed. Oh, they are terrible creatures! Even the people here are terrified of them. But if anyone dies, or if some poor burglar breaks in, and sees these people, and might tell—"

"Yes? Go on."

"Then they send for the others, the Dark Men."

"Good heavens!"

"Yes, and they put the body in Surgical Supplies—or the burglar, all tied up, if it's a burglar—and they send for these others, and then they all hide, and in they come, the others— Oh! they're like pieces of blackness. I saw them once. It was terrible."

"And then?"

"They go in, to where the dead person is, or the poor burglar. And they have wax there—and all sorts of things. And when they're gone there's just one of these wax models left, on the table. And then our people put a dress on it, or a bathing suit, and they mix it up with all the others, and nobody ever knows."

"But aren't they heavier than the others, these wax models? You would think they'd be heavier."

"No. They're not heavier. I think there's a lot of them— gone."

"Oh, dear! So they were going to do that to you, when you were a little child?"

"Yes, only Mrs. Vanderpant said I was to be her maid."

"I don't like these people, Ella."

"Nor do I. I wish I could see a bird."

"Why don't you go into the pet-shop?"

"It wouldn't be the same. I want to see it on a twig, with leaves."

"Ella, let us meet often. Let us creep away down here and meet. I will tell you about birds, and twigs and leaves."

MAY 1

For the last few nights the store has been feverish with the shivering whisper of a huge crush at Bloomingdale's. Tonight was the night.

"Not changed yet? We leave on the stroke of two." Roscoe has appointed himself, or been appointed, my guide or my guard.

"Roscoe, I am still a greenhorn. I dread the streets."

"Nonsense! There's nothing to it. We slip out by two's and three's, stand on the sidewalk, pick up a taxi. Were you never out late in the old days? If so, you must have seen us, many a time."

"Good heavens, I believe I have! And often wondered where you came from. And it was from here! But, Roscoe, my brow is burning. I find it hard to breathe. I fear a cold."

"In that case you must certainly remain behind. Our whole party would be disgraced in the unfortunate event of a sneeze."

I had relied on their rigid etiquette, so largely based on fear of discovery, and I was right. Soon they were gone, drifting out like leaves aslant on the wind. At once I dressed in flannel slacks, canvas shoes, and a tasteful sport shirt, all new in stock today. I found a quiet spot, safely off the track beaten by the night-watchman. There, in a model's lifted hand, I set a wide fern frond culled from the florist's shop, and at once had a young, spring tree. The carpet was sandy, sandy as a lake-side beach. A snowy napkin; two cakes, each with a cherry on it; I had only to imagine the lake and to find Ella.

"Why, Charles, what's this?"

"I'm a poet, Ella, and when a poet meets a girl like you he thinks of a day in the country. Do you see this tree? Let's call it *our* tree. There's the lake—the prettiest lake imaginable. Here is grass, and there are flowers. There are birds, too, Ella. You told me you like birds."

"Oh, Charles, you're so sweet. I feel I hear them singing."

"And here's our lunch. But before we eat, go behind the rock there, and see what you find."

I heard her cry out in delight when she saw the summer dress I had put there for her. When she came back the spring day smiled to see her, and the lake shone brighter than before. "Ella, let us have lunch. Let us have fun. Let us have a swim. I can just imagine you in one of those new bathing suits."

"Let's just sit there, Charles, and talk."

So we sat and talked, and the time was gone like a dream. We might have stayed there, forgetful of everything, had it not been for the spider.

"Charles, what are you doing?"

"Nothing, my dear. Just a naughty little spider, crawling over your knee. Purely imaginary, of course, but that sort are sometimes the worst. I had to try to catch him."

"Don't, Charles! It's late. It's terribly late. They'll be back any minute. I'd better go home."

I took her home to the kitchenware on the sub-ground floor, and kissed her good-day. She offered me her cheek. This troubles me.

MAY 10

"Ella, I love you."

I said it to her just like that. We have met many times. I have dreamt of her by day. I have not even kept up my journal. Verse has been out of the question.

"Ella, I love you. Let us move into the trousseau department. Don't look so dismayed, darling. If you like, we will go right away from here. We will live in that little restaurant in Central Park. There are thousands of birds there."

"Please—please don't talk like that!"

"But I love you with all my heart."

"You mustn't."

"But I find I must. I can't help it. Ella, you don't love another?"

She wept a little. "Oh, Charles, I do."

"Love another, Ella? One of these? I thought you dreaded them all. It must be Roscoe. He is the only one that's any way human. We talk of art, life, and such things. And he has stolen your heart!''

"No, Charles, no. He's just like the rest, really. I hate them all. They make me shudder.''

"Who is it, then?''

"It's him.''

"Who?''

"The night-watchman.''

"Impossible!''

"No. He smells of the sun.''

"Oh, Ella, you have broken my heart.''

"Be my friend, though.''

"I will. I'll be your brother. How did you fall in love with him?''

"Oh, Charles, it was so wonderful. I was thinking of birds, and I was careless. Don't tell on me, Charles. They'll punish me.''

"No. No. Go on.''

"I was careless, and there he was, coming round the corner. And there was no place for me; I had this blue dress on. There were only some wax models in their underthings.''

"Please go on.''

"I couldn't help it. I slipped off my dress and stood still.''

"I see.''

"And he stopped just by me, Charles. And he looked at me. And he touched my cheek.''

"Did he notice nothing?''

"No. It was cold. But Charles, he said—he said—'Say, honey, I wish they made 'em like you on Eighth Avenue.' Charles, wasn't that a lovely thing to say?''

"Personally, I should have said Park Avenue.''

"Oh, Charles, don't get like these people here. Sometimes I think you're getting like them. It doesn't matter what street, Charles; it was a lovely thing to say.''

"Yes, but my heart's broken. And what can you do about him? Ella, he belongs to another world.''

"Yes, Charles, Eighth Avenue. I want to go there. Charles, are you truly my friend?"

"I'm your brother, only my heart's broken."

"I'll tell you. I will. I'm going to stand there again. So he'll see me."

"And then?"

"Perhaps he'll speak to me again."

"My dearest Ella, you are torturing yourself. You are making it worse."

"No, Charles. Because I shall answer him. He will take me away."

"Ella, I can't bear it."

"Ssh! There is someone coming. I shall see birds—real birds, Charles—and flowers growing. They're coming. You must go."

MAY 13

The last three days have been torture. This evening I broke. Roscoe had joined me. He sat eying me for a long time. He put his hand on my shoulder.

He said, "You're looking seedy, old fellow. Why don't you go over to Wanamaker's for some skiing?"

His kindness compelled a frank response. "It's deeper than that, Roscoe. I'm done for. I can't eat, I can't sleep. I can't write, man, I can't even write."

"What is it? Day starvation?"

"Roscoe—it's love."

"Not one of the staff, Charles, or the customers? That's absolutely forbidden."

"No, it's not that, Roscoe. But just as hopeless."

"My dear old fellow, I can't bear to see you like this. Let me help you. Let me share your trouble."

Then it came out. It burst out. I trusted him. I think I trusted him. I really think I had no intention of betraying Ella, of spoiling her escape, of keeping her here till her heart turned towards me. If I had, it was subconscious, I swear it.

But I told him all. All! He was sympathetic, but I detected a sly reserve in his sympathy. "You will respect my confidence. Roscoe? This is to be a secret between us."

"As secret as the grave, old chap."

And he must have gone straight to Mrs. Vanderpant. This evening the atmosphere has changed. People flicker to and fro, smiling nervously, horribly, with a sort of frightened sadistic exaltation. When I speak to them they answer evasively, fidget, and disappear. An informal dance has been called off. I cannot find Ella. I will creep out. I will look for her again.

LATER

Heaven! It has happened. I went in desperation to the manager's office, whose glass front overlooks the whole shop. I watched till midnight. Then I saw a little group of them, like ants bearing a victim. They were carrying Ella. They took her to the surgical department. They took other things.

And, coming back here, I was passed by a flittering, whispering horde of them, glancing over their shoulders in a thrilled ecstasy of panic, making for their hiding places. I, too, hid myself. How can I describe the dark inhuman creatures that passed me, silent as shadows? They went there—where Ella is.

What can I do? There is only one thing. I will find the watchman. I will tell him. He and I will save her. And if we are overpowered—Well, I will leave this on a counter. Tomorrow, if we live, I can recover it.

If not, look in the windows. Look for the three new figures: two men, one rather sensitive-looking, and a girl. She has blue eyes, like periwinkle flowers, and her upper lip is lifted a little.

Look for us.

Smoke them out! Obliterate them! Avenge us!

M. R. James

THE ASH-TREE

M. R. James was the master of the ghost story in which an evil from the distant past persists into the present and is visited upon us as a legacy. His antiquarian ghost stories are a body of work that codified a main tradition of horror for the twentieth century. The weight of the past haunts us in Jamesian fiction, a bleak, stern moral landscape rich in detail. "The Ash-Tree" is thematically interesting in contrast to Hawthorne and Wellman as a witchcraft story. James looks back to J. S. Le Fanu as his paradigm (he is responsible for the modern revival of interest in Le Fanu, through his famous edition of Le Fanu stories, *Madame Crowl's Ghost*, 1923), but the on-stage horror at the climax of "The Ash-Tree" is James' own contribution, striking and monstrous, to the genre.

Everyone who has travelled over Eastern England knows the smaller country-houses with which it is studded—the rather dark little buildings, usually in the Italian style, surrounded with parks of some eighty to a hundred acres. For me they have always had a very strong attraction, with the grey paling of split oak, the noble trees, the meres with their reed-beds, and the line of distant woods. Then, I like the pillared portico—perhaps stuck on to a red-brick Queen Anne house which has been faced with stucco to bring it into line

with the "Grecian" taste of the end of the eighteenth century; the hall inside, going up to the roof, which hall ought
always to be provided with a gallery and a small organ. I like
the library, too, where you may find anything from a Psalter
of the thirteenth century to a Shakespeare quarto. I like the
pictures, of course; and perhaps most of all I like fancying
what life in such a house was when it was first built, and in
the piping times of landlords' prosperity, and not least now,
when, if money is not so plentiful, taste is more varied and
life quite as interesting. I wish to have one of these houses
and enough money to keep it together and entertain my
friends in it modestly.

But this is a digression. I have to tell you of a curious series
of events which happened in such a house as I have tried to
describe. It is Castringham Hall in Suffolk. I think a good
deal has been done to the building since the period of my
story, but the essential features I have sketched are still
there—Italian portico, square block of white house, older inside than out, park with fringe of woods, and mere. The one
feature that marked out the house from a score of others is
gone. As you looked at it from the park, you saw on the right
a great old ash-tree growing within half a dozen yards of the
wall, and almost or quite touching the building with its
branches. I suppose it had stood there ever since Castringham
ceased to be a fortified place, and since the moat was filled
in and the Elizabethan dwelling-house built. At any rate, it
had well-nigh attained its full dimensions in the year 1690.

In that year the district in which the Hall is situated was
the scene of a number of witch-trails. It will be long, I think,
before we arrive at a just estimate of the amount of solid
reason—if there was any—which lay at the root of the universal fear of witches in old times. Whether the persons accused of this offence really did imagine that they were
possessed of unusual power of any kind; or whether they had
the will at least, if not the power, of doing mischief to their
neighbours; or whether all the confessions, of which there
are so many, were extorted by the mere cruelty of the witch-

finders—these are questions which are not, I fancy, yet solved. And the present narrative gives me pause. I cannot altogether sweep it away as mere invention. The reader must judge for himself.

Castringham contributed a victim to the *auto-da-fe*. Mrs. Mothersole was her name, and she differed from the ordinary run of village witches only in being rather better off and in a more influential position. Efforts were made to save her by several reputable farmers of the parish. They did their best to testify to her character, and showed considerable anxiety as to the verdict of the jury.

But what seems to have been fatal to the woman was the evidence of the then proprietor of Castringham Hall—Sir Matthew Fell. He deposed to having watched her on three different occasions from his window, at the full of the moon, gathering sprigs "from the ash-tree near my house." She had climbed into the branches, clad only in her shift, and was cutting off small twigs with a peculiarly curved knife, and as she did so she seemed to be talking to herself. On each occasion Sir Matthew had done his best to capture the woman, but she had always taken alarm at some accidental noise he had made, and all he could see when he got down to the garden was a hare running across the path in the direction of the village.

On the third night he had been at the pains to follow at his best speed, and had gone straight to Mrs. Mothersole's house; but he had had to wait a quarter of an hour battering at her door, and then she had come out very cross, and apparently very sleepy, as if just out of bed; and he had no good explanation to offer of his visit.

Mainly on this evidence, though there was much more of a less striking and unusual kind from other parishioners, Mrs. Mothersole was found guilty and condemned to die. She was hanged a week after the trial, with five or six more unhappy creatures, at Bury St. Edmunds.

Sir Matthew Fell, then Deputy-Sheriff, was present at the execution. It was a damp, drizzly March morning when the cart made its way up the rough grass hill outside Northgate, where the gallows stood. The other victims were apathetic or broken down with misery; but Mrs. Mothersole was, as in life so in death, of a very different temper. Her "poysonous Rage," as a reporter of the time puts it, "did so work upon the Bystanders—yea, even upon the Hangman—that it was constantly affirmed of all that saw her that she presented the living Aspect of a mad Divell. Yet she offer'd no Resistance to the Officers of the Law; onely she looked upon those that laid Hands upon her with so direfull and venomous an Aspect that—as one of them afterwards assured me—the meer Thought of it preyed inwardly upon his Mind for six Months after."

However, all that she is reported to have said were the seemingly meaningless words: "There will be guests at the Hall." Which she repeated more than once in an undertone.

Sir Matthew Fell was not unimpressed by the bearing of the woman. He had some talk upon the matter with the Vicar of his parish, with whom he travelled home after the assize business was over. His evidence at the trial had not been very willingly given; he was not specially infected with the witch-finding mania, but he declared, then and afterwards, that he could not give any other account of the matter than that he had given, and that he could not possibly have been mistaken as to what he saw. The whole transaction had been repugnant to him, for he was a man who liked to be on pleasant terms with those about him; but he saw a duty to be done in this business, and he had done it. That seems to have been the gist of his sentiments, and the Vicar applauded it, as any reasonable man must have done.

A few weeks after, when the moon of May was at the full, Vicar and Squire met again in the park, and walked to the Hall together. Lady Fell was with her mother, who was dangerously ill, and Sir Matthew was alone at home; so the Vicar, Mr. Crome, was easily persuaded to take a late supper at the Hall.

Sir Matthew was not very good company this evening. The

talk ran chiefly on family and parish matters, and, as luck would have it, Sir Matthew made a memorandum in writing of certain wishes or intentions of his regarding his estates, which afterwards proved exceedingly useful.

When Mr. Crome thought of starting for home, about half past nine o'clock, Sir Matthew and he took a preliminary turn on the gravelled walk at the back of the house. The only incident that struck Mr. Crome was this: they were in sight of the ash-tree which I described as growing near the windows of the building, when Sir Matthew stopped and said:

"What is that that runs up and down the stem of the ash? It is never a squirrel? They will all be in their nests by now."

The Vicar looked and saw the moving creature, but he could make nothing of its colour in the moonlight. The sharp outline, however, seen for an instant, was imprinted on his brain, and he could have sworn, he said, though it sounded foolish, that, squirrel or not, it had more than four legs.

Still, not much was to be made of the momentary vision, and the two men parted. They may have met since then, but it was not for a score of years.

Next day Sir Matthew Fell was not downstairs at six in the morning, as was his custom, nor at seven, nor yet at eight. Hereupon the servants went and knocked at his chamber door. I need not prolong the description of their anxious listenings and renewed batterings on the panels. The door was opened at last from the outside, and they found their master dead and black. So much you have guessed. That there were any marks of violence did not at the moment appear; but the window was open.

One of the men went to fetch the parson, and then by his directions rode on to give notice to the coroner. Mr. Crome himself went as quick as he might to the Hall, and was shown to the room where the dead man lay. He has left some notes among his papers which show how genuine a respect and sorrow was felt for Sir Matthew, and there is also this passage, which I transcribe for the sake of the light it throws upon the course of events, and also upon the common beliefs of the time:

"There was not any the least Trace of an Entrance having been forc'd to the Chamber: but the Casement stood open, as my poor Friend would always have it in this Season. He had his Evening Drink of small Ale in a silver vessel of about a pint measure, and tonight had not drunk it out. This Drink was examined by the Physician from Bury, a Mr. Hodgkins, who could not, however, as he afterwards declar'd upon his Oath, before the Coroner's quest, discover that any matter of a venomous kind was present in it. For, as was natural, in the great Swelling and Blackness of the Corpse, there was talk made among the Neighbours of Poyson. The Body was very much Disorder'd as it laid in the Bed, being twisted after so extream a sort as gave too probable Conjecture that my worthy Friend and Patron had expir'd in great Pain and Agony. And what is as yet unexplain'd, and to myself the Argument of some Horrid and Artfull Designe in the Perpetrators of this Barbarous Murther, was this, that the Women which were entrusted with the laying-out of the Corpse and washing it, being both sad Pearsons and very well Respected in their Mournful Profession, came to me in a great Pain and Distress both of Mind and Body, saying, what was indeed confirmed upon the first View, that they had no sooner touch'd the Breast of the Corpse with their naked Hands than they were sensible of a more than ordinary violent Smart and Acheing in their Palms, which, with their whole Forearms, in no long time swell'd so immoderately, the Pain still continuing, that, as afterwards proved, during many weeks they were forc'd to lay by the exercise of their Calling; and yet no mark seen on the Skin.

"Upon hearing this, I sent for the Physician, who was still in the House, and we made as careful a Proof as we were able by the Help of a small Magnifying Lens of Crystal of the condition of the Skinn on this Part of the Body: but could not detect with the Instrument we had any Matter of Importance beyond a couple of small Punctures or Pricks, which we then concluded were the Spotts by which the Poyson might be introduced, remembering that Ring of *Pope Borgia*, with other known Specimens of the Horrid Act of the Italian Poysoners of the last age.

"So much is to be said of the Symptoms seen on the Corpse. As to what I am to add, it is meerly my own Experiment, and to be left to Posterity to judge whether there be anything of Value therein. There was on the Table by the Beddside a Bible of the small size, in which my Friend—punctuall as in Matters of less Moment, so in this more weighty one—used nightly, and upon his First Rising, to read a sett Portion. And I taking it up—not without a Tear duly paid to him wich from the Study of this poorer Adumbration was now pass'd to the contemplation of its great Originall—it came into my Thoughts, as at such moments of Helplessness we are prone to catch at any the least Glimmer that makes promise of Light, to make trial of that old and by many accounted Superstitious Practice of drawing the *Sortes*; of which a Principall Instance, in the case of his late Sacred Majesty the Blessed Martyr King *Charles* and my Lord *Falkland*, was now much talked of. I must needs admit that by my Trial not much Assistance was afforded me: yet, as the Cause and Origin of these Dreadful Events may hereafter be search'd out, I set down the Results, in the case it may be found that they pointed the true Quarter of the Mischief to a quicker Intelligence than my own.

"I made, then, three trials, opening the Book and placing my Finger upon certain Words: which gave in the first these words, from Luke xiii. 7, *Cut it down*; in the second. Isaiah xiii. 20, *It shall never be inhabited*; and upon the third Experiment, Job xxxix. 30, *Her young ones also suck up blood.*"

This is all that need be quoted from Mr. Crome's papers. Sir Matthew Fell was duly coffined and laid into the earth, and his funeral sermon, preached by Mr. Crome on the following Sunday, has been printed under the title of "The Unsearchable Way; or, England's Danger and the Malicious

Dealings of Antichrist,'' it being the Vicar's view, as well as that most commonly held in the neighbourhood, that the Squire was the victim of a recrudescence of the Popish Plot.

His son, Sir Matthew the second, succeeded to the title and estates. And so ends the first act of the Castringham tragedy. It is to be mentioned, though the fact is not surprising, that the new Baronet did not occupy the room in which his father had died. Nor, indeed, was it slept in by anyone but an occasional visitor during the whole of his occupation. He died in 1735, and I do not find that anything particular marked his reign, save a curiously constant mortality among his cattle and live-stock in general, which showed a tendency to increase slightly as time went on.

Those who are interested in the details will find a statistical account in a letter to the *Gentlemen's Magazine* of 1772, which draws the facts from the Baronet's own papers. He put an end to it at last by a very simple expedient, that of shutting up all his beasts in sheds at night, and keeping no sheep in his park. For he had noticed that nothing was ever attacked that spent the night indoors. After that the disorder confined itself to wild birds, and beasts of chase. But as we have no good account of the symptoms, and as all-night watching was quite unproductive of any clue, I do not dwell on what the Suffolk farmers called the "Castringham sickness."

The second Sir Matthew died in 1735, as I said, and was duly succeeded by his son, Sir Richard. It was in his time that the great family pew was built out on the north side of the parish church. So large were the Squire's ideas that several of the graves on that unhallowed side of the building had to be disturbed to satisfy his requirements. Among them was that of Mrs. Mothersole, the position of which was accurately known, thanks to a note of a plan of the church and yard, both made by Mr. Crome.

A certain amount of interest was excited in the village when it was known that the famous witch, who was still remembered by a few, was to be exhumed. And the feeling of surprise, and indeed disquiet, was very strong when it was found that, though her coffin was fairly sound and unbroken, there was no trace whatever inside it of body, bones, or dust. Indeed, it is a curious phenomenon, for at the time of her burying no such things were dreamt of as resurrection-men, and it is difficult to conceive any rational motive for stealing a body otherwise than for the uses of the dissecting-room.

The incident revived for a time all the stories of witch-trials and of the exploits of the witches, dormant for forty years, and Sir Richard's orders that the coffin should be burnt were thought by a good many to be rather foolhardy, though they were duly carried out.

Sir Richard was a pestilent innovator, it is certain. Before his time the Hall had been a fine block of the mellowest red brick; bur Sir Richard had travelled in Italy and become infected with the Italian taste, and, having more money than his predecessors, he determined to leave an Italian palace where he had found an English house. So stucco and ashlar masked the brick; some indifferent Roman marbles were planted about in the entrance-hall and gardens; a reproduction of the Sibyl's temple at Tivoli was erected on the opposite bank of the mere; and Castringham took an entirely new, and, I must say, a less engaging, aspect. But it was much admired, and served as a model to a good many of the neighbouring gentry in after-years.

One morning (it was in 1754) Sir Richard woke after a night of discomfort. It had been windy, and his chimney had smoked persistently, and yet it was so cold that he must keep up a fire. Also something had so rattled about the window that no man could get a moment's peace. Further, there was the prospect of several guests of position arriving in the course of the day, who would expect sport of some kind, and the inroads of the distemper (which continued among his game) had been lately so serious that he was afraid for his reputation as a game-preserver. But what really touched him most nearly was the other matter of his sleepless night. He could certainly not sleep in that room again.

That was the chief subject of his meditations at breakfast, and after it he began a systematic examination of the rooms to see which would suit his notions best. It was long before he found one. This had a window with an eastern aspect and that with a northern; this door the servants would be always passing, and he did not like the bedstead in that. No, he must have a room with a western look-out, so that the sun could not wake him early, and it must be out of the way of the business of the house. The housekeeper was at the end of her resources.

"Well, Sir Richard," she said, "you know that there is but the one room like that in the house."

"Which may that be?" said Sir Richard.

"And that is Sir Matthew's—the West Chamber."

"Well, put me in there, for there I'll lie tonight," said her master. "Which way is it? Here, to be sure"; and he hurried off.

"Oh, Sir Richard, but no one has slept there these forty years. The air has hardly been changed since Sir Matthew died there."

Thus she spoke, and rustled after him.

"Come, open the door, Mrs. Chiddock. I'll see the chamber, at least."

So it was opened, and, indeed, the smell was very close and earthy. Sir Richard crossed to the window, and, impatiently, as was his wont, threw the shutters back, and flung open the casement. For this end of the house was one which the alterations had barely touched, grown up as it was with the great ash-tree, and being otherwise concealed from view.

"Air it, Mrs. Chiddock, all today, and move my bed-furniture in in the afternoon. Put the Bishop of Kilmore in my old room."

"Pray, Sir Richard," said a new voice, breaking in on his speech, "might I have the favour of a moment's interview?"

Sir Richard turned around and saw a man in black in the doorway, who bowed.

"I must ask your indulgence for this intrusion, Sir Richard. You will, perhaps, hardly remember me. My name is William Crome, and my grandfather was Vicar in your grandfather's time."

"Well, sir," said Sir Richard, "the name of Crome is always a passport to Castringham. I am glad to renew a friendship of two generations' standing. In what can I serve you? for your hour of calling—and, if I do not mistake you, your bearing—shows you to be in some haste."

"That is no more than the truth, sir. I am riding from Norwich to Bury St. Edmunds with what haste I can make, and I have called in on my way to leave with you some papers which we have but just come upon in looking over what my grandfather left at his death. It is thought you may find some matters of family interest in them."

"You are mighty obliging, Mr. Crome, and, if you will be so good as to follow me to the parlour, and drink a glass of wine, we will take a first look at these same papers together. And you, Mrs. Chiddock, as I said, be about airing this chamber . . . Yes, it is here my grandfather died . . . Yes, the tree, perhaps, does make the place a little dampish . . . No; I do not wish to listen to any more. Make no difficulties, I beg. You have your orders—go. Will you follow me, sir?"

They went to the study. The packet which young Mr. Crome had brought—he was then just become a Fellow of Clare Hall in Cambridge, I may say, and subsequently brought out a respectable edition of Polyaenus—contained among other things the notes which the old Vicar had made upon the occasion of Sir Matthew Fell's death. And for the first time Sir Richard was confronted with the enigmatical *Sortes Biblicae* which you have heard. They amused him a good deal.

"Well," he said, "my grandfather's Bible gave one prudent piece of advice—*Cut it down*. If that stands for the ash-tree, he may rest assured I shall not neglect it. Such a nest of catarrhs and agues was never seen."

The parlour contained the family books, which, pending the arrival of a collection which Sir Richard had made in

Italy, and the building of a proper room to receive them, were not many in number.

Sir Richard looked up from the paper to the bookcase.

"I wonder," says he, "whether the old prophet is there yet? I fancy I see him."

Crossing the room, he took out a dumpy Bible, which, sure enough, bore on the flyleaf the inscription: "To Matthew Fell, from his Loving Godmother, Anne Aldous, 2 September 1659."

"It would be no bad plan to test him again, Mr. Crome. I will wager we get a couple of names in the Chronicles. H'm! what have we here? 'Thou shalt seek me in the morning, and I shall not be.' Well, well! Your grandfather would have made a fine omen of that, hey? No more prophets for me! They are all in a tale. And now, Mr. Crome, I am infinitely obliged to you for your packet. You will, I fear, be impatient to get on. Pray allow me—another glass."

So with offers of hospitality, which were genuinely meant (for Sir Richard thought well of the young man's address and manner), they parted.

In the afternoon came the guests—the Bishop of Kilmore, Lady Mary Hervey, Sir William Kentfield, etc. Dinner at five, wine, cards, supper, and dispersal to bed.

Next morning Sir Richard is disinclined to take his gun with the rest. He talks with the Bishop of Kilmore. This prelate, unlike a good many of the Irish Bishops of his day, had visited his see, and, indeed, resided there, for some considerable time. This morning, as the two were walking along the terrace and talking over the alterations and improvements in the house, the Bishop said, pointing to the window of the West Room:

"You could never get one of my Irish flock to occupy that room, Sir Richard."

"Why is that, my lord? It is, in fact, my own."

"Well, our Irish peasantry will always have it that it brings the worst of luck to sleep near an ash-tree, and you have a fine growth of ash not two yards from your chamber window.

Perhaps," the Bishop went on, with a smile, "it has given you a touch of its quality already, for you do not seem, if I may say it, so much the fresher for your night's rest as your friends would like to see you."

"That, or something else, it is true, cost me my sleep from twelve to four, my lord. But the tree is to come down tomorrow, so I shall not hear much more from it."

"I applaud your determination. It can hardly be wholesome to have the air you breathe strained, as it were, through all that leafage."

"Your lordship is right there, I think. But I had not my window open last night. It was rather the noise that went on—no doubt from the twigs sweeping the glass—that kept me open-eyed."

"I think that can hardly be, Sir Richard. Here—you see it from this point. None of these nearest branches even can touch your casement unless there were a gale, and there was none of that last night. They miss the panes by a foot."

"No, sir, true. What, then, will it be, I wonder, that scratched and rustled so—ay, and covered the dust on my sill with lines and marks?"

At last they agreed that the rats must have come up through the ivy. That was the Bishop's idea, and Sir Richard jumped at it.

So the day passed quietly, and night came, and the party dispersed to their rooms, and wished Sir Richard a better night.

And now we are in his bedroom, with the light out and the Squire in bed. The room is over the kitchen, and the night outside still and warm, so the window stands open.

There is very little light about the bedstead, but there is a strange movement there; it seems as if Sir Richard were moving his head rapidly to and fro with only the slightest possible sound. And now you would guess, so deceptive is the half-darkness, that he had several heads, round and brownish which move back and forward, even as low as his chest. It is a horrible illusion. Is it nothing more? There! something drops off the bed with a soft plump, like a kitten, and is out of the window in a flash; another—four—and after that there is quiet again.

Thou shalt seek me in the morning, and I shall not be.

As with Sir Matthew, so with Sir Richard—dead and black in his bed!

A pale and silent party of guests and servants gathered under the window when the news was known. Italian poisoners, Popish emissaries, infected air—all these and more guesses were hazarded, and the Bishop of Kilmore looked at the tree, in the fork of whose lower boughs a white tom-cat was crouching, looking down the hollow which years had gnawed in the trunk. It was watching something inside the tree with great interest.

Suddenly it got up and craned over the hole. Then a bit of the edge on which it stood gave way, and it went slithering in. Everyone looked up at the noise of the fall.

It is known to most of us that a cat can cry; but few of us have heard, I hope, such a yell as came out of the trunk of the great ash. Two or three screams there were—the witnesses are not sure which—and then a slight and muffled noise of some commotion or struggling was all that came. But Lady Mary Hervey fainted outright, and the housekeeper stopped her ears and fled till she fell on the terrace.

The Bishop of Kilmore and Sir William Kentfield stayed. Yet even they were daunted, though it was only at the cry of a cat; and Sir William swallowed once or twice before he could say:

"There is something more than we know of in that tree, my lord. I am for an instant search."

And this was agreed upon. A ladder was brought, and one of the gardeners went up, and, looking down the hollow, could detect nothing but a few dim indications of something moving. They got a lantern, and let it down by a rope.

"We must get at the bottom of this. My life upon it, my lord, but the secret of these terrible deaths is there."

Up went the gardener again with the lantern, and let it

down the hole cautiously. They saw the yellow light upon his face as he bent over, and saw his face struck with an incredulous terror and loathing before he cried out in a dreadful voice and fell back from the ladder—where, happily, he was caught by two of the men—letting the lantern fall inside the tree.

He was in a dead faint, and it was some time before any word could be got from him.

By then they had something else to look at. The lantern must have broken at the bottom, and the light in it caught upon dry leaves and rubbish that lay there, for in a few minutes a dense smoke began to come up, and then flame; and, to be short, the tree was in a blaze.

The bystanders made a ring at some yards' distance, and Sir William and the Bishop sent men to get what weapons and tools they could; for, clearly, whatever might be using the tree as its lair would be forced out by the fire.

So it was. First, at the fork, they saw a round body covered with fire—the size of man's head—appear very suddenly, then seem to collapse and fall back. This, five or six times; then a similar ball leapt into the air and fell on the grass, where after a moment it lay still. The Bishop went as near as he dared to it, and saw—what but the remains of an enormous spider, veinous and seared! And, as the fire burned lower down, more terrible bodies like this began to break out from the trunk, and it was seen that these were covered with greyish hair.

All that day the ash burned, and until it fell to pieces the men stood about it, and from time to time killed the brutes as they darted out. At last there was a long interval when none appeared, and they cautiously closed in and examined the roots of the tree.

"They found," says the Bishop of Kilmore, "below it a rounded hollow place in the earth, wherein were two or three bodies of these creatures that had plainly been smothered by the smoke; and, what is to be more curious, at the side of this den, against the wall, was crouching the anatomy or skeleton of a human being, with the skin dried upon the bones, having some remains of black hair, which was pronounced by those that examined it to be undoubtedly the body of a woman, and clearly dead for a period of fifty years.''

Lucy Clifford

THE NEW MOTHER

Lucy Clifford was a Victorian writer of children's fantasies. "The New Mother" is from *Anyhow Stories, Moral
and Otherwise* (London, 1882). It is a curious example
of the often-noted tendency of Victorian morality to be
at odds in an unsettling way with human psychology.
"Step on a crack, break your mother's back," or step
out of line and you will be punished horribly, out of all
proportion to the sin, seems to be the moral, familiar
from horrid children's rhymes. It represents herein the
whole tradition of tales calculated to terrify and horrify
children into good behavior through moral allegory. The
allegory may be awry, but the horror is real.

I

The children were always called Blue-Eyes and the Turkey. The elder one was like her dear father who was far
away at sea; for the father had the bluest of blue eyes, and
so gradually his little girl came to be called after them. The
younger one had once, while she was still almost a baby,
cried bitterly because a turkey that lived near the cottage
suddenly vanished in the middle of the winter; and to console
her she had been called by its name.

Now the mother and Blue-Eyes and the Turkey and the

baby all lived in a lonely cottage on the edge of the forest. It was a long way to the village, nearly a mile and a half, and the mother had to work hard and had not time to go often herself to see if there was a letter at the post-office from the dear father, and so very often in the afternoon she used to send the two children. They were very proud of being able to go alone. When they came back tired with the long walk, there would be the mother waiting and watching for them, and the tea would be ready, and the baby crowing with delight; and if by any chance there was a letter from the sea, then they were happy indeed. The cottage room was so cosy: the walls were as white as snow inside as well as out. The baby's high chair stood in one corner, and in another there was a cupboard, in which the mother kept all manner of surprises.

"Dear children," the mother said one afternoon late in the autumn, "it is very chilly for you to go to the village, but you must walk quickly, and who knows but what you may bring back a letter saying that dear father is already on his way to England. Don't be long," the mother said, as she always did before they started. "Go the nearest way and don't look at any strangers you meet, and be sure you do not talk with them."

"No, mother," they answered; and then she kissed them and called them dear good children, and they joyfully started on their way.

The village was gayer than usual, for there had been a fair the day before. "Oh, I *do* wish we had been here yesterday," Blue-Eyes said as they went on to the grocer's, which was also the post-office. The post-mistress was very busy and just said "No letter for you to-day." Then Blue-Eyes and the Turkey turned away to go home. They had left the village and walked some way, and then they noticed, resting against a pile of stones by the wayside, a strange wild-looking girl, who seemed very unhappy. So they thought they would ask her if they could do anything to help her, for they were kind children and sorry indeed for any one in distress.

The girl seemed to be about fifteen years old. She was dressed in very ragged clothes. Round her shoulders there was an old brown shawl. She wore no bonnet. Her hair was coal-black and hung down uncombed and unfastened. She had something hidden under her shawl; on seeing them coming towards her, she carefully put it under her and sat upon it. She sat watching the children approach, and did not move or stir till they were within a yard of her; then she wiped her eyes just as if she had been crying bitterly, and looked up.

The children stood still in front of her for a moment, staring at her. "Are you crying?" they asked shyly.

To their surprise she said in a most cheerful voice, "Oh dear, no! quite the contrary. Are you?"

"Perhaps you have lost yourself?" they said gently.

But the girl answered promptly, "Certainly not. Why, you have just found me. Besides," she added, "I live in the village."

The children were surprised at this, for they had never seen her before, and yet they thought they knew all the village folk by sight.

Then the Turkey, who had an inquiring mind, put a question. "What are you sitting on?" she asked.

"On a peardrum," the girl answered.

"What is a peardrum?" they asked.

"I am surprised at your not knowing," the girl answered. "Most people in good society have one." And then she pulled it out and showed it to them. It was a curious instrument, a good deal like a guitar in shape; it had three strings, but only two pegs by which to tune them. But the strange thing about the peardrum was not the music it made, but a little square box attached to one side.

"Where did you get it?" the children asked.

"I bought it," the girl answered.

"Didn't it cost a great deal of money?" they asked.

"Yes," answered the girl slowly, nodding her head, "it cost a great deal of money. I am very rich," she added.

"You don't look rich," they said, in as polite a voice as possible.

"Perhaps not," the girl answered cheerfully.

At this, the children gathered courage, and ventured to remark, "You look rather shabby."

"Indeed?" said the girl in a voice of one who had heard a pleasant but surprising statement. "A little shabbiness is very respectable," she added in a satisfied voice. "I must really tell them this," she continued. And the children wondered what she meant. She opened the little box by the side of the peardrum, and said, just as if she were speaking to some one who could hear her, "They say I look rather shabby; it is quite lucky isn't it?"

"Why, you are not speaking to any one!" they said, more surprised than ever.

"Oh dear, yes! I am speaking to them both."

"Both?" they said, wondering.

"Yes. I have here a little man dressed as a peasant, and a little woman to match. I put them on the lid of the box, and when I play they dance most beautifully."

"Oh! let us see; do let us see!" the children cried.

Then the village girl looked at them doubtfully. "Let you see!" she said slowly. "Well, I am not sure that I can. Tell me, are you good?"

"Yes, yes," they answered eagerly, "we are very good!"

"Then it's quite impossible," she answered, and resolutely closed the lid of the box.

They stared at her in astonishment. "But we are good," they cried, thinking she must have misunderstood them. "We are very good. Then can't you let us see the little man and woman?"

"Oh dear, no!" the girl answered. "I only show them to naughty children. And the worse the children the better do the man and woman dance."

She put the peardrum carefully under her ragged cloak, and prepared to go on her way. "I really could not have believed that you were good," she said reproachfully, as if they had accused themselves of some great crime. "Well, good day."

"Oh, but we will be naughty," they said in despair.

"I am afraid you couldn't," she answered, shaking her head. "It requires a great deal of skill to be naughty well."

And swiftly she walked away, while the children felt their eyes fill with tears, and their hearts ache with disappointment.

"If we had only been naughty," they said, "we should have seen them dance."

"Suppose," said the Turkey, "we try to be naughty today; perhaps she would let us see them to-morrow."

"But, oh!" said Blue-Eyes, "I don't know how to be naughty; no one ever taught me."

The Turkey thought for a few minutes in silence. "I think I can be naughty if I try," she said. "I'll try to-night."

"Oh, don't be naughty without me!" she cried. "It would be so unkind of you. You know I want to see the little man and woman just as much as you do. You are very, very unkind."

And so, quarreling and crying, they reached their home.

Now, when their mother saw them, she was greatly astonished, and, fearing they were hurt, ran to meet them.

"Oh, my children, oh, my dear, dear children," she said; "what is the matter?"

But they did not dare tell their mother about the village girl and the little man and woman, so they answered, "Nothing is the matter," and cried all the more.

"Poor children!" the mother said to herself, "They are tired, and perhaps they are hungry; after tea they will be better." And she went back to the cottage, and made the fire blaze; and she put the kettle on to boil, and set the tea-things on the table. Then she went to the little cupboard and took out some bread and cut it on the table, and said in a loving voice, "Dear little children, come and have your tea. And see, there is the baby waking from her sleep; she will crow at us while we eat."

But the children made no answer to the dear mother; they only stood still by the window and said nothing.

"Come, children," the mother said again. "Come, Blue-Eyes, and come, my Turkey; here is nice sweet bread for tea." Then suddenly she looked up and saw that the Turkey's eyes were full of tears.

"Turkey!" she exclaimed, "my dear little Turkey! what is the matter? Come to mother, my sweet." And putting the baby down, she held out her arms, and the Turkey ran swiftly into them.

"Oh, mother," she sobbed, "Oh, dear mother! I do so want to be naughty. I do so want to be very, very naughty."

And then Blue-Eyes left her chair also, and rubbing her face against her mother's shoulder, cried sadly. "And so do I, mother. Oh, I'd give anything to be very, very naughty."

"But, my dear children," said the mother, in astonishment, "Why do you want to be naughty?"

"Because we do; oh, what shall we do?" they cried together.

"I should be very angry if you were naughty. But you could not be, for you love me," the mother answered.

"Why couldn't we?" they asked.

Then the mother thought a while before she answered; and she seemed to be speaking rather to herself than to them.

"Because if one loves well," she said gently, "one's love is stronger than all bad feelings in one, and conquers them."

"We don't know what you mean," they cried; "and we do love you; but we want to be naughty."

"Then I should know you did not love me," the mother said.

"If we were very, very, very naughty, and wouldn't be good, what then?"

"Then," said the mother sadly—and while she spoke her eyes filled with tears, and a sob almost choked her—"then," she said, "I should have to go away and leave you, and to send home a new mother, with glass eyes and wooden tail."

II

"Good-day," said the village girl, when she saw Blue-Eyes and the Turkey approach. She was again sitting by the heap of stones, and under her shawl the peardrum was hidden.

"Are the little man and woman there?" the children asked.

"Yes, thank you for inquiring after them," the girl answered; "they are both here and quite well. The little woman has heard a secret—she tells it while she dances."

"Oh do let us see," they entreated.

"Quite impossible, I assure you," the girl answered promptly. "You see, you are good."

"Oh!" said Blue-Eyes, sadly; "but mother says if we are naughty she will go away and send home a new mother, with glass eyes and a wooden tail."

"Indeed," said the girl, still speaking in the same unconcerned voice, "that is what they all say. They all threaten that kind of thing. Of course really there are no mothers with glass eyes and wooden tails; they would be much too expensive to make." And the common sense of this remark the children saw at once.

"We think you might let us see the little man and woman dance."

"The kind of thing you would think," remarked the village girl.

"But will you if we are naughty?" they asked in despair.

"I fear you could not be naughty—that is, really—even if you tried," she said scornfully.

"But if we are very naughty tonight, will you let us see them to-morrow?"

"Questions asked to-day are always best answered to-morrow," the girl said, and turned round as if to walk on. "Good-day," she said blithely; "I must really go and play a little to myself."

For a few minutes the children stood looking after her,

then they broke down and cried. The Turkey was the first to wipe away her tears. "Let us go home and be very naughty," she said; "then perhaps she will let us see them to-morrow."

And that afternoon the dear mother was sorely distressed, for, instead of sitting at their tea as usual with smiling happy faces, they broke their mugs and threw their bread and butter on the floor, and when the mother told them to do one thing they carefully did another, and only stamped their feet with rage when she told them to go upstairs until they were good.

"Do you remember what I told you I should do if you were very, very naughty?" she asked sadly.

"Yes, we know, but it isn't true," they cried. "There is no mother with a wooden tail and glass eyes, and if there were we should just stick pins into her and send her away; but there is none."

Then the mother became really angry, and sent them off to bed, but instead of crying and being sorry at her anger, they laughed for joy, and sat up and sang merry songs at the top of their voices.

The next morning quite early, without asking leave from the mother, the children got up and ran off as fast as they could to look for the village girl. She was sitting as usual by the heap of stones with the peardrum under her shawl.

"Now please show us the little man and woman," they cried, "and let us hear the peardrum. We were very naughty last night." But the girl kept the peardrum carefully hidden.

"So you say," she answered. "You were not half naughty enough. As I remarked before, it requires a great deal of skill to be naughty well."

"But we broke our mugs, we threw our bread and butter on the floor, we did everything we could to be tiresome."

"Mere trifles," answered the village girl scornfully. "Did you throw cold water on the fire, did you break the clock, did you pull all the tins down from the walls, and throw them on the floor?"

"No," exclaimed the children, aghast, "we did not do that."

"I thought not," the girl answered. "So many people mistake a little noise and foolishness for real naughtiness." And before they could say another word she had vanished.

"We'll be much worse," the children cried, in despair. "We'll go and do all the things she says"; and then they went home and did all these things. And when the mother saw all that they had done she did not scold them as she had the day before, but she just broke down and cried, and said sadly—

"Unless you are good to-morrow, my poor Blue-Eyes and Turkey, I shall indeed have to go away and come back no more, and the new mother I told you of will come to you."

They did not believe her; yet their hearts ached when they saw how unhappy she looked, and they thought within themselves that when they once had seen the little man and woman dance, they would be good to the dear mother for ever afterwards.

The next morning, before the birds were stirring, the children crept out of the cottage and ran across the fields. They found the village girl sitting by the heap of stones, just as if it were her natural home.

"We have been very naughty," they cried. "We have done all the things you told us; now will you show us the little man and woman?" The girl looked at them curiously. "You really seem quite excited," she said in her usual voice. "You should be calm."

"We have done all the things you told us," the children cried again, "and we do so long to hear the secret. We have been so very naughty, and mother says she will go away to-day and send home a new mother if we are not good."

"Indeed," said the girl. "Well, let me see. When did your mother say she would go?"

"But if she goes, what shall we do?" they cried in despair. "We don't want her to go; we love her very much."

"You had better go back and be good, you are really not clever enough to be anything else; and the little woman's secret is very important; she never tells it for make-believe naughtiness.''

"But we did all the things you told us," the children cried.

"You didn't throw the looking-glass out of the window, or stand the baby on its head."

"No, we didn't do that," the children gasped.

"I thought not," the girl said triumphantly. "Well, good-day. I shall not be here to-morrow."

"Oh, but don't go away," they cried. "Do let us see them just once."

"Well, I shall go past your cottage at eleven o'clock this morning," the girl said. "Perhaps I shall play the peardrum as I go by."

"And will you show us the man and woman?" they asked.

"Quite impossible, unless you have really deserved it; make-believe naughtiness is only spoilt goodness. Now if you break the looking-glass and do the things that are desired . . ."

"Oh, we will," they cried. "We will be very naughty till we hear you coming."

Then again the children went home, and were naughty, oh, so very very naughty that the dear mother's heart ached and her eyes filled with tears, and at last she went upstairs and slowly put on her best gown and her new sun-bonnet, and she dressed the baby all in its Sunday clothes, and then she came down and stood before Blue-Eyes and the Turkey, and just as she did so the Turkey threw the looking-glass out of the window, and it fell with a loud crash upon the ground.

"Good-bye, my children," the mother said sadly, kissing them. "The new mother will be home presently. Oh, my poor children!" and then weeping bitterly, the mother took the baby in her arms and turned to leave the house.

"But mother, we will be good at half-past eleven, come back at half-past eleven," they cried, "and we'll both be good; we must be naughty till eleven o'clock." But the mother only picked up the little bundle in which she had tied up her cotton apron, and went slowly out at the door. Just by the corner of the fields she stopped and turned, and waved her handkerchief, all wet with tears, to the children at the window; she made the baby kiss its hand; and in a moment mother and baby had vanished from their sight.

Then the children felt their hearts ache with sorrow, and they cried bitterly, and yet they could not believe that she had gone. And the broken clock struck eleven, and suddenly there was a sound, a quick, clanging, jangling sound, with a strange discordant note at intervals. They rushed to the open window, and there they saw the village girl dancing along and playing as she did so.

"We have done all you told us," the children called. "Come and see; and now show us the little man and woman."

The girl did not cease her playing or her dancing, but she called out in a voice that was half speaking half singing. "You did it all badly. You threw the water on the wrong side of the fire, the tin things were not quite in the middle of the room, the clock was not broken enough, you did not stand the baby on its head."

She was already passing the cottage. She did not stop singing, and all she said sounded like part of a terrible song. "I am going to my own land," the girl sang, "to the land where I was born."

"But our mother is gone," the children cried; "our dear mother will she ever come back?"

"No," sang the girl, "she'll never come back. She took a boat upon the river; she is sailing to the sea; she will meet your father once again, and they will go sailing on."

Then the girl, her voice getting fainter and fainter in the distance, called out once more to them. "Your new mother is coming. She is already on her way; but she only walks slowly, for her tail is rather long, and her spectacles are left behind; but she is coming, she is coming—coming—coming."

The last word died away; it was the last one they ever heard the village girl utter. On she went, dancing on.

Then the children turned, and looked at each other and at the little cottage home, that only a week before had been so bright and happy, so cosy and spotless. The fire was out, the clock all broken and spoilt. And there was the baby's high chair, with no baby to sit in it; there was the cupboard on the wall, and never a sweet loaf on its shelf; and there were the broken mugs, and the bits of bread tossed about, and the greasy boards which the mother had knelt down to scrub until they were as white as snow. In the midst of all stood the children, looking at the wreck they had made, their eyes blinded with tears, and their poor little hands clasped in misery.

"I don't know what we shall do if the new mother comes," cried Blue-Eyes. "I shall never, never like any other mother."

The Turkey stopped crying for a minute, to think what should be done. "We will bolt the door and shut the window; and we won't take any notice when she knocks."

All through the afternoon they sat watching and listening for fear of the new mother, but they saw and heard nothing of her, and gradually they became less and less afraid lest she could come. They fetched a pail of water and washed the floor; they found some rag, and rubbed the tins; they picked up the broken mugs and made the room as neat as they could. There was no sweet loaf to put on the table, but perhaps the mother would bring something from the village, they thought. At last all was ready, and Blue-Eyes and the Turkey washed their faces and their hands, and then sat and waited, for of course they did not believe what the village girl had said about their mother sailing away.

Suddenly, while they were sitting by the fire, they heard a sound as of something heavy being dragged along the ground outside, and then there was a loud and terrible knocking at the door. The children felt their hearts stand still. They knew it could not be their own mother, for she would have turned the handle and tried to come in without any knocking at all.

Again there came a loud and terrible knocking.

"She'll break the door down if she knocks so hard," cried Blue-Eyes.

"Go and put your back to it," whispered the Turkey, "and I'll peep out of the window and try to see if it is really the new mother."

So in fear and trembling Blue-Eyes put her back against the door, and the Turkey went to the window. She could just see a black satin poke bonnet with a frill round the edge, and a long bony arm carrying a black leather bag. From beneath the bonnet there flashed a strange bright light, and Turkey's heart sank and her cheeks turned pale, for she knew it was the flashing of two glass eyes. She crept up to Blue-Eyes. "It is—it is—it is!" she whispered, her voice shaking with fear, "it is the new mother!"

Together they stood with the two little backs against the door. There was a long pause. They thought perhaps the new mother had made up her mind that there was no one at home to let her in, and would go away, but presently the two children heard through the thin wooden door the new mother move a little, and then say to herself—"I must break the door open with my tail."

For one terrible moment all was still, but in it the children could almost hear her lift up her tail, and then, with a fearful blow, the little painted door was cracked and splintered. With a shriek the children darted from the spot and fled through the cottage, and out at the back door into the forest beyond. All night long they stayed in the darkness and the cold, and all the next day and the next, and all through the cold, dreary days and the long dark nights that followed.

They are there still, my children. All through the long weeks and months they have been there, with only green rushes for their pillows and only the brown dead leaves to cover them, feeding on the wild strawberries in the summer, or on the nuts when they hang green; on the blackberries when they are no longer sour in the autumn, and in the winter on the little red berries that ripen in the snow. They wander about among the tall dark firs or beneath the great trees beyond. Sometimes they stay to rest beside the little pool near the copse, and they long and long, with a longing that is greater than words can say, to see their own dear mother again, just once again, to tell her that they'll be good for evermore—just once again.

And still the new mother stays in the little cottage, but the windows are closed and the doors are shut, and no one knows what the inside looks like. Now and then, when the darkness has fallen and the night is still, hand in hand Blue-Eyes and the Turkey creep up near the home in which they once were so happy, and with beating hearts they watch and listen; sometimes a blinding flash comes through the window, and they know it is the light from the new mother's glass eyes, or they hear a strange muffled noise, and they know it is the sound of her wooden tail as she drags it along the floor.

Russell Kirk

THERE'S A LONG, LONG TRAIL A-WINDING

Russell Kirk is one of the most articulate Conservatives in the U.S. and also one of the contemporary masters of the Gothic, the supernatural and the uncanny in fiction. He is the great living exponent of the Christian moral allegory in the horror mode. His approach is set forth in an essay appendix to his first collection, *The Surly Sullen Bell* (1962), "A Cautionary Note on the Ghostly Tale." Kirk and T. S. Eliot were close friends and they shared an intellectual and emotional commitment to the Christian supernatural that informs all of Kirk's fiction. "There's a Long, Long Trail A-Winding" is one of Kirk's later works and the winner of the World Fantasy Award for best short fiction of the year in 1977. It epitomizes the overtly allegorical mode in contemporary horror (stories written as allegory as opposed to stories, such as much of the works of Stephen King, that may be interpreted using the moral coordinates of the allegorical method). Kirk's body of work in this mode makes him the C. S. Lewis of the supernatural genre in our day.

Then he said unto the disciples, It is impossible but that offenses will come; but woe unto him, through whom they come!

It were better for him that a millstone were hanged about his neck, and he cast into the sea, than that he should offend one of these little ones.

Luke 17:1–2

Along the vast empty six-lane highway, the blizzard swept as if it meant to swallow all the sensual world. Frank Sarsfield, massive though he was, scudded like a heavy kite before that overwhelming wind. On his thick white hair the snow clotted and tried to form a Phrygian cap; the big flakes so swirled about his Viking face that he scarcely could make out the barren country on either side of the road.

Somehow he must get indoors. Racing for sanctuary, the last automobile had swept unheeding past his thumb two hours ago, doubtless bound for the county town some twenty miles eastward. Westward among the hills, the highway must be blocked by snowdrifts now. This was an unkind twelfth of January. "Blow, blow, thou winter wind!" Twilight being almost upon him, soon he must find lodging or else freeze stiff by the roadside.

He had walked more than thirty miles that day. Having in his pocket the sum of twenty-nine dollars and thirty cents, he could have put up at either of the two motels he had passed, had they not been closed for the winter. Well, as always, he was decently dressed—a good wash-and-wear suit and a neat black overcoat. As always, he was shaven and clean and civil-spoken. Surely some farmer or villager would take him in, if he knocked with a ten-dollar bill in his fist. People sometimes mistook him for a stranded well-to-do motorist, and sometimes he took the trouble to undeceive them.

But where to apply? This was depopulated country, its forests gone to the sawmills long before, its mines worked out. The freeway ran through the abomination of desolation. He did not prefer to walk the freeways, but on such a day as this there were no cars on the lesser roads.

He had run away from a hardscrabble New Hampshire farm

when he was fourteen, and ever since then, except for brief working intervals, he had been either on the roads or in the jails. Now his sixtieth birthday was imminent. There were few men bigger than Frank Sarsfield, and none more solitary. Where was a friendly house?

For a few moments, the rage of the snow slackened; he stared about. Away to the left, almost a mile distant, he made out a grim high clump of buildings on rising ground, a wall enclosing them; the roof of the central building was gone. Sarsfield grinned, knowing what that complex must be: a derelict prison. He had lodged in prisons altogether too many nights.

His hand sheltering his eyes from the north wind, he looked to his right. Down in a snug valley, beside a narrow river and broad marshes, he could perceive a village or hamlet: a white church-tower, three or four commercial buildings, some little houses, beyond them a park of bare maple trees. The old highway must have run through or near this forgotten place, but the new freeway had sealed it off. There was no sign of a freeway exit to the settlement; probably it could be reached by car only along some detouring country lane. In such a little decayed town there would be folk willing to accept him for the sake of his proffered ten dollars—or, better, simply for charity's sake and talk with an amusing stranger who could recite every kind of poetry.

He scrambled heavily down the embankment. At this point, praise be, no tremendous wire fence kept the haughty new highway inviolable. His powerful thighs took him through the swelling drifts, though his heart pounded as the storm burst upon him afresh.

The village was more distant than he had thought. He passed panting through old fields half-grown up to poplar and birch. A little to the west he noticed what seemed to be old mine-workings, with fragments of brick buildings. He clambered upon an old railroad bed, its rails and ties taken up; perhaps the new freeway had dealt the final blow to the rails. Here the going was somewhat easier.

Mingled with the wind's shriek, did he hear a church-bell now? Could they be holding services at the village in this weather? Presently he came to a burnt-out little railway depot, on its platform signboard still the name ''Anthonyville.'' Now he walked on a street of sorts, but no car-tracks or footprints sullied the snow.

Anthonyville Free Methodist Church hulked before him. Indeed the bell was swinging, and now and again faintly ringing in the steeple; but it was the wind's mockery, a knell for the derelict town of Anthonyville. The church door was slamming in the high wind, flying open again, and slamming once more, like a perpetual-motion machine, the glass being gone from the church windows. Sarsfield trudged past the skeletal church.

The front of Emmons's General Store was boarded up, and so was the front of what may have been a drugstore. The village hall was a wreck. The school may have stood upon those scanty foundations which protruded from the snow. And from no chimney of the decrepit cottages and cabins along Main Street—the only street—did any smoke rise.

Sarsfield never had seen a deader village. In an upper window of what looked like a livery-stable converted into a garage, a faded cardboard sign could be read—

REMEMBER YOUR FUTURE
BACK THE TOWNSEND PLAN

Was no one at all left here—not even some gaunt old couple managing on Social Security? He might force his way into one of the stores or cottages—though on principle and prudence he generally steered clear of possible charges of breaking and entering—but that would be cold comfort. In poor Anthonyville there must remain some living soul.

His mittened hands clutching his red ears, Sarsfield had plodded nearly to the end of Main Street. Anthonyville was Endsville, he saw now: river and swamp and new highway cut it off altogether from the rest of the frozen world, except for the drift-obliterated country road that twisted southward, Lord knew whither. He might count himself lucky to find a stove, left behind in some shack, that he could feed with boards ripped from walls.

Main Street ended at that grove or park of old maples. Just a sugarbush, like those he had tapped in his boyhood under his father's rough command? No: had the trees not been leafless, he might not have discerned the big stone house among the trees, the only substantial building remaining to Anthonyville. But see it he did for one moment, before the blizzard veiled it from him. There were stone gateposts, too, and a bronze tablet set into one of them. Sarsfield brushed the snowflakes from the inscription: "Tamarack House."

Stumbling among the maples toward this promise, he almost collided with a tall glacial boulder. A similar boulder rose a few feet to his right, the pair of them halfway between gateposts and house. There was a bronze tablet on this boulder, too, and he paused to read it:

SACRED TO THE MEMORY OF
JEROME ANTHONY
JULY 4, 1836–JANUARY 14, 1915
BRIGADIER-GENERAL IN THE CORPS OF ENGINEERS,
ARMY OF THE REPUBLIC, FOUNDER OF THIS TOWN
ARCHITECT OF ANTHONYVILLE STATE PRISON
WHO DIED AS HE HAD LIVED, WITH HONOR

> *"And there will I keep you forever,*
> *Yes, forever and a day,*
> *Till the walls shall crumble in ruin,*
> *And moulder in dust away."*

There's an epitaph for a prison architect, Sarsfield thought. It was too bitter an evening for inspecting the other boulder, and he hurried toward the portico of Tamarack House. This was a very big house indeed, a bracketed house, built all of squared fieldstone with beautiful glints to the masonry. A cupola topped it.

Once, come out of the cold into a public library, Sarsfield had pored through a picture-book about American architectural styles. There was a word for this sort of house. Was it "Italianate"? Yes, it rose in his memory—he took pride in no quality except his power of recollection. Yes, that was the word. Had he visited this house before? He could not account for a vague familiarity. Perhaps there had been a photograph of this particular house in that library book.

Every window was heavily shuttered, and no smoke rose from any of the several chimneys. Sarsfield went up to the stone steps to confront the oaken front door.

It was a formidable door, but it seemed as if at some time it had been broken open, for long ago a square of oak with a different grain had been mortised into the area round lock and keyhole. There was a gigantic knocker with a strange face worked upon it. Sarsfield knocked repeatedly.

No one answered. Conceivably the storm might have made his pounding inaudible to any occupants, but who could spend the winter in a shuttered house without fires? Another bronze plaque was screwed to the door:

TAMARACK HOUSE
PROPERTY OF THE ANTHONY FAMILY TRUST
GUARDED BY PROTECTIVE SERVICE

Sarsfield doubted the veracity of the last line. He made his way round to the back. No one answered those back doors, either, and they too were locked.

But presently he found what he had hoped for: an oldfangled slanting cellar door, set into the foundations. It was not wise to enter without permission, but at least he might accomplish it without breaking. His fingers, though clumsy, were strong as the rest of him. After much trouble and with help from the Boy Scout knife that he carried, he pulled the pins out of the cellar door's three hinges and scrambled down into the darkness. With the passing of the years, he had become something of a jailhouse lawyer—though those young inmates bored him with their endless chatter about Miranda and Escobedo. And now he thought of the doctrine called "defense of necessity." If caught, he could say that self-preservation from freezing is the first necessity; besides, they might not take him for a bum.

Faint light down the cellar steps—he would replace the hinge-pins later—showed him an inner door at the foot. That door was hooked, though hooked only. With a sigh, Sarsfield put his shoulder to the door; the hook clattered to the stone floor inside; and he was master of all he surveyed.

In that black cellar he found no light-switch. Though he never smoked, he carried matches for such emergencies. Having lit one, he discovered a providential kerosene lamp on a table, with enough kerosene still in it. Sarsfield went lamp-lit through the cellars and up more stone stairs into a pantry. "Anybody home?" he called. It was an eerie echo.

He would make sure before exploring, for he dreaded shotguns. How about a cheerful song? In that chill pantry, Sarsfield bellowed a tune formerly beloved at Rotary Clubs. Once a waggish Rotarian, after half an hour's talk with the hobo extraordinary, had taken him to Rotary for lunch and commanded him to tell tales of the road and to sing the members a song. Frank Sarsfield's untutored voice was loud enough when he wanted it to be, and he sang the song he had sung to Rotary:

> *"There's a long, long trail a-winding*
> *into the land of my dreams,*
> *Where the nightingale is singing*
> *and the white moon beams;*
> *There's a long, long night of waiting*
> *until my dreams all come true,*
> *Till the day when I'll be walking*
> *down that long, long trail to you!"*

No response: no cry, no footstep, not a rustle. Even in so big a house, they couldn't have failed to hear his song, sung in a voice fit to wake the dead. Father O'Malley had called Frank's voice "stentorian"—a good word, though he was not just sure what it meant. He liked that last line, though he'd no one to walk to; he'd repeat it:

> "Till the day when I'll be walking
> down that long, long trail to you!"

It was all right. Sarsfield went into the dining room, where he found a splendid long walnut table, chairs with embroidered seats, a fine sideboard and china cabinet, and a high Venetian chandelier. The china was in that cabinet, and the silverware was in that sideboard. But in no room of Tamarack House was any living soul.

Sprawled in a big chair before the fireplace in the Sunday parlor, Sarsfield took the chill out of his bones. The woodshed, connected with the main house by a passage from the kitchen, was half filled with logs—not first-rate fuel, true, for they had been stacked there three or four years ago, to judge by the fungi upon them, but burnable after he had collected old newspapers and chopped kindling. He had crisscrossed elm and birch to make a noble fire.

It was not very risky to let white woodsmoke eddy from the chimneys, for it would blend with the driving snow and the blast would dissipate it at once. Besides, Anthonyville's population was zero. From the cupola atop the house, in another lull of the blizzard, he had looked over the icy countryside and had seen no inhabited farmhouse up the forgotten dirt road—which, anyway, was hopelessly blocked by drifts today. There was no approach for vehicles from the freeway, while river and marsh protected the rear. He speculated that Tamarack House might be inhabited summers, though not in any very recent summer. The "Protective Service" probably consisted of a farmer who made a fortnightly inspection in fair weather.

It was good to hole up in a remote county where burglars seemed unknown as yet. Frank Sarsfield restricted his own depredations to church poor-boxes (Catholic, preferably, he being no Protestant) and then under defense of necessity, after a run of unsuccessful mendicancy. He feared and detested strong thieves, so numerous nowadays; to avoid them and worse than thieves, he steered clear of the cities, roving to little places which still kept crime in the family, where it belonged.

He had dined, and then washed the dishes dutifully. The kitchen wood-range still functioned, and so did the hard-water and soft-water hand pumps in the scullery. As for food, there was enough to feed a good-sized prison: the shelves of the deep cellar cold-room threatened to collapse under the weight of glass jars full of jams, jellies, preserved peaches, apricots, applesauce, pickled pork, pickled trout, and many more good things, all redolent of his New England youth. Most of the jars had neat paper labels, all giving the year of canning, some of name of the canner; on the front shelves, the most recent date he had found was 1968, on a little pot of strawberry jam, and below it was the name "Allegra" in a feminine hand.

Everything in this house lay in apple-pie order—though Sarsfield wondered how long the plaster would keep from cracking, with Tamarack House unheated in winter. He felt positively virtuous for lighting fires, one here in the Sunday parlor, another in the little antique iron stove in the bedroom he had chosen for himself at the top of the house.

He had poked into every handsome room of Tamarack House, with the intense pleasure of a small boy who had found his way into an enchanted castle. Every room was satisfying, well-furnished (he was warming by the fire two sheets from the linen closet, for his bed), and wondrously old-fashioned. There was no electric light, no central heating, no bathroom; there was an indoor privy, at the back of the woodshed, but no running water unless one counted the hand pumps. There was an oldfangled wall telephone: Frank tried, greatly daring, for the operator, but it was dead. He had found a crystal-set radio that didn't work. This was an old lady's house, surely, and the old lady hadn't visited it for some years, but perhaps her relatives kept it in order as a "holiday home" or in hope of selling it—at ruined Anthonyville, a forlorn hope. He had discovered two canisters of tea, a jar full of coffee beans, and ten gallons of kerosene. How thoughtful!

Perhaps the old lady was dead, buried under the other boulder among the maples in front of the house. Perhaps she had been the General's daughter—but no, not if the General had been born in 1836. Why those graves in the lawn? Sarsfield had heard of farm families, near medical schools in the old days, who had buried their dead by the house for fear of body-snatchers; but that couldn't apply at Anthonyville. Well, there were family graveyards, but this must be one of the smallest.

The old General who built this house had died on January fourteenth. Day after tomorrow, January fourteenth would come round again, and it would be Frank Sarsfield's sixtieth birthday. "I drink your health in water, General," Sarsfield said aloud, raising his cut-glass goblet taken from the china cabinet. There was no strong drink in the house, but that didn't distress Sarsfield, for he never touched it. His mother had warned him against it—and sure enough, the one time he had drunk a good deal of wine, when he was new to the road, he had got sick. "Thanks, General, for your hospitality." Nobody responded to his toast.

His mother had been a saint, the neighbors had said, and his father a drunken devil. He had seen neither of them after he ran away. He had missed his mother's funeral because he hadn't known of her death until months after; he had missed his father's, long later, because he chose to miss it, though that omission cost him sleepless nights now. Sarsfield slept poorly at best. Almost always there were nightmares.

Yet perhaps he would sleep well enough tonight in that little garret room near the cupola. He had found that several of the bedrooms in Tamarack House had little metal plates over their doorways. There were "The General's Room" and "Father's Room" and "Mama's Room" and "Alice's Room" and "Allegra's Room" and "Edith's Room." By a happy coincidence, the little room at the top of the back stair, on the garret floor of the house was labelled "Frank's Room." But he'd not chosen it for that only. At the top of the house, one was safer from sheriffs or burglars. And through the sky-light—there was only a frieze window—a man could get to the roof of the main block. From that roof, one could de-scend to the woodshed roof by a fire-escape of iron rungs fixed in the stone outer wall; and from the woodshed, it was an easy drop to the ground. After that, the chief difficulty would be to run down Main Street and then get across the freeway without being detected, while people searched the house for you. Talk of Goldilocks and the Three Bears! Much experience had taught Sarsfield such forethought.

Had that other Frank, so commemorated over the bedroom door, been a son or a servant? Presumably a son—though Sarsfield had found no pictures of boys in the old velvet-covered album in the Sunday parlor, nor any of manservants. There were many pictures of the General, a little roosterlike man with a beard; and of Father, portly and pleasant-faced; and of Mama, elegant; and of three small girls, who must be Alice and Allegra and Edith. He had liked especially the photographs of Allegra, since he had tasted her strawberry jam. All the girls were pretty, but Allegra—who must be about seven in most of the pictures—was really charming, with long ringlets and kind eyes and a delicate mouth that curved upward at its corners.

Sarsfield adored little girls and distrusted big girls. His mother had cautioned him against bad women, so he had kept away from such. Because he liked peace, he never had married—not that he could have married anyway, because that would have tied him to one place, and he was too clumsy

to earn money at practically anything except dish-washing for
summer hotels. Not marrying had meant that he could have
no little daughters like Allegra.

Sometimes he had puzzled the prison psychiatrists. In
prison it was well to play stupid. He had refrained cunningly
from reciting poetry to the psychiatrists. So after testing him
they wrote him down as "dull normal" and he was assigned
to labor as "gardener"—which meant going round the prison
yards picking up trash by a stick with a nail in the end of it.
That was easy work, and he detested hard work. Yet when
there was truly heavy work to be done in prison, sometimes
he would come forward to shovel tons of coal or carry hods
of brick or lift big blocks into place. That, too, was his cunning: it impressed the other jailbirds with his enormous
strength, so that the gangs left him alone.

"Yes, you're a loner, Frank Sarsfield," he said to himself,
aloud. He looked at himself in that splendid Sunday-parlor
mirror, which stretched from floor to ceiling. He saw a man
overweight but lean enough of face, standing six feet six,
built like a bear, a strong nose, some teeth missing, a strong
chin, and rather wild light-blue eyes. He was an uncommon
sort of bum. Deliberately he looked at his image out of the
corners of his eyes—as was his way, because he was nonviolent, and eye-contact might mean trouble.

"You look like a Viking, Frank," old Father O'Malley had
told him once, "but you ought to have been a monk."

"Oh, Father," he had answered, "I'm too much of a fool
for a monk."

"Well," said Father O'Malley, "you're no more fool than
many a brother, and you're celibate, and continent, I take it.
Yet it's late for that now. Look out you don't turn berserker,
Frank. Go to confession, sometime, to a priest that doesn't
know you, if you'll not go to me. If you'd confess, you'd not
be haunted."

But he seldom went to mass, and never to confession. All
those church boxes pilfered, his mother and father abandoned, his sister neglected, all the ghastly humbling of him-

self before policemen, all the horror and shame of the prisons! There could be no grace for him now. *"There's a long, long trail a-winding into the land of my dreams. . . ."* What dreams! He had looked up "berserker" in Webster. But he wouldn't ever do that sort of thing: a man had to keep a control upon himself, and besides he was a coward, and he loved peace.

Nearly all the other prisoners had been brutes, guilty as sin, guilty as Miranda or Escobedo. Once, sentenced for rifling a church safe, he had been put into the same cell with a man who had murdered his wife by taking off her head. The head never had been found. Sarsfield had dreamed of that head in such short intervals of sleep as he had enjoyed while the wife-killer was his cellmate. Nearly all night, every night, he had lain awake surreptitiously watching the murderer in the opposite bunk, and feeling his own neck now and again. He had been surprised and pleased when eventually the wife-killer had gone hysterical and obtained assignment to another cell. The murderer had told the guards that he just couldn't stand being watched all night by that terrible giant who never talked.

Only one of the prison psychiatrists had been pleasant or bright, and that had been the old doctor born in Vienna who went round from penitentiary to penitentiary checking on the psychiatric staffs. The old doctor had taken a liking to him, and had written a report to accompany Frank's petition for parole. Three months later, in a parole office, the parole officer had gone out hurriedly for a quarter of an hour, and Sarsfield had taken the chance to read his own file that the parole man had left in a folder on his desk.

"Francis Sarsfield has a memory that almost can be described as photographic"—so had run one line in the Vienna doctor's report. When he read that, Sarsfield had known that the doctor was a clever doctor. "He suffers chiefly from an arrest of emotional development, and may be regarded as a rather bright small boy in some respects. His three temporarily successful escapes from prison suggest that his intelligence has been much underrated. On at least one of those three occasions, he could have eluded the arresting officer had he been willing to resort to violence. Sarsfield repeatedly describes himself as nonviolent and has no record of aggression while confined, nor in connection with any of the offenses for which he was arrested. On the contrary, he seems timid and withdrawn, and might become a victim of assaults in prison, were it not for his size, strength, and power of voice.''

Sarsfield had been pleased enough by that paragraph, but a little puzzled by what followed:

''In general, Sarsfield is one of those recidivists who ought not to be confined, were any alternative method now available for restraining them from petty offenses against property. Not only does he lack belligerence against men, but apparently he is quite clean of any record against women and children. It seems that he does not indulge in autoeroticism, either—perhaps because of strict instruction by his R.C. mother during his formative years.

''I add, however, that conceivably Sarsfield is not fundamentally so gentle as his record indicates. He can be energetic in self-defence when pushed to the wall. In his youth occasionally he was induced, for the promise of five dollars or ten dollars, to stand up as an amateur against some travelling professional boxer. He admits that he did not fight hard, and cried when he was badly beaten. Nevertheless, I am inclined to suspect a potentiality for violence, long repressed but not totally extinguished by years of 'humbling himself,' in his phrase. This possibility is not so certain as to warrant additional detention, even though three years of Sarsfield's sentence remain unexpired.''

Yes, he had memorized nearly the whole of that old doctor's analysis, which had got his parole for him. There had been the concluding paragraphs:

''Francis Sarsfield is oppressed by a haunting sense of personal guilt. He is religious to the point of superstition, an R.C., and appears to believe himself damned. Although worldly-wise in a number of respects, he retains an almost unique innocence in others. His frequent humor and candor account for his success, much of the time, at begging. He has read much during his wanderings and terms of confinement. He has a strong taste for good poetry of the popular sort, and has accumulated a mass of miscellaneous information, much of it irrelevant to the life he leads.

"Although occasionally moody and even surly, most of the time he subjects himself to authority, and will work fairly well if closely supervised. He possesses no skills of any sort, unless some knack for woodchopping, acquired while he was enrolled in the Civilian Conservation Corps, can be considered a marketable skill. He appears to be incorrigibly footloose, and therefore confinement is more unpleasant to him than to most prisoners. It is truly remarkable that he continues to be rational enough, his isolation and heavy guilt-complex considered.

"Sometimes evasive when he does not desire to answer questions, nevertheless he rarely utters a direct lie. His personal modesty may be described as excessive. His habits of cleanliness are commendable, if perhaps of origins like Lady Macbeth's.

"Despite his strength, he is a diabetic and suffers from a heart murmur, sometimes painful.

"Only in circumstances so favorable as to be virtually unobtainable could Sarsfield succeed in abstaining from the behavior-pattern that has led to his repeated prosecution and imprisonment. The excessive crowding of this penitentiary considered, however, I strongly recommend that he be released upon parole. Previous psychiatric reports concerning this inmate have been shallow and erroneous, I regret to note. Perhaps Sarsfield's chief psychological difficulty is that, from obscure causes, he lacks emotional communication with other adults, although able to maintain cordial and healthy relations with small children. He is very nearly a solipsist, which in large part may account for his inability to make firm decisions or pursue any regular occupation. In contradiction of previous analyses of Sarsfield, he should not be described as 'dull normal' intellectually. Francis Xavier Sarsfield distinctly is neither dull nor normal.''

Sarsfield had looked up ''solipsist,'' but hadn't found himself much the wiser. He didn't think himself the only existent thing—not most of the time, anyway. He wasn't sure that the old doctor had been real, but he knew that his mother had been real before she went straight to Heaven. He knew that his nightmares probably weren't real; but sometimes, while awake, he could see things that other men couldn't. In a house like this, he could glimpse little unaccountable movements out of the corners of his eyes, but it wouldn't do to worry about those. He was afraid of those things which other people couldn't see, yet not so frightened of them as most people were. Some of the other inmates had called him Crazy Frank, and it had been hard to keep down his temper. If you could perceive *more* existent things, though not flesh-and-blood things, than psychiatrists or convicts could—why, were you a solipsist?

There was no point in puzzling over it. Dad had taken him out of school to work on the farm when he hadn't yet finished the fourth grade, so words like ''solipsist'' didn't mean much to him. Poets' words, though, he mostly understood. He had picked up a rhyme that made children laugh when he told it to them:

> *"Though you don't know it,*
> *You're a poet.*
> *Your feet show it:*
> *They're Longfellows."*

That wasn't very good poetry, but Henry Wadsworth Longfellow was a good poet. They must have loved Henry Wadsworth Longfellow in this house, and especially ''The Children's Hour,'' because of those three little girls named Alice, Allegra, and Edith, and those lines on the General's boulder. Allegra: that's the prettiest of all names ever, and it means "merry," someone had told him.

He looked at the cheap wristwatch he had bought, besides the wash-and-wear suit, with his last dishwashing money from that Lake Superior summer hotel. Well, midnight! It's up the wooden hill for you, Frank Sarsfield, to your snug little room under the rafters. If anybody comes to Tamarack House tonight, it's out the skylight and through the snow for you, Frank, my boy—and no tiny reindeer. If you want to survive, in prison or out of it, you stick to your own business and let other folks stew in their own juice.

Before he closed his eyes, he would pray for Mother's soul—not that she really needed it—and then say the little Scottish prayer he had found in a children's book:

"From ghosties and ghoulies, long-leggitie beasties, and things that go bump in the night, good Lord deliver us!"

The next morning, the morning before his birthday, Frank Sarsfield went up the circular stair to the cupola, even before making his breakfast of pickled trout and peaches and strong coffee. The wind had gone down, and it was snowing only lightly now, but the drifts were immense. Nobody would make his way to Anthonyville and Tamarack House this day; the snowplows would be busy elsewhere.

From this height he could see the freeway, and nothing seemed to be moving along it. The dead village lay to the north of him. To the east were river and swamp, the shores lined with those handsome tamaracks, the green gone out of them, which had given this house its name. Everything in sight belonged to Frank.

He had dreamed during the night, the wind howling and whining round the top of the house, and he had known he was dreaming, but it had been even stranger than usual, if less horrible.

In his dream, he had found himself in the dining room of Tamarack House. He had not been alone. The General and Father and Mama and the three little girls had been dining happily at the long table, and he had waited on them. In the kitchen an old woman who was the cook, and a girl who cleaned, had eaten by themselves. But when he had finished filling the family's plates, he had sat down at the end of the table, as if he had been expected to do that.

The family had talked among themselves and even to him as he ate, but somehow he had not been able to hear what they said to him. Suddenly he had pricked up his ears, though, because Allegra had spoken to him.

"Frank," she had said, all mischief, "why do they call you Punkinhead?"

The old General had frowned at the head of the table, and Mama had said, "Allegra, don't speak that way to Frank!"

But he had grinned at Allegra, if slightly hurt, and had told the little girl, "Because some men think I've got a head like a jack-o'-lantern's and not even seeds inside it."

"Nonsense, Frank," Mama had put in, "you have a very handsome head."

"You've got a pretty head, Frank," the three little girls had told him then, almost in chorus, placatingly. Allegra had come round the table to make her peace. "There's going to be a big surprise for you tomorrow, Frank," she had whispered to him. And then she had kissed him on the cheek.

That had waked him. Most of the rest of that howling night he had lain awake trying to make sense of his dream, but he couldn't. The people in it had been more real than the people he met on the long, long trail.

Now he strolled through the house again, admiring everything. It was almost as if he had seen the furniture and pictures and the carpets long, long ago. The house must be over a century old, and many of the good things in it must go back to the beginning. He would have two or three more days here until the roads were cleared. There were no newspapers to tell him about the great storm, of course, and no radio that worked; but that didn't matter.

He found a great big handsome *Complete Works of Henry Wadsworth Longfellow*, in red morocco, and an illustrated copy of the *Rubaiyat*. He didn't need to read it, because he had memorized all the quatrains once. There was a black silk ribbon as marker between the pages, and he opened it there— at Quatrain 44, it turned out:

> *"Why, if the Soul can fling the Dust aside,*
> *And naked on the Air of Heaven ride,*
> *Were't not a Shame—were't not a Shame for him*
> *In this clay carcass crippled to abide?"*

That old Vienna doctor, Frank suspected, hadn't believed in immortal souls. Frank Sarsfield knew better. But also Frank suspected that his soul never would ride, naked or clothed, on the Air of Heaven. Souls! That put him in mind of his sister, a living soul that he had forsaken. He ought to write her a letter on this the eve of his sixtieth birthday.

Frank travelled light, his luggage being mostly a safety razor, a hairbrush, and a comb; he washed his shirt and socks and underclothes every night, and often his wash-and-wear suit, too. But he did carry with him a few sheets of paper and a ballpoint pen. Sitting down at the library table—he had built a fire in the library stove also, there being no lack of logs—he began to write to Mary Sarsfield, alone in the rotting farmhouse in New Hampshire. His spelling wasn't good, he knew, but today he was careful at his birthday letter, using the big old dictionary with the General's bookplate in it.

To write that letter took most of the day. Two versions were discarded. At last Frank had done the best he could.

"Dearest Mary my sister,

"Its been nearly 9 years since I came to visit you and borrowed the $78 from you and went away again and never paid it back. I guess you don't want to see your brother Frank again after what I did that time and other times but the Ethiopian can not change his skin nor the leopard his spots and when some man like a

Jehovahs Witness or that rancher with all the cash gives me quite a lot of money I mean to send you what I owe but the post office isnt handy at the time and so I spend it on presents for little kids I meet and buying new clothes and such so I never get around to sending you that $78 Mary. Right now I have $29 and more but the post office at this place is folded up and by the time I get to the next town the money will be mostly gone and so it goes. I guess probably you need the money and Im sorry Mary but maybe some day I will win in the lottery and then Ill give you the thousands of dollars I win.

"Well Mary its been 41 years and 183 days since Mother passed away and here I am 60 years old tomorrow and you getting on toward 56. I pray that your cough is better and that your son and my nephew Jack is doing better than he was in Tallahassee Florida. Some time Mary if you would write to me c/o Father Justin O'Malley in Albatross Michigan where he is pastor now I would stop by his rectory and get your letter and read it with joy. But I know Ive been a very bad brother and I dont blame you Mary if you never get around to writing your brother Frank.

"Mary Ive been staying out of jails and working a little here and there along the road. Now Mary do you know what I hate most about those prisons? Why not being on the road you will say. No Mary the worst thing is the foul language the convicts use from morning till night. Taking the name of their Lord in vain is the least they do. There is a foul curse word in every sentence. I wasn't brought up that way any more than you Mary and I will not revile woman or child. It is like being in H——to hear it.

"Im not in bad shape except the diabetes is no better but I take my pills for it when I can buy them and dont have to take needles for it and my heart hurts me dreadfully bad sometimes when I lift heavy things hours on end and sometimes it hurts me worse at night when Ive been just lying there thinking of the life Ive led and how I ought to pay you the $78 and pay back other folks that helped me too. I owe Father O'Malley $497.11 now altogether and I keep track of it in my head and when the lottery ticket wins he will not be forgot.

"Some people have been quite good to me and I still can make them laugh and I recite to them and generally I start my reciting with what No Person of Quality wrote hundreds of years ago

'Seven wealthy towns contend for Homer dead
 Through which the living Homer begged his bread.'

"They like that and also usually they like Thomas Grays Elegy in a Country Churchyard leaving the world to darkness and to me and I recite all of that and sometimes some of the Quatrains of Omar. At farms when they ask me I chop wood for these folks and I help with the dishes but I still break a good many as you learned Mary 9 years ago but I didnt mean to do it Mary because I am just clumsy in all ways. Oh yes I am good at reciting Frosts Stopping by Woods and his poem about the Hired Man. I have been reading the poetical works of Thomas Stearns Eliot so I can recite his The Hollow Men or much of it and also his Book of Practical Cats which is comical when I come to college towns and some professor or his wife gives me a sandwich and maybe $2 and maybe a ride to the next town.

"Where I am now Mary I ought to study the poems of John Greenleaf Whittier because theres been a real blizzard maybe the biggest in the state for many years and Im Snowbound. Years ago I tried to memorize all that poem but I got only part way for it is a whopper of a poem.

"I dont hear much good Music Mary because of course at the motels there isnt any phonograph or tape recorder. Id like to hear some good string quartet or maybe old folk songs well sung for music hath charms to soothe the savage breast. Theres an old Edison at the house where Im staying now and what do you know they have a record of a song you and I used to sing together Theres a Long Long Trail A Winding. Its about the newest record in this house. Ill play it again soon thinking of you Mary my sister. O there is a long long night of waiting.

"Mary right now Im at a big fine house where the people have gone away for awhile and I watch the house for them and keep some of the rooms warm. Let me assure you Mary I wont take anything from this good old house when I go. These are nice people I know and I just came in out of the storm and Im very found of their 3 sweet little girls. I remember what you looked like when I ran way first and you looked like one of them called Alice. The one I like best though is Allegra because she makes mischief and laughs a lot but is innocent.

"I came here just yesterday but it seems as if Id lived in this house before but of course I couldnt have and I feel at home here. Nothing in this house could scare me much. You might not like it Mary because of little noises and glimpses you get but its a lovely house and as you know I like old places that have been lived in lots.

"By the way Mary once upon a time Father O'Malley told me that to the Lord all time is eternally present. I think this means everything that happens in the world in any day goes on all at once. So God sees what went on in this house long ago and whats going on in this house today all at the same time. Its just as well we dont see through Gods eyes because then wed know everything thats going to happen to us and because I'm such a sinner I dont want to know. Father O'Malley says that God may forgive me everything and have something special in store for me but I dont think so because why should He?

"And Father O'Malley says that maybe some people work out their Purgatory here on earth and I might be one of these. He says we are spirits in the prisonhouse of the body which is like we were serving Time in the world here below and maybe God forgave me long ago and Im just waiting my time and paying for what I did and it will be alright in the end. Or maybe Im being given some second chance to set things right but as Father O'Malley put it to do that Id have to fortify my Will and do some Signal Act of contrition. Father O'Malley even says I might not have to do the Act actually if only I just made up my mind to do it really and truly because what God counts is the intention. But I think people who are in Purgatory must know they are climbing up and have hope and Mary I think Im going down down down even though Ive stayed out of prisons some time now.

"Father O'Malley tells me that for everybody the battle is won or lost already in Gods sight and that though Satan thinks he has a good chance to conquer actually Satan has lost forever but doesnt know it. Mary I never did anybody any good but only harm to ones that loved me. If just once before I die I could do one Signal Act that was truly good then God might love me and let me have the Beatific Vision. Yet Mary I know Im weak of will and a coward and lazy and Ive missed my chance forever.

"Well Mary my only sister Ive bored you long enough and I just wanted to say hello and tell you to be of good cheer. Im sorry I whined and complained like a little boy about my health because Im still strong and deserve all the pain I get. Mary if you can forgive your big brother who never grew up please pray for me some time because nobody else does except possibly Father O'Malley when he isnt busy with other prayers.

I pray for Mother every night and every other night for you and once a month for Dad. You were a good little girl and sweet. Now I will say good bye and ask your pardon for bothering you with my foolishness. Also Im sorry your friends found out I was just a hobo when I was with you 9 years ago and I dont blame you for being angry with me then for talking too much and I know I wasnt fit to lodge in your house. There arent many of us old real hobos left only beatniks and such that cant walk or chop wood and I guess that is just as well. It is a degrading life Mary but I cant stop walking down that long long trail not knowing where it ends.

>   "Your Loving Brother
>   "Francis (Frank)

"P.S.: I dont wish to mislead so I will add Mary that
        the people who own this house didnt exactly
        ask me in but its alright because I wont do any
        harm here but a little good if I can. Good night
        again Mary."

Now he needed an envelope, but he had forgotten to take one from the last motel, where the Presbyterian minister had put him up. There must be some in Tamarack House, and one would not be missed, and that would not be very wrong because he would take nothing else. He found no envelopes in the drawer of the library table: so he went up the stairs and almost knocked at the closed door of Allegra's Room. Foolish! He opened the door gently.

He had admired Allegra's small rosewood desk. In its drawer was a leather letter-folder, the kind with a blotter, he found, and in the folder were several small pages, in a woman's hand, a trifle shaky. He started to sit down to read Allegra's letter that was never sent to anybody, but it passed through his mind that his great body might break the delicate rosewood chair that belonged to Allegra, so he read the letter

standing. It was dated January 14, 1969. On that birthday of
his, he had been in Joliet prison.

How beautifully Allegra wrote!

"Darling Celia,

"This is a lonely day at Tamarack House, just fifty-
four years after your great-great-grandfather the General died, so I am writing to my grand-niece to tell you
how much I hope you will be able to come up to Anthonyville and stay with me next summer—if I still am
here. The doctor says that only God knows whether I
will be. Your grandmother wants me to come down
your way to stay with her for the rest of this winter, but
I can't bear to leave Tamarack House at my age, for
they might have to put me in a rest-home down there
and then I wouldn't see this old house again.

"I am all right, really, because kind Mr. Connor
looks in every day, and Mrs. Williams comes every
other day to clean. I am not sick, my little girl, but
simply older than my years, and running down. When
you come up next summer, God willing, I will make
you that soft toast you like, and perhaps Mr. Connor
will turn the crank for the ice-cream, and I may try to
make some preserves with you to help me.

"You weren't lonely, were you, when you stayed with
me last summer for a whole month? Of course there
are fewer than a hundred people left in Anthonyville
now, and most of those are old. They say that there will
be practically nobody living in the town a few years
from now, when the new highway is completed and the
old one is abandoned. There were more than two thousand people here in town and roundabout, a few years
after the General built Tamarack House! But first the
lumber industry gave out, and then the mines were exhausted, and the prison-break in 1915 scared many away
forever. There are no passenger trains now, and they

say the railway line will be pulled out altogether when the new freeway—they have just begun building it to the east—is ready for traffic. But we still have the maples and the tamaracks, and there are ever so many raccoons and opossums and squirrels for you to watch—and a lynx, I think, and an otter or two, and many deer.

"Celia, last summer you asked me about the General's death and all the things that happened then, because you had heard something of them from your Grandmother Edith. But I didn't wish to frighten you, so I didn't tell you everything. You are older now, and you have a right to know, because when you grow up you will be one of the trustees of the Anthony Family Trust, and then this old house will be in your charge when I am gone. Tamarack House is not at all frightening, except a little in the morning on every January 14. I do hope that you and the other trustees will keep the house always, with the money that Father left to me—he was good at making money, even though the forests vanished and the mines failed, by his investments in Chicago—and which I am leaving to the Family Trust. I've kept the house just as it was, for the sake of the General's memory and because I love it that way.

"You asked just what happened on January 14, 1915. There were seven people who slept in the house that month—not counting Cook and Cynthia (who was a kind of nannie to us girls and also cleaned), because they slept at their houses in the village. In the house, of course, was the General, my grandfather, your great-great-grandfather, who was nearly eighty years old. Then there were Father and Mama, and the three of us little sisters, and dear Frank.

"Alice and sometimes even that baby Edith used to tease me in those days by screaming, 'Frank's Allegra's sweetheart! Frank's Allegra's sweetheart!' I used to chase them, but I suppose it was true: he liked me best. Of course he was about sixty years old, though not so old as I am now, and I was a little thing. He used to take me through the swamps and show me the muskrats' houses. The first time he took me on such a trip, Mama raised her eyebrows when he was out of the room, but the General said, 'I'll warrant Frank; I have his papers.' Alice and Edith might just as well have shouted, 'Frank's Allegra's slave!' He read to me—oh, Robert Louis Stevenson's poems and all sorts of books. I never had another sweetheart, partly because almost all the young men left Anthonyville as I grew up when there was no work for them here, and the ones that remained didn't please Mama.

"We three sisters used to play Creepmouse with Frank, I remember well. We would be the Creepmice, and would sneak up and scare him when he wasn't watching, and he would pretend to be terrified. He made up a little song for us—or, rather, he put words to some tune he had borrowed:

'Down, down, down in Creepmouse Town
  All the lamps are low,
  And the little rodent feet
  Softly come and go

'There's a rat in Creepmouse Town
  And a bat or two:
  Everything in Creepmouse Town
  Would swiftly frighten you!'

"Do you remember, Celia, that the General was State Supervisor of Prisons and Reformatories for time out of mind? He was a good architect, too, and designed Anthonyville State Prison, without taking any fee for himself, as a model prison. Some people in the capital said that he did it to give employment to his county, but really it was because the site was so isolated that it would be difficult for convicts to escape.

"The General knew Frank's last name, but he never

told the rest of us. Frank had been in Anthonyville State Prison at one time, and later other prisons, and the General had taken him out of one of those other prisons on parole, having known Frank when he was locked up at Anthonyville. I never learned what Frank had done to be sentenced to prison, but he was gentle with me and everybody else, until that early morning of January 14.

"The General was amused by Frank, and said that Frank would be better off with us than anywhere else. So Frank became our hired man, and chopped the firewood for us, and kept the fires going in the stoves and fireplaces, and sometimes served at dinner. In summer he was supposed to scythe the lawns, but of course summer didn't come. Frank arrived by train at Anthonyville Station in October, and we gave him the little room at the top of the house.

"Well, on January 12 Father went off to Chicago on business. We still had the General. Every night he barred the shutters on the ground floor, going round to all the rooms by himself. Mama knew he did it because there was a rumor that some life convicts at the Prison 'had it in' for the Supervisor of Prisons, although the General had retired five years earlier. Also they may have thought he kept a lot of money in the house—when actually, what with the timber gone and the mines going, in those times we were rather hard pressed and certainly kept our money in the bank at Duluth. But we girls didn't know why the General closed the shutters, except that it was one of the General's rituals. Besides, Anthonyville State Prison was supposed to be escape-proof. It was just that the General always took precautions, though ever so brave.

"Just before dawn, Celia, on the cold morning of January 14, 1915, we all were waked by the siren of the Prison, and we all rushed downstairs in our night-clothes, and we could see that part of the Prison was afire. Oh, the sky was red! The General tried to telephone the Prison, but he couldn't get through, and later it turned out that the lines had been cut.

"Next—it all happened so swiftly—we heard shouting somewhere down Main Street, and then guns went off. The General knew what that meant. He had got his trousers and his boots on, and now he struggled with his old military overcoat, and he took his old army revolver. 'Lock the door behind me, girl,' he told Mama. She cried and tried to pull him back inside, but he went down into the snow, nearly eighty though he was.

"Only three or four minutes later, we heard the shots. The General had met the convicts at the gate. It was still dark, and the General had cataracts on his eyes. They say he fired first, and missed. Those bad men had broken into Mr. Emmons's store and taken guns and axes and whiskey. They shot the General—shot him again and again and again.

"The next thing we knew, they were chopping at our front door with axes. Mama hugged us.

"Celia dear, writing all this has made me so silly! I feel a little odd, so I must go lie down for an hour or two before telling you the rest. Celia, I do hope you will love this old house as much as I have. If I'm not here when you come up, remember that where I have gone I will know the General and Father and Mama and Alice and poor dear Frank, and will be ever so happy with them. Be a good little girl, my Celia."

The letter ended there, unsigned.

Frank clumped downstairs to the Sunday parlor. He was crying, for the first time since he had fought that professional heavyweight on October 19, 1943. Allegra's letter—if only she'd finished it! What had happened to those little girls, and Mama, and that other Frank? He thought of something from the Holy Bible: "It were better for him that a millstone were hanged about his neck, and he cast into the sea, than that he should offend one of these little ones."

Already it was almost evening. He lit the wick in the cranberry-glass lamp that hung from the middle of the parlor ceiling, standing on a chair to reach it. Why not enjoy more light? On a whim, he arranged upon the round table four silver candlesticks that had rested above the fireplace. He needed three more, and those he fetched from the dining room. He lit every candle in the circle: one for the General, one for Father, one for Mama, one for Alice, one for Allegra, one for Edith—one for Frank.

The dear names of those little girls! He might as well recite aloud, it being good practice for the approaching days on the long, long trail:

> *"I hear in the chamber above me*
> *The patter of little feet,*
> *The sound of a door that is opened,*
> *And voices soft and sweet. . . ."*

Here he ceased. Had he heard something in the passage— or "descending the broad hall stair"? Because of the wind outside, he could not be certain. It cost him a gritting of his teeth to rise and open the parlor door. Of course no one could be seen in the hall or on the stair. "Crazy Frank," men had called him at Joliet and other prisons: he had clenched his fists, but had kept a check upon himself. Didn't Saint Paul say that the violent take Heaven by storm? Perhaps he had barked up the wrong tree; perhaps he would be spewed out of His mouth for being too peaceful.

Shutting the door, he went back to the fireside. Those lines of Longfellow had been no evocation. He put "The Long, Long Trail" on the old phonograph again, strolling about the room until the record ran out. There was an old print of a Great Lakes schooner on one wall that he liked. Beside it, he noticed, there seemed to be some pellets embedded in a

closet door-jamb, but painted over, as if someone had fired
a shotgun in the parlor in the old days. "The violent take it
by storm . . ." He admired the grand piano; perhaps Allegra
had learned to play it. There was one or two big notches or
gashes along one edge of the piano, varnished over, hard
though that wood was. Then Frank sank into the big chair
again and stared at the burning logs.

Just how long he had dozed, he did not know. He woke
abruptly. Had he heard a whisper, the faintest whisper? He
tensed to spring up. But before he could move, he saw reflections in the tall mirror.

Something had moved in the corner by the bookcase. No
doubt about it; that small something had stirred again. Also
something crept behind one of the satin sofas, and something
else lurked near the piano. All these were at his back: he saw
the reflections in the glass, as in a glass darkly, more alarming
than physical forms. In this high shadowy room, the light of
the kerosene lamp and of the seven candles did not suffice.

From near the bookcase, the first of them emerged into
candlelight; then came the second, and the third. They were
giggling, but he could not hear them—only see their faces,
and those not clearly. He was unable to stir, and the goose-
flesh prickled all over him, and his hair rose at the back of
his big head.

They were three little girls, barefoot, in their long muslin
nightgowns, ready for bed. One may have been as much as
twelve years old, and the smallest was little more than a baby.
The middle one was Allegra, tiny even for her tender years,
and a little imp: he knew, he knew! They were playing
Creepmouse.

The three of them stole forward, Allegra in the lead, her
eyes alight. He could see them plain now, and the dread was
ebbing out of him. He might have risen and turned to greet
them across the great gulf of time, but any action—why, what
might it do to these little ones? Frank sat frozen in his chair,
looking at the nimble reflections in the mirror, and nearer

they came, perfectly silent. Allegra vanished from the glass, which meant that she must be standing just behind him.

He must please them. Could he speak? He tried, and the lines came out hoarsely:

> *"Down, down, down in Creepmouse Town*
> *All the lamps are low,*
> *And the little rodent feet . . ."*

He was not permitted to finish. Wow! There came a light tug at the curly white hair on the back of his head. Oh, to talk with Allegra, the imp! Reckless, he heaved his bulk out of the chair, and swung round—too late.

The parlor door was closing. But from the hall came another whisper, ever so faint, ever so unmistakable: "Good night, Frank!" There followed subdued giggles, scampering, and then the silence once more.

He strode to the parlor door. The hall was empty again, and the broad stair. Should he follow them up? No, all three would be abed now. Should he knock at Mama's Room, muttering, "Mrs. Anthony, are the children all right?" No, he hadn't the nerve for that, and it would be presumptuous. He had been given one moment of perception, and no more.

Somehow he knew that they would not go so far as the garret floor. Ah, he needed fresh air! He snuffed out lamp and candles, except for one candlestick—Allegra's—that he took with him. Out into the hall he went. He unfastened the front door with that oaken patch about the middle of it, and stepped upon the porch, leaving the burning candle just within the hall. The wind had risen again, bringing still more snow. It was black as sin outside, and the temperature must be thirty below.

To him the wind bore one erratic peal of the desolate church-bell of Anthonyville, and then another. How strong the blast must be through that belfry! Frank retreated inside from that unfathomable darkness and that sepulchral bell which seemed to toll for him. He locked the thick door behind him and screwed up his courage for the expedition to his room at the top of the old house.

But why shudder? He loved them now, Allegra most of all. Up the broad stairs to the second floor he went, hearing only his own clumsy footfalls, and past the clay-sealed doors of the General and Father and Mama and Alice and Allegra and Edith. No one whispered, no one scampered.

In Frank's Room, he rolled himself in his blankets and quilt (had Allegra helped stitch the patchwork?), and almost at once the consciousness went out of him, and he must have slept dreamless for the first night since he was a farm boy.

So profound had been his sleep, deep almost as death, that the siren may have been wailing for some minutes before at last it roused him. Frank knew that horrid sound: it had called for him thrice before, as he fled from prisons. Who wanted him now? He heaved his ponderous body out of the warm bed. The candle that he had brought up from the Sunday parlor and left burning all night was flickering in its socket, but by that flame he could see the hour on his watch: seven o'clock, too soon for dawn.

Through the narrow skylight, as he flung on his clothes, the sky glowed an unnatural red, though it was long before sunup. The prison siren ceased to wail, as if choked off. Frank lumbered to the little frieze-window, and saw to the north, perhaps two miles distant, a monstrous mass of flame shooting high into the air. The prison was afire.

Then came shots outside: first the bark of a heavy revolver, followed irregularly by blasts of shotguns or rifles. Frank was lacing his boots with a swiftness uncongenial to him. He got into his overcoat as there came a crashing and battering down below. That sound, too, he recognized, wood-chopper that he had been: axes shattering the front door.

Amid this pandemonium, Frank was too bewildered to grasp altogether where he was or even how this catastrophe might be fitted into the pattern of time. All that mattered was flight; the scheme of his escape remained clear in his mind.

Pull up the chair below the skylight, heave yourself out to the upper roof, descend those iron rungs to the woodshed roof, make for the other side of the freeway, then—why, then you must trust to circumstance, Frank. It's that long, long trail a-winding for you.

Now he heard a woman screaming within the house, and slipped and fumbled in his alarm. He had got upon the chair, opened the skylight, and was trying to obtain a good grip on the icy outer edge of the skylight-frame, when someone knocked and kicked at the door of Frank's Room.

Yet those were puny knocks and kicks. He was about to heave himself upward when, in a relative quiet—the screaming had ceased for a moment—he heard a little shrill voice outside his door, urgently pleading: "Frank, Frank, let me in!"

He was arrested in flight as though great weights had been clamped to his ankles. That little voice he knew, as if it were part of him: Allegra's voice.

For a brief moment he still meant to scramble out the skylight. But the sweet little voice was begging. He stumbled off the chair, upset it, and was at the door in one stride.

"Is that you, Allegra?"

"Open it, Frank, *please* open it!"

He turned the key and pulled the bolt. On the threshold the little girl stood, indistinct by the dying candlelight, terribly pale, all tears, frantic.

Frank snatched her up. Ah, this was the dear real Allegra Anthony, all warm and soft and sobbing, flesh and blood! He kissed her cheek gently.

She clung to him in terror, and then squirmed loose, tugging at his heavy hand: "Oh, Frank, come on! Come downstairs! They're hurting Mama!"

"Who is, little girl?" He held her tiny hand, his body quivering with dread and indecision. "Who's down there, Allegra?"

"The bad men! *Come on*, Frank!" Braver than he, the

little thing plunged back down the garret stair into the black-ness below.

"Allegra! Come back here—come back now!" He bel-lowed it, but she was gone.

Up two flights of stairs, there poured to him a tumult of shrieks, curses, laughter, breaking noises. Several men were below, their speech slurred and raucous. He did not need Allegra to tell him what kind of men they were, for he heard prison slang and prison foulness, and he shook all over. There still was the skylight.

He would have turned back to that hole in the roof, had not Allegra squealed in pain somewhere on the second floor. Dazed, trembling, unarmed, Frank went three steps down the garret staircase. "Allegra! Little girl! What is it, Allegra?"

Someone was charging up the stair toward him. It was a burly man in the prison uniform, a lighted lantern in one hand and a glittering axe in the other. Frank had no time to turn. The man screeched obscenely at him, and swung that axe.

In those close quarters, wielded by a drunken man, it was a chancy weapon. The edge shattered the plaster wall; the flat of the blade thumped upon Frank's shoulder. Frank, lurching forward, took the man by the throat with a mighty grip. They all tumbled pellmell down the steep stairs—the two men, the axe, the lantern.

Frank's ursine bulk landed atop the stranger's body, and Frank heard his adversary's bones crunch. The lantern had broken and gone out. The convict's head hung loose on his shoulders, Frank found as he groped for the axe. Then he trampled over the fallen man and flung himself along the corridor, gripping the axe-helve. "Allegra! Allegra girl!"

From the head of the main stair, he could see that the lamps and candles were burning in the hall and in the rooms of the ground floor. All three children were down there, wail-ing, and above their noise rose Mama's shrieks again. A mob of men were stamping, breaking things, roaring with amuse-ment and desire, shouting filth. A bottle shattered.

His heart pounding as if it would burst out of his chest, Frank hurried rashly down that stair and went, all crimson with fury, into the Sunday parlor, the double-bitted axe swinging in his hand. They all were there: the little girls, Mama, and five wild men. "Stop that!" Frank roared with all the power of his lungs. "You let them go!"

Everyone in the parlor stood transfixed at that summons like the Last Trump. Allegra had been tugging pathetically at the leg of a dark man who gripped her mother's waist, and the other girls sputtered and sobbed, cornered, as a tall man poured a bottle of whiskey over them. Mrs. Anthony's gown was ripped nearly its whole length, and a third man was bending her backward by her long hair, as if he would snap her spine. Near the hall door stood a man like a long lean rat, the Rat of Creepmouse Town, a shotgun on his arm, gape-jawed at Frank's intervention. Guns and axes lay scattered about the Turkey carpet. By the fireplace, a fifth man had been heating the poker in the flames.

For that tableau-moment, they all stared astonished at the raving giant who had burst upon them; and the giant, puffing, stared back with his strange blue eyes. "Oh, Frank!" Allegra sobbed: it was more command than entreaty—as if, Frank thought in a flash of insane mirth, he were like the boy in the fairy tale who could cry confidently, "All heads off but mine!"

He knew what these men were, the rats and bats of Creepmouse Town: the worst men in any prison, lifers who had made their hell upon earth, killers all of them and worse than killers. The rotten damnation showed in all those flushed and drunken faces. Then the dark man let go of Mama and said in relief, with a coughing laugh, "Hell, it's only old Punkinhead Frank, clowning again! Have some fun for yourself, Frank boy!"

"Hey, Frank," Ratface asked, his shotgun crooked under his arm, "where'd the old man keep his money?"

Frank towered there perplexed, the berserker-lust draining out of him, almost bashful—and frightened worse than ever before in all his years on the trail. What should he shout now?

What should he do? Who was he to resist such perfect evil? They were five to one, and those five were fiends from down under, and that one a coward. Long ago he had been weighed in the balance and found wanting.

Mama was the first to break the tableau. Her second captor had relaxed his clutch upon her hair, and she prodded the little girls before her, and she leaped for the door.

The hair-puller was after her at once, but she bounded past Ratface's shotgun, which had wavered toward Frank, and Alice and Edith were ahead of her. Allegra, her eyes wide and desperate, tripped over the rung of a broken chair. Everything happened in half a second. The hair-puller caught Allegra by her little ankle.

Then Frank bellowed again, loudest in all his life, and he swung his axe high above his head and downward, a skillful dreadful stroke, catching the hair-puller's arm just below the shoulder. At once the man began to scream and spout, while Allegra fled after her mother.

Falling, the hair-puller collided with Ratface, spoiling his aim, but one barrel of the shotgun fired, and Frank felt pain in his side. His bloody axe on high, he hulked between the five men and the door.

All the men's faces were glaring at Frank, incredulously, as if demanding how he dared stir against them. Three convicts were scrabbling tipsily for weapons on the floor. As Frank strode among them, he saw the expression on those faces change from gloating to desperation. Just as his second blow descended, there passed through his mind a kind of fleshly collage of death he had seen once at a farmyard gate: the corpses of five weasels nailed to a gatepost by the farmer, their frozen open jaws agape like damned souls in Hell.

"All heads off but mine!" Frank heard himself braying. "All heads off but mine!" He hacked and hewed, his own screams of lunatic fury drowning their screams of terror.

For less than three minutes, shots, thuds, shrieks, crashes, terrible wailing. They could not get past him to the doorway.

"Come on!" Frank was raging as he stood in the middle

of the parlor. "Come on, who's next? All heads off but mine! Who's next?"

There came no answer but a ghastly rattle from one of the five heaps that littered the carpet. Blood-soaked from hair to boots, the berserker towered alone, swaying where he stood.

His mind began to clear. He had been shot twice, Frank guessed, and the pain at his heart was frightful. Into his frantic consciousness burst all the glory of what he had done, and all the horror.

He became almost rational; he must count the dead. One upstairs, five here. One, two, three, four, five heaps. That was correct: all present and accounted for, Frank boy, Punkinhead Frank, Crazy Frank: all dead and accounted for. Had he thought that thought before? Had he taken that mock roll before? Had he wrought this slaughter twice over, twice in this same old room?

But where were Mama and the little girls? They mustn't see this blood-splashed inferno of a parlor. He was looking at himself in the tall mirror, and he saw a bear-man loathsome with his own blood and others' blood. He looked like the Wild Man of Borneo. In abhorrence he flung his axe aside. Behind him sprawled the reflections of the hacked dead.

Fighting down his heart pain, he reeled into the hall. "Little girls! Mrs. Anthony! Allegra, oh, Allegra!" His voice was less strong. "Where are you? It's safe now!"

They did not call back. He labored up the main stair, clutching his side. "Allegra, speak to your Frank!" They were in none of the bedrooms.

He went up the garret stair, then, whatever the agony, and beyond Frank's Room to the cupola stair, and ascended that slowly, gasping hard. They were not in the cupola. Might they have run out among the trees? In that cold dawn, he stared on every side; he thought his sight was beginning to fail.

He could see no one outside the house. The drifts still choked the street beyond the gateposts, and those two boulders protruded impassive from untrodden snow. Back down the flights of stairs he made his way, clutching at the rail, at the wall.

Surely the little girls hadn't strayed into that parlor butcher-shop? He bit his lip and peered into the Sunday parlor.

The bodies all were gone. The splashes and ropy strands of blood all were gone. Everything stood in perfect order, as if violence never had touched Tamarack House. The sun was rising, and sunlight filtered through the shutters. Within fifteen minutes, the trophies of his savage victory had disappeared.

It was like the recurrent dream which had tormented Frank when he was little: he separated from Mother in the dark, wandering solitary in empty lanes, no soul alive in all the universe but little Frank. Yet those tremendous axe blows had severed living flesh and blood, and for one moment, there on the stairs, he had held in his arms a tiny quick Allegra; of that reality he did not doubt at all.

Wonder subduing pain, he staggered to the front door. It stood unshattered. He drew the bar and turned the key, and went down the stone steps into the snow. He was weak now, and did not know where he was going. Had he done a Signal Act? Might the Lord give him one parting glimpse of little Allegra, some-where among these trees? He slipped in a drift, half rose, sank again, crawled. He found himself at the foot of one of those boulders—the farther one, the stone he had not inspected.

The snow had fallen away from the face of the bronze tablet. Clutching the boulder, Frank drew himself up. By bringing his eyes very close to the tablet, he could read the words, a dying man panting against deathless bronze:

IN LOVING MEMORY OF
FRANK
A SPIRIT IN PRISON, MADE FOR ETERNITY
WHO SAVED US AND DIED FOR US
JANUARY 14, 1915

"Why, if the Soul can fling the Dust aside,
And naked on the Air of Heaven ride,
    Were't not a Shame—were't not a Shame for him
In this clay carcass crippled to abide?"

H. P. Lovecraft

THE CALL OF CTHULHU

Between Poe and King, the great American master of horror is H. P. Lovecraft. As a critic, his *Supernatural Horror in Literature* is the most important essay on horror literature. His influence as mentor and correspondent on his generation was overwhelming and is still felt. His emphasis on cosmic scale, his New England antiquarianism and his elevated and florid style, his consistent juxtaposition of the supernatural to the rational, combined to make him a literary outcast in his day. But his reputation has grown steadily in France (as did Poe's) and, in spite of Edmund Wilson's attempt to dispose of him once and for all in the 1940s, persists in the U.S. Lovecraft rejected conventional morality and the supernatural and yearned to have been born in the eighteenth century a rationalist. But "The Call of Cthulhu" is about a cosmic evil that waits to overcome us with "such terrifying vistas of reality, and of our frightful position therein, that we shall either go mad from the revelation or flee from the deadly light into the peace and safety of a new dark age." Psychologically interesting, but not about the psychological life of characters, concerned with the nature of reality, but with no doubt as to its nature, "The Call of Cthulhu" is about "some things man was not meant to know." Lovecraft was the giant of the pulp horror story and *Weird Tales* was the magazine where much of his work found a home, along with the stories of his friends and correspondents such as Clark Ashton Smith, Frank Belknap Long, Robert E. Howard, throughout the 1920s and 1930s. The influence of the

"Lovecraft circle" was dominant until the 1940s and remained strong in *Weird Tales* until its demise in the 1950s.

(Found Among the Papers of the Late Francis Wayland Thurston, of Boston)

"Of such great powers or beings there may be conceivably a survival . . . a survival of a hugely remote period when . . . consciousness was manifested, perhaps, in shapes and forms long since withdrawn before the tide of advancing humanity . . . forms of which poetry and legend alone have caught a flying memory and called them gods, monsters, mythical beings of all sorts and kinds. . . ."

—Algernon Blackwood

I The Horror in Clay

The most merciful thing in the world, I think, is the inability of the human mind to correlate all its contents. We live on a placid island of ignorance in the midst of black seas of infinity, and it was not meant that we should voyage far. The sciences, each straining in its own direction, have hitherto harmed us little; but some day the piecing together of dissociated knowledge will open up such terrifying vistas of reality, and of our frightful position therein, that we shall either go mad from the revelation or flee from the deadly light into the peace and safety of a new dark age.

Theosophists have guessed at the awesome grandeur of the cosmic cycle wherein our world and human race form transient incidents. They have hinted at strange survivals in terms which would freeze the blood if not masked by a bland optimism. But it is not from them that there came the single glimpse of forbidden aeons which chills me when I think of it and maddens me when I dream of it. That glimpse, like all dread glimpses of truth, flashed out from an accidental piecing together of separated things—in this case an old newspaper item and the notes of a dead professor. I hope that no one else will accomplish this piecing out; certainly, if I live, I shall never knowingly supply a link in so hideous a chain. I think that the professor, too, intended to keep silent regarding the part he knew, and that he would have destroyed his notes had not sudden death seized him.

My knowledge of the thing began in the winter of 1926-27 with the death of my grand-uncle George Gammell Angell, Professor Emeritus of Semitic Languages in Brown University, Providence, Rhode Island. Professor Angell was widely known as an authority on ancient inscriptions, and had frequently been resorted to by the heads of prominent museums; so that his passing at the age of ninety-two may be recalled by many. Locally, interest was intensified by the obscurity of the cause of death. The professor had been stricken whilst returning from the Newport boat; falling suddenly, as witnesses said, after having been jostled by a nautical-looking negro who had come from one of the queer dark courts on the precipitous hillside which formed a short cut from the waterfront to the deceased's home in Williams Street. Physicians were unable to find any visible disorder, but concluded after perplexed debate that some obscure lesion of the heart, induced by the brisk ascent of so steep a hill by so elderly a man, was responsible for the end. At the time I saw no reason to dissent from this dictum, but latterly I am inclined to wonder—and more than wonder.

As my grand-uncle's heir and executor, for he died a childless widower, I was expected to go over his papers with some thoroughness; and for that purpose moved his entire set of files and boxes to my quarters in Boston. Much of the material which I correlated will be later published by the American Archaeological Society, but there was one box which I found exceedingly puzzling, and which I felt much adverse from shewing to other eyes. It had been locked, and I did not find the key till it occurred to me to examine the personal ring which the professor carried always in his pocket. Then indeed I succeeded in opening it, but when I did so seemed only to be confronted by a greater and more closely locked barrier. For what could be the meaning of the queer clay bas-relief and the disjointed jottings, ramblings, and cuttings which I found? Had my uncle, in his latter years, become credulous of the most superficial impostures? I resolved to search out the eccentric sculptor responsible for this apparent disturbance of an old man's peace of mind.

The bas-relief was a rough rectangle less than an inch thick and about five by six inches in area; obviously of modern origin. Its designs, however, were far from modern in atmosphere and suggestion; for although the vagaries of cubism and futurism are many and wild, they do not often reproduce that cryptic regularity which lurks in prehistoric writing. And writing of some kind the bulk of these designs seemed certainly to be; though my memory, despite much familiarity with the papers and collections of my uncle, failed in any way to identify this particular species, or even to hint at its remotest affiliations.

Above these apparent hieroglyphics was a figure of evidently pictorial intent, though its impressionistic execution forbade a very clear idea of its nature. It seemed to be a sort of monster, or symbol representing a monster, of a form which only a diseased fancy could conceive. If I say that my somewhat extravagant imagination yielded simultaneous pictures of an octopus, a dragon, and a human caricature, I shall not be unfaithful to the spirit of the thing. A pulpy, tentacled head surmounted a grotesque and scaly body with rudimentary wings; but it was the *general outline* of the whole which made it most shockingly frightful. Behind the figure was a vague suggestion of a Cyclopean architectural background.

The writing accompanying this oddity was, aside from a stack of press cuttings, in Professor Angell's most recent hand; and made no pretence to literary style. What seemed to be the main document was headed "CTHULHU CULT" in characters painstakingly printed to avoid the erroneous reading of a word so unheard-of. This manuscript was divided into two sections, the first of which was headed "1925—Dream and Dream Work of H. A. Wilcox, 7 Thomas St., Providence, R.I.," and the second, "Narrative of Inspector John R. Legrasse, 121 Bienville St., New Orleans, La., at 1908 A. A. S. Mtg.—Notes on Same, & Prof. Webb's Acct." The other manuscript papers were all brief notes, some of them accounts of the queer dreams of different persons, some of them citations from theosophical books and magazines (notably W. Scott-Elliot's *Atlantis and the Lost Lemuria*), and the rest comments on long-surviving secret societies and hidden cults, with references to passages in such mythological and anthropological source-books as Frazer's *Golden Bough* and Miss Murray's *Witch-Cult in Western Europe*. The cuttings largely alluded to outré mental illnesses and outbreaks of group folly or mania in the spring of 1925.

The first half of the principal manuscript told a very peculiar tale. It appears that on March 1st, 1925, a thin, dark young man of neurotic and excited aspect had called upon Professor Angell bearing the singular clay bas-relief, which was then exceedingly damp and fresh. His card bore the name of Henry Anthony Wilcox, and my uncle had recognised him as the youngest son of an excellent family slightly known to him, who had latterly been studying sculpture at the Rhode Island School of Design and living alone at the Fleur-de-Lys Building near that institution. Wilcox was a precocious youth of known genius but great eccentricity, and had from childhood excited attention through the strange stories and odd dreams he was in the habit of relating. He called himself "psychically hypersensitive," but the staid folk of the ancient commercial city dismissed him as merely "queer." Never mingling much with his kind, he had dropped gradually from social visibility, and was now known only to a small group of aesthetes from other towns. Even the Providence Art Club, anxious to preserve its conservatism, had found him quite hopeless.

On the occasion of the visit, ran the professor's manuscript, the sculptor abruptly asked for the benefit of his host's archaeological knowledge in identifying the hieroglyphics on the bas-relief. He spoke in a dreamy, stilted manner which suggested pose and alienated sympathy; and my uncle shewed some sharpness in replying, for the conspicuous freshness of the tablet implied kinship with anything but archaeology. Young Wilcox's rejoinder, which impressed my uncle enough to make him recall and record it verbatim, was of a fantastically poetic cast which must have typified his whole conversation, and which I have since found highly characteristic of him. He said, "It is new, indeed, for I made it last night in a dream of strange cities; and dreams are older than brooding Tyre, or the contemplative Sphinx, or garden-girdled Babylon."

It was then that he began that rambling tale which suddenly played upon a sleeping memory and won the fevered interest of my uncle. There had been a slight earthquake tremor the night before, the most considerable felt in New England for some years; and Wilcox's imagination had been keenly affected. Upon retiring, he had had an unprecedented dream of great Cyclopean cities of titan blocks and sky-flung monoliths, all dripping with green ooze and sinister with latent horror. Hieroglyphics had covered the walls and pillars, and from some undetermined point below had come a voice that was not a voice; a chaotic sensation which only fancy could transmute into sound, but which he attempted to render by the almost unpronounceable jumble of letters, "*Cthulhu fhtagn.*"

This verbal jumble was the key to the recollection which excited and disturbed Professor Angell. He questioned the sculptor with scientific minuteness; and studied with almost frantic intensity the bas-relief on which the youth had found himself working, chilled and clad only in his nightclothes, when waking had stolen bewilderingly over him. My uncle blamed his old age, Wilcox afterward said, for his slowness in recognising both hieroglyphics and pictorial design. Many of his questions seemed highly out-of-place to his visitor, especially those which tried to connect the latter with strange cults or societies; and Wilcox could not understand the repeated promises of silence which he was offered in exchange for an admission of membership in some widespread mystical or paganly religious body. When Professor Angell became convinced that the sculptor was indeed ignorant of any cult or system of cryptic lore, he besieged his visitor with demands for future reports of dreams. This bore regular fruit, for after the first interview the manuscript records daily calls of the young man, during which he related startling fragments of nocturnal imagery whose burden was always some terrible Cyclopean vista of dark and dripping stone, with a subterrene voice or intelligence shouting monotonously in enigmatical sense-impacts uninscribable save as gibberish. The two sounds most frequently repeated are those rendered by the letters "*Cthulhu*" and "*R'lyeh*."

On March 23d, the manuscript continued, Wilcox failed to appear; and inquiries at his quarters revealed that he had been stricken with an obscure sort of fever and taken to the home of his family in Waterman Street. He had cried out in the night, arousing several other artists in the building, and had manifested since then only alternations of unconsciousness and delirium. My uncle at once telephoned the family, and from that time forward kept close watch of the case; calling often at the Thayer Street office of Dr. Tobey, whom he learned to be in charge. The youth's febrile mind, apparently, was dwelling on strange things; and the doctor shuddered now and then as he spoke of them. They included not only a repetition of what he had formerly dreamed, but touched wildly on a gigantic thing "miles high" which walked or lumbered about. He at no time fully described this object, but occasional frantic words, as repeated by Dr. Tobey, convinced the professor that it must be identical with the nameless monstrosity he had sought to depict in his dream-sculpture. Reference to this object, the doctor added, was invariably a prelude to the young man's subsidence into lethargy. His temperature, oddly enough, was not greatly above normal; but his whole condition was otherwise such as to suggest true fever rather than mental disorder.

On April 2nd at about 3 p.m. every trace of Wilcox's malady suddenly ceased. He sat upright in bed, astonished to find himself at home and completely ignorant of what had happened in dream or reality since the night of March 22nd. Pronounced well by his physician, he returned to his quarters in three days; but to Professor Angell he was of no further assistance. All traces of strange dreaming had vanished with his recovery, and my uncle kept no record of his night-thoughts after a week of pointless and irrelevant accounts of thoroughly usual visions.

Here the first part of the manuscript ended, but references to certain of the scattered notes gave me much material for thought—so much, in fact, that only the ingrained scepticism then forming my philosophy can account for my continued distrust of the artist. The notes in question were those descriptive of the dreams of various persons covering the same period as that in which young Wilcox had had his strange visitations. My uncle, it seems, had quickly instituted a prodigiously far-flung body of inquiries amongst nearly all the friends whom he could question without impertinence, asking for nightly reports of their dreams, and the dates of any notable visions for some time past. The reception of his request seems to have been varied; but he must, at the very least, have received more responses than any ordinary man could have handled without a secretary. This original correspondence was not preserved, but his notes formed a thorough and really significant digest. Average people in society and business—New England's traditional "salt of the earth"—gave an almost completely negative result, though scattered cases of uneasy but formless nocturnal impressions appear

here and there, always between March 23d and April 2nd—
the period of young Wilcox's delirium. Scientific men were
little more affected, though four cases of vague description
suggest fugitive glimpses of strange landscapes, and in one
case there is mentioned a dread of something abnormal.

It was from the artists and poets that the pertinent answers
came, and I know that panic would have broken loose had
they been able to compare notes. As it was, lacking their
original letters, I half suspected the compiler of having asked
leading questions, or of having edited the correspondence in
corroboration of what he had latently resolved to see. That
is why I continued to feel that Wilcox, somehow cognisant
of the old data which my uncle had possessed, had been
imposing on the veteran scientist. These responses from
aesthetes told a disturbing tale. From February 28th to April
2nd a large proportion of them had dreamed very bizarre
things, the intensity of the dreams being immeasurably the
stronger during the period of the sculptor's delirium. Over a
fourth of those who reported anything, reported scenes and
half-sounds not unlike those which Wilcox had described;
and some of the dreamers confessed acute fear of the gigantic
nameless thing visible toward the last. One case, which the
note describes with emphasis, was very sad. The subject, a
widely known architect with leanings toward theosophy and
occultism, went violently insane on the date of young Wilcox's seizure, and expired several months later after incessant
screamings to be saved from some escaped denizen of hell.
Had my uncle referred to these cases by name instead of
merely by number, I should have attempted some corroboration and personal investigation; but as it was, I succeeded
in tracing down only a few. All of these, however, bore out
the notes in full. I have often wondered if all the objects of
the professor's questioning felt as puzzled as did this fraction.
It is well that no explanation shall ever reach them.

The press cuttings, as I have intimated, touched on cases
of panic, mania, and eccentricity during the given period.
Professor Angell must have employed a cutting bureau, for

the number of extracts was tremendous and the sources scattered throughout the globe. Here was a nocturnal suicide in London, where a lone sleeper had leaped from a window after a shocking cry. Here likewise a rambling letter to the editor of a paper in South America, where a fanatic deduces a dire future from visions he has seen. A despatch from California describes a theosophist colony as donning white robes en masse for some "glorious fulfilment" which never arrives, whilst items from India speak guardedly of serious native unrest toward the end of March. Voodoo orgies multiply in Hayti, and African outposts report ominous mutterings. American officers in the Philippines find certain tribes bothersome about this time, and New York policemen are mobbed by hysterical Levantines on the night of March 22–23. The west of Ireland, too, is full of wild rumour and legendry, and a fantastic painter named Ardois-Bonnot hangs a blasphemous "Dream Landscape" in the Paris spring salon of 1926. And so numerous are the recorded troubles in insane asylums, that only a miracle can have stopped the medical fraternity from noting strange parallelisms and drawing mystified conclusions. A weird bunch of cuttings, all told; and I can at this date scarcely envisage the callous rationalism with which I set them aside. But I was then convinced that young Wilcox had known of the older matters mentioned by the professor.

II   The Tale of Inspector Legrasse

The older matters which had made the sculptor's dream and bas-relief so significant to my uncle formed the subject of the second half of his long manuscript. Once before, it appears, Professor Angell had seen the hellish outlines of the nameless monstrosity, puzzled over the unknown hieroglyphics, and heard the ominous syllables which can be rendered only as "*Cthulhu*"; and all this in so stirring and horrible a connexion that it is small wonder he pursued young Wilcox with queries and demands for data.

This earlier experience had come in 1908, seventeen years before, when the American Archaeological Society held its annual meeting in St. Louis. Professor Angell, as befitted one of his authority and attainments, had had a prominent part in all the deliberations; and was one of the first to be approached by the several outsiders who took advantage of the convocation to offer questions for correct answering and problems for expert solution.

The chief of these outsiders, and in a short time the focus of interest for the entire meeting, was a commonplace-looking middle-aged man who had travelled all the way from New Orleans for certain special information unobtainable from any local source. His name was John Raymond Legrasse, and he was by profession an Inspector of Police. With him he bore the subject of his visit, a grotesque, repulsive, and apparently very ancient stone statuette whose origin he was at a loss to determine. It must not be fancied that Inspector Legrasse had the least interest in archaeology. On the contrary, his wish for enlightenment was prompted by purely professional considerations. The statuette, idol, fetish, or whatever it was, had been captured some months before in the wooded swamps south of New Orleans during a raid on a supposed voodoo meeting; and so singular and hideous were the rites connected with it, that the police could not but realise that they had stumbled on a dark cult totally unknown to them, and infinitely more diabolic than even the blackest of the African voodoo circles. Of its origin, apart from the erratic and unbelievable tales extorted from the captured members, absolutely nothing was to be discovered; hence the anxiety of the police for any antiquarian lore which might help them to place the frightful symbol, and through it track down the cult to its fountain-head.

Inspector Legrasse was scarcely prepared for the sensation which his offering created. One sight of the thing had been enough to throw the assembled men of science into a state of tense excitement, and they lost no time in crowding around him to gaze at the diminutive figure whose utter strangeness and air of genuinely abysmal antiquity hinted so potently at unopened and archaic vistas. No recognised school of sculpture had animated this terrible object, yet centuries and even thousands of years seemed recorded in its dim and greenish surface of unplaceable stone.

The figure, which was finally passed slowly from man to man for close and careful study, was between seven and eight inches in height, and of exquisitely artistic workmanship. It represented a monster of vaguely anthropoid outline, but with an octopus-like head whose face was a mass of feelers, a scaly, rubbery-looking body, prodigious claws on hind and fore feet, and long, narrow wings behind. This thing, which seemed instinct with a fearsome and unnatural malignancy, was of a somewhat bloated corpulence, and squatted evilly on a rectangular block or pedestal covered with undecipherable characters. The tips of the wings touched the back edge of the block, the seat occupied the centre, whilst the long, curved claws of the doubled-up, crouching hind legs gripped the front edge and extended a quarter of the way down toward the bottom of the pedestal. The cephalopod head was bent forward, so that the ends of the facial feelers brushed the backs of huge fore paws which clasped the croucher's elevated knees. The aspect of the whole was abnormally life-like, and the more subtly fearful because its source was so totally unknown. Its vast, awesome, and incalculable age was unmistakable; yet not one link did it shew with any known type of art belonging to civilisation's youth—or indeed to any other time. Totally separate and apart, its very material was a mystery; for the soapy, greenish-black stone with its golden or iridescent flecks and striations resembled nothing familiar to geology or mineralogy. The characters along the base were equally baffling; and no member present, despite a representation of half the world's expert learning in this field, could form the least notion of even their remotest linguistic kinship. They, like the subject and material, belonged to something frightfully suggestive of old and unhallowed cycles of life in which our world and our conceptions have no part.

And yet, as the members severally shook their heads and confessed defeat at the Inspector's problem, there was one man in that gathering who suspected a touch of bizarre familiarity in the monstrous shape and writing, and who presently told with some diffidence of the odd trifle he knew. This person was the late William Channing Webb, Professor of Anthropology in Princeton University, and an explorer of no slight note. Professor Webb had been engaged, forty-eight years before, in a tour of Greenland and Iceland in search of some Runic inscriptions which he failed to unearth; and whilst high up on the West Greenland coast had encountered a singular tribe or cult of degenerate Esquimaux whose religion, a curious form of devil-worship, chilled him with its deliberate bloodthirstiness and repulsiveness. It was a faith of which other Esquimaux knew little, and which they mentioned only with shudders, saying that it had come down from horribly ancient aeons before ever the world was made. Besides nameless rites and human sacrifices there were certain queer hereditary rituals addressed to a supreme elder devil or *tornasuk*; and of this Professor Webb had taken a careful phonetic copy from an aged *angekok* or wizard-priest, expressing the sounds in Roman letters as best he knew how. But just now of prime significance was the fetish which this cult had cherished, and around which they danced when the aurora leaped high over the ice cliffs. It was, the professor stated, a very crude bas-relief of stone, comprising a hideous picture and some cryptic writing. And so far as he could tell, it was a rough parallel in all essential features of the bestial thing now lying before the meeting.

This data, received with suspense and astonishment by the assembled members, proved doubly exciting to Inspector Legrasse; and he began at once to ply his informant with questions. Having noted and copied an oral ritual among the swamp cult-worshippers his men had arrested, he besought the professor to remember as best he might the syllables taken down amongst the diabolist Esquimaux. There then followed an exhaustive comparison of details, and a moment of really

awed silence when both detective and scientist agreed on the
virtual identity of the phrase common to two hellish rituals
so many worlds of distance apart. What, in substance, both
the Esquimau wizards and the Louisiana swamp-priests had
chanted to their kindred idols was something very like this—
the word-divisions being guessed at from traditional breaks
in the phrase as chanted aloud:

"Ph'nglui mglw'nafh Cthulhu R'lyeh wgah'nagl fhtagn."

Legrasse had one point in advance of Professor Webb, for
several among his mongrel prisoners had repeated to him
what older celebrants had told them the words meant. This
text, as given, ran something like this:

"In his house at R'lyeh dead Cthulhu waits dreaming."

And now, in response to a general and urgent demand,
Inspector Legrasse related as fully as possible his experience
with the swamp worshippers; telling a story to which I could
see my uncle attached profound significance. It savoured of
the wildest dreams of mythmaker and theosophist, and disclosed an astonishing degree of cosmic imagination among
such half-castes and pariahs as might be least expected to
possess it.

On November 1st, 1907, there had come to the New Orleans police a frantic summons from the swamp and lagoon
country to the south. The squatters there, mostly primitive
but good-natured descendants of Lafitte's men, were in the
grip of stark terror from an unknown thing which had stolen
upon them in the night. It was voodoo, apparently, but voodoo of a more terrible sort than they had ever known; and
some of their women and children had disappeared since the
malevolent tom-tom had begun its incessant beating far within
the black haunted woods where no dweller ventured. There
were insane shouts and harrowing screams, soul-chilling
chants and dancing devil-flames; and, the frightened messen-
ger added, the people could stand it no more.

So a body of twenty police, filling two carriages and an
automobile, had set out in the late afternoon with the shivering squatter as a guide. At the end of the passable road they

alighted, and for miles splashed on in silence through the terrible cypress woods where day never came. Ugly roots and malignant hanging nooses of Spanish moss beset them, and now and then a pile of dank stones or fragment of a rotting wall intensified by its hint of morbid habitation a depression which every malformed tree and every fungous islet combined to create. At length the squatter settlement, a miserable huddle of huts, hove in sight; and hysterical dwellers ran out to cluster around the group of bobbing lanterns. The muffled beat of tom-toms was now faintly audible far, far ahead; and a curdling shriek came at infrequent intervals when the wind shifted. A reddish glare, too, seemed to filter through the pale undergrowth beyond endless avenues of forest night. Reluctant even to be left alone again, each one of the cowed squatters refused point-blank to advance another inch toward the scene of unholy worship, so Inspector Legrasse and his nineteen colleagues plunged on unguided into black arcades of horror that none of them had ever trod before.

The region now entered by the police was one of traditionally evil repute, substantially unknown and untraversed by white men. There were legends of a hidden lake unglimpsed by mortal sight, in which dwelt a huge, formless white polypous thing with luminous eyes; and squatters whispered that bat-winged devils flew up out of caverns in inner earth to worship it at midnight. They said it had been there before D'Iberville, before La Salle, before the Indians, and before even the wholesome beasts and birds of the woods. It was nightmare itself, and to see it was to die. But it made men dream, and so they knew enough to keep away. The present voodoo orgy was, indeed, on the merest fringe of this abhorred area, but that location was bad enough; hence perhaps the very place of the worship had terrified the squatters more than the shocking sounds and incidents.

Only poetry or madness could do justice to the noises heard by Legrasse's men as they ploughed on through the black morass toward the red glare and the muffled tom-toms. There are vocal qualities peculiar to men, and vocal qualities peculiar to beasts; and it is terrible to hear the one when the source should yield the other. Animal fury and orgiastic licence here whipped themselves to daemoniac heights by howls and squawking ecstasies that tore and reverberated through those nighted woods like pestilential tempests from the gulfs of hell. Now and then the less organised ululation would cease, and from what seemed a well-drilled chorus of hoarse voices would rise in sing-song chant that hideous phrase or ritual:

"Ph'nglui mglw'nafh Cthulhu R'lyeh wgah'nagl fhtagn."

Then the men, having reached a spot where the trees were thinner, came suddenly in sight of the spectacle itself. Four of them reeled, one fainted, and two were shaken into a frantic cry which the mad cacophony of the orgy fortunately deadened. Legrasse dashed swamp water on the face of the fainting man, and all stood trembling and nearly hypnotised with horror.

In a natural glade of the swamp stood a grassy island of perhaps an acre's extent, clear of trees and tolerably dry. On this now leaped and twisted a more indescribable horde of human abnormality than any but a Sime or an Angarola could paint. Void of clothing, this hybrid spawn were braying, bellowing, and writhing about a monstrous ring-shaped bonfire; in the centre of which, revealed by occasional rifts in the curtain of flame, stood a great granite monolith some eight feet in height; on top of which, incongruous in its diminutiveness, rested the noxious carven statuette. From a wide circle of ten scaffolds set up at regular intervals with the flame-girt monolith as a centre hung, head downward, the oddly marred bodies of the helpless squatters who had disappeared. It was inside this circle that the ring of worshippers jumped and roared, the general direction of the mass motion being from left to right in endless Bacchanal between the ring of bodies and the ring of fire.

It may have been only imagination and it may have been only echoes which induced one of the men, an excitable Spaniard, to fancy he heard antiphonal responses to the ritual from some far and unillumined spot deeper within the wood of ancient legendry and horror. This man, Joseph D. Galvez, I later met and questioned; and he proved distractingly imaginative. He indeed went so far as to hint of the faint beating of great wings, and of a glimpse of shining eyes and a mountainous white bulk beyond the remotest trees—but I suppose he had been hearing too much native superstition.

Actually, the horrified pause of the men was of comparatively brief duration. Duty came first; and although there must have been nearly a hundred mongrel celebrants in the throng, the police relied on their firearms and plunged determinedly into the nauseous rout. For five minutes the resultant din and chaos were beyond description. Wild blows were struck, shots were fired, and escapes were made; but in the end Legrasse was able to count some forty-seven sullen prisoners, whom he forced to dress in haste and fall into line between two rows of policemen. Five of the worshippers lay dead, and two severely wounded ones were carried away on improvised stretchers by their fellow-prisoners. The image on the monolith, of course, was carefully removed and carried back by Legrasse.

Examined at headquarters after a trip of intense strain and weariness, the prisoners all proved to be men of a very low, mixed-blooded, and mentally aberrant type. Most were seamen, and a sprinkling of negroes and mulattoes, largely West Indians or Brava Portuguese from the Cape Verde Islands, gave a colouring of voodooism to the heterogeneous cult. But before many questions were asked, it became manifest that something far deeper and older than negro fetichism was involved. Degraded and ignorant as they were, the creatures held with surprising consistency to the central idea of their loathsome faith.

They worshipped, so they said, the Great Old Ones who lived ages before there were any men, and who came to the young world out of the sky. Those Old Ones were gone now, inside the earth and under the sea; but their dead bodies had told their secrets in dreams to the first men, who formed a cult which had never died. This was that cult, and the prisoners said it had always existed and always would exist, hidden in distant wastes and dark places all over the world until the time when the great priest Cthulhu, from his dark house in the mighty city of R'lyeh under the water, should rise and bring the earth again beneath his sway. Some day he would call, when the stars were ready, and the secret cult would always be waiting to liberate him.

Meanwhile no more must be told. There was a secret which even torture could not extract. Mankind was not absolutely alone among the conscious things of earth, for shapes came out of the dark to visit the faithful few. But these were not the Great Old Ones. No man had ever seen the Old Ones. The carven idol was great Cthulhu, but none might say whether or not the others were precisely like him. No one could read the old writing now, but things were told by word of mouth. The chanted ritual was not the secret—that was never spoken aloud, only whispered. The chant meant only this: "In his house at R'lyeh dead Cthulhu waits dreaming."

Only two of the prisoners were found sane enough to be hanged, and the rest were committed to various institutions. All denied a part in the ritual murders, and averred that the killing had been done by Black Winged Ones which had come to them from their immemorial meeting-place in the haunted wood. But of those mysterious allies no coherent account could ever be gained. What the police did extract, came mainly from an immensely aged mestizo named Castro, who claimed to have sailed to strange ports and talked with undying leaders of the cult in the mountains of China.

Old Castro remembered bits of hideous legend that paled the speculations of theosophists and made man and the world seem recent and transient indeed. There had been aeons when other Things ruled on the earth, and They had had great cities. Remains of Them, he said the deathless Chinamen had told him, were still to be found as Cyclopean stones on islands in the Pacific. They all died vast epochs of time before men came, but there were arts which could revive Them when the stars had come round again to the right positions in the cycle of eternity. They had, indeed, come themselves from the stars, and brought Their images with Them.

These Great Old Ones, Castro continued, were not composed altogether of flesh and blood. They had shape—for did not this star-fashioned image prove it?—but that shape was not made of matter. When the stars were right, They could plunge from world to world through the sky; but when the stars were wrong, They could not live. But although They no longer lived, They would never really die. They all lay in stone houses in Their great city of R'lyeh, preserved by the spells of mighty Cthulhu for a glorious resurrection when the stars and the earth might once more be ready for Them. But at that time some force from outside must serve to liberate Their bodies. The spells that preserved Them intact likewise prevented Them from making an initial move, and They could only lie awake in the dark and think whilst uncounted millions of years rolled by. They knew all that was occurring in the universe, for Their mode of speech was transmitted thought. Even now They talked in Their tombs. When, after infinities of chaos, the first men came, the Great Old Ones spoke to the sensitive among them by moulding their dreams; for only thus could Their language reach the fleshly minds of mammals.

Then, whispered Castro, those first men formed the cult around small idols which the Great Ones shewed them; idols brought in dim aeras from dark stars. That cult would never die till the stars came right again, and the secret priests would take great Cthulhu from His tomb to revive His subjects and resume His rule of earth. The time would be easy to know, for then mankind would have become as the Great Old Ones; free and wild and beyond good and evil, with laws and morals thrown aside and all men shouting and killing and revelling in joy. Then the liberated Old Ones would teach them new ways to shout and kill and revel and enjoy themselves, and all the earth would flame with a holocaust of ecstasy and freedom. Meanwhile the cult, by appropriate rites, must keep alive the memory of those ancient ways and shadow forth the prophecy of their return.

In the elder time chosen men had talked with the entombed Old Ones in dreams, but then something had happened. The great stone city R'lyeh, with its monoliths and sepulchres, had sunk beneath the waves; and the deep waters, full of the one primal mystery through which not even thought can pass, had cut off the spectral intercourse. But memory never died, and high-priests said that the city would rise again when the stars were right. Then came out of the earth the black spirits of earth, mouldy and shadowy, and full of dim rumours picked up in caverns beneath forgotten sea-bottoms. But of them old Castro dared not speak much. He cut himself off hurriedly, and no amount of persuasion or subtlety could elicit more in this direction. The *size* of the Old Ones, too, he curiously declined to mention. Of the cult, he said that he thought the centre lay amid the pathless deserts of Arabia, where Irem, the City of Pillars, dreams hidden and untouched. It was not allied to the European witch-cult, and was virtually unknown beyond its members. No book had ever really hinted of it, though the deathless Chinamen said that there were double meanings in the *Necronomicon* of the mad Arab Abdul Alhazred which the initiated might read as they chose, especially the must-discussed couplet:

> "That is not dead which can eternal lie,
> And with strange aeons even death may die."

Legrasse, deeply impressed and not a little bewildered, had inquired in vain concerning the historic affiliations of the cult. Castro, apparently, had told the truth when he said that it was wholly secret. The authorities at Tulane University could shed no light upon either cult or image, and now the detective had come to the highest authorities in the country and met with no more than the Greenland tale of Professor Webb.

The feverish interest aroused at the meeting by Legrasse's

tale, corroborated as it was by the statuette, is echoed in the subsequent correspondence of those who attended; although scant mention occurs in the formal publications of the society. Caution is the first care of those accustomed to face occasional charlatanry and imposture. Legrasse for some time lent the image to Professor Webb, but at the latter's death it was returned to him and remains in his possession, where I viewed it not long ago. It is truly a terrible thing, and unmistakably akin to the dream-sculpture of young Wilcox.

That my uncle was excited by the tale of the sculptor I did not wonder, for what thoughts must arise upon hearing, after a knowledge of what Legrasse had learned of the cult, of a sensitive young man who had *dreamed* not only the figure and exact hieroglyphics of the swamp-found image and the Greenland devil tablet, but had come *in his dreams* upon at least three of the precise words of the formula uttered alike by Esquimau diabolists and mongrel Louisianans? Professor Angell's instant start on an investigation of the utmost thoroughness was eminently natural; though privately I suspected young Wilcox of having heard of the cult in some indirect way, and of having invested a series of dreams to heighten and continue the mystery at my uncle's expense. The dream-narratives and cuttings collected by the professor were, of course, strong corroboration; but the rationalism of my mind and the extravagance of the whole subject led me to adopt what I thought the most sensible conclusions. So, after thoroughly studying the manuscript again and correlating the theosophical and anthropological notes with the cult narrative of Legrasse, I made a trip to Providence to see the sculptor and give him the rebuke I thought proper for so boldly imposing upon a learned and aged man.

Wilcox still lived alone in the Fleur-de-Lys Building in Thomas Street, a hideous Victorian imitation of seventeenth-century Breton architecture which flaunts its stuccoed front amidst the lovely colonial houses on the ancient hill, and under the very shadow of the finest Georgian steeple in America. I found him at work in his rooms, and at once conceded from the specimens scattered about that his genius is indeed profound and authentic. He will, I believe, some time be heard from as one of the great decadents; for he has crystallised in clay and will one day mirror in marble those nightmares and phantasies which Arthur Machen evokes in prose, and Clark Ashton Smith makes visible in verse and in painting.

Dark, frail, and somewhat unkempt in aspect, he turned languidly at my knock and asked me my business without rising. When I told him who I was, he displayed some interest; for my uncle had excited his curiosity in probing his strange dreams, yet had never explained the reason for the study. I did not enlarge his knowledge in this regard, but sought with some subtlety to draw him out. In a short time I became convinced of his absolute sincerity, for he spoke of the dreams in a manner none could mistake. They and their subconscious residuum had influenced his art profoundly, and he shewed me a morbid statue whose contours almost made me shake with the potency of its black suggestion. He could not recall having seen the original of this thing except in his own dream bas-relief, but the outlines had formed themselves insensibly under his hands. It was, no doubt, the giant shape he had raved of in delirium. That he really knew nothing of the hidden cult, save from what my uncle's relentless catechism had let fall, he soon made clear; and again I strove to think of some way in which he could possibly have received the weird impressions.

He talked of his dreams in a strangely poetic fashion; making me see with terrible vividness the damp Cyclopean city of slimy green stone—whose *geometry*, he oddly said, was *all wrong*—and hear with frightened expectancy the ceaseless, half-mental calling from underground: *"Cthulhu fhtagn,"* *"Cthulhu fhtagn."* These words had formed part of that dread ritual which told of dead Cthulhu's dream-vigil in his stone vault at R'lyeh, and I felt deeply moved despite my rational beliefs. Wilcox, I was sure, had heard of the cult in some casual way, and had soon forgotten it amidst the mass of his equally weird reading and imagining. Later, by virtue of its sheer impressiveness, it had found subconscious expression in dreams, in the bas-relief, and in the terrible statue I now beheld; so that his imposture upon my uncle had been a very innocent one. The youth was of a type, at once slightly affected and slightly ill-mannered, which I could never like; but I was willing enough now to admit both his genius and his honesty. I took leave of him amicably, and wish him all the success his talent promises.

The matter of the cult still remained to fascinate me, and at times I had visions of personal fame from researches into its origin and connexions. I visited New Orleans, talked with Legrasse and others of that old-time raiding-party, saw the frightful image, and even questioned such of the mongrel prisoners as still survived. Old Castro, unfortunately, had been dead for some years. What I now heard so graphically at first-hand, though it was really no more than a detailed confirmation of what my uncle had written, excited me afresh; for I felt sure that I was on the track of a very real, very secret, and very ancient religion whose discovery would make me an anthropologist of note. My attitude was still one of absolute materialism, *as I wish it still were,* and I discounted with almost inexplicable perversity the coincidence of the dream notes and odd cuttings collected by Professor Angell.

One thing I began to suspect, and which I now fear I *know,* is that my uncle's death was far from natural. He fell on a narrow hill street leading up from an ancient waterfront swarming with foreign mongrels, after a careless push from a negro sailor. I did not forget the mixed blood and marine pursuits of the cult-members in Louisiana, and would not be surprised to learn of secret methods and poison needles as ruthless and as anciently known as the cryptic rites and beliefs. Legrasse and his men, it is true, have been let alone; but in Norway a certain seaman who saw things is dead. Might not the deeper inquiries of my uncle after encountering the sculptor's data have come to sinister ears? I think Professor Angell died because he knew too much, or because he was likely to learn too much. Whether I shall go as he did remains to be seen, for I have learned much now.

III   The Madness from the Sea

If heaven ever wishes to grant me a boon, it will be a total effacing of the results of a mere chance which fixed my eye on a certain stray piece of shelf-paper. It was nothing on which I would naturally have stumbled in the course of my daily round, for it was an old number of an Australian journal, the *Sydney Bulletin* for April 18, 1925. It had escaped even the cutting bureau which had at the time of its issuance been avidly collecting material for my uncle's research.

I had largely given over my inquiries into what Professor Angell called the "Cthulhu cult," and was visiting a learned friend in Paterson, New Jersey; the curator of a local museum and a mineralogist of note. Examining one day the reserve specimens roughly set on the storage shelves in a rear room of the museum, my eye was caught by an odd picture in one of the old papers spread beneath the stones. It was the *Sydney Bulletin* I have mentioned, for my friend has wide affiliations in all conceivable foreign parts; and the picture was a half-tone cut of a hideous stone image almost identical with that which Legrasse had found in the swamp.

Eagerly clearing the sheet of its precious contents, I scanned the item in detail; and was disappointed to find it of only moderate length. What it suggested, however, was of portentous significance to my flagging quest; and I carefully tore it out for immediate action. It read as follows:

MYSTERY DERELICT FOUND AT SEA

Vigilant Arrives With Helpless Armed
New Zealand Yacht in Tow.
One Survivor and Dead Man Found Aboard. Tale of
Desperate Battle and Deaths at Sea.

Rescued Seaman Refuses
Particulars of Strange Experience.
Odd Idol Found in His Possession. Inquiry
to Follow.

The Morrison Co.'s freighter *Vigilant*, bound from
Valparaiso, arrived this morning at its wharf in Darling
Harbour, having in tow the battled and disabled but
heavily armed steam yacht *Alert* of Dunedin, N. Z.,
which was sighted April 12th in S. Latitude 34° 21',
W. Longitude 152° 17' with one living and one dead
man aboard.

The *Vigilant* left Valparaiso March 25th, and on April
2nd was driven considerably south of her course by exceptionally heavy storms and monster waves. On April
12th the derelict was sighted; and though apparently
deserted, was found upon boarding to contain one survivor in a half-delirious condition and one man who
had evidently been dead for more than a week. The
living man was clutching a horrible stone idol of unknown origin, about a foot in height, regarding whose
nature authorities at Sydney University, the Royal Society, and the Museum in College Street all profess
complete bafflement, and which the survivor says he
found in the cabin of the yacht, in a small carved shrine
of common pattern.

This man, after recovering his senses, told an exceedingly strange story of piracy and slaughter. He is
Gustaf Johansen, a Norwegian of some intelligence, and
had been second mate of the two-masted schooner
Emma of Auckland, which sailed for Callao February
20th with a complement of eleven men. The *Emma*, he
says, was delayed and thrown widely south of her course
by the great storm of March 1st, and on March 22nd,
in S. Latitude 49° 51', W. Longitude 128° 34', encountered the *Alert*, manned by a queer and evil-looking
crew of Kanakas and half-castes. Being ordered per-

emptorily to turn back, Capt. Collins refused; where-upon the strange crew began to fire savagely and without warning upon the schooner with a pecularily heavy battery of brass cannon forming part of the yacht's equipment. The *Emma*'s men shewed fight, says the survivor, and though the schooner began to sink from shots beneath the waterline they managed to heave alongside their enemy and board her, grappling with the savage crew on the yacht's deck, and being forced to kill them all, the number being slightly superior, because of their particularly abhorrent and desperate though rather clumsy mode of fighting.

Three of the *Emma*'s men, including Capt. Collins and First Mate Green, were killed; and the remaining eight under Second Mate Johansen proceeded to navigate the captured yacht, going ahead in their original direction to see if any reason for their ordering back had existed. The next day, it appears, they raised and landed on a small island, although none is known to exist in that part of the ocean; and six of the men some-how died ashore, though Johansen is queerly reticent about this part of his story, and speaks only of their falling into a rock chasm. Later, it seems, he and one companion boarded the yacht and tried to manage her, but were beaten about by the storm of April 2nd. From that time till his rescue on the 12th the man remembers little, and he does not even recall when William Briden, his companion, died. Briden's death reveals no appar-ent cause, and was probably due to excitement or ex-posure. Cable advices from Dunedin report that the *Alert* was well known there as an island trader, and bore an evil reputation along the waterfront. It was owned by a curious group of half-castes whose frequent meetings and night trips to the woods attracted no little curiosity; and it had set sail in great haste just after the storm and earth tremors of March 1st. Our Auckland correspondent gives the *Emma* and her crew an excellent reputation, and Johansen is described as a sober and worthy man. The admiralty will institute an inquiry on the whole matter beginning tomorrow, at which every effort will be made to induce Johansen to speak more freely than he has done hitherto.

This was all, together with the picture of the hellish image; but what a train of ideas it started in my mind! Here were new treasuries of data on the Cthulhu Cult, and evidence that it had strange interests at sea as well as on land. What motive prompted the hybrid crew to order back the *Emma* as they sailed about with their hideous idol? What was the unknown island on which six of the *Emma*'s crew had died, and about which the mate Johansen was so secretive? What had the vice-admiralty's investigation brought out, and what was known of the noxious cult in Dunedin? And most marvellous of all, what deep and more than natural linkage of dates was this which gave a malign and now undeniable significance to the various turns of events so carefully noted by my uncle?

March 1st—our February 28th according to the International Date Line—the earthquake and storm had come. From Dunedin the *Alert* and her noisome crew had darted eagerly forth as if imperiously summoned, and on the other side of the earth poets and artists had begun to dream of a strange, dank Cyclopean city whilst a young sculptor had moulded in his sleep the form of the dreaded Cthulhu. March 23d the crew of the *Emma* landed on an unknown island and left six men dead; and on that date the dreams of sensitive men assumed a heightened vividness and darkened with dread of a giant monster's malign pursuit, whilst an architect had gone mad and a sculptor had lapsed suddenly into delirium! And what of this storm of April 2nd—the date on which all dreams of the dank city ceased, and Wilcox emerged unharmed from the bondage of strange fever? What of all this—and of those hints of old Castro about the sunken, star-born Old Ones and their coming reign; their faithful cult *and their mastery of dreams*? Was I tottering on the brink of cosmic horrors beyond man's power to bear? If so, they must be horrors of the mind alone, for in some way the second of April had put a stop to whatever monstrous menace had begun its siege of mankind's soul.

That evening, after a day of hurried cabling and arranging, I bade my host adieu and took a train for San Francisco. In less than a month I was in Dunedin; where, however, I found that little was known of the strange cult-members who had lingered in the old sea-taverns. Waterfront scum was far too common for special mention; though there was vague talk about one inland trip these mongrels had made, during which faint drumming and red flame were noted on the distant hills. In Auckland I learned that Johansen had returned *with yellow hair turned white* after a perfunctory and inconclusive questioning at Sydney, and had thereafter sold his cottage in West Street and sailed with his wife to his old home in Oslo. Of his stirring experience he would tell his friends no more than he had told the admiralty officials, and all they could do was to give me his Oslo address.

After that I went to Sydney and talked profitlessly with seamen and members of the vice-admiralty court. I saw the *Alert*, now sold and in commercial use, at Circular Quay in Sydney Cove, but gained nothing from its non-committal bulk. The crouching image with its cuttlefish head, dragon body, scaly wings, and hieroglyphed pedestal, was preserved in the Museum at Hyde Park; and I studied it long and well, finding it a thing of balefully exquisite workmanship, and with the same utter mystery, terrible antiquity, and unearthly strangeness of material which I had noted in Legrasse's smaller specimen. Geologists, the curator told me, had found it a monstrous puzzle; for they vowed that the world held no rock like it. Then I thought with a shudder of what old Castro had told Legrasse about the primal Great Ones: "They had come from the stars, and had brought Their images with Them."

Shaken with such a mental revolution as I had never before known, I now resolved to visit Mate Johansen in Olso. Sailing for London, I reembarked at once for the Norwegian capital; and one autumn day landed at the trim wharves in the shadow of the Egeberg. Johansen's address, I discovered, lay in the Old Town of King Harold Haardrada, which kept alive the name of Oslo during all the centuries that the greater city masqueraded as "Christiana." I made the brief trip by taxicab, and knocked with palpitant heart at the door of a neat and ancient building with plastered front. A sad-faced woman in black answered my summons, and I was stung with disappointment when she told me in halting English that Gustaf Johansen was no more.

He had not long survived his return, said his wife, for the doings at sea in 1925 had broken him. He had told her no more than he had told the public, but had left a long manuscript—of "technical matters" as he said—written in English, evidently in order to safeguard her from the peril of casual perusal. During a walk through a narrow lane near the Gothenburg dock, a bundle of papers falling from an attic window had knocked him down. Two Lascar sailors at once helped him to his feet, but before the ambulance could reach him he was dead. Physicians found no adequate cause for the end, and laid it to heart trouble and a weakened constitution.

I now felt gnawing at my vitals that dark terror which will never leave me till I, too, am at rest; "accidentally" or otherwise. Persuading the widow that my connexion with her husband's "technical matters" was sufficient to entitle me to his manuscript, I bore the document away and began to read it on the London boat. It was a simple, rambling thing—a naive sailor's effort at a post-facto diary—and strove to recall day by day that last awful voyage. I cannot attempt to transcribe it verbatim in all its cloudiness and redundance, but I will tell its gist enough to shew why the sound of the water against the vessel's sides became so unendurable to me that I stopped my ears with cotton.

Johansen, thank God, did not know quite all, even though he saw the city and the Thing, but I shall never sleep calmly again when I think of the horrors that lurk ceaselessly behind life in time and in space, and of those unhallowed blasphemies from elder stars which dream beneath the sea, known and favoured by a nightmare cult ready and eager to loose them on the world whenever another earthquake shall heave their monstrous stone city again to the sun and air.

Johansen's voyage had begun just as he told it to the vice-admiralty. The *Emma*, in ballast, had cleared Auckland on February 20th, and had felt the full force of that earthquake-born tempest which must have heaved up from the sea-bottom the horrors that filled men's dreams. Once more under control, the ship was making good progress when held up by the *Alert* on March 22nd, and I could feel the mate's regret as he wrote of her bombardment and sinking. Of the swarthy cult-fiends on the *Alert* he speaks with significant horror. There was some peculiarly abominable quality about them which made their destruction seem almost a duty, and Johansen shews ingenuous wonder at the charge of ruthlessness brought against his party during the proceedings of the court of inquiry. Then, driven ahead by curiosity in their captured yacht under Johansen's command, the men sight a great stone pillar sticking out of the sea, and in S. Latitude 47° 9', W. Longitude 126° 43' come upon a coast-line of mingled mud, ooze, and weedy Cyclopean masonry which can be nothing less than the tangible substance of earth's supreme terror—the nightmare corpse-city of R'lyeh, that was built in measureless aeons behind history by the vast, loathsome shapes that seeped down from the dark stars. There lay great Cthulhu and his hordes, hidden in green slimy vaults and sending out at last, after cycles incalculable, the thoughts that spread fear to the dreams of the sensitive and called imperiously to the faithful to come on a pilgrimage of liberation and restoration. All this Johansen did not suspect, but God knows he soon saw enough!

I suppose that only a single mountain-top, the hideous monolith-crowned citadel whereon great Cthulhu was buried, actually emerged from the waters. When I think of the *extent* of all that may be brooding down there I almost wish to kill myself forthwith. Johansen and his men were awed by the cosmic majesty of this dripping Babylon of elder daemons, and must have guessed without guidance that it was nothing of this or of any sane planet. Awe at the unbelievable size of the greenish stone blocks, at the dizzying height of the great carven monolith, and at the stupefying identity of the colossal statues and bas-reliefs with the queer image found in the shrine on the *Alert*, is poignantly visible in every line of the mate's frightened description.

Without knowing what futurism is like, Johansen achieved something very close to it when he spoke of the city; for instead of describing any definite structure or building, he dwells only on broad impressions of vast angles and stone surfaces—surfaces too great to belong to any thing right or proper for this earth, and impious with horrible images and hieroglyphs. I mention his talk about *angles* because it suggests something Wilcox had told me of his awful dreams. He had said that the *geometry* of the dream-place he saw was abnormal, non-Euclidean, and loathsomely redolent of spheres and dimensions apart from ours. Now an unlettered seaman felt the same thing whilst gazing at the terrible reality.

Johansen and his men landed at a sloping mud-bank on this monstrous Acropolis, and clambered slipperily up over titan oozy blocks which could have been no mortal staircase. The very sun of heaven seemed distorted when viewed through the polarising miasma welling out from this sea-soaked perversion, and twisted menace and suspense lurked leeringly in those crazily elusive angles of carven rock where a second glance shewed concavity after the first shewed convexity.

Something very like fright had come over all the explorers before anything more definite than rock and ooze and weed was seen. Each would have fled had he not feared the scorn of the others, and it was only half-heartedly that they searched—vainly, as it proved—for some portable souvenir to bear away.

It was Rodriguez the Portuguese who climbed up the foot of the monolith and shouted of what he had found. The rest followed him, and looked curiously at the immense carved door with the now familiar squid-dragon bas-relief. It was, Johansen said, like a great barn-door; and they all felt that it was a door because of the ornate lintel, threshold, and jambs around it, though they could not decide whether it lay flat like a trap-door or slantwise like an outside cellar-door. As Wilcox would have said, the geometery of the place was all wrong. One could not be sure that the sea and the ground were horizontal, hence the relative position of everything else seemed phantasmally variable.

Briden pushed at the stone in several places without result. Then Donovan felt over it delicately around the edge, pressing each point separately as he went. He climbed interminably along the grotesque stone moulding—that is, one would call it climbing if the thing was not after all horizontal—and the men wondered how any door in the universe could be so vast. Then, very softly and slowly, the acre-great panel began to give inward at the top; and they saw that it was balanced. Donovan slid or somehow propelled himself down or along the jamb and rejoined his fellows, and everyone watched the queer recession of the monstrously carven portal. In this phantasy of prismatic distortion it moved anomalously in a diagonal way, so that all the rules of matter and perspective seemed upset.

The aperture was black with a darkness almost material. That tenebrousness was indeed a *positive quality*; for it obscured such parts of the inner walls as ought to have been revealed, and actually burst forth like smoke from its aeon-long imprisonment, visibly darkening the sun as it slunk away into the shrunken and gibbous sky on flapping membraneous wings. The odour arising from the newly opened depths was intolerable, and at length the quick-eared Hawkins thought he heard a nasty, slopping sound down there. Everyone listened, and everyone was listening still when It lumbered slobberingly into sight and gropingly squeezed Its gelatinous green immensity through the black doorway into the tainted outside air of that poison city of madness.

Poor Johansen's handwriting almost gave out when he wrote of this. Of the six men who never reached the ship, he thinks two perished of pure fright in that accursed instant. The Thing cannot be described—there is no language for such abysms of shrieking and immemorial lunacy, such eldritch contradictions of all matter, force, and cosmic order. A mountain walked or stumbled. God! What wonder that across the earth a great architect went mad, and poor Wilcox raved with fever in that telepathic instant? The Thing of the idols, the green, sticky spawn of the stars, had awaked to claim his own. The stars were right again, and what an age-old cult had failed to do by design, a band of innocent sailors had done by accident. After vigintillions of years great Cthulhu was loose again, and ravening for delight.

Three men were swept up by the flabby claws before anybody turned. God rest them, if there be any rest in the universe. They were Donovan, Guerrera, and Angstrom. Parker slipped as the other three were plunging frenziedly over endless vistas of green-crusted rock to the boat, and Johansen swears he was swallowed up by an angle of masonry which shouldn't have been there; an angle which was acute, but behaved as if it were obtuse. So only Briden and Johansen reached the boat, and pulled desperately for the *Alert* as the mountainous monstrosity flopped down the slimy stones and hesitated floundering at the edge of the water.

Steam had not been suffered to go down entirely, despite the departure of all hands for the shore; and it was the work of only a few moments of feverish rushing up and down between wheel and engines to get the *Alert* under way. Slowly, amidst the distorted horrors of that indescribable scene, she began to churn the lethal waters; whilst on the masonry of that charnel shore that was not of earth the titan Thing from the stars slavered and gibbered like Polypheme cursing the fleeing ship of Odysseus. Then, bolder than the storied Cyclops, great Cthulhu slid greasily into the water and began to pursue with vast wave-raising strokes of cosmic potency. Briden looked back and went mad, laughing shrilly as he kept on laughing at intervals till death found him one night in the cabin whilst Johansen was wandering deliriously.

But Johansen had not given out yet. Knowing that the Thing could surely overtake the *Alert* until steam was fully up, he resolved on a desperate chance; and, setting the engine for full speed, ran lightning-like on deck and reversed the wheel. There was a mighty eddying and foaming in the noisome brine, and as the steam mounted higher and higher the brave Norwegian drove his vessel head on against the pursuing jelly which rose above the unclean froth like the stern of a daemon galleon. The awful squid-head with writhing feelers came nearly up to the bowsprit of the sturdy yacht, but Johansen drove on relentlessly. There was a bursting as of an exploding bladder, a slushy nastiness as of a cloven sunfish, a stench as of a thousand opened graves, and a sound that the chronicler would not put on paper. For an instant the ship was befouled by an acrid and blinding green cloud, and then there was only a venomous seething astern; where—God in heaven!—the scattered plasticity of that nameless sky-spawn was nebulously *recombining* in its hateful original form, whilst its distance widened every second as the *Alert* gained impetus from its mounting steam.

That was all. After that Johansen only brooded over the idol in the cabin and attended to a few matters of food for himself and the laughing maniac by his side. He did not try to navigate after the first bold flight, for the reaction had taken something out of his soul. Then came the storm of April 2nd, and a gathering of the clouds about his consciousness. There is a sense of spectral whirling through liquid gulfs of infinity, of dizzying rides through reeling universes on a comet's tail, and of hysterical plunges from the pit to the moon and from the moon back again to the pit, all livened by a cachinnating chorus of the distorted, hilarious elder gods and the green, bat-winged mocking imps of Tartarus.

Out of that dream came rescue—the *Vigilant*, the vice-admiralty court, the streets of Dunedin, and the long voyage back home to the old house by the Egeberg. He could not tell—they would think him mad. He would write of what he knew before death came, but his wife must not guess. Death would be a boon if only it could blot out the memories.

That was the document I read, and now I have placed it in the tin box beside the bas-relief and the papers of Professor Angell. With it shall go this record of mine—this test of my own sanity, wherein is pieced together that which I hope may never be pieced together again. I have looked upon all that the universe has to hold of horror, and even the skies of spring and the flowers of summer must ever afterward be poison to me. But I do not think my life will be long. As my uncle went, as poor Johansen went, so I shall go. I know too much, and the cult still lives.

Cthulhu still lives, too, I suppose, again in that chasm of stone which has shielded him since the sun was young. His accursed city is sunken once more, for the *Vigilant* sailed over the spot after the April storm; but his ministers on earth still bellow and prance and slay around idol-capped monoliths in lonely places. He must have been trapped by the sinking whilst within his black abyss, or else the world would by now be screaming with fright and frenzy. Who knows the end? What has risen may sink, and what has sunk may rise. Loathsomeness waits and dreams in the deep, and decay spreads over the tottering cities of men. A time will come—but I must not and cannot think! Let me pray that, if I do not survive this manuscript, my executors may put caution before audacity and see that it meets no other eye.

Shirley Jackson

THE SUMMER PEOPLE

A significant portion of the major work of Shirley Jackson is horror fiction. Aside from her novels, *The Sundial*, *The Haunting of Hill House* and the National Book Award winner, *We Have Always Lived in the Castle*, much of her short fiction is particularly fine horror. She chose to work often in the specialized area of the house story, of which *The Haunting of Hill House* is perhaps the most perfect example yet written. She told me in conversation in 1962 that she had a complete run of *Unknown* magazine. "It's the best," she said. Her influence on horror in the novel form continues to grow in the two decades since her death. Stephen King, in *Danse Macabre*, featured *The Haunting of Hill House* as one of his ten best since World War II. "The Summer People" is another of Jackson's house stories. Mr. and Mrs. Allison have broken a rule and will be punished. This tale is an interesting comparison to Lucy Clifford's "The New Mother." Here, however, the irony is overt, since we have the form of the moral tale without the morality at all.

The Allisons' country cottage, seven miles from the nearest town, was set prettily on a hill; from three sides it looked down on soft trees and grass that seldom, even at midsummer, lay still and dry. On the fourth side was the

lake, which touched against the wooden pier the Allisons had
to keep repairing, and which looked equally well from the
Allisons' front porch, their side porch or any spot on the
wooden staircase leading from the porch down to the water.
Although the Allisons loved their summer cottage, looked
forward to arriving in the early summer and hated to leave in
the fall, they had not troubled themselves to put in any improvements, regarding the cottage itself and the lake as improvement enough for the life left to them. The cottage had
no heat, no running water except the precarious supply from
the backyard pump and no electricity. For seventeen summers, Janet Allison had cooked on a kerosene stove, heating
all their water; Robert Allison had brought buckets full of
water daily from the pump and read his paper by kerosene
light in the evenings and they had both, sanitary city people,
become stolid and matter-of-fact about their backhouse. In
the first two years they had gone through all the standard
vaudeville and magazine jokes about backhouses and by now,
when they no longer had frequent guests to impress, they had
subsided to a comfortable security which made the backhouse, as well as the pump and the kerosene, an indefinable
asset to their summer life.

In themselves, the Allisons were ordinary people. Mrs.
Allison was fifty-eight years old and Mr. Allison sixty; they
had seen their children outgrow the summer cottage and go
on to families of their own and seashore resorts; their friends
were either dead or settled in comfortable year-round houses,
their nieces and nephews vague. In the winter they told one
another they could stand their New York apartment while
waiting for the summer; in the summer they told one another
that the winter was well worth while, waiting to get to the
country.

Since they were old enough not to be ashamed of regular
habits, the Allisons invariably left their summer cottage the
Tuesday after Labor Day, and were as invariably sorry when
the months of September and early October turned out to be
pleasant and almost insufferably barren in the city; each year

they recognized that there was nothing to bring them back to New York, but it was not until this year that they overcame their traditional inertia enough to decide to stay at the cottage after Labor Day.

"There isn't really anything to take us back to the city," Mrs. Allison told her husband seriously, as though it were a new idea, and he told her, as though neither of them had ever considered it, "We might as well enjoy the country as long as possible."

Consequently, with much pleasure and a slight feeling of adventure, Mrs. Allison went into their village the day after Labor Day and told those natives with whom she had dealings, with a pretty air of breaking away from tradition, that she and her husband had decided to stay at least a month longer at their cottage.

"It isn't as though we had anything to take us back to the city," she said to Mr. Babcock, her grocer. "We might as well enjoy the country while we can."

"Nobody ever stayed at the lake past Labor Day before," Mr. Babcock said. He was putting Mrs. Allison's groceries into a large cardboard carton, and he stopped for a minute to look reflectively into a bag of cookies. "Nobody," he added.

"But the city!" Mrs. Allison always spoke of the city to Mr. Babcock as though it were Mr. Babcock's dream to go there. "It's so hot—you've really no idea. We're always sorry when we leave."

"Hate to leave," Mr. Babcock said. One of the most irritating native tricks Mrs. Allison had noticed was that of taking a trivial statement and rephrasing it downwards, into an even more trite statement. "I'd hate to leave myself," Mr. Babcock said, after deliberation, and both he and Mrs. Allison smiled. "But I never heard of anyone ever staying out at the lake after Labor Day before."

"Well, we're going to give it a try," Mrs. Allison said, and Mr. Babcock replied gravely, "Never know till you try."

Physically, Mrs. Allison decided, as she always did when leaving the grocery after one of her inconclusive conversations with Mr. Babcock, physically, Mr. Babcock could model for a statue of Daniel Webster, but mentally . . . it was horrible to think into what old New England Yankee stock had degenerated. She said as much to Mr. Allison when she got into the car, and he said, "It's generations of inbreeding. That and the bad land."

Since this was their big trip into town, which they made only once every two weeks to buy things they could not have delivered, they spent all day at it, stopping to have a sandwich in the newspaper and soda shop, and leaving packages heaped in the back of the car. Although Mrs. Allison was able to order groceries delivered regularly, she was never able to form any accurate idea of Mr. Babcock's current stock by telephone, and her lists of odds and ends that might be procured was always supplemented, almost beyond their need, by the new and fresh local vegetables Mr. Babcock was selling temporarily, or the packaged candy which had just come in. This trip Mrs. Allison was tempted, too, by the set of glass baking dishes that had found themselves completely by chance in the hardware and clothing and general store, and which had seemingly been waiting there for no one but Mrs. Allison, since the country people, with their instinctive distrust of anything that did not look as permanent as trees and rocks and sky, had only recently begun to experiment in aluminum baking dishes instead of ironware, and had, apparently within the memory of local inhabitants, discarded stoneware in favor of iron.

Mrs. Allison had the glass baking dishes carefully wrapped, to endure the uncomfortable ride home over the rocky road that led up to the Allisons' cottage, and while Mr. Charley Walpole, who, with his younger brother Albert, ran the hardware-clothing-general store (the store itself was called Johnson's, because it stood on the site of the old Johnson cabin, burned fifty years before Charley Walpole was born), laboriously unfolded newspapers to wrap around the dishes, Mrs. Allison said, informally, "Course, I *could* have waited and gotten those dishes in New York, but we're not going back so soon this year."

"Heard you was staying on," Mr. Charley Walpole said. His old fingers fumbled maddeningly with the thin sheets of newspaper, carefully trying to isolate only one sheet at a time, and he did not look up at Mrs. Allison as he went on, "Don't know about staying on up there to the lake. Not after Labor Day."

"Well, you know," Mrs. Allison said, quite as though he deserved an explanation, "it just seemed to us that we've been hurrying back to New York every year, and there just wasn't any need for it. You know what the city's like in the fall." And she smiled confidingly up at Mr. Charley Walpole.

Rhythmically he wound string around the package. He's giving me a piece long enough to save, Mrs. Allison thought, and she looked away quickly to avoid giving any sign of impatience. "I feel sort of like we belong here, more," she said. "Staying on after everyone else has left." To prove this, she smiled brightly across the store at a woman with a familiar face, who might have been the woman who sold berries to the Allisons one year, or the woman who occasionally helped in the grocery and was probably Mr. Babcock's aunt.

"Well," Mr. Charley Walpole said. He shoved the package a little across the counter, to show that it was finished and that for a sale well made, a package well wrapped, he was willing to accept pay. "Well," he said again. "Never been summer people before, at the lake after Labor Day."

Mrs. Allison gave him a five-dollar bill, and he made change methodically, giving great weight even to the pennies. "Never after Labor Day," he said, and nodded at Mrs. Allison, and went soberly along the store to deal with two women who were looking at cotton house dresses.

As Mrs. Allison passed on her way out she heard one of the women say acutely, "Why is one of them dresses one dollar and thirty-nine cents and this one here is only ninety-eight?"

"They're great people," Mrs. Allison told her husband as they went together down the sidewalk after meeting at the door of the hardware store. "They're so solid, and so reasonable, and so *honest*."

"Makes you feel good, knowing there are still towns like this," Mr. Allison said.

"You know, in New York," Mrs. Allison said, "I might have paid a few cents less for these dishes, but there wouldn't have been anything sort of *personal* in the transaction."

"Staying on to the lake?" Mrs. Martin, in the newspaper and sandwich shop, asked the Allisons. "Heard you was staying on."

"Thought we'd take advantage of the lovely weather this year," Mr. Allison said.

Mrs. Martin was a comparative newcomer to the town; she had married into the newspaper and sandwich shop from a neighboring farm, and had stayed on after her husband's death. She served bottled soft drinks, and fried egg and onion sandwiches on thick bread, which she made on her own stove at the back of the store. Occasionally when Mrs. Martin served a sandwich it would carry with it the rich fragrance of the stew or the pork chops cooking alongside for Mrs. Martin's dinner.

"I don't guess anyone's ever stayed out there so long before," Mrs. Martin said. "Not after Labor Day, anyway."

"I guess Labor Day is when they usually leave," Mr. Hall, the Allisons' nearest neighbor, told them later, in front of Mr. Babcock's store, where the Allisons were getting into their car to go home. "Surprised you're staying on."

"It seemed a shame to go so soon," Mrs. Allison said. Mr. Hall lived three miles away; he supplied the Allisons with butter and eggs, and occasionally, from the top of their hill, the Allisons could see the lights in his house in the early evening before the Halls went to bed.

"They usually leave Labor Day," Mr. Hall said.

The ride home was long and rough; it was beginning to get dark, and Mr. Allison had to drive very carefully over the dirt road by the lake. Mrs. Allison lay back against the seat, pleasantly relaxed after a day of what seemed whirlwind shopping compared with their day-to-day existence; the new glass baking dishes lurked agreeably in her mind, and the half bushel of red eating apples, and the package of colored thumbtacks with which she was going to put up new shelf edging in the kitchen. "Good to get home," she said softly as they came in sight of their cottage, silhouetted above them against the sky.

"Glad we decided to stay on," Mr. Allison agreed.

Mrs. Allison spent the next morning lovingly washing her baking dishes, although in his innocence Charley Walpole had neglected to notice the chip in the edge of one; she decided, wastefully, to use some of the red eating apples in a pie for dinner, and, while the pie was in the oven and Mr. Allison was down getting the mail, she sat out on the little lawn the Allisons had made at the top of the hill, and watched the changing lights on the lake, alternating gray and blue as clouds moved quickly across the sun.

Mr. Allison came back a little out of sorts; it always irritated him to walk the mile to the mail box on the state road and come back with nothing, even though he assumed that the walk was good for his health. This morning there was nothing but a circular from a New York department store, and their New York paper, which arrived erratically by mail from one to four days later than it should, so that some days the Allisons might have three papers and frequently none. Mrs. Allison, although she shared with her husband the annoyance of not having mail when they so anticipated it, pored affectionately over the department store circular, and made a mental note to drop in at the store when she finally went back to New York, and check on the sale of wool blankets; it was hard to find good ones in pretty colors nowadays. She debated saving the circular to remind herself, but after thinking about getting up and getting into the cottage to put it away safely somewhere, she dropped it into the grass beside her chair and lay back, her eyes half closed.

"Looks like we might have some rain," Mr. Allison said, squinting at the sky.

"Good for the crops," Mrs. Allison said laconically, and they both laughed.

The kerosene man came the next morning while Mr. Allison was down getting the mail; they were getting low on kerosene and Mrs. Allison greeted the man warmly; he sold kerosene and ice, and, during the summer, hauled garbage away for the summer people. A garbage man was only necessary for improvident city folk; country people had no garbage.

"I'm glad to see you," Mrs. Allison told him. "We were getting pretty low."

The kerosene man, whose name Mrs. Allison had never learned, used a hose attachment to fill the twenty-gallon tank which supplied light and heat and cooking facilities for the Allisons; but today, instead of swinging down from his truck and unhooking the hose from where it coiled affectionately around the cab of the truck, the man stared uncomfortably at Mrs. Allison, his truck motor still going.

"Thought you folks'd be leaving," he said.

"We're staying on another month," Mrs. Allison said brightly. "The weather was so nice, and it seemed like—"

"That's what they told me," the man said. "Can't give you no oil, though."

"What do you mean?" Mrs. Allison raised her eyebrows. "We're just going to keep on with our regular—"

"After Labor Day," the man said. "I don't get so much oil myself after Labor Day."

Mrs. Allison reminded herself, as she had frequently to do when in disagreement with her neighbors, that city manners were no good with country people; you could not expect to overrule a country employee as you could a city worker, and Mrs. Allison smiled engagingly as she said, "But can't you get extra oil, at least while we stay?"

"You see," the main said. He tapped his finger exasperatingly against the car wheel as he spoke. "You see," he said slowly, "I order this oil. I order it down from maybe fifty, fifty-five miles away. I order back in June, how much I'll need for the summer. Then I order again . . . oh, about November. Round about now it's starting to get pretty short." As though the subject were closed, he stopped tapping his finger and tightened his hands on the wheel in preparation for departure.

"But can't you give us *some*?" Mrs. Allison said. "Isn't there anyone else?"

"Don't know as you could get oil anywheres else right now," the man said consideringly. "*I* can't give you none." Before Mrs. Allison could speak, the truck began to move; then it stopped for a minute and he looked at her through the back window of the cab. "Ice?" he called. "I could let you have some ice."

Mrs. Allison shook her head; they were not terribly low on ice, and she was angry. She ran a few steps to catch up with the truck, calling, "Will you try to get us some? Next week?"

"Don't see's I can," the man said. "After Labor Day, it's harder." The truck drove away, and Mrs. Allison, only comforted by the thought that she could probably get kerosene from Mr. Babcock or, at worst, the Halls, watched it go with anger. "Next summer," she told herself, "just let *him* trying coming around next summer!"

There was no mail again, only the paper, which seemed to be coming doggedly on time, and Mr. Allison was openly cross when he returned. When Mrs. Allison told him about the kerosene man he was not particularly impressed.

"Probably keeping it all for a high price during the winter," he commented. "What's happened to Anne and Jerry, do you think?"

Anne and Jerry were their son and daughter, both married, one living in Chicago, one in the far west; their dutiful weekly letters were late; so late, in fact, that Mr. Allison's annoyance at the lack of mail was able to settle on a legitimate grievance. "Ought to realize how we wait for their letters," he said. "Thoughtless, selfish children. Ought to know better."

"Well, dear," Mrs. Allison said placatingly. Anger at Anne and Jerry would not relieve her emotions toward the kerosene man. After a few minutes she said, "Wishing won't bring the mail, dear. I'm going to go call Mr. Babcock and tell him to send up some kerosene with my order."

"At least a postcard," Mr. Allison said as she left.

As with most of the cottage's inconveniences, the Allisons no longer noticed the phone particularly, but yielded to its eccentricities without conscious complaint. It was a wall phone, of a type still seen in only few communities; in order to get the operator, Mrs. Allison had first to turn the side-crank and ring once. Usually it took two or three tries to force the operator to answer, and Mrs. Allison, making any kind of telephone call, approached the phone with resignation and a sort of desperate patience. She had to crank the phone three times this morning before the operator answered, and then it was still longer before Mr. Babcock picked up the receiver at his phone in the corner of the grocery behind the meat table. He said "Store?" with the rising inflection that seemed to indicate suspicion of anyone who tried to communicate with him by means of this unreliable instrument.

"This is Mrs. Allison, Mr. Babcock. I thought I'd give you my order a day early because I wanted to be sure and get some—"

"What say, Mrs. Allison?"

Mrs. Allison raised her voice a little; she saw Mr. Allison, out on the lawn, turn in his chair and regard her sympathetically. "I said, Mr. Babcock, I thought I'd call in my order early so you could send me—"

"Mrs. Allison?" Mr. Babcock said. "You'll come and pick it up?"

"Pick it up?" In her surprise Mrs. Allison let her voice drop back to its normal tone and Mr. Babcock said loudly, "What's that, Mrs. Allison?"

"I thought I'd have you send it out as usual," Mrs. Allison said.

"Well, Mrs. Allison," Mr. Babcock said, and there was a pause while Mrs. Allison waited, staring past the phone over her husband's head out into the sky. "Mrs. Allison," Mr. Babcock went on finally, "I'll tell you, my boy's been working for me went back to school yesterday, and now I got no one to deliver. I only got a boy delivering summers, you see."

"I thought you *always* delivered," Mrs. Allison said.

"Not after Labor Day, Mrs. Allison," Mr. Babcock said firmly, "you never been here after Labor Day before, so's you wouldn't know, of course."

"Well," Mrs. Allison said helplessly. Far inside her mind she was saying, over and over, can't use city manners on country folk, no use getting mad.

"Are you *sure*?" she asked finally. "Couldn't you just send out an order today, Mr. Babcock?"

"Matter of fact," Mr. Babcock said, "I guess I couldn't, Mrs. Allison. It wouldn't hardly pay, delivering, with no one else out at the lake."

"What about Mr. Hall?" Mrs. Allison asked suddenly, "the people who live about three miles away from us out here? Mr. Hall could bring it out when he comes."

"Hall?" Mr. Babcock said. "John Hall? They've gone to visit her folks upstate, Mrs. Allison."

"But they bring all our butter and eggs," Mrs. Allison said, appalled.

"Left yesterday," Mr. Babcock said. "Probably didn't think you folks would stay on up there."

"But I told Mr. Hall . . ." Mrs. Allison started to say, and then stopped. "I'll send Mr. Allison in after some groceries tomorrow," she said.

"You got all you need till then," Mr. Babcock said, satisfied; it was not a question, but a confirmation.

After she hung up, Mrs. Allison went slowly out to sit again in her chair next to her husband. "He won't deliver," she said. "You'll have to go in tomorrow. We've got just enough kerosene to last till you get back."

"He should have told us sooner," Mr. Allison said.

It was not possible to remain troubled long in the face of the day; the country had never seemed more inviting, and the lake moved quietly below them, among the trees, with the almost incredible softness of a summer picture. Mrs. Allison sighed deeply, in the pleasure of possessing for themselves that sight of the lake, with the distant green hills beyond, the gentleness of the small wind through the trees.

The weather continued fair; the next morning Mr. Allison, duly armed with a list of groceries, with "kerosene" in large letters at the top, went down the path to the garage, and Mrs. Allison began another pie in her new baking dishes. She had mixed the crust and was starting to pare the apples when Mr. Allison came rapidly up the path and flung open the screen door into the kitchen.

"Damn car won't start," he announced, with the end-of-the-tether voice of a man who depends on a car as he depends on his right arm.

"What's wrong with it?" Mrs. Allison demanded, stopping with the paring knife in one hand and an apple in the other. "It was all right on Tuesday."

"Well," Mr. Allison said between his teeth, "it's not all right on Friday."

"Can you fix it?" Mrs. Allison asked.

"No," Mr. Allison said, "I can not. Got to call someone, I guess.

"Who?" Mrs. Allison asked.

"Man runs the filling station, I guess." Mr. Allison moved purposefully toward the phone. "He fixed it last summer one time."

A little apprehensive, Mrs. Allison went on paring apples absentmindedly, while she listened to Mr. Allison with the phone, ringing, waiting, ringing, waiting, finally giving the number to the operator, then waiting again and giving the number again, giving the number a third time, and then slamming down the receiver.

"No one there," he announced as he came into the kitchen.

"He's probably gone out for a minute," Mrs. Allison said nervously; she was not quite sure what made her so nervous, unless it was the probability of her husband's losing his temper completely. "He's there alone, I imagine, so if he goes out there's no one to answer the phone."

"That must be it," Mr. Allison said with heavy irony. He slumped into one of the kitchen chairs and watched Mrs. Allison paring apples. After a minute, Mrs. Allison said soothingly, "Why don't you go down and get the mail and then call him again?"

Mr. Allison debated and then said, "Guess I might as well." He rose heavily and when he got to the kitchen door he turned and said, "But if there's no mail—" and leaving an awful silence behind him, he went off down the path.

Mrs. Allison hurried with her pie. Twice she went to the window to glance at the sky to see if there were clouds coming up. The room seemed unexpectedly dark, and she herself felt in the state of tension that precedes a thunderstorm, but both times when she looked the sky was clear and serene, smiling indifferently down on the Allisons' summer cottage as well as on the rest of the world. When Mrs. Allison, her pie ready for the oven, went a third time to look outside, she saw her husband coming up the path; he seemed more cheerful, and when he saw her, he waved eagerly and held a letter in the air.

"From Jerry," he called as soon as he was close enough for her to hear him, "at last—a letter!" Mrs. Allison noticed with concern that he was no longer able to get up the gentle slope of the path without breathing heavily; but then he was in the doorway, holding out the letter. "I saved it till I got here," he said.

Mrs. Allison looked with an eagerness that surprised her on the familiar handwriting of her son; she could not imagine why the letter excited her so, except that it was the first they had received in so long; it would be a pleasant, dutiful letter, full of the doings of Alice and the children, reporting progress with his job, commenting on the recent weather in Chicago, closing with love from all; both Mr. and Mrs. Allison could, if they wished, recite a pattern letter from either of their children.

Mr. Allison slit the letter open with great deliberation, and then he spread it out on the kitchen table and they leaned down and read it together.

"Dear Mother and Dad," it began, in Jerry's familiar, rather childish, handwriting, *"Am glad this goes to the lake as usual, we always thought you came back too soon and ought to stay up there as long as you could. Alice says that now that you're not as young as you used to be and have no demands on your time, fewer friends, etc., in the city, you ought to get what fun you can while you can. Since you two are both happy up there, it's a good idea for you to stay."*

Uneasily Mrs. Allison glanced sideways at her husband; he was reading intently, and she reached out and picked up the empty envelope, not knowing exactly what she wanted from it. It was addressed quite as usual, in Jerry's handwriting, and was postmarked Chicago. Of course it's postmarked Chicago, she thought quickly, why would they want to postmark it anywhere else? When she looked back down at the letter, her husband had turned the page, and she read on with him: *"—and of course if they get measles, etc., now, they will be better off later. Alice is well, of course, me too. Been playing a lot of bridge lately with some people you don't know, named Carruthers. Nice young couple, about our age. Well, will close now as I guess it bores you to hear about things so far away. Tell Dad old Dickson, in our Chicago office, died. He used to ask about Dad a lot. Have a good time up at the lake, and don't bother about hurrying back. Love from all of us, Jerry."*

"Funny," Mr. Allison commented.

"It doesn't sound like Jerry," Mrs. Allison said in a small voice. "He never wrote anything like . . ." she stopped.

"Like what?" Mr. Allison demanded. "Never wrote anything like what?"

Mrs. Allison turned the letter over, frowning. It was impossible to find any sentence, any word, even, that did not sound like Jerry's regular letters. Perhaps it was only that the letter was so late, or the unusual number of dirty fingerprints on the envelope.

"I don't *know*," she said impatiently.

"Going to try that phone call again," Mr. Allison said.

Mrs. Allison read the letter twice more, trying to find a phrase that sounded wrong. Then Mr. Allison came back and said, very quietly, "Phone's dead."

"What?" Mrs. Allison said, dropping the letter.

"Phone's dead," Mr. Allison said.

The rest of the day went quickly; after a lunch of crackers and milk, the Allisons went to sit outside on the lawn, but their afternoon was cut short by the gradually increasing storm clouds that came up over the lake to the cottage, so that it was as dark as evening by four o'clock. The storm delayed, however, as though in loving anticipation of the moment it would break over the summer cottage, and there was an occasional flash of lightning, but no rain. In the evening Mr. and Mrs. Allison, sitting close together inside their cottage, turned on the battery radio they had brought with them from New York. There were no lamps lighted in the cottage, and the only light came from the lightning outside and the small square glow from the dial of the radio.

The slight framework of the cottage was not strong enough to withstand the city noises, the music and the voices, from the radio, and the Allisons could hear them far off echoing across the lake, the saxophones in the New York dance band wailing over the water, the flat voice of the girl vocalist going inexorably out into the clean country air. Even the announcer, speaking glowingly of the virtues of razor blades, was no more than an inhuman voice sounding out from the Allisons' cottage and echoing back, as though the lake and the hills and the trees were returning it unwanted.

During one pause between commercials, Mrs. Allison turned and smiled weakly at her husband. "I wonder if we're supposed to . . . *do* anything," she said.

"No," Mr. Allison said consideringly. "I don't think so. Just wait."

Mrs. Allison caught her breath quickly, and Mr. Allison said, under the trivial melody of the dance band beginning again, "The car had been tampered with, you know. Even I could see that."

Mrs. Allison hesitated a minute and then said very softly, "I suppose the phone wires were cut."

"I imagine so," Mr. Allison said.

After a while, the dance music stopped and they listened attentively to a news broadcast, the announcer's rich voice telling them breathlessly of a marriage in Hollywood, the latest baseball scores, the estimated rise in food prices during the coming week. He spoke to them, in the summer cottage, quite as though they still deserved to hear news of a world that no longer reached them except through the fallible batteries on the radio, which were already beginning to fade, almost as though they still belonged, however tenuously, to the rest of the world.

Mrs. Allison glanced out the window at the smooth surface of the lake, the black masses of the trees, and the waiting storm, and said conversationally, "I feel better about that letter of Jerry's."

"I knew when I saw the light down at the Hall place last night," Mr. Allison said.

The wind, coming up suddenly over the lake, swept around the summer cottage and slapped hard at the windows. Mr. and Mrs. Allison involuntarily moved closer together, and with the first sudden crash of thunder, Mr. Allison reached out and took his wife's hand. And then, while the lightning flashed outside, and the radio faded and sputtered, the two old people huddled together in their summer cottage and waited.

Harlan Ellison

THE WHIMPER OF WHIPPED DOGS

Harlan Ellison, the popular fantasist, when he writes in the horror mode, is a conduit through whom the horrors of everyday life are transformed into fictions that re-awaken us, reconnect us to those daily horrors to which we have become desensitized by conventional wisdom and by habit. Ellison strives for extreme effects. Stephen King has called him the greatest contemporary horror writer: "He sums up, for me, the finest elements of the term . . . in his short stories of fantasy and horror, he strikes closest to all those things which horrify and amuse us (sometimes both at the same time) in our present lives." (*Danse Macabre*, p. 369) "The Whimper of Whipped Dogs" is a violent fantasia on everyday life in the big city with a dystopian moral and is one of the landmarks of contemporary horror fiction. It won for Ellison an Edgar Award in 1974 from the Mystery Writers of America and remains his quintessential work of horror.

On the night after the day she had stained the louvered window shutters of her new apartment on East 52nd Street, Beth saw a woman slowly and hideously knifed to death in the courtyard of her building. She was one of twenty-six witnesses to the ghoulish scene, and, like them, she did nothing to stop it.

She saw it all, every moment of it, without break and with no impediment to her view. Quite madly, the thought crossed her mind as she watched in horrified fascination, that she had the sort of marvelous line of observation Napoleon had sought when he caused to have constructed at the *Comédie-Française* theaters, a curtained box at the rear, so he could watch the audience as well as the stage. The night was clear, the moon was full, she had just turned off the 11:30 movie on channel 2 after the second commercial break, realizing she had already seen Robert Taylor in *Westward the Women*, and had disliked it the first time; and the apartment was quite dark.

She went to the window, to raise it six inches for the night's sleep, and she saw the woman stumble into the courtyard. She was sliding along the wall, clutching her left arm with her right hand. Con Ed had installed mercury-vapor lamps on the poles; there had been sixteen assaults in seven months; the courtyard was illuminated with a chill purple glow that made the blood streaming down the woman's left arm look black and shiny. Beth saw every detail with utter clarity, as though magnified a thousand power under a microscope, solarized as if it had been a television commercial.

The woman threw back her head, as if she were trying to scream, but there was no sound. Only the traffic on First Avenue, late cabs foraging for singles paired for the night at Maxwell's Plum and Friday's and Adam's Apple. But that was over there, beyond. Where *she* was, down there seven floors below, in the courtyard, everything seemed silently suspended in an invisible force-field.

Beth stood in the darkness of her apartment, and realized she had raised the window completely. A tiny balcony lay just over the low sill; now not even glass separated her from the sight; just the wrought-iron balcony railing and seven floors to the courtyard below.

The woman staggered away from the wall, her head still thrown back, and Beth could see she was in her mid-thirties, with dark hair cut in a shag; it was impossible to tell if she was pretty: terror had contorted her features and her mouth was a twisted black slash, opened but emitting no sound. Cords stood out in her neck. She had lost one shoe, and her steps were uneven, threatening to dump her to the pavement.

The man came around the corner of the building, into the courtyard. The knife he held was enormous—or perhaps it only seemed so: Beth remembered a bone-handled fish knife her father had used one summer at the lake in Maine: it folded back on itself and locked, revealing eight inches of serrated blade. The knife in the hand of the dark man in the courtyard seemed to be similar.

The woman saw him and tried to run, but he leaped across the distance between them and grabbed her by the hair and pulled her head back as though he would slash her throat in the next reaper-motion.

Then the woman screamed.

The sound skirled up into the courtyard like bats trapped in an echo chamber, unable to find a way out, driven mad. It went on and on . . .

The man struggled with her and she drove her elbow into his sides and he tried to protect himself, spinning her around by her hair, the terrible scream going up and up and never stopping. She came loose and he was left with a fistful of hair torn out by the roots. As she spun out, he slashed straight across and opened her up just below the breasts. Blood sprayed through her clothing and the man was soaked; it seemed to drive him even more berserk. He went at her again, as she tried to hold herself together, the blood pouring down over her arms.

She tried to run, teetered against the wall, slid sidewise, and the man struck the brick surface. She was away, stumbling over a flower bed, falling, getting to her knees as he threw himself on her again. The knife came up in a flashing arc that illuminated the blade strangely with purple light. And still she screamed.

Lights came on in dozens of apartments and people appeared at windows.

He drove the knife to the hilt into her back, high on the right shoulder. He used both hands.

Beth caught it all in jagged flashes—the man, the woman, the knife, the blood, the expressions on the faces of those watching from the windows. Then lights clicked off in the windows, but they still stood there, watching.

She wanted to yell, to scream, "What are you doing to that woman?" But her throat was frozen, two iron hands that had been immersed in dry ice for ten thousand years clamped around her neck. She could feel the blade sliding into her own body.

Somehow—it seemed impossible but there it was down there, happening somehow—the woman struggled erect and *pulled* herself off the knife. Three steps, she took three steps and fell into the flower bed again. The man was howling now, like a great beast, the sounds inarticulate, bubbling up from his stomach. He fell on her and the knife went up and came down, then again, and again, and finally it was all a blur of motion, and her scream of lunatic bats went on till it faded off and was gone.

Beth stood in the darkness, trembling and crying, the sight filling her eyes with horror. And when she could no longer bear to look at what he was doing down there to the unmoving piece of meat over which he worked, she looked up and around at the windows of darkness where the others still stood—even as she had stood—and somehow she could see their faces, bruise-purple with the dim light from the mercury lamps, and there was a universal sameness to their expressions. The women stood with their nails biting into the upper arms of their men, their tongues edging from the corners of their mouths; the men were wild-eyed and smiling. They all looked as though they were at cock fights. Breathing deeply. Drawing some sustenance from the grisly scene below. An exhalation of sound, deep, deep, as though from caverns beneath the earth. Flesh pale and moist.

And it was then that she realized the courtyard had grown foggy, as though mist off the East River had rolled up 52nd

Street in a veil that would obscure the details of what the knife and the man were still doing . . . endlessly doing it . . . long after there was any joy in it . . . still doing it . . . again and again . . .

But the fog was unnatural, thick and gray and filled with tiny scintillas of light. She stared at it, rising up in the empty space of the courtyard. Bach in the cathedral, stardust in a vacuum chamber.

Beth saw eyes.

There, up there, at the ninth floor and higher, two great eyes, as surely as night and the moon, there were *eyes*. And— a face? Was that a face, could she be sure, was she imagining it . . . a face? In the roiling vapors of chill fog something lived, something brooding and patient and utterly malevolent had been summoned up to witness what was happening down there in the flower bed. Beth tried to look away, but could not. The eyes, those primal burning eyes, filled with an abysmal antiquity yet frighteningly bright and anxious like the eyes of a child; eyes filled with tomb depths, ancient and new, chasm-filled, burning, gigantic and deep as an abyss, holding her, compelling her. The shadow play was being staged not only for the tenants in their windows, watching and drinking of the scene, but for some *other*. Not on frigid tundra or waste moors, not in subterranean caverns or on some faraway world circling a dying sun, but here, in the city, here the eyes of that *other* watched.

Shaking with the effort, Beth wrenched her eyes from those burning depths up there beyond the ninth floor, only to see again the horror that had brought that *other*. And she was struck for the first time by the awfulness of what she was witnessing, she was released from the immobility that had held her like a coelacanth in shale, she was filled with the blood thunder pounding against the membranes of her mind: she had *stood* there! She had done nothing, nothing! A woman had been butchered and she had said nothing, done nothing. Tears had been useless, tremblings had been pointless, she *had done nothing*!

Then she heard hysterical sounds midway between laughter and giggling, and as she stared up into that great face rising in the fog and chimneysmoke of the night, she heard *herself* making those deranged gibbon noises and from the man below a pathetic, trapped sound, like the whimper of whipped dogs.

She was staring up into that face again. She hadn't wanted to see it again—ever. But she was locked with those smoldering eyes, overcome with the feeling that they were childlike, though she *knew* they were incalculably ancient.

Then the butcher below did an unspeakable thing and Beth reeled with dizziness and caught the edge of the window before she could tumble out onto the balcony; she steadied herself and fought for breath.

She felt herself being looked at, and for a long moment of frozen terror she feared she might have caught the attention of that face up there in the fog. She clung to the window, feeling everything growing faraway and dim, and stared straight across the court. She *was* being watched. Intently. By the young man in the seventh-floor window across from her own apartment. Steadily, he was looking at her. Through the strange fog with its burning eyes feasting on the sight below, he was staring at her.

As she felt herself blacking out, in the moment before unconsciousness, the thought flickered and fled that there was something terribly familiar about his face.

It rained the next day. East 52nd Street was slick and shining with the oil rainbows. The rain washed the dog turds into the gutters and nudged them down and down to the catchbasin openings. People bent against the slanting rain, hidden beneath umbrellas, looking like enormous, scurrying black mushrooms. Beth went out to get the newspapers after the police had come and gone.

The news reports dwelled with loving emphasis on the twenty-six tenants of the building who had watched in cold interest as Leona Ciarelli, 37, of 455 Fort Washington Avenue, Manhattan, had been systematically stabbed to death by Burton H. Wells, 41, an unemployed electrician, who had been subsequently shot to death by two off-duty police officers when he burst into Michael's Pub on 55th Street, covered with blood and brandishing a knife that authorities later identified as the murder weapon.

She had thrown up twice that day. Her stomach seemed incapable of retaining anything solid, and the taste of bile lay along the back of her tongue. She could not blot the scenes of the night before from her mind; she re-ran them again and again, every movement of that reaper arm playing over and over as though on a short loop of memory. The woman's head thrown back for silent screams. The blood. Those eyes in the fog.

She was drawn again and again to the window, to stare down into the courtyard and the street. She tried to superimpose over the bleak Manhattan concrete the view from her window in Swann House at Bennington: the little yard and another white, frame dormitory; the fantastic apple trees; and from the other window the rolling hills and gorgeous Vermont countryside; her memory skittered through the change of seasons. But there was always concrete and the rain-slick streets; the rain on the pavement was black and shiny as blood.

She tried to work, rolling up the tambour closure of the old rolltop desk she had bought on Lexington Avenue and hunching over the graph sheets of choreographer's charts. But Labanotation was merely a Jackson Pollock jumble of arcane hieroglyphics to her today, instead of the careful representation of eurhythmics she had studied four years to perfect. And before that, Farmington.

The phone rang. It was the secretary from the Taylor Dance Company, asking when she would be free. She had to beg off. She looked at her hand, lying on the graph sheets of figures Laban had devised, and she saw her fingers trembling. She had to beg off. Then she called Guzman at the Downtown Ballet Company, to tell him she would be late with the charts.

"My God, lady, I have ten dancers sitting around in a rehearsal hall getting their leotards sweaty! What do you expect me to do?"

She explained what had happened the night before. And as she told him, she realized the newspapers had been justified in holding that tone against the twenty-six witnesses to the death of Leona Ciarelli. Paschal Guzman listened, and when he spoke again, his voice was several octaves lower, and he spoke more slowly. He said he understood and she could take a little longer to prepare the charts. But there was a distance in his voice, and he hung up while she was thanking him.

She dressed in an argyle sweater vest in shades of dark purple, and a pair of fitted khaki gabardine trousers. She had to go out, to walk around. To do what? To think about other things. As she pulled on the Fred Braun chunky heels, she idly wondered if that heavy silver bracelet was still in the window of Georg Jensen's. In the elevator, the young man from the window across the courtyard stared at her. Beth felt her body begin to tremble again. She went deep into the corner of the box when he entered behind her.

Between the fifth and fourth floors, he hit the *off* switch and the elevator jerked to a halt.

Beth stared at him and he smiled innocently.

"Hi. My name's Gleeson, Ray Gleeson, I'm in 714."

She wanted to demand he turn the elevator back on, by what right did he pre*sume* to do such a thing, what did he mean by this, turn it on at once or suffer the consequences. That was what she *wanted* to do. Instead, from the same place she had heard the glibbering laughter the night before, she heard her voice, much smaller and much less possessed than she had trained it to be, saying, "Beth O'Neill, I live in 701."

The thing about it, was that *the elevator was stopped*. And she was frightened. But he leaned against the paneled wall, very well dressed, shoes polished, hair combed and probably blown dry with a hand dryer, and he *talked* to her as if they were across a table at L'Argenteuil. "You just moved in, huh?"

"About two months ago."

"Where did you go to school? Bennington or Sarah Lawrence?"

"Bennington. How did you know?"

He laughed, and it was a nice laugh. "I'm an editor at a religious book publisher; every year we get half a dozen Bennington, Sarah Lawrence, Smith girls. They come hopping in like grasshoppers, ready to revolutionize the publishing industry."

"What's wrong with that? You sound like you don't care for them."

"Oh, I *love* them, they're marvelous. They think they know how to write better than the authors we publish. Had one darlin' little item who was given galleys of three books to proof, and she rewrote all three. I think she's working as a table-swabber in a Horn & Hardart's now."

She didn't reply to that. She would have pegged him as an anti-feminist, ordinarily, if it had been anyone else speaking. But the eyes. There was something terribly familiar about his face. She was enjoying the conversation; she rather liked him.

"What's the nearest big city to Bennington?"

"Albany, New York. About sixty miles."

"How long does it take to drive there?"

"From Bennington? About an hour and a half."

"Must be a nice drive, that Vermont country, really pretty. They went coed, I understand. How's that working out?"

"I don't know, really."

"You don't know?"

"It happened around the time I was graduating."

"What did you major in?"

"I was a dance major, specializing in Labanotation. That's the way you write choreography."

"It's all electives, I gather. You don't have to take anything required, like sciences, for example." He didn't change tone as he said, "That was a terrible thing last night. I saw you watching. I guess a lot of us were watching. It was a really terrible thing.''

She nodded dumbly. Fear came back.

"I understand the cops got him. Some nut, they don't even know why he killed her, or why he went charging into that bar. It was really an awful thing. I'd very much like to have dinner with you one night soon, if you're not attached.''

"That would be all right.''

"Maybe Wednesday. There's an Argentinian place I know. You might like it.''

"That would be all right.''

"Why don't you turn on the elevator, and we can go,'' he said, and smiled again. She did it, wondering why she had stopped the elevator in the first place.

On her third date with him, they had their first fight. It was at a party thrown by a director of television commercials. He lived on the ninth floor of their building. He had just done a series of spots for *Sesame Street* (the letters "U" for Underpass, "T" for Tunnel, lowercase "b" for boats, "c" for cars; the numbers 1 to 6 and the numbers 1 to 20; the words *light* and *dark*) and was celebrating his move from the arena of commercial tawdriness (and its attendant $75,000 a year) to the sweet fields of educational programming (and its accompanying descent into low-pay respectability). There was a logic in his joy Beth could not quite understand, and when she talked with him about it, in a far corner of the kitchen, his arguments didn't seem to parse. But he seemed happy, and his girlfriend, a long-legged ex-model from Philadelphia, continued to drift to him and away from him, like some exquisite undersea plant, touching his hair and kissing his neck, murmuring words of pride and barely submerged sexuality. Beth found it bewildering, though the celebrants were all bright and lively.

In the living room, Ray was sitting on the arm of the sofa, hustling a stewardess named Luanne. Beth could tell he was hustling; he was trying to look casual. When he *wasn't* hustling, he was always intense, about everything. She decided to ignore it, and wandered around the apartment, sipping at a Tanqueray and tonic.

There were framed prints of abstract shapes clipped from a calendar printed in Germany. They were in metal Bonniers frames.

In the dining room a huge door from a demolished building somewhere in the city had been handsomely stripped, teaked and refinished. It was now the dinner table.

A Lightolier fixture attached to the wall over the bed swung out, levered up and down, tipped, and its burnished globe-head revolved a full three hundred and sixty degrees.

She was standing in the bedroom, looking out the window, when she realized *this* had been one of the rooms in which light had gone on, gone off; one of the rooms that had contained a silent watcher at the death of Leona Ciarelli.

When she returned to the living room, she looked around more carefully. With only three or four exceptions—the stewardess, a young married couple from the second floor, a stockbroker from Hemphill, Noyes—*everyone* at the party had been a witness to the slaying.

"I'd like to go," she told him.

"Why, aren't you having a good time?" asked the stewardess, a mocking smile crossing her perfect little face.

"Like all Bennington ladies," Ray said, answering for Beth, "she is enjoying herself most by not enjoying herself at all. It's a trait of the anal retentive. Being here in someone else's apartment, she can't empty ashtrays or rewind the toilet paper roll so it doesn't hang a tongue, and being tightassed, her nature demands we go.

"All right, Beth, let's say our goodbyes and take off. The Phantom Rectum strikes again."

She slapped him and the stewardess's eyes widened. But the smile remained frozen where it had appeared.

He grabbed her wrist before she could do it again. "Garbanzo beans, baby," he said, holding her wrist tighter than necessary.

They went back to her apartment, and after sparring silently with kitchen cabinet doors slammed and the television being tuned too loud, they got to her bed, and he tried to perpetuate the metaphor by fucking her in the ass. He had her on elbows and knees before she realized what he was doing; she struggled to turn over and he rode her bucking and tossing without a sound. And when it was clear to him that she would never permit it, he grabbed her breast from underneath and squeezed so hard she howled in pain. He dumped her on her back, rubbed himself between her legs a dozen times, and came on her stomach.

Beth lay with her eyes closed and an arm thrown across her face. She wanted to cry, but found she could not. Ray lay on her and said nothing. She wanted to rush to the bathroom and shower, but he did not move, till long after his semen had dried on their bodies.

"Who did you date at college?" he asked.

"I didn't date anyone very much." Sullen.

"No heavy makeouts with wealthy lads from Williams and Dartmouth . . . no Amherst intellectuals begging you to save them from creeping faggotry by permitting them to stick their carrots in your sticky little slit?"

"Stop it!"

"Come on, baby, it couldn't all have been knee socks and little round circle-pins. You don't expect me to believe you didn't get a little mouthful of cock from time to time. It's only, what? about fifteen miles to Williamstown? I'm sure the Williams werewolves were down burning the highway to your cunt on weekends; you can level with old Uncle Ray. . . ."

"Why are you like this?!" She started to move, to get away from him, and he grabbed her by the shoulder, forced her to lie down again. Then he rose up over her and said, "I'm like this because I'm a New Yorker, baby. Because I live in this fucking city every day. Because I have to play patty-cake with the ministers and other sanctified holy-joe assholes who want their goodness and lightness tracts published by the Blessed

Sacrament Publishing and Storm Window Company of 277 Park Avenue, when what I *really* want to do is toss the stupid psalm-suckers out the thirty-seventh-floor window and listen to them quote chapter-and-worse all the way down. Because I've lived in this great big snapping dog of a city all my life and I'm mad as a mudfly, for chrissakes!''

She lay unable to move, breathing shallowly, filled with a sudden pity and affection for him. His face was white and strained, and she knew he was saying things to her that only a bit too much Almadén and exact timing would have let him say.

"What do you expect from me," he said, his voice softer now, but no less intense, "do you expect kindness and gentility and understanding and a hand on *your* hand when the smog burns your eyes? I can't do it, I haven't got it. No one has it in this cesspool of a city. Look around you; what do you think is happening here? They take rats and they put them in boxes and when there are too many of them, some of the little fuckers go out of their minds and start gnawing the rest to death. *It ain't no different here, baby!* It's rat time for everybody in this madhouse. You can't expect to jam as many people into this stone thing as we do, with buses and taxis and dogs shitting themselves scrawny and noise night and day and no money and not enough places to live and no place to go to have a decent think . . . you can't do it without making the time right for some godforsaken other kind of thing to be born! You can't hate everyone around you, and kick every beggar and nigger and *mestizo* shithead, you can't have cabbies stealing from you and taking tips they don't deserve, and then cursing you, you can't walk in the soot till your collar turns black, and your body stinks with the smell of flaking brick and decaying brains, you can't do it without calling up some kind of awful—''

He stopped.

His face bore the expression of a man who has just received brutal word of the death of a loved one. He suddenly lay down, rolled over, and turned off.

She lay beside him, trembling, trying desperately to remember where she had seen his face before.

He didn't call her again, after the night of the party. And when they met in the hall, he pointedly turned away, as though he had given her some obscure chance and she had refused to take it. Beth thought she understood: though Ray Gleeson had not been her first affair, he had been the first to reject her so completely. The first to put her not only out of his bed and his life, but even out of his world. It was as though she were invisible, not even beneath contempt, simply not there.

She busied herself with other things.

She took on three new charting jobs for Guzman and a new group that had formed on Staten Island, of all places. She worked furiously and they gave her new assignments; they even paid her.

She tried to decorate the apartment with a less precise touch. Huge poster blowups of Merce Cunningham and Martha Graham replaced the Brueghel prints that had reminded her of the view looking down the hill toward Williams. The tiny balcony outside her window, the balcony she had steadfastly refused to stand upon since the night of the slaughter, the night of the fog with eyes, that balcony she swept and set about with little flower boxes in which she planted geraniums, petunias, dwarf zinnias, and other hardy perennials. Then, closing the window, she went to give herself, to involve herself in this city to which she had brought her ordered life.

And the city responded to her overtures:

Seeing off an old friend from Bennington, at Kennedy International, she stopped at the terminal coffee shop to have a sandwich. The counter—like a moat—surrounded a center service island that had huge advertising cubes rising above it on burnished poles. The cubes proclaimed the delights of Fun City. *New York Is a Summer Festival*, they said, and *Joseph Papp Presents Shakespeare in Central Park* and *Visit the Bronx Zoo* and *You'll Adore Our Contentious but Lovable Cabbies*. The food emerged from a window far down the service area and moved slowly on a conveyor belt through the hordes of screaming waitresses who slathered the counter with redolent washcloths. The lunchroom had all the charm and dignity of a steel-rolling mill, and approximately the same noise level. Beth ordered a cheeseburger that cost a dollar and a quarter, and a glass of milk.

When it came, it was cold, the cheese unmelted, and the patty of meat resembling nothing so much as a dirty scouring pad. The bun was cold and untoasted. There was no lettuce under the patty.

Beth managed to catch the waitress's eye. The girl approached with an annoyed look. "Please toast the bun and may I have a piece of lettuce?" Beth said.

"We dun' do that," the waitress said, turning half away as though she would walk in a moment.

"You don't do what?"

"We dun' toass the bun here."

"Yes, but I *want* the bun toasted," Beth said firmly.

"An' you got to pay for extra lettuce."

"If I was asking for *extra* lettuce," Beth said, getting annoyed, "I would pay for it, but since there's *no* lettuce here, I don't think I should be charged extra for the first piece."

"We dun' do that."

The waitress started to walk away. "Hold it," Beth said, raising her voice just enough so the assembly-line eaters on either side stared at her. "You mean to tell me I have to pay a dollar and a quarter and I can't get a piece of lettuce or even get the bun toasted?"

"Ef you dun' like it . . ."

"Take it back."

"You gotta pay for it, you order it."

"I said take it back, I don't want the fucking thing!"

The waitress scratched it off the check. The milk cost 27¢ and tasted going-sour. It was the first time in her life that Beth had said *that* word aloud.

At the cashier's stand, Beth said to the sweating man with the felt-tip pens in his shirt pocket, "Just out of curiosity, are you interested in complaints?"

"No!" he said, snarling, quite literally snarling. He did not look up as he punched out 73¢ and it came rolling down the chute.

The city responded to her overtures:

It was raining again. She was trying to cross Second Avenue, with the light. She stepped off the curb and a car came sliding through the red and splashed her. "Hey!" she yelled.

"Eat shit, sister!" the driver yelled back, turning the corner.

Her boots, her legs and her overcoat were splattered with mud. She stood trembling on the curb.

The city responded to her overtures:

She emerged from the building at One Astor Place with her big briefcase full of Laban charts; she was adjusting her rain scarf about her head. A well-dressed man with an attaché case thrust the handle of his umbrella up between her legs from the rear. She gasped and dropped her case.

The city responded and responded and responded.

Her overtures altered quickly.

The old drunk with the stippled cheeks extended his hand and mumbled words. She cursed him and walked on up Broadway past the beaver film houses.

She crossed against the lights on Park Avenue, making hackies slam their brakes to avoid hitting her; she used *that* word frequently now.

When she found herself having a drink with a man who had elbowed up beside her in the singles' bar, she felt faint and knew she should go home.

But Vermont was so far away.

Nights later. She had come home from the Lincoln Center ballet, and gone straight to bed. Lying half-asleep in her bedroom, she heard an alien sound. One room away, in the living room, in the dark, there was a sound. She slipped out of bed and went to the door between the rooms. She fumbled silently for the switch on the lamp just inside the living room, and found it, and clicked it on. A black man in a leather car coat was trying to get *out* of the apartment. In that first flash of light filling the room she noticed the television set beside him on the floor as he struggled with the door, she noticed the police lock and bar had been broken in a new and clever manner *New York* magazine had not yet reported in a feature article on apartment ripoffs, she noticed that he had gotten his foot tangled in the telephone cord that she had requested be extra-long so she could carry the instrument into the bathroom, I don't want to miss any business calls when the shower is running; she noticed all things in perspective and one thing with sharpest clarity: the expression on the burglar's face.

There was something familiar in that expression.

He almost had the door open, but now he closed it, and slipped the police lock. He took a step toward her.

Beth went back, into the darkened bedroom.

The city responded to her overtures.

She backed against the wall at the head of the bed. Her hand fumbled in the shadows for the telephone. His shape filled the doorway, light, all light behind him.

In silhouette it should not have been possible to tell, but somehow she knew he was wearing gloves and the only marks he would leave would be deep bruises, very blue, almost black, with the tinge under them of blood that had been stopped in its course.

He came for her, arms hanging casually at his sides. She tried to climb over the bed, and he grabbed her from behind, ripping her nightgown. Then he had a hand around her neck and he pulled her backward. She fell off the bed, landed at his feet and his hold was broken. She scuttled across the floor and for a moment she had the respite to feel terror. She was going to die, and she was frightened.

He trapped her in the corner between the closet and the bureau and kicked her. His foot caught her in the thigh as she folded tighter, smaller, drawing her legs up. She was cold.

Then he reached down with both hands and pulled her erect by her hair. He slammed her head against the wall. Everything slid up in her sight as though running off the edge of the world. He slammed her head against the wall again, and she felt something go soft over her right ear.

When he tried to slam her a third time she reached out blindly for his face and ripped down with her nails. He howled in pain and she hurled herself forward, arms wrapping themselves around his waist. He stumbled backward and in a tangle of thrashing arms and legs they fell out onto the little balcony.

Beth landed on the bottom, feeling the window boxes jammed up against her spine and legs. She fought to get to her feet, and her nails hooked into his shirt under the open jacket, ripping. Then she was on her feet again and they struggled silently.

He whirled her around, bent her backward across the wrought-iron railing. Her face was turned outward.

They were standing in their windows, watching.

Through the fog she could see them watching. Through the fog she recognized their expressions. Through the fog she heard them breathing in unison, bellows breathing of expectation and wonder. Through the fog.

And the black man punched her in the throat. She gagged and started to black out and could not draw air into her lungs. Back, back, he bent her further back and she was looking up, straight up, toward the ninth floor and higher . . .

Up there: eyes.

The words Ray Gleeson had said in a moment filled with what he had become, with the utter hopelessness and finality of the choice the city had forced on him, the words came back. *You can't live in this city and survive unless you have protection . . . you can't live this way, like rats driven mad, without making the time right for some godforsaken other*

*kind of thing to be born . . . you can't do it without calling
up some kind of awful . . .*

God! A new God, an ancient God come again with the
eyes and hunger of a child, a deranged blood God of fog and
street violence. A God who needed worshippers and offered
the choices of death as a victim or life as an eternal witness
to the deaths of *other* chosen victims. A God to fit the times,
a God of streets and people.

She tried to shriek, to appeal to Ray, to the director in the
bedroom window of his ninth-floor apartment with his long-
legged Philadelphia model beside him and his fingers inside
her as they worshipped in their holiest of ways, to the others
who had been at the party that had been Ray's offer of a
chance to join their congregation. She wanted to be saved
from having to make that choice.

But the black man had punched her in the throat, and now
his hands were on her, one on her chest, the other in her
face, the smell of leather filling her where the nausea could
not. And she understood Ray had *cared*, had wanted her to
take the chance offered; but she had come from a world of
little white dormitories and Vermont countryside; it was not
a real world. *This* was the real world and up there was the
God who ruled this world, and she had rejected him, had
said no to one of his priests and servitors. *Save me! Don't
make me do it!*

She knew she had to call out, to make appeal, to try and
win the approbation of that God. *I can't . . . save me!*

She struggled and made terrible little mewing sounds trying to summon the words to cry out, and suddenly she crossed
a line, and screamed up into the echoing courtyard with a
voice Leona Ciarelli had never known enough to use.

"Him! Take him! Not me! I'm yours, I love you, I'm yours!
Take him, not me, please not me, take him, take him, I'm
yours!"

And the black man was suddenly lifted away, wrenched off
her, and off the balcony, whirled straight up into the fog-

thick air in the courtyard, as Beth sank to her knees on the ruined flower boxes.

She was half-conscious, and could not be sure she saw it just that way, but up he went, end over end, whirling and spinning like a charred leaf.

And the form took firmer shape. Enormous paws with claws and shapes that no animal she had ever seen had ever possessed, and the burglar, black, poor, terrified, whimpering like a whipped dog, was stripped of his flesh. His body was opened with a thin incision, and there was a rush as all the blood poured from him like a sudden cloudburst, and yet he was still alive, twitching with the involuntary horror of a frog's leg shocked with an electric current. Twitched, and twitched again as he was torn piece by piece to shreds. Pieces of flesh and bone and half a face with an eye blinking furiously, cascaded down past Beth, and hit the cement below with sodden thuds. And still he was alive, as his organs were squeezed and musculature and bile and shit and skin were rubbed, sandpapered together and let fall. It went on and on, as the death of Leona Ciarelli had gone and on, and she understood with the blood-knowledge of survivors *at any cost* that the reason the witnesses to the death of Leona Ciarelli had done nothing was not that they had been frozen with horror, that they didn't want to get involved, or that they were inured to death by years of television slaughter.

They were worshippers at a black mass the city had demanded be staged; not once, but a thousand times a day in this insane asylum of steel and stone.

Now she was on her feet, standing half-naked in her ripped nightgown, her hands tightening on the wrought-iron railing, begging to see more, to drink deeper.

Now she was one of them, as the pieces of the night's sacrifice fell past her, bleeding and screaming.

Tomorrow the police would come again, and they would question her, and she would say how terrible it had been, that burglar, and how she fought, afraid he would rape her and kill her, and how he had fallen, and she had no idea how he had been so hideously mangled and ripped apart, but a seven-storey fall, after all . . .

Tomorrow she would not have to worry about walking in the streets, because no harm could come to her. Tomorrow she could even remove the police lock. Nothing in the city could do her any further evil, because she had made the only choice. She was now a dweller in the city, now wholly and richly a part of it. Now she was taken to the bosom of her God.

She felt Ray beside her, standing beside her, holding her, protecting her, his hand on her naked backside, and she watched the fog swirl up and fill the courtyard, fill the city, fill her eyes and her soul and her heart with its power. As Ray's naked body pressed tightly inside her, she drank deeply of the night, knowing whatever voices she heard from this moment forward would be the voices not of whipped dogs, but those of strong, meat-eating beasts.

At last she was unafraid, and it was so good, so very good *not* to be afraid.

"When inward life dries up, when feeling decreases and apathy increases, when one cannot affect or even genuinely touch another person, violence flares up as a daimonic necessity for contact, a mad drive forcing touch in the most direct way possible."

—Rolly May, *Love and Will*

Nathaniel Hawthorne

Young Goodman Brown

Perhaps the original horror in American myth grows out of the witchcraft trials in Puritan New England, our own regional version of the Spanish Inquisition. Nathaniel Hawthorne was the greatest American writer drawn to the matter of the Puritans and their moral horrors. It has been pointed out that the Puritan sermon, with its hair-raising images of hell and damnation, was the characteristic mode of horror literature in the U.S. before the invention of the short story. Hawthorne's awareness of horror and its effects underpins one of the great allegories of good and evil, "Young Goodman Brown." The irony that the new world of God's chosen few nurtured in its bosom its opposite, devil worship, literally or metaphorically, endures. There is more than a hint of the world of Hawthorne in Stephen King's "The Reach."

Young Goodman Brown came forth at sunset into the street at Salem village; but put his head back, after crossing the threshold, to exchange a parting kiss with his young wife. And Faith, as the wife was aptly named, thrust her own pretty head into the street, letting the wind play with the pink ribbons of her cap while she called to Goodman Brown.

"Dearest heart," whispered she, softly and rather sadly,

when her lips were close to his ear, "prithee put off your journey until sunrise and sleep in your own bed tonight. A lone woman is troubled with such dreams and such thoughts that she's afeard of herself sometimes. Pray tarry with me this night, dear husband, of all nights in the year."

"My love and my Faith," replied young Goodman Brown, "of all nights in the year, this one night must I tarry away from thee. My journey, as thou callest it, forth and back again, must needs be done 'twixt now and sunrise. What, my sweet, pretty wife, dost thou doubt me already, and we but three months married?"

"Then God bless you!" said Faith, with the pink ribbons, "and may you find all well when you come back."

"Amen!" cried Goodman Brown. "Say thy prayers, dear Faith, and go to bed at dusk, and no harm will come to thee."

So they parted; and the young man pursued his way until, being about to turn the corner by the meetinghouse, he looked back and saw the head of Faith still peeping after him with a melancholy air, in spite of her pink ribbons.

"Poor little Faith!" thought he, for his heart smote him. "What a wretch am I to leave her on such an errand! She talks of dreams, too. Methought as she spoke there was trouble in her face, as if a dream had warned her what work is to be done tonight. But no, no; 'twould kill her to think it. Well, she's a blessed angel on earth; and after this one night I'll cling to her skirts and follow her to heaven."

With this excellent resolve for the future, Goodman Brown felt himself justified in making more haste on his present evil purpose. He had taken a dreary road, darkened by all the gloomiest trees of the forest, which barely stood aside to let the narrow path creep through, and closed immediately behind. It was all as lonely as could be; and there is this peculiarity in such a solitude, that the traveler knows not who may be concealed by the innumerable trunks and the thick boughs overhead; so that with lonely footsteps he may yet be passing through an unseen multitude.

"There may be a devilish Indian behind every tree," said Goodman Brown to himself; and he glanced fearfully behind him as he added, "What if the devil himself should be at my very elbow!"

His head being turned back, he passed a crook of the road, and, looking forward again, beheld the figure of a man, in grave and decent attire, seated at the foot of an old tree. He arose at Goodman Brown's approach and walked onward side by side with him.

"You are late, Goodman Brown," said he. "The clock of the Old South was striking as I came through Boston, and that is full fifteen minutes agone."

"Faith kept me back awhile," replied the young man, with a tremor in his voice, caused by the sudden appearance of his companion, though not wholly unexpected.

It was now deep dusk in the forest, and deepest in that part of it where these two were journeying. As nearly as could be discerned, the second traveler was about fifty years old, apparently in the same rank of life as Goodman Brown, and bearing a considerable resemblance to him, though perhaps more in expression than features. Still they might have been taken for father and son. And yet, though the elder person was as simply clad as the younger, and as simple in manner, too, he had an indescribable air of one who knew the world, and who would not have felt abashed at the Governor's dinner table or in King William's court, were it possible that his affairs should call him thither. But the only thing about him that could be fixed upon as remarkable was his staff, which bore the likeness of a great black snake, so curiously wrought that it might almost be seen to twist and wriggle itself like a living serpent. This, of course, must have been an ocular deception, assisted by the uncertain light.

"Come, Goodman Brown," cried his fellow traveler, "this is a dull pace for the beginning of a journey. Take my staff, if you are so soon weary."

"Friend," said the other, exchanging his slow pace for a full stop, "having kept covenant by meeting thee here, it is my purpose now to return whence I came. I have scruples touching the matter thou wot'st of.''

"Sayest thou so?" replied he of the serpent, smiling apart. "Let us walk on, nevertheless, reasoning as we go; and if I convince thee not, thou shalt turn back. We are but a little way in the forest yet."

"Too far! too far!" exclaimed the goodman, unconsciously resuming his walk. "My father never went into the woods on such an errand, nor his father before him. We have been a race of honest men and good Christians since the days of the martyrs; and shall I be the first of the name of Brown that ever took this path and kept—"

"Such company, thou wouldst say," observed the elder person, interpreting his pause. "Well said, Goodman Brown! I have been as well acquainted with your family as with ever a one among the Puritans; and that's no trifle to say. I helped your grandfather, the constable, when he lashed the Quaker woman so smartly through the streets of Salem; and it was I that brought your father a pitch-pine knot, kindled at my own hearth, to set fire to an Indian village, in King Philip's war. They were my good friends, both; and many a pleasant walk have we had along this path, and returned merrily after midnight. I would fain be friends with you for their sake."

"If it be as thou sayest," replied Goodman Brown, "I marvel they never spoke of these matters; or, verily, I marvel not, seeing that the least rumor of the sort would have driven them from New England. We are a people of prayer, and good works to boot, and abide no such wickedness."

"Wickedness or not," said the traveler with the twisted staff, "I have a very general acquaintance here in New England. The deacons of many a church have drunk the communion wine with me; the selectmen of divers towns make me their chairman; and a majority of the Great and General Court are firm supporters of my interest. The Governor and I, too—But these are state secrets."

"Can this be so?" cried Goodman Brown, with a stare of amazement at his undisturbed companion. "Howbeit, I have nothing to do with the Governor and council; they have their own ways, and are no rule for a simple husbandman like me. But, were I to go on with thee, how should I meet the eye of that good old man, our minister, at Salem village? Oh, his voice would make me tremble both Sabbath day and lecture day.''

Thus far the elder traveler had listened with due gravity; but now burst into a fit of irrepressible mirth, shaking himself so violently that his snakelike staff actually seemed to wriggle in sympathy.

''Ha! ha! ha!'' shouted he again and again; then composing himself, ''Well, go on, Goodman Brown, go on; but, prithee, don't kill me with laughing.''

''Well, then, to end the matter at once,'' said Goodman Brown, considerably nettled, ''there is my wife, Faith. It would break her dear little heart; and I'd rather break my own.''

''Nay, if that be the case,'' answered the other, ''e'en go thy ways, Goodman Brown. I would not for twenty old women like the one hobbling before us that Faith should come to any harm.''

As he spoke, he pointed his staff at a female figure on the path, in whom Goodman Brown recognized a very pious and exemplary dame, who had taught him his catechism in youth, and was still his moral and spiritual adviser, jointly with the minister and Deacon Gookin.

''A marvel, truly, that Goody Cloyse should be so far in the wilderness at nightfall,'' said he. ''But with your leave, friend, I shall take a cut through the woods until we have left this Christian woman behind. Being a stranger to you, she might ask whom I was consorting with and whither I was going.''

''Be it so,'' said his fellow traveler. ''Betake you to the woods, and let me keep the path.''

Accordingly, the young man turned aside, but took care to watch his companion, who advanced softly along the road until he had come within a staff's length of the old dame.

She, meanwhile, was making the best of her way, with singular speed for so aged a woman, and mumbling some indistinct words—a prayer, doubtless—as she went. The traveler put forth his staff and touched her withered neck with what seemed the serpent's tail.

"The devil!" screamed the pious old lady.

"Then Goody Cloyse knows her old friend?" observed the traveler, confronting her and leaning on his writhing stick.

"Ah, forsooth, and is it your worship indeed?" cried the good dame. "Yea, truly is it, and in the very image of my old gossip Goodman Brown, the grandfather of the silly fellow that now is. But—would your worship believe it?—my broomstick hath strangely disappeared, stolen, as I suspect, by that unhanged witch, Goody Cory, and that, too, when I was all anointed with the juice of smallage, and cinquefoil, and wolfsbane—"

"Mingled with fine wheat and the fat of a newborn babe," said the shape of old Goodman Brown.

"Ah, your worship knows the recipe," cried the old lady, cackling aloud. "So, as I was saying, being all ready for the meeting, and no horse to ride on, I made up my mind to foot it; for they tell me there is a nice young man to be taken into communion tonight. But now your good worship will lend me your arm, and we shall be there in a twinkling."

"That can hardly be," answered her friend. "I may not spare you my arm, Goody Cloyse; but here is my staff, if you will."

So saying, he threw it down at her feet, where, perhaps, it assumed life, being one of the rods which its owner had formerly lent to the Egyptian magi. Of this fact, however, Goodman Brown could not take cognizance. He had cast up his eyes in astonishment, and, looking down again, beheld neither Goody Cloyse nor the serpentine staff, but his fellow traveler alone, who waited for him as calmly as if nothing had happened.

"That old woman taught me my catechism," said the

young man; and there was a world of meaning in this simple comment.

They continued to walk onward, while the elder traveler exhorted his companion to make good speed and persevere in the path, discoursing so aptly that his arguments seemed rather to spring up in the bosom of his auditor than to be suggested by himself. As they went, he plucked a branch of maple to serve for a walking stick, and began to strip it of the twigs and little boughs, which were wet with evening dew. The moment his fingers touched them, they became strangely withered and dried up as with a week's sunshine. Thus the pair proceeded, at a good free pace, until suddenly, in a gloomy hollow of the road, Goodman Brown sat himself down on the stump of a tree and refused to go any farther.

"Friend," said he, stubbornly, "my mind is made up. Not another step will I budge on this errand. What if a wretched old woman do choose to go to the devil when I thought she was going to heaven: is that any reason why I should quit my dear Faith and go after her?"

"You will think better of this by and by," said his acquaintance, composedly. "Sit here and rest yourself awhile; and when you feel like moving again, there is my staff to help you along."

Without more words, he threw his companion the maple stick, and was as speedily out of sight as if he had vanished into the deepening gloom. The young man sat a few moments by the roadside, applauding himself greatly, and thinking with how clear a conscience he should meet the minister in his morning walk, nor shrink from the eye of good old Deacon Gookin. And what calm sleep would be his that very night, which was to have been spent so wickedly, but so purely and sweetly now, in the arms of Faith! Amidst these pleasant and praiseworthy meditations, Goodman Brown heard the tramp of horses along the road, and deemed it advisable to conceal himself within the verge of the forest, conscious of the guilty purpose that had brought him thither, though now so happily turned from it.

On came the hoof tramps and the voices of the riders, two grave old voices, conversing soberly as they drew near. These mingled sounds appeared to pass along the road, within a few yards of the young man's hiding place; but, owing doubtless to the depth of the gloom at that particular spot, neither the travelers nor their steeds were visible. Though their figures brushed the small boughs by the wayside, it could not be seen that they intercepted, even for a moment, the faint gleam from the strip of bright sky athwart which they must have passed. Goodman Brown alternately crouched and stood on tiptoe, pulling aside the branches and thrusting forth his head as far as he durst without discerning so much as a shadow. It vexed him the more, because he could have sworn, were such a thing possible, that he recognized the voices of the minister and Deacon Gookin, jogging along quietly, as they were wont to do, when bound to some ordination or ecclesiastical council. While yet within hearing, one of the riders stopped to pluck a switch.

"Of the two, reverend sir," said the voice like the deacon's, "I had rather miss an ordination dinner than tonight's meeting. They tell me that some of our community are to be here from Falmouth and beyond, and others from Connecticut and Rhode Island, besides several of the Indian powwows, who, after their fashion, know almost as much deviltry as the best of us. Moreover, there is a goodly young woman to be taken into communion."

"Mighty well, Deacon Gookin!" replied the solemn old tones of the minister. "Spur up, or we shall be late. Nothing can be done, you know, until I get on the ground."

The hoofs clattered again; and the voices, talking so strangely in the empty air, passed on through the forest, where no church had ever been gathered or solitary Christian prayed. Whither, then, could these holy men be journeying so deep into the heathen wilderness? Young Goodman Brown caught hold of a tree for support, being ready to sink down on the ground, faint and overburdened with the heavy sickness of his heart. He looked up to the sky, doubting whether there really was a heaven above him. Yet there was the blue arch, and the stars brightening in it.

"With heaven above and Faith below, I will yet stand firm against the devil!" cried Goodman Brown.

While he still gazed upward into the deep arch of the firmament and had lifted his hands to pray, a cloud, though no wind was stirring, hurried across the zenith and hid the brightening stars. The blue sky was still visible, except directly overhead, where this black mass of cloud was sweeping swiftly northward. Aloft in the air, as if from the depths of the cloud, came a confused and doubtful sound of voices. Once the listener fancied that he could distinguish the accents of townspeople of his own, men and women, both pious and ungodly, many of whom he had met at the communion table, and had seen others rioting at the tavern. The next moment, so indistinct were the sounds, he doubted whether he had heard aught but the murmur of the old forest, whispering without a wind. Then came a stronger swell of those familiar tones, heard daily in the sunshine at Salem village, but never until now from a cloud of night. There was one voice, of a young woman, uttering lamentations, yet with an uncertain sorrow, and entreating for some favor, which, perhaps, it would grieve her to obtain; and all the unseen multitude, both saints and sinners, seemed to encourage her onward.

"Faith!" shouted Goodman Brown, in a voice of agony and desperation; and the echoes of the forest mocked him, crying, "Faith! Faith!" as if bewildered wretches were seeking her all through the wilderness.

The cry of grief, rage, and terror was yet piercing the night, when the unhappy husband held his breath for a response. There was a scream, drowned immediately in a louder murmur of voices, fading into far-off laughter, as the dark cloud swept away, leaving the clear and silent sky above Goodman Brown. But something fluttered lightly down through the air and caught on the branch of a tree. The young man seized it, and beheld a pink ribbon.

"My Faith is gone!" cried he, after one stupefied moment.

"There is no good on earth; and sin is but a name. Come, devil; for to thee is this world given."

And, maddened with despair, so that he laughed loud and long, did Goodman Brown grasp his staff and set forth again, at such a rate that he seemed to fly along the forest path rather than to walk or run. The road grew wilder and drearier and more faintly traced, and vanished at length, leaving him in the heart of the dark wilderness, still rushing onward with the instinct that guides mortal man to evil. The whole forest was peopled with frightful sounds—the creaking of the trees, the howling of wild beasts, and the yell of Indians; while sometimes the wind tolled like a distant church bell, and sometimes gave a broad roar around the traveler, as if all Nature were laughing him to scorn. But he was himself the chief horror of the scene, and shrank not from its other horrors.

"Ha! ha! ha!" roared Goodman Brown when the wind laughed at him. "Let us hear which will laugh loudest. Think not to frighten me with your deviltry. Come witch, come wizard, come Indian powwow, come devil himself, and here comes Goodman Brown. You may as well fear him as he fear you."

In truth, all through the haunted forest there could be nothing more frightful than the figure of Goodman Brown. On he flew among the black pines, brandishing his staff with frenzied gestures, now giving vent to an inspiration of horrid blasphemy, and now shouting forth such laughter as set all the echoes of the forest laughing like demons around him. The fiend in his own shape is less hideous than when he rages in the breast of man. Thus sped the demoniac on his course, until, quivering among the trees, he saw a red light before him, as when the felled trunks and branches of a clearing have been set on fire, and throw up their lurid blaze against the sky, at the hour of midnight. He paused, in a lull of the tempest that had driven him onward, and heard the swell of what seemed a hymn, rolling solemnly from a distance with the weight of many voices. He knew the tune; it was a familiar one in the choir of the village meetinghouse. The verse died heavily away, and was lengthened by a chorus, not of human voices, but of all the sounds of the benighted wilderness pealing in awful harmony together. Goodman Brown cried out, and his cry was lost to his own ear by its unison with the cry of the desert.

In the interval of silence, he stole forward until the light glared full upon his eyes. At one extremity of an open space, hemmed in by the dark wall of the forest, arose a rock, bearing some rude, natural resemblance either to an altar or a pulpit, and surrounded by four blazing pines, their tops aflame, their stems untouched, like candles at an evening meeting. The mass of foliage that had overgrown the summit of the rock was all on fire, blazing high into the night and fitfully illuminating the whole field. Each pendent twig and leafy festoon was in a blaze. As the red light arose and fell, a numerous congregation alternately shone forth, then disappeared in shadow, and again grew, as it were, out of the darkness, peopling the heart of the solitary woods at once.

"A grave and dark-clad company," quoth Goodman Brown.

In truth they were such. Among them, quivering to and fro between gloom and splendor, appeared faces that would be seen next day at the council board of the province, and others which, Sabbath after Sabbath, looked devoutly heavenward, and benignantly over the crowded pews, from the holiest pulpits in the land. Some affirm that the lady of the Governor was there. At least, there were high dames well known to her, and wives of honored husbands, and widows, a great multitude, and ancient maidens, all of excellent repute, and fair young girls, who trembled lest their mothers should espy them. Either the sudden gleams of light flashing over the obscure field bedazzled Goodman Brown, or he recognized a score of the church members of Salem village famous for their especial sanctity. Good old Deacon Gookin had arrived, and waited at the skirts of that venerable saint, his revered pastor. But, irreverently consorting with these grave, reputable, and pious people, these elders of the church, these chaste dames and dewy virgins, there were men of dissolute lives and women of spotted fame, wretches given over to all mean and filthy vice, and suspected even of horrid crimes. It was strange to see that the good shrank not from the wicked, nor were the sinners abashed by the saints. Scattered also among their pale-faced enemies were the Indian priests, or powwows, who had often scared their native forest with more hideous incantations than any known to English witchcraft.

"But where is Faith?" thought Goodman Brown; and, as hope came into his heart, he trembled.

Another verse of the hymn arose, a slow and mournful strain, such as the pious love, but joined to words which expressed all that our nature can conceive of sin, and darkly hinted at far more. Unfathomable to mere mortals is the lore of fiends. Verse after verse was sung; and still the chorus of the desert swelled between like the deepest tone of a mighty organ; and with the final peal of that dreadful anthem there came a sound, as if the roaring wind, the rushing streams, the howling beasts, and every other voice of the unconcerted wilderness were mingling and according with the voice of guilty man in homage to the prince of all. The four blazing pines threw up a loftier flame, and obscurely discovered shapes and visages of horror on the smoke wreaths above the impious assembly. At the same moment, the fire on the rock shot redly forth and formed a glowing arch above its base, where now appeared a figure. With reverence be it spoken, the figure bore no slight similitude, both in garb and manner, to some grave divine of the New England churches.

"Bring forth the converts!" cried a voice that echoed through the field and rolled into the forest.

At the word, Goodman Brown stepped forth from the shadow of the trees and approached the congregation, with whom he felt a loathful brotherhood by the sympathy of all that was wicked in his heart. He could have well-nigh sworn that the shape of his own dead father beckoned him to advance, looking downward from a smoke wreath, while a woman, with dim features of despair, threw out her hand to warn him back. Was it his mother? But he had no power to retreat one step, nor to resist, even in thought, when the minister and good old Deacon Gookin seized his arms and led him to the blazing rock. Thither came also the slender form of a veiled female, led between Goody Cloyse, that pious teacher of the catechism, and Martha Carrier, who had received the devil's promise to be queen of hell. A rampant hag was she. And there stood the proselytes beneath the canopy of fire.

"Welcome, my children," said the dark figure, "to the communion of your race. Ye have found thus young your nature and your destiny. My children, look behind you!"

They turned; and flashing forth, as it were, in a sheet of flame, the fiend-worshippers were seen; the smile of welcome gleamed darkly on every visage.

"There," resumed the sable form, "are all whom ye have reverenced from youth. Ye deemed them holier than yourselves, and shrank from your own sin, contrasting it with their lives of righteousness and prayerful aspirations heavenward. Yet here are they all in my worshiping assembly. This night it shall be granted you to know their secret deeds: how hoary-bearded elders of the church have whispered wanton words to the young maids of their households; how many a woman, eager for widows' weeds, has given her husband a drink at bedtime and let him sleep his last sleep in her bosom; how beardless youths have made haste to inherit their fathers' wealth; and how fair damsels—blush not, sweet ones—have dug little graves in the garden, and bidden me, the sole guest, to an infant's funeral. By the sympathy of your human hearts for sin ye shall scent out all the places—whether in church, bedchamber, street, field, or forest—where crime has been committed, and shall exult to behold the whole earth one stain of guilt, one mighty blood spot. Far more than this. It shall be yours to penetrate, in every bosom, the deep mystery of sin, the fountain of all wicked arts, and which inexhaustibly supplies more evil impulses than human power—than my power at its utmost—can make manifest in deeds. And now, my children, look upon each other."

They did so; and, by the blaze of the hell-kindled torches, the wretched man beheld his Faith, and the wife her husband, trembling before that unhallowed altar.

"Lo, there ye stand, my children," said the figure, in a deep and solemn tone, almost sad with its despairing awfulness, as if his once angelic nature could yet mourn for our miserable race. "Depending upon one another's hearts, ye had still hoped that virtue were not all a dream. Now are ye undeceived. Evil is the nature of mankind. Evil must be your only happiness. Welcome again, my children, to the communion of your race."

"Welcome," repeated the fiend-worshipers, in one cry of despair and triumph.

And there they stood, the only pair, as it seemed, who were yet hesitating on the verge of wickedness in this dark world. A basin was hollowed, naturally, in the rock. Did it contain water, reddened by the lurid light? or was it blood? or, perchance, a liquid flame? Herein did the shape of evil dip his hand and prepare to lay the mark of baptism upon their foreheads, that they might be partakers of the mystery of sin, more conscious of the secret guilt of others, both in deed and thought, than they could now be of their own. The husband cast one look at his pale wife, and Faith at him. What polluted wretches would the next glance show them to each other, shuddering alike at what they disclosed and what they saw!

"Faith! Faith!" cried the husband, "look up to heaven, and resist the wicked one."

Whether Faith obeyed he knew not. Hardly had he spoken when he found himself amid calm night and solitude, listening to a roar of the wind which died heavily away through the forest. He staggered against the rock, and felt it chill and damp; while a hanging twig, that had been all on fire, besprinkled his cheek with the coldest dew.

The next morning, young Goodman Brown came slowly

into the street of Salem village, staring around him like a bewildered man. The good old minister was taking a walk along the graveyard to get an appetite for breakfast and meditate his sermon, and bestowed a blessing, as he passed, on Goodman Brown. He shrank from the venerable saint as if to avoid an anathema. Old Deacon Gookin was at domestic worship, and the holy words of his prayer were heard through the open window. "What God doth the wizard pray to?" quoth Goodman Brown. Goody Cloyse, that excellent old Christian, stood in the early sunshine at her own lattice, catechizing a little girl who had brought her a pint of morning's milk. Goodman Brown snatched away the child as from the grasp of the fiend himself. Turning the corner by the meetinghouse, he spied the head of Faith, with the pink ribbons, gazing anxiously forth, and bursting into such joy at sight of him that she skipped along the street and almost kissed her husband before the whole village. But Goodman Brown looked sternly and sadly into her face, and passed on without a greeting.

Had Goodman Brown fallen asleep in the forest and only dreamed a wild dream of a witch meeting?

Be it so if you will; but alas! it was a dream of evil omen for young Goodman Brown. A stern, a sad, a darkly meditative, a distrustful, if not a desperate man did he become from the night of that fearful dream. On the Sabbath day, when the congregation were singing a holy psalm, he could not listen because an anthem of sin rushed loudly upon his ear and drowned all the blessed strain. When the minister spoke from the pulpit with power and fervid eloquence, and, with his hand on the open Bible, of the sacred truths of our religion, and of saintlike lives and triumphant deaths, and of future bliss or misery unutterable, then did Goodman Brown turn pale, dreading lest the roof should thunder down upon the gray blasphemer and his hearers. Often, awaking suddenly at midnight, he shrank from the bosom of Faith; and at morning or eventide, when the family knelt down at prayer, he scowled and muttered to himself, and gazed sternly at his wife, and turned away. And when he had lived long, and was borne to his grave a hoary corpse, followed by Faith, an aged woman, and children and grandchildren, a goodly procession, besides neighbors not a few, they carved no hopeful verse upon his tombstone, for his dying hour was gloom.

J. Sheridan Le Fanu

MR. JUSTICE HARBOTTLE

Le Fanu and Poe are, according to Jack Sullivan, "the
first short story writers in English to work out carefully
planned aesthetic strategies of horror. They were also
among the first to write modern short stories. Their habitual strict attention to unity of mood and economy of
means is a quality we take for granted in short fiction
today, but it was virtually unknown to their more didac-
tically inclined contemporaries." (*Horror Literature*, pp.
221–22) Sullivan goes on to maintain that "Le Fanu was
more revolutionary than Poe, for he began the process
of dismantling the Gothic props and placing the supernatural tale in everyday settings." M. R. James and his
progeny derive from Le Fanu, and James considered him
the very greatest of ghost story writers. But he was not
a notable popular success in his day; his books are
among the very rarest in all nineteenth-century literature.
His masterpieces include "Carmilla," "Green Tea," "The
Room in the Dragon Volant," and a number of others,
including "Mr. Justice Harbottle" offered here. Both Poe
and Le Fanu offered examinations of the human psyche
in abnormal circumstances characteristically in their stories, but in Le Fanu there is unquestionably supernatural
evil at work, against an evil man, Judge Harbottle.

PROLOGUE

On this case Doctor Hesselius has inscribed nothing more than the words, "Harman's Report," and a simple reference to his own extraordinary Essay on "The Interior Sense, and the Conditions of the Opening thereof."

The reference is to Vol. I., Section 317, Note Z^a. The note to which reference is thus made, simply says: "There are two accounts of the remarkable case of the Honourable Mr. Justice Harbottle, one furnished to me by Mrs. Trimmer, of Tunbridge Wells (June, 1805); the other at a much later date, by Anthony Harman, Esq. I much prefer the former; in the first place, because it is minute and detailed, and written, it seems to me, with more caution and knowledge; and in the next, because the letters from Dr. Hedstone, which are embodied in it, furnish matter of the highest value to a right apprehension of the nature of the case. It was one of the best declared cases of an opening of the interior sense, which I have met with. It was affected too, by the phenomenon, which occurs so frequently as to indicate a law of these eccentric conditions; that is to say, it exhibited what I may term, the contagious character of this sort of intrusion of the spirit-world upon the proper domain of matter. So soon as the spirit-action has established itself in the case of one patient, its developed energy begins to radiate, more or less effectually, upon others. The interior vision of the child was opened; as was, also, that of its mother, Mrs. Pyneweck; and both the interior vision and hearing of the scullery-maid, were opened on the same occasion. After-appearances are the result of the law explained in Vol. II., Section 17 to 49. The common centre of association, simultaneously recalled, unites, or *re*-unites, as the case may be, for a period measured, as we see, in Section 37. The *maximum* will extend to days, the *minimum* is little more than a second. We see the operation of this principle perfectly displayed, in certain cases of lunacy, of epilepsy, of catalepsy, and of mania, of a peculiar and painful character, though unattended by incapacity of business.''

The memorandum of the case of Judge Harbottle, which was written by Mrs. Trimmer, of Tunbridge Wells, which Doctor Hesselius thought the better of the two, I have been unable to discover among his papers. I found in his escritoire a note to the effect that he had lent the Report of Judge Harbottle's case, written by Mrs. Trimmer, to Dr. F. Heyne. To that learned and able gentleman accordingly I wrote, and received from him, in his reply, which was full of alarms and regrets, on account of the uncertain safety of that ''valuable MS.,'' a line written long since by Dr. Hesselius, which completely exonerated him, inasmuch as it acknowledged the safe return of the papers. The narrative of Mr. Harman, is therefore, the only one available for this collection. The late Dr. Hesselius, in another passage of the note that I have cited, says, ''As to the facts (non-medical) of the case, the narrative of Mr. Harman exactly tallies with that furnished by Mrs. Trimmer.'' The strictly scientific view of the case would scarcely interest the popular reader; and, possibly, for the purposes of this selection, I should, even had I both papers to choose between, have preferred that of Mr. Harman, which is given, in full, in the following pages.

I   The Judge's House

Thirty years ago, an elderly man, to whom I paid quarterly a small annuity charged on some property of mine, came on the quarter-day to receive it. He was a dry, sad, quiet man, who had known better days, and had always maintained an unexceptionable character. No better authority could be imagined for a ghost story.

He told me one, though with a manifest reluctance; he was drawn into the narration by his choosing to explain what I should not have remarked, that he had called two days earlier than that week after the strict day of payment, which he had usually allowed to elapse. His reason was a sudden determination to change his lodgings, and the consequent necessity of paying his rent a little before it was due.

He lodged in a dark street in Westminster, in a spacious old house, very warm, being wainscoted from top to bottom, and furnished with no undue abundance of windows, and those fitted with thick sashes and small panes.

This house was, as the bills upon the windows testified, offered to be sold or let. But no one seemed to care to look at it.

A thin matron, in rusty black silk, very taciturn, with large, steady, alarmed eyes, that seemed to look in your face, to read what you might have seen in the dark rooms and passages through which you had passed, was in charge of it, with a solitary "maid-of-all-work" under her command. My poor friend had taken lodgings in this house, on account of their extraordinary cheapness. He had occupied them for nearly a year without the slightest disturbance, and was the only tenant, under rent, in the house. He had two rooms; a sitting-room and a bed-room with a closet opening from it, in which he kept his books and papers locked up. He had gone to his bed, having also locked the outer door. Unable to sleep, he had lighted a candle, and after having read for a time, had laid the book beside him. He heard the old clock at the stair-head strike one; and very shortly after, to his alarm, he saw the closet door, which he thought he had locked, open stealthily, and a slight dark man, particularly sinister, and somewhere about fifty, dressed in mourning of a very antique fashion, such as a suit as we see in Hogarth, entered the room on tip-toe. He was followed by an elder man, stout, and blotched with scurvy, and whose features, fixed as a corpse's, were stamped with dreadful force with a character of sensuality and villainy.

This old man wore a flowered silk dressing-gown and ruffles, and he remarked a gold ring on his finger, and on his head a cap of velvet, such as, in the days of perukes, gentlemen wore in undress.

This direful old man carried in his ringed and ruffled hand a coil of rope; and these two figures crossed the floor diagonally, passing the foot of his bed, from the closet door at the farther end of the room, at the left, near the window, to the door opening upon the lobby, close to the bed's head, at his right.

He did not attempt to describe his sensations as these figures passed so near him. He merely said, that so far from sleeping in that room again, no consideration the world could offer would induce him so much as to enter it again alone, even in the daylight. He found both doors, that of the closet, and that of the room opening upon the lobby, in the morning fast locked as he had left them before going to bed.

In answer to a question of mine, he said that neither appeared the least conscious of his presence. They did not seem to glide, but walked as living men do, but without any sound, and he felt a vibration on the floor as they crossed it. He so obviously suffered from speaking about the apparitions, that I asked him no more questions.

There were in his description, however, certain coincidences so very singular, as to induce me, by that very post, to write to a friend much my senior, then living in a remote part of England, for the information which I knew he could give me. He had himself more than once pointed out that old house to my attention, and told me, though very briefly, the strange story which I now asked him to give me in greater detail.

His answer satisfied me; and the following pages convey its substance.

Your letter (he wrote) tells me you desire some particulars about the closing years of the life of Mr. Justice Harbottle, one of the judges of the Court of Common Pleas. You refer, of course, to the extraordinary occurrences that made that period of his life long after a theme for "winter tales" and metaphysical speculation. I happen to know perhaps more than any other man living of those mysterious particulars.

The old family mansion, when I revisited London, more

than thirty years ago, I examined for the last time. During the years that have passed since then, I hear that improvement, with its preliminary demolitions, has been doing wonders for the quarter of Westminster in which it stood. If I were quite certain that the house had been taken down, I should have no difficulty about naming the street in which it stood. As what I have to tell, however, is not likely to improve its letting value, and as I should not care to get into trouble, I prefer being silent on that particular point.

How old the house was, I can't tell. People said it was built by Roger Harbottle, a Turkey merchant, in the reign of King James I. I am not a good opinion upon such questions; but having been in it, though in its forlorn and deserted state, I can tell you in a general way what it was like. It was built of dark-red brick, and the door and windows were faced with stone that had turned yellow by time. It receded some feet from the line of the other houses in the street; and it had a florid and fanciful rail of iron about the broad steps that invited your ascent to the hall-door, in which were fixed, under a file of lamps among scrolls and twisted leaves, two immense "extinguishers," like the conical caps of fairies, into which, in old times, the footmen used to thrust their flambeaux when their chairs or coaches had set down their great people, in the hall or at the steps, as the case might be. That hall is panelled up to the ceiling, and has a large fire-place. Two or three stately old rooms open from it at each side. The windows of these are tall, with many small panes. Passing through the arch at the back of the hall, you come upon the wide and heavy well-staircase. There is a back staircase also. The mansion is large, and has not as much light, by any means, in proportion to its extent, as modern houses enjoy. When I saw it, it had long been untenanted, and had the gloomy reputation beside of a haunted house. Cobwebs floated from the ceilings or spanned the corners of the cornices, and dust lay thick over everything. The windows were stained with the dust and rain of fifty years, and darkness had thus grown darker.

When I made it my first visit, it was in company with my father, when I was still a boy, in the year 1808. I was about twelve years old, and my imagination impressible, as it always is at that age. I looked about me with great awe. I was here in the very centre and scene of those occurrences which I had heard recounted at the fireside at home, with so delightful a horror.

My father was an old bachelor of nearly sixty when he married. He had, when a child, seen Judge Harbottle on the bench in his robes and wig a dozen times at least before his death, which took place in 1748, and his appearance made a powerful and unpleasant impression, not only on his imagination, but upon his nerves.

The Judge was at that time a man of some sixty-seven years. He had a great mulberry-coloured face, a big, carbuncled nose, fierce eyes, and a grim and brutal mouth. My father, who was young at the time, thought it the most formidable face he had ever seen; for there were evidences of intellectual power in the formation and lines of the forehead. His voice was loud and harsh, and gave effect to the sarcasm which was his habitual weapon on the bench.

This old gentleman had the reputation of being about the wickedest man in England. Even on the bench he now and then showed his scorn of opinion. He had carried cases his own way, it was said, in spite of counsel, authorities, and even of juries, by a sort of cajolery, violence, and bamboozling, that somehow confused and overpowered resistance. He had never actually committed himself; he was too cunning to do that. He had the character of being, however, a dangerous and unscrupulous judge; but his character did not trouble him. The associates he chose for his hours of relaxation cared as little as he did about it.

II Mr. Peters

One night during the session of 1746 this old Judge went down in his chair to wait in one of the rooms of the House of Lords for the result of a division in which he and his order were interested.

This over, he was about to return to his house close by, in his chair; but the night had become so soft and fine that he changed his mind, sent it home empty, and with two footmen, each with a flambeau, set out on foot in preference. Gout had made him rather a slow pedestrian. It took him some time to get through the two or three streets he had to pass before reaching his house.

In one of those narrow streets of tall houses, perfectly silent at that hour, he overtook, slowly as he was walking, a very singular-looking old gentleman.

He had a bottle-green coat on, with a cape to it, and large stone buttons, a broad-leafed low-crowned hat, from under which a big powdered wig escaped; he stooped very much, and supported his bending knees with the aid of a crutch-handled cane, and so shuffled and tottered along painfully.

"I ask your pardon, sir," said this old man, in a very quavering voice, as the burly Judge came up with him, and he extended his hand feebly towards his arm.

Mr. Justice Harbottle saw that the man was by no means poorly dressed, and his manner that of a gentleman.

The Judge stopped short, and said, in his harsh peremptory tones, "Well, sir, how can I serve you?"

"Can you direct me to Judge Harbottle's house? I have some intelligence of the very last importance to communicate to him."

"Can you tell it before witnesses?" asked the Judge.

"By no means; it must reach *his* ear only," quavered the old man earnestly.

"If that be so, sir, you have only to accompany me a few steps farther to reach my house, and obtain a private audience; for I am Judge Harbottle."

With this invitation the infirm gentleman in the white wig complied very readily; and in another minute the stranger stood in what was then termed the front parlour of the Judge's house, *tête-à-tête* with that shrewd and dangerous functionary.

He had to sit down, being very much exhausted, and unable for a little time to speak; and then he had a fit of coughing, and after that a fit of gasping; and thus two or three minutes passed, during which the Judge dropped his roquelaure on an arm-chair, and threw his cocked-hat over that.

The venerable pedestrian in the white wig quickly recovered his voice. With closed doors they remained together for some time.

There were guests waiting in the drawing-rooms, and the sound of men's voices laughing, and then of a female voice singing to a harpsichord, were heard distinctly in the hall over the stairs; for old Judge Harbottle had arranged one of his dubious jollifications, such as might well make the hair of godly men's heads stand upright for that night.

This old gentleman in the powdered white wig, that rested on his stooped shoulders, must have had something to say that interested the Judge very much; for he would not have parted on easy terms with the ten minutes and upward which that conference filched from the sort of revelry in which he most delighted, and in which he was the roaring king, and in some sort the tyrant also, of his company.

The footman who showed the aged gentleman out observed that the Judge's mulberry-coloured face, pimples and all, were bleached to a dingy yellow, and there was the abstraction of agitated thought in his manner, as he bid the stranger goodnight. The servant saw that the conversation had been of serious import, and that the Judge was frightened.

Instead of stumping upstairs forthwith to his scandalous hilarities, his profane company, and his great china bowl of punch—the identical bowl from which a bygone Bishop of London, good easy man, had baptised this Judge's grandfather, now clinking round the rim with silver ladles, and hung with scrolls of lemon-peel—instead, I say, of stumping and clambering up the great staircase to the cavern of his Circean enchantment, he stood with his big nose flattened against the window-pane, watching the progress of the feeble old man, who clung stiffly to the iron rail as he got down, step by step, to the pavement.

The hall-door had hardly closed, when the old Judge was in the hall bawling hasty orders, with such stimulating expletives as old colonels under excitement sometimes indulge in now-a-days, with a stamp or two of his big foot, and a waving of his clenched fist in the air. He commanded the footman to overtake the old gentleman in the white wig, to offer him his protection on his way home, and in no case to show his face again without having ascertained where he lodged, and who he was, and all about him.

"By——, sirrah! if you fail me in this, you doff my livery to-night!"

Forth bounced the stalwart footman, with his heavy cane under his arm, and skipped down the steps, and looked up and down the street after the singular figure, so easy to recognize.

What were his adventures I shall not tell you just now.

The old man, in the conference to which he had been admitted in that stately panelled room, had just told the Judge a very strange story. He might be himself a conspirator; he might possibly be crazed; or possibly his whole story was straight and true.

The aged gentleman in the bottle-green coat, on finding himself alone with Mr. Justice Harbottle, had become agitated. He said,

"There is, perhaps you are not aware, my lord, a prisoner in Shrewsbury jail, charged with having forged a bill of exchange for a hundred and twenty pounds, and his name is Lewis Pyneweck, a grocer of that town."

"Is there?" says the Judge, who knew well that there was.

"Yes, my lord," says the old man.

"Then you had better say nothing to affect this case. If you do, by——I'll commit you! for I'm to try it,'' says the Judge, with his terrible look and tone.

''I am not going to do anything of the kind, my lord; of him or his case I know nothing, and care nothing. But a fact has come to my knowledge which it behoves you to well consider.''

''And what may that fact be?'' inquired the Judge; ''I'm in haste, sir, and beg you will use dispatch.''

''It has come to my knowledge, my lord, that a secret tribunal is in process of formation, the object of which is to take cognisance of the conduct of the judges; and first, of *your* conduct, my lord: it is a wicked conspiracy.''

''Who are of it?'' demands the Judge.

''I know not a single name as yet. I know but the fact, my lord; it is most certainly true.''

''I'll have you before the Privy Council, sir,'' says the Judge.

''That is what I most desire; but not for a day or two, my lord.''

''And why so?''

''I have not as yet a single name, as I told your lordship; but I expect to have a list of the most forward men in it, and some other papers connected with the plot, in two or three days.''

''You said one or two just now.''

''About that time, my lord.''

''Is this a Jacobite plot?''

''In the main I think it is, my lord.''

''Why, then, it is political. I have tried no State prisoners, nor am like to try any such. How, then, doth it concern me?''

''From what I can gather, my lord, there are those in it who desire private revenges upon certain judges.''

''What do they call their cabal?''

''The High Court of Appeal, my lord.''

''Who are you, sir? What is your name?''

''Hugh Peters, my Lord.''

''That should be a Whig name?''

"It is, my lord."

"Where do you lodge, Mr. Peters?"

"In Thames Street, my lord, over against the sign of the 'Three Kings.' "

" 'Three Kings'? Take care one be not too many for you, Mr. Peters! How come you, an honest Whig, as you say, to be privy to a Jacobite plot? Answer me that."

"My lord, a person in whom I take an interest has been seduced to take a part in it; and being frightened at the unexpected wickedness of their plans, he is resolved to become an informer for the Crown."

"He resolves like a wise man, sir. What does he say of the persons? Who are in the plot? Doth he know them?"

"Only two, my lord; but he will be introduced to the club in a few days, and he will then have a list, and more exact information of their plans, and above all of their oaths, and their hours and places of meeting, with which he wishes to be acquainted before they can have any suspicions of his intentions. And being so informed, to whom, think you, my lord, had he best go then?"

"To the king's attorney-general straight. But you say this concerns me, sir, in particular? How about this prisoner, Lewis Pyneweck? Is he one of them?"

"I can't tell, my lord; but for some reason, it is thought your lordship will be well advised if you try him not. For if you do, it is feared 'twill shorten your days."

"So far as I can learn, Mr. Peters, this business smells pretty strong of blood and treason. The king's attorney-general will know how to deal with it. When shall I see you again, sir?"

"If you give me leave, my lord, either before your lordship's court sits, or after it rises, to-morrow. I should like to come and tell your lordship what has passed."

"Do so, Mr. Peters, at nine o'clock to-morrow morning. And see you play me no trick, sir, in this matter; if you do, by——, sir, I'll lay you by the heels!"

"You need fear no trick from me, my lord; had I not

wished to serve you, and acquit my own conscience, I never would have come all this way to talk with your lordship.''

"I'm willing to believe you, Mr. Peters; I'm willing to believe you, sir.''

And upon this they parted.

"He has either painted his face, or he is consumedly sick,'' thought the old Judge.

The light had shone more effectually upon his features as he turned to leave the room with a low bow, and they looked, he fancied, unnaturally chalky.

"D——him!'' said the Judge ungraciously, as he began to scale the stairs: ''he has half-spoiled my supper.''

But if he had, no one but the Judge himself perceived it, and the evidence was all, as any one might perceive, the other way.

III   Lewis Pyneweck

In the meantime the footman dispatched in pursuit of Mr. Peters speedily overtook that feeble gentleman. The old man stopped when he heard the sound of pursuing steps, but any alarms that may have crossed his mind seemed to disappear on his recognizing the livery. He very gratefully accepted the proffered assistance, and placed his tremulous arm within the servant's for support. They had not gone far, however, when the old man stopped suddenly, saying,

"Dear me! as I live, I have dropped it. You heard it fall. My eyes, I fear, won't serve me, and I'm unable to stoop low enough; but if *you* will look, you shall have half the find. It is a guinea; I carried it in my glove.''

The street was silent and deserted. The footman had hardly descended to what he termed his "hunkers,'' and begun to search the pavement about the spot which the old man indicated, when Mr. Peters, who seemed very much exhausted, and breathed with difficulty, struck him a violent blow, from above, over the back of the head with a heavy instrument, and then another; and leaving him bleeding and senseless in the gutter, ran like a lamplighter down a lane to the right, and was gone.

When, an hour later, the watchman brought the man in livery home, still stupid and covered with blood, Judge Harbottle cursed his servant roundly, swore he was drunk, threatened him with an indictment for taking bribes to betray his master, and cheered him with a perspective of the broad street leading from the Old Bailey to Tyburn, the cart's tail, and the hangman's lash.

Notwithstanding this demonstration, the Judge was pleased. It was a disguised "affidavit man," or footpad, no doubt, who had been employed to frighten him. The trick had fallen through.

A "court of appeal," such as the false Hugh Peters had indicated, with assassination for its sanction, would be an uncomfortable institution for a "hanging judge" like the Honourable Justice Harbottle. That sarcastic and ferocious administrator of the criminal code of England, at that time a rather pharisaical, bloody and heinous system of justice, had reasons of his own for choosing to try that very Lewis Pyneweck, on whose behalf this audacious trick was devised. Try him he would. No man living should take that morsel out of his mouth.

Of Lewis Pyneweck, of course, so far as the outer world could see, he knew nothing. He would try him after his fashion, without fear, favour, or affection.

But did he not remember a certain thin man, dressed in mourning, in whose house, in Shrewsbury, the Judge's lodgings used to be, until a scandal of his ill-treating his wife came suddenly to light? A grocer with a demure look, a soft step, and a lean face as dark as mahogany, with a nose sharp and long, standing ever so little awry, and a pair of dark steady brown eyes under thinly-traced black brows—a man whose thin lips wore always a faint unpleasant smile.

Had not that scoundrel an account to settle with the Judge? had he not been troublesome lately? and was not his name

Lewis Pyneweck, some time grocer in Shrewsbury, and now prisoner in the jail of that town?

The reader may take it, if he pleases, as a sign that Judge Harbottle was a good Christian, that he suffered nothing ever from remorse. That was undoubtedly true. He had, nevertheless, done this grocer, forger, what you will, some five or six years before, a grievous wrong; but it was not that, but a possible scandal, and possible complications, that troubled the learned Judge now.

Did he not, as a lawyer, know, that to bring a man from his shop to the dock, the chances must be at least ninety-nine out of a hundred that he is guilty.

A weak man like his learned brother Withershins was not a judge to keep the high-roads safe, and make crime tremble. Old Judge Harbottle was the man to make the evil-disposed quiver, and to refresh the world with showers of wicked blood, and thus save the innocent, to the refrain of the ancient saw he loved to quote:

> Foolish pity
> Ruins a city.

In hanging that fellow he could not be wrong. The eye of a man accustomed to look upon the dock could not fail to read "villain" written sharp and clear in his plotting face. Of course he would try him, and no one else should.

A saucy-looking woman, still handsome, in a mob-cap gay with blue ribbons, in a saque of flowered silk, with lace and rings on, much too fine for the Judge's housekeeper, which nevertheless she was, peeped into his study next morning, and, seeing the Judge alone, stepped in.

"Here's another letter from him, come by the post this morning. Can't you do nothing for him?" she said wheedlingly, with her arm over his neck, and her delicate finger and thumb fiddling with the lobe of his purple ear.

"I'll try," said Judge Harbottle, not raising his eyes from the paper he was reading.

"I knew you'd do what I asked you," she said.

The Judge clapt his gouty claw over his heart, and made her an ironical bow.

"What," she asked, "will you do?"

"Hang him," said the Judge with a chuckle.

"You don't mean to; no, you don't, my little man," said she, surveying herself in a mirror on the wall.

"I'm d——d but I think you're falling in love with your husband at last!" said Judge Harbottle.

"I'm blest but I think you're growing jealous of him," replied the lady with a laugh. "But no; he was always a bad one to me; I've done with him long ago."

"And he with you, by George! When he took your fortune, and your spoons, and your ear-rings, he had all he wanted of you. He drove you from his house; and when he discovered you had made yourself comfortable, and found a good situation, he'd have taken your guineas, and your silver, and your ear-rings over again, and then allowed you half-a-dozen years more to make a new harvest for his mill. You don't wish him good; if you say you do, you lie."

She laughed a wicked, saucy laugh, and gave the terrible Rhadamanthus a playful tap on the chops.

"He wants me to send him money to fee a counsellor," she said, while her eyes wandered over the pictures on the wall, and back again to the looking-glass; and certainly she did not look as if his jeopardy troubled her very much.

"Confound his impudence, the *scoundrel*!" thundered the old Judge, throwing himself back in his chair, as he used to do *in furore* on the bench, and the lines of his mouth looked brutal, and his eyes ready to leap from their sockets. "If you answer his letter from my house to please yourself, you'll write your next from somebody else's to please me. You understand, my pretty witch, I'll not be pestered. Come, no pouting; whimpering won't do. You don't care a brass farthing for the villain, body or soul. You came here but to make a row. You are one of Mother Carey's chickens; and where you come, the storm is up. Get you gone, baggage! get you *gone!*" he repeated, with a stamp; for a knock at the hall-door made her instantaneous disappearance indispensable.

I need hardly say that the venerable Hugh Peters did not appear again. The Judge never mentioned him. But oddly enough, considering how he laughed to scorn the weak invention which he had blown into dust at the very first puff, his white-wigged visitor and the conference in the dark front parlour was often in his memory.

His shrewd eye told him that allowing for change of tints and such disguises as the playhouse affords every night, the features of this false old man, who had turned out too hard for his tall footman, were identical with those of Lewis Pyneweck.

Judge Harbottle made his registrar call upon the crown solicitor, and tell him that there was a man in town who bore a wonderful resemblance to a prisoner in Shrewsbury jail named Lewis Pyneweck, and to make inquiry through the post forthwith whether any one was personating Pyneweck in prison, and whether he had thus or otherwise made his escape.

The prisoner was safe, however, and no question as to his identity.

IV   Interruption in Court

In due time Judge Harbottle went circuit; and in due time the judges were in Shrewsbury. News travelled slowly in those days, and newspapers, like the wagons and stage-coaches, took matters easily. Mrs. Pyneweck, in the Judge's house, with a diminished household—the greater part of the Judge's servants having gone with him, for he had given up riding circuit, and travelled in his coach in state—kept house rather solitarily at home.

In spite of quarrels, in spite of mutual injuries—some of them, inflicted by herself, enormous—in spite of a married life of spited bickerings—a life in which there seemed no love or liking or forbearance, for years—now that Pyneweck stood in near danger of death, something like remorse came suddenly upon her. She knew that in Shrewsbury were transacting the scenes which were to determine his fate. She knew she did not love him; but she could not have supposed, even a fortnight before, that the hour of suspense could have affected her so powerfully.

She knew the day on which the trial was expected to take place. She could not get it out of her head for a minute; she felt faint as it drew towards evening.

Two or three days passed; and then she knew that the trial must be over by this time. There were floods between London and Shrewsbury, and news was long delayed. She wished the floods would last for ever. It was dreadful waiting to hear; dreadful to know that the event was over, and that she could not hear till self-willed rivers subsided; dreadful to know that they must subside and the news come at last.

She had some vague trust in the Judge's good-nature, and much in the resources of chance and accident. She had contrived to send the money he wanted. He would not be without legal advice and energetic and skilled support.

At last the news did come—a long arrear all in a gush: a letter from a female friend in Shrewsbury; a return of the sentences, sent up for the Judge; and most important, because most easily got at, being told with great aplomb and brevity, the long-deferred intelligence of the Shrewsbury Assizes in the *Morning Advertiser*. Like an impatient reader of a novel, who reads the last page first, she read with dizzy eyes the list of the executions.

Two were respited, seven were hanged; and in that capital catalogue was this line:

"Lewis Pyneweck—forgery."

She had to read it half-a-dozen times over before she was sure she understood it. Here was the paragraph:

Sentence, Death—7

Executed accordingly, on Friday the 13th instant, to wit:

Thomas Primer, *alias* Duck—highway robbery.

Flora Guy—stealing to the value of IIs. 6d.

Arthur Pounden—burglary.

Matilda Mummery—riot.

Lewis Pyneweck—forgery, bill of exchange.

And when she reached this, she read it over and over, feeling very cold and sick.

This buxom housekeeper was known in the house as Mrs. Carwell—Carwell being her maiden name, which she had resumed.

No one in the house except its master knew her history. Her introduction had been managed craftily. No one suspected that it had been concerted between her and the old reprobate in scarlet and ermine.

Flora Carwell ran up the stairs now, and snatched her little girl, hardly seven years of age, whom she met on the lobby, hurriedly up in her arms, and carried her into her bedroom, without well knowing what she was doing, and sat down, placing the child before her. She was not able to speak. She held the child before her, and looked in the little girl's wondering face, and burst into tears of horror.

She thought the Judge could have saved him. I daresay he could. For a time she was furious with him, and hugged and kissed her bewildered little girl, who returned her gaze with large round eyes.

That little girl had lost her father, and knew nothing of the matter. She had been always told that her father was dead long ago.

A woman, coarse, uneducated, vain, and violent, does not reason, or even feel, very distinctly; but in these tears of consternation were mingling a self-upbraiding. She felt afraid of that little child.

But Mrs. Carwell was a person who lived not upon sentiment, but upon beef and pudding; she consoled herself with punch; she did not trouble herself long even with resentments; she was a gross and material person, and could not mourn over the irrevocable for more than a limited number of hours, even if she would.

Judge Harbottle was soon in London again. Except the gout, this savage old epicurean never knew a day's sickness. He laughed, and coaxed, and bullied away the young woman's faint upbraidings, and in a little time Lewis Pyneweck troubled her no more; and the Judge secretly chuckled over the perfectly fair removal of a bore, who might have grown little by little into something very like a tyrant.

It was the lot of the Judge whose adventures I am now recounting to try criminal cases at the Old Bailey shortly after his return. He had commenced his charge to the jury in a case of forgery, and was, after his wont, thundering dead against the prisoner, with many a hard aggravation and cynical gibe, when suddenly all died away in silence, and, instead of looking at the jury, the eloquent Judge was gaping at some person in the body of the court.

Among the persons of small importance who stand and listen at the sides was one tall enough to show with a little prominence; a slight mean figure, dressed in seedy black, lean and dark of visage. He had just handed a letter to the crier, before he caught the Judge's eye.

That Judge described, to his amazement, the features of Lewis Pyneweck. He has the usual faint thin-lipped smile; and with his blue chin raised in air, and as it seemed quite unconscious of the distinguished notice he has attracted, he was stretching his low cravat with his crooked fingers, while he slowly turned his head from side to side—a process which enabled the Judge to see distinctly a stripe of swollen blue round his neck, which indicated, he thought, the grip of the rope.

This man, with a few others, had got a footing on a step, from which he could better see the court. He now stepped down, and the Judge lost sight of him.

His lordship signed energetically with his hand in the direction in which this man had vanished. He turned to the tipstaff. His first effort to speak ended in a gasp. He cleared his throat, and told the astounded official to arrest that man who had interrupted the court.

"He's but this moment gone down *there*. Bring him in custody before me, within ten minutes' time, or I'll strip your gown from your shoulders and fine the sheriff!" he thundered, while his eyes flashed round the court in search of the functionary.

Attorneys, counsellors, idle spectators, gazed in the direction in which Mr. Justice Harbottle had shaken his gnarled old hand. They compared notes. Not one had seen any one making a disturbance. They asked one another if the Judge was losing his head.

Nothing came of the search. His lordship concluded his charge a great deal more tamely; and when the jury retired, he stared round the court with a wandering mind, and looked as if he would not have given sixpence to see the prisoner hanged.

V Caleb Searcher

The Judge had received the letter; had he known from whom it came, he would no doubt have read it instantaneously. As it was he simply read the direction:

> *To the Honourable*
> *The Lord Justice*
> *Elijah Harbottle,*
> *One of his Majesty's Justices of*
> *the Honourable Court of Common Pleas.*

It remained forgotten in his pocket till he reached home. When he pulled out that and others from the capacious pocket of his coat, it had its turn, as he sat in his library in his thick silk dressing-gown; and then he found its contents to be a closely-written letter, in a clerk's hand, and an enclosure in "secretary hand," as I believe the angular scrivinary of law-writings in those days were termed, engrossed on a bit of parchment about the size of this page. The letter said:

Mr. Justice Harbottle,—My Lord,

I am ordered by the High Court of Appeal to acquaint your lordship, in order to your better preparing yourself for your trial, that a true bill hath been sent down, and the indictment lieth against your lordship for the murder of one Lewis Pyneweck of Shrewsbury, citizen, wrongfully executed for the forgery of a bill of exchange, on the——th day of——last, by reason of the wilful perversion of the evidence, and the undue pressure put upon the jury, together with the illegal admission of evidence by your lordship, well knowing the same to be illegal, by all which the promoter of the prosecution of the said indictment, before the High Court of Appeal, hath lost his life.

And the trial of the said indictment, I am farther ordered to acquaint your lordship, is fixed for the 10th day of——next ensuing, by the right honourable the Lord Chief-Justice Twofold, of the court aforesaid, to wit, the High Court of Appeal, on which day it will most certainly take place. And I am farther to acquaint your lordship, to prevent any surprise or miscarriage, that your case stands first for the said day, and that the said High Court of Appeal sits day and night, and never rises; and herewith, by order of the said court, I furnish your lordship with a copy (extract) of the record in this case, except of the indictment, whereof, notwithstanding, the substance and effect is supplied to your lordship in this Notice. And farther I am to inform you, that in case the jury then to try your lordship should find you guilty, the right honourable the Lord Chief-Justice will, in passing sentence of death upon you, fix the day of execution for the 10th day of——, being one calendar month from the day of your trial.

It was signed by   Caleb Searcher,
Officer of the Crown Solicitor in the
Kingdom of Life and Death.

The Judge glanced through the parchment.

" 'Sblood! Do they think a man like me is to be bamboozled by their buffoonery?"

The Judge's coarse features were wrung into one of his sneers; but he was pale. Possibly, after all, there was a conspiracy on foot. It was queer. Did they mean to pistol him in his carriage? or did they only aim at frightening him?

Judge Harbottle had more than enough of animal courage. He was not afraid of highwaymen, and he had fought more than his share of duels, being a foul-mouthed advocate while he held briefs at the bar. No one questioned his fighting qualities. But with respect to this particular case of Pyneweck, he lived in a house of glass. Was there not his pretty, dark-eyed, over-dressed housekeeper, Mrs. Flora Carwell? Very easy for people who knew Shrewsbury to identify Mrs. Pyneweck, if once put upon the scent; and had he not stormed and worked hard in that case? Had he not made it hard sailing for the prisoner? Did he not know very well what the bar thought of it? It would be the worst scandal that ever blasted Judge.

So much there was intimidating in the matter but nothing more. The Judge was a little bit gloomy for a day or two after, and more testy with every one than usual.

He locked up the papers; and about a week after he asked his housekeeper, one day, in the library:

"Had your husband never a brother?"

Mrs. Carwell squalled on this sudden introduction of the funereal topic, and cried exemplary "piggins full," as the Judge used pleasantly to say. But he was in no mood for trifling now, and he said sternly:

"Come, madam! this wearies me. Do it another time; and give me an answer to my question." So she did.

Pyneweck had no brother living. He once had one; but he died in Jamaica.

"How do you know he is dead?" asked the Judge.

"Because he told me so."

"Not the dead man."

"Pyneweck told me so."

"Is that all?" sneered the Judge.

He pondered this matter; and time went on. The Judge was growing a little morose, and less enjoying. The subject struck nearer to his thoughts than he fancied it could have done. But so it is with most undivulged vexations, and there was no one to whom he could tell this one.

It was now the ninth; and Mr. Justice Harbottle was glad. He knew nothing would come of it. Still it bothered him; and to-morrow would see it well over.

[What of the paper I have cited? No one saw it during his life; no one, after his death. He spoke of it to Dr. Hedstone; and what purported to be "a copy," in the old Judge's hand-writing, was found. The original was nowhere. Was it a copy of an illusion, incident to brain disease? Such is my belief.]

VI   Arrested

Judge Harbottle went this night to the play at Drury Lane. He was one of those old fellows who care nothing for late hours, and occasional knocking about in pursuit of pleasure. He had appointed with two cronies of Lincoln's Inn to come home in his coach with him to sup after the play.

They were not in his box, but were to meet him near the entrance, and get into his carriage there; and Mr. Justice Harbottle, who hated waiting, was looking a little impatiently from the window.

The Judge yawned.

He told the footman to watch for Counsellor Thavies and Counsellor Beller, who were coming; and, with another yawn, he laid his cocked hat on his knees, closed his eyes, leaned back in his corner, wrapped his mantle closer about him, and began to think of pretty Mrs. Abington.

And being a man who could sleep like a sailor, at a moment's notice, he was thinking of taking a nap. Those fellows had no business to keep a judge waiting.

He heard their voices now. Those rake-hell counsellors were laughing, and bantering, and sparring after their wont. The carriage swayed and jerked, as one got in, and then again as the other followed. The door clapped, and the coach was now jogging and rumbling over the pavement. The Judge was a little bit sulky. He did not care to sit up and open his eyes. Let them suppose he was asleep. He heard them laugh with more malice than good-humour, he thought, as they observed it. He would give them a d——d hard knock or two when they got to his door, and till then he would counterfeit his nap.

The clocks were chiming twelve. Beller and Thavies were silent as tombstones. They were generally loquacious and merry rascals.

The Judge suddenly felt himself roughly seized and thrust from his corner into the middle of the seat, and opening his eyes, instantly he found himself between his two companions.

Before he could blurt out the oath that was at his lips, he saw that they were two strangers—evil-looking fellows, each with a pistol in his hand, and dressed like Bow Street officers.

The Judge clutched at the check-string. The coach pulled up. He stared about him. They were not among houses; but through the windows, under a broad moonlight, he saw a black moor stretching lifelessly from right to left, with rotting trees, pointing fantastic branches in the air, standing here and there in groups, as if they held up their arms and twigs like fingers, in horrible glee at the Judge's coming.

A footman came to the window. He knew his long face and sunken eyes. He knew it was Dingly Chuff, fifteen years ago a footman in his service, whom he had turned off at a moment's notice, in a burst of jealousy, and indicted for a missing spoon. The man had died in prison of the jail-fever.

The Judge drew back in utter amazement. His armed companions signed mutely; and they were again gliding over this unknown moor.

The bloated and gouty old man, in his horror considered the question of resistance. But his athletic days were long over. This moor was a desert. There was no help to be had. He was in the hands of strange servants, even if his recognition turned out to be a delusion, and they were under the command of his captors. There was nothing for it but submission, for the present.

Suddenly the coach was brought nearly to a standstill, so that the prisoner saw an ominous sight from the window.

It was a gigantic gallows beside the road; it stood three-sided, and from each of its three broad beams at top depended in chains some eight or ten bodies, from several of which the cere-clothes had dropped away, leaving the skeletons swinging lightly by their chains. A tall ladder reached to the summit of the structure, and on the peat beneath lay bones.

On top of the dark transverse beam facing the road, from which, as from the other two completing the triangle of death, dangled a row of these unfortunates in chains, a hangman, with a pipe in his mouth, much as we see him in the famous print of the "Idle Apprentice," though here his perch was ever so much higher, was reclining at his ease and listlessly shying bones, from a little heap at his elbow, at the skeletons that hung round, bringing down now a rib or two, now a hand, now half a leg. A long-sighted man could have discerned that he was a dark fellow, lean; and from continually looking down on the earth from the elevation over which, in another sense, he always hung, his nose, his lips, his chin were pendulous and loose, and drawn down into a monstrous grotesque.

This fellow took his pipe from his mouth on seeing the coach, stood up, and cut some solemn capers high on his beam, and shook a new rope in the air, crying with a voice high and distant as the caw of a raven hovering over a gibbet, "A rope for Judge Harbottle!"

The coach was now driving on at its old swift pace.

So high a gallows as that, the Judge had never, even in his most hilarious moments, dreamed of. He thought he must be raving. And the dead footman! He shook his ears and strained his eyelids; but if he was dreaming, he was unable to awake himself.

There was no good in threatening these scoundrels. A *brutum fulmen* might bring a real one on his head.

Any submission to get out of their hands; and then heaven and earth he would move to unearth and hunt them down.

Suddenly they drove round a corner of a vast white building, and under a *porte-cochère*.

VII   Chief Justice Twofold

The Judge found himself in a corridor lighted with dingy oil lamps, the walls of bare stone; it looked like a passage in a prison. His guards placed him in the hands of other people. Here and there he saw bony and gigantic soldiers passing to and fro, with muskets over their shoulders. They looked straight before them, grinding their teeth, in bleak fury, with no noise but the clank of their shoes. He saw these by glimpses, round corners, and at the ends of passages, but he did not actually pass them by.

And now, passing under a narrow doorway, he found himself in the dock, confronting a judge in his scarlet robes, in a large court-house. There was nothing to elevate this Temple of Themis above its vulgar kind elsewhere. Dingy enough it looked, in spite of candles lighted in decent abundance. A case had just closed, and the last juror's back was seen escaping through the door in the wall of the jury-box. There were some dozen barristers, some fiddling with pen and ink, others buried in briefs, some beckoning, with the plumes of their pens, to their attorneys, of whom there were no lack;

there were clerks to-ing and fro-ing, and the officers of the court, and the registrar, who was handing up a paper to the judge; and the tipstaff, who was presenting a note at the end of his wand to a king's counsel over the heads of the crowd between. If this was the High Court of Appeal, which never rose day or night, it might account for the pale and jaded aspect of everybody in it. An air of indescribable gloom hung upon the pallid features of all the people here; no one ever smiled; all looked more or less secretly suffering.

"The King against Elijah Harbottle!" shouted the officer.

"Is the appellant Lewis Pyneweck in court?" asked Chief-Justice Twofold, in a voice of thunder, that shook the woodwork of the court, and boomed down the corridors.

Up stood Pyneweck from his place at the table.

"Arraign the prisoner!" roared the Chief: and Judge Harbottle felt the panels of the dock round him, and the floor, and the rails quiver in the vibrations of that tremendous voice.

The prisoner, *in limine*, objected to this pretended court, as being a sham, and non-existent in point of law; and then, that, even if it were a court constituted by law (the Judge was growing dazed), it had not and could not have any jurisdiction to try him for his conduct on the bench.

Whereupon the chief-justice laughed suddenly, and every one in court, turning round upon the prisoner, laughed also, till the laugh grew and roared all round like a deafening acclamation; he saw nothing but glittering eyes and teeth, a universal stare and grin; but though all the voices laughed, not a single face of all those that concentrated their gaze upon him looked like a laughing face. The mirth subsided as suddenly as it began.

The indictment was read. Judge Harbottle actually pleaded! He pleaded "Not Guilty." A jury were sworn. The trial proceeded. Judge Harbottle was bewildered. This could not be real. He must be either mad, or *going* mad, he thought.

One thing could not fail to strike even him. This Chief-Justice Twofold, who was knocking him about at every turn with sneer and gibe, and roaring him down with his tremendous voice, was a dilated effigy of himself; an image of Mr. Justice Harbottle, at least double his size, and with all his fierce colouring, and his ferocity of eye and visage, enhanced awfully.

Nothing the prisoner could argue, cite, or state, was permitted to retard for a moment the march of the case towards its catastrophe.

The chief-justice seemed to feel his power over the jury, and to exult and riot in the display of it. He glared at them, he nodded at them; he seemed to have established an understanding with them. The lights were faint in that part of the court. The jurors were mere shadows, sitting in rows; the prisoner could see a dozen pair of white eyes shining, coldly, out of the darkness; and whenever the judge in his charge, which was contemptuously brief, nodded and grinned and gibed, the prisoner could see, in the obscurity, by the dip of all these rows of eyes together, that the jury nodded in acquiescence.

And now the charge was over, the huge chief-justice leaned back panting and gloating on the prisoner. Every one in the court turned about, and gazed with steadfast hatred on the man in the dock. From the jury-box where the twelve sworn brethren were whispering together, a sound in the general stillness like a prolonged ''hiss-s-s!'' was heard; and then, in answer to the challenge of the officer, ''How say you, gentlemen of the jury, guilty or not guilty?'' came in a melancholy voice the finding, ''Guilty.''

The place seemed to the eyes of the prisoner to grow gradually darker and darker, till he could discern nothing distinctly but the lumen of the eyes that were turned upon him from every bench and side and corner and gallery of the building. The prisoner doubtless thought that he had quite enough to say, and conclusive, why sentence of death should not be pronounced upon him; but the lord chief-justice puffed it contemptuously away, like so much smoke, and proceeded to pass sentence of death upon the prisoner, having named the tenth of the ensuing month for his execution.

Before he had recovered the stun of this ominous farce, in obedience to the mandate, "Remove the prisoner," he was led from the dock. The lamps seemed all to have gone out, and there were stoves and charcoal-fires here and there, that threw a faint crimson light on the walls of the corridors through which he passed. The stones that composed them looked now enormous, cracked and unhewn.

He came into a vaulted smithy, where two men, naked to the waist, with heads like bulls, round shoulders, and the arms of giants, were welding red-hot chains together with hammers that pelted like thunderbolts.

They looked on the prisoner with fierce red eyes, and rested on their hammers for a minute; and said the elder to his companion, "Take out Elijah Harbottle's gyves"; and with a pincers he plucked the end which lay dazzling in the fire from the furnace.

"One end locks," said he, taking the cool end of the iron in one hand, while with the grip of a vice he seized the leg of the Judge, and locked the ring round his ankle. "The other," he said with a grin, "is welded."

The iron band that was to form the ring for the other leg lay still red hot upon the stone floor, with brilliant sparks sporting up and down its surface.

His companion, in his gigantic hands, seized the old Judge's other leg, and pressed his foot immovably to the stone floor; while his senior, in a twinkling, with a masterly application of pincers and hammer, sped the glowing bar round his ankle so tight that the skin and sinews smoked and bubbled again, and old Judge Harbottle uttered a yell that seemed to chill the very stones, and make the iron chains quiver on the wall.

Chains, vaults, smiths, and smithy all vanished in a moment; but the pain continued. Mr. Justice Harbottle was suffering torture all round the ankle on which the infernal smiths had just been operating.

His friends, Thavies and Beller were startled by the Judge's roar in the midst of their elegant trifling about a marriage *à-la-mode* case which was going on. The Judge was in panic as well as pain. The street lamps and the light of his own hall door restored him.

"I'm very bad," growled he between his set teeth; "my foot's blazing. Who was he that hurt my foot? 'Tis the gout—'tis the gout!" he said, awaking completely. "How many hours have we been coming from the playhouse? 'Sblood, what has happened on the way? I've slept half the night!"

There had been no hitch or delay, and they had driven home at a good pace.

The Judge, however, was in gout; he was feverish too; and the attack, though very short, was sharp; and when, in about a fortnight, it subsided, his ferocious joviality did not return. He could not get this dream, as he chose to call it, out of his head.

VIII   Somebody Has Got Into the House

People remarked that the Judge was in the vapours. His doctor said he should go for a fortnight to Buxton.

Whenever the Judge fell into a brown study, he was always conning over the terms of the sentence pronounced upon him in his vision—"in one calendar month from the date of this day"; and then the usual form, "and you shall be hanged by the neck till you are dead," etc. "That will be the 10th—I'm not much in the way of being hanged. I know what stuff dreams are, and I laugh at them; but this is continually in my thoughts, as if it forecast misfortune of some sort. I wish the day my dream gave me were passed and over. I wish I were well purged of my gout. I wish I were as I used to be. 'Tis nothing but vapours, nothing but a maggot." The copy of the parchment and letter which had announced his trial with many a snort and sneer he would read over and over again, and the scenery and people of his dream would rise about him in places the most unlikely, and steal him in a moment from all that surrounded him into a world of shadows.

The Judge had lost his iron energy and banter. He was growing taciturn and morose. The Bar remarked the change, as well they might. His friends thought him ill. The doctor said he was troubled with hypochondria, and that his gout was still lurking in his system, and ordered him to that ancient haunt of crutches and chalk-stones, Buxton.

The Judge's spirits were very low; he was frightened about himself; and he described to his housekeeper, having sent for her to his study to drink a dish of tea, his strange dream in his drive home from Drury Lane Playhouse. He was sinking into the state of nervous dejection in which men lose their faith in orthodox advice, and in despair consult quacks, astrologers, and nursery story-tellers. Could such a dream mean that he was to have a fit, and so die on the 10th? She did not think so. On the contrary, it was certain some good luck must happen on that day.

The Judge kindled; and for the first time for many days, he looked for a minute or two like himself, and he tapped her on the cheek with the hand that was not in flannel.

"Odsbud! odsheart! you dear rogue! I had forgot. There is young Tom—yellow Tom, my nephew, you know, lies sick at Harrogate; why shouldn't he go that day as well as another, and if he does, I get an estate by it? Why, lookee, I asked Doctor Hedstone yesterday if I was like to take a fit any time, and he laughed, and swore I was the last man in town to go off that way."

The Judge sent most of his servants down to Buxton to make his lodgings and all things comfortable for him. He was to follow in a day or two.

It was now the 9th; and the next day well over, he might laugh at his visions and auguries.

On the evening of the 9th, Dr. Hedstone's footman knocked at the Judge's door. The Doctor ran up the dusky stairs to the drawing-room. It was a March evening, near the hour of sunset, with an east wind whistling sharply through the chimney-stacks. A wood fire blazed cheerily on the hearth. And Judge Harbottle, in what was then called a brigadier-wig, with his red roquelaure on, helped the glowing effect of the darkened chamber, which looked red all over like a room on fire.

The Judge had his feet on a stool, and his huge grim purple face confronted the fire, and seemed to pant and swell, as the blaze alternately spread upward and collapsed. He had fallen again among his blue devils, and was thinking of retiring from the Bench, and of fifty other gloomy things.

But the Doctor, who was an energetic son of Æsculapius, would listen to no croaking, told the Judge he was full of gout, and in his present condition no judge even of his own case, but promised him leave to pronounce on all those melancholy questions, a fortnight later.

In the meantime the Judge must be very careful. He was over-charged with gout, and he must not provoke an attack, till the waters of Buxton should do that office for him, in their own salutary way.

The Doctor did not think him perhaps quite so well as he pretended, for he told him he wanted rest, and would be better if he went forthwith to his bed.

Mr. Gerningham, his valet, assisted him, and gave him his drops; and the Judge told him to wait in his bedroom till he should go to sleep.

Three persons that night had specially odd stories to tell.

The housekeeper had got rid of the trouble of amusing her little girl at this anxious time, by giving her leave to run about the sitting-rooms and look at the pictures and china, on the usual condition of touching nothing. It was not until the last gleam of sunset had for some time faded, and the twilight had so deepened that she could no longer discern the colours on the china figures on the chimneypiece or in the cabinets, that the child returned to the housekeeper's room to find her mother.

To her she related, after some prattle about the china, and the pictures, and the Judge's two grand wigs in the dressing-room off the library, an adventure of an extraordinary kind.

In the hall was placed, as was customary in those times, the sedan-chair which the master of the house occasionally used, covered with stamped leather, and studded with gilt nails, and with its red silk blinds down. In this case, the doors of this old-fashioned conveyance were locked, the windows up, and, as I said, the blinds down, but not so closely that the curious child could not peep underneath one of them, and see into the interior.

A parting beam from the setting sun, admitted through the window of a back room, shot obliquely through the open door, and lighting on the chair, shone with a dull transparency through the crimson blind.

To her surprise, the child saw in the shadow a thin man, dressed in black, seated in it; he had sharp dark features; his nose, she fancied, a little awry, and his brown eyes were looking straight before him; his hand was on his thigh, and he stirred no more than the waxen figure she had seen at Southwark fair.

A child so often lectured for asking questions, and on the propriety of silence, and the superior wisdom of its elders, that it accepts most things at last in good faith; and the little girl acquiesced respectfully in the occupation of the chair by this mahogany-faced person as being all right and proper.

It was not until she asked her mother who this man was, and observed her scared face as she questioned her more minutely upon the appearance of the stranger, that she began to understand that she had seen something unaccountable.

Mrs. Carwell took the key of the chair from its nail over the footman's shelf, and led the child by the hand up to the hall, having a lighted candle in her other hand. She stopped at a distance from the chair, and placed the candlestick in the child's hand.

"Peep in, Margery, again, and try if there's anything there," she whispered; "hold the candle near the blind so as to throw its light through the curtain."

The child peeped, this time with a very solemn face, and intimated at once that he was gone.

"Look again, and be sure," urged her mother.

The little girl was quite certain; and Mrs. Carwell, with her mob-cap of lace and cherry-coloured ribbons, and her dark brown hair, not yet powdered, over a very pale face, unlocked the door, looked in, and beheld emptiness.

"All a mistake, child, you see."

"*There!* ma'am! see there! He's gone round the corner," said the child.

"Where?" said Mrs. Carwell, stepping backward a step.

"Into that room."

"Tut, child! 'twas the shadow," cried Mrs. Carwell, angrily, because she was frightened. "I moved the candle." But she clutched one of the poles of the chair, which leant against the wall in the corner, and pounded the floor furiously with one end of it, being afraid to pass the open door the child had pointed to.

The cook and two kitchen-maids came running upstairs, not knowing what to make of the unwonted alarm.

They all searched the room; but it was still and empty, and no sign of any one's having been there.

Some people may suppose that the direction given to her thoughts by this odd little incident will account for a very strange illusion which Mrs. Carwell herself experienced about two hours later.

IX   The Judge Leaves His House

Mrs. Flora Carwell was going up the great staircase with a posset for the Judge in a china bowl, on a little silver tray.

Across the top of the well-staircase there runs a massive oak rail; and, raising her eyes accidentally, she saw an extremely odd-looking stranger, slim and long, leaning carelessly over with a pipe between his finger and thumb. Nose, lips, and chin seemed all to droop downward into extraordinary length, as he leant his odd peering face over the banister. In his other hand he held a coil of rope, one end of which escaped from under his elbow and hung over the rail.

Mrs. Carwell, who had no suspicion at the moment, that he was not a real person, and fancied that he was some one employed in cording the Judge's luggage, called to know what he was doing there.

Instead of answering, he turned about, and walked across the lobby, at about the same leisurely pace at which she was ascending, and entered a room, into which she followed him. It was an uncarpeted and unfurnished chamber. An open trunk lay upon the floor empty, and beside it the coil of rope; but except herself there was no one in the room.

Mrs. Carwell was very much frightened, and now concluded that the child must have seen the same ghost that had just appeared to her. Perhaps, when she was able to think it over, it was a relief to believe so; for the face, figure, and dress described by the child were awfully like Pyneweck; and this certainly was not he.

Very much scared and very hysterical, Mrs. Carwell ran down to her room, afraid to look over her shoulder, and got some companions about her, and wept, and talked, and drank more than one cordial, and talked and wept again, and so on, until, in those early days, it was ten o'clock, and time to go to bed.

A scullery-maid remained up finishing some of her scouring and "scalding" for some time after the other servants—who, as I said, were few in number—that night had got to their beds. This was a low-browed, broad-faced, intrepid wench with black hair, who did not "vally a ghost not a button," and treated the housekeeper's hysterics with measureless scorn.

The old house was quiet now. It was near twelve o'clock, no sounds were audible except the muffled wailing of the wintry winds, piping high among the roofs and chimneys, or rumbling at intervals, in under gusts, through the narrow channels of the street.

The spacious solitudes of the kitchen level were awfully

dark, and this sceptical kitchen-wench was the only person now up and about in the house. She hummed tunes to herself, for a time; and then stopped and listened; and then resumed her work again. At last, she was destined to be more terrified than even was the housekeeper.

There was a back kitchen in this house, and from this she heard, as if coming from below its foundations, a sound like heavy strokes, that seemed to shake the earth beneath her feet. Sometimes a dozen in sequence, at regular intervals; sometimes fewer. She walked out softly into the passage, and was surprised to see a dusky glow issuing from this room, as if from a charcoal fire.

The room seemed thick with smoke.

Looking in she very dimly beheld a monstrous figure, over a furnace, beating with a mighty hammer the rings and rivets of a chain.

The strokes, swift and heavy as they looked, sounded hollow and distant. The man stopped, and pointed to something on the floor, that, through the smoky haze, looked, she thought, like a dead body. She remarked no more; but the servants in the room close by, startled from their sleep by a hideous scream, found her in a swoon on the flags, close to the door, where she had just witnessed this ghastly vision.

Startled by the girl's incoherent asseverations that she had seen the Judge's corpse on the floor, two servants having first searched the lower part of the house, went rather frightened up-stairs to inquire whether their master was well. They found him, not in his bed, but in his room. He had a table with candles burning at his bedside, and was getting on his clothes again; and he swore and cursed at them roundly in his old style, telling them that he had business, and that he would discharge on the spot any scoundrel who should dare to disturb him again.

So the invalid was left to his quietude.

In the morning it was rumoured here and there in the street that the Judge was dead. A servant was sent from the house three doors away, by Counsellor Traverse, to inquire at Judge Harbottle's hall-door.

The servant who opened it was pale and reserved, and would only say that the Judge was ill. He had had a dangerous accident; Doctor Hedstone had been with him at seven o'clock in the morning.

There were averted looks, short answers, pale and frowning faces, and all the usual signs that there was a secret that sat heavily upon their minds, and the time for disclosing which had not yet come. That time would arrive when the coroner had arrived, and the mortal scandal that had befallen the house could be no longer hidden. For that morning Mr. Justice Harbottle had been found hanging by the neck from the banister at the top of the great staircase, and quite dead.

There was not the smallest sign of any struggle or resistance. There had not been heard a cry or any other noise in the slightest degree indicative of violence. There was medical evidence to show that, in his atrabilious state, it was quite on the cards that he might have made away with himself. The jury found accordingly that it was a case of suicide. But to those who were acquainted with the strange story which Judge Harbottle had related to at least two persons, the fact that the catastrophe occurred on the morning of March 10th seemed a startling coincidence.

A few days after, the pomp of a great funeral attended him to the grave; and so, in the language of Scripture, "the rich man died, and was buried."

Ray Bradbury

THE CROWD

For just over a decade, from the early 1940s to the late
1950s, Ray Bradbury produced an extraordinary body
of work in the short story form, stories of science fiction,
fantasy and horror, work that was quickly recognized as
a significant contribution to American literature. The
thread of dark fantasy is woven throughout his works.
His first book, the collection *Dark Carnival* (Arkham
House, 1947), was primarily supernatural horror fiction
and his later masterpieces, *The Martian Chronicles*
(1950), *The Illustrated Man* (1951), *The Golden Apples
of the Sun* (1953), *The October Country* (1955) and
Something Wicked This Way Comes (1959), all contain
horror stories in his characteristic mode: overt moral
consciousness in the face of evil. The ordinary man is
faced with an evil just too big and organized to overcome. It is interesting to compare "The Crowd" to Harlan Ellison's "The Whimper of Whipped Dogs."

Mr. Spallner put his hands over his face.
    There was the feeling of movement in space, the
beautifully tortured scream, the impact and tumbling of the
car with wall, through wall, over and down like a toy, and
him hurled out of it. Then—silence.
    The crowd came running. Faintly, where he lay, he heard

them running. He could tell their ages and their sizes by
the sound of their numerous feet over the summer grass and
on the lined pavement, and over the asphalt street, and picking through the cluttered bricks to where his car hung half
into the night sky, still spinning its wheels with senseless
centrifuge.

Where the crowd came from he didn't know. He struggled
to remain aware and then the crowd faces hemmed in upon
him, hung over him like the large glowing leaves of down-
bent trees. They were a ring of shifting, compressing, changing faces over him, looking down, looking down, reading the
time of his life or death by his face, making his face into a
moon-dial, where the moon cast a shadow from his nose out
upon his cheek to tell the time of breathing or not breathing
any more ever.

How swiftly a crowd comes, he thought, like the iris of an
eye compressing in out of nowhere.

A siren. A police voice. Movement. Blood trickled from
his lips and he was being moved into an ambulance. Someone said, "Is he dead?" And someone else said, "No, he's
not dead." And a third person said, "He won't die, he's not
going to die." And he saw the faces of the crowd beyond
him in the night, and he knew by their expressions that he
wouldn't die. And that was strange. He saw a man's face,
thin, bright, pale; the man swallowed and bit his lips, very
sick. There was a small woman, too, with red hair and too
much red on her cheeks and lips. And a little boy with a
freckled face. Others' faces. An old man with a wrinkled
upper lip, an old woman, with a mole upon her chin. They
had all come from—where? Houses, cars, alleys, from the
immediate and the accident-shocked world. Out of alleys and
out of hotels and out of streetcars and seemingly out of nothing they came.

The crowd looked at him and he looked back at them and
did not like them at all. There was a vast wrongness to them.
He couldn't put his finger on it. They were far worse than
this machine-made thing that happened to him now.

The ambulance doors slammed. Through the windows he saw the crowd looking in, looking in. That crowd that always came so fast, so strangely fast, to form a circle, to peer down, to probe, to gawk, to question, to point, to disturb, to spoil the privacy of a man's agony by their frank curiosity.

The ambulance drove off. He sank back and their faces still stared into his face, even with his eyes shut.

The car wheels spun in his mind for days. One wheel, four wheels, spinning, spinning, and whirring, around and around.

He knew it was wrong. Something wrong with the wheels and the whole accident and the running of feet and the curiosity. The crowd faces mixed and spun into the wild rotation of the wheels.

He awoke.

Sunlight, a hospital room, a hand taking his pulse.

"How do you feel?" asked the doctor.

The wheels faded away. Mr. Spallner looked around.

"Fine—I guess."

He tried to find words. About the accident. "Doctor?"

"Yes?"

"That crowd—was it last night?"

"Two days ago. You've been here since Thursday. You're all right, though. You're doing fine. Don't try and get up."

"That crowd. Something about wheels, too. Do accidents make people, well, a—little off?"

"Temporarily, sometimes."

He lay staring up at the doctor. "Does it hurt your time sense?"

"Panic sometimes does."

"Makes a minute seem like an hour, or maybe an hour seem like a minute?"

"Yes."

"Let me tell you then." He felt the bed under him, the sunlight on his face. "You'll think I'm crazy. I was driving too fast, I know. I'm sorry now. I jumped the curb and hit that wall. I was hurt and numb, I know, but I still remember

things. Mostly—the crowd.'' He waited a moment and then
decided to go on, for he suddenly knew what it was that
bothered him. ''The crowd got there too quickly. Thirty seconds after the smash they were all standing over me and staring at me . . . it's not right they should run that fast, so late
at night. . . .''

''You only think it was thirty seconds,'' said the doctor.
''It was probably three or four minutes. Your senses—''

''Yeah, I know—my senses, the accident. But I was conscious! I remember one thing that puts it all together and
makes it funny. God, so damned funny. The wheels of my
car, upside down. The wheels were still spinning when the
crowd got there!''

The doctor smiled.

The man in bed went on. ''I'm positive! The wheels were
spinning and spinning fast—the front wheels! Wheels don't
spin very long, friction cuts them down. And these were really spinning!''

''You're confused,'' said the doctor.

''I'm not confused. That street was empty. Not a soul in
sight. And then the accident and the wheels still spinning and
all those faces over me, quick, in no time. And the way they
looked down at me, I *knew* I wouldn't die. . . .''

''Simple shock,'' said the doctor, walking away into the
sunlight.

They released him from the hospital two weeks later. He
rode home in a taxi. People had come to visit him during his
two weeks on his back, and to all of them he had told his
story, the accident, the spinning wheels, the crowd. They had
all laughed with him concerning it, and passed it off.

He leaned forward and tapped on the taxi window.

''What's wrong?''

The cabbie looked back. ''Sorry, boss. This is one helluva
town to drive in. Got an accident up ahead. Want me to
detour?''

''Yes. No. No! Wait. Go ahead. Let's—let's take a look.''

The cab moved forward, honking.

"Funny damn thing," said the cabbie. "Hey, *you*! Get that fleatrap out the way!" Quieter, "Funny thing—more damn people. Nosy people."

Mr. Spallner looked down and watched his fingers tremble on his knee. "You noticed that, too?"

"Sure," said the cabbie. "All the time. There's always a crowd. You'd think it was their own mother got killed."

"They come running awfully fast," said the man in the back of the cab.

"Same way with a fire or an explosion. Nobody around. Boom. Lotsa people around. I dunno."

"Ever seen an accident—at night?"

The cabbie nodded. "Sure. Don't make no difference. There's always a crowd."

The wreck came in view. A body lay on the pavement. You knew there was a body even if you couldn't see it. Because of the crowd. The crowd with its back toward him as he sat in the rear of the cab. With its back toward him. He opened the window and almost started to yell. But he didn't have the nerve. If he yelled they might turn around.

And he was afraid to see their faces.

"I seem to have a penchant for accidents," he said, in his office. It was late afternoon. His friend sat across the desk from him, listening. "I got out of the hospital this morning and first thing on the way home, we detoured around a wreck."

"Things run in cycles," said Morgan.

"Let me tell you about my accident."

"I've heard it. Heard it all."

"But it was funny, you must admit."

"I must admit. Now how about a drink?"

They talked on for half an hour or more. All the while they talked, at the back of Spallner's brain a small watch ticked, a watch that never needed winding. It was the memory of a few little things. Wheels and faces.

At about five-thirty there was a hard metal noise in the street. Morgan nodded and looked out and down. "What'd I tell you? Cycles. A truck and a cream-colored Cadillac. Yes, yes."

Spallner walked to the window. He was very cold and as he stood there, he looked at his watch, at the small minute hand. One two three four five seconds—people running—eight nine ten eleven twelve—from all over, people came running—fifteen sixteen seventeen eighteen seconds—more people, more cars, more horns blowing. Curiously distant, Spallner looked upon the scene as an explosion in reverse, the fragments of the detonation sucked back to the point of impulsion. Nineteen, twenty, twenty-one seconds and the crowd was there. Spallner made a gesture down at them, wordless.

The crowd had gathered so fast.

He saw a woman's body a moment before the crowd swallowed it up.

Morgan said, "You look lousy. Here. Finish your drink."

"I'm all right, I'm all right. Let me alone. I'm all right. Can you see those people? Can you see any of them? I wish we could see them closer."

Morgan cried out, "Where in hell are you going?"

Spallner was out the door, Morgan after him, and down the stairs, as rapidly as possible. "Come along, and hurry."

"Take it easy, you're not a well man!"

They walked out on to the street. Spallner pushed his way forward. He thought he saw a red-haired woman with too much red color on her cheeks and lips.

"There!" He turned wildly to Morgan. "Did you see her?"

"See *who*?"

"Damn it; she's gone. The crowd closed in!"

The crowd was all around, breathing and looking and shuffling and mixing and mumbling and getting in the way when he tried to shove through. Evidently the red-haired woman had seen him coming and run off.

He saw another familiar face! A little freckled boy. But there are many freckled boys in the world. And, anyway, it was no use, before Spallner reached him, this little boy ran away and vanished among the people.

"Is she dead?" a voice asked. "Is she dead?"

"She's dying," someone else replied. "She'll be dead before the ambulance arrives. They shouldn't have moved her. They shouldn't have moved her."

All the crowd faces—familiar, yet unfamiliar, bending over, looking down, looking down.

"Hey, mister, stop pushing."

"Who you shovin', buddy?"

Spallner came back out, and Morgan caught hold of him before he fell. "You damned fool. You're still sick. Why in hell'd you have to come down here?" Morgan demanded.

"I don't know, I really don't. They moved her, Morgan, someone moved her. You should never move a traffic victim. It kills them. It kills them."

"Yeah. That's the way with people. The idiots."

Spallner arranged the newspaper clippings carefully.

Morgan looked at them. "What's the idea? Ever since your accident you think every traffic scramble is part of you. What are these?"

"Clippings of motor-car crackups, and photos. Look at them. Not at the cars," said Spallner, "but at the crowds around the cars." He pointed. "Here. Compare this photo of a wreck in the Wilshire District with one in Westwood. No resemblance. But now take this Westwood picture and align it with one taken in the Westwood District ten years ago." Again he motioned. "This woman is in both pictures."

"Coincidence. The woman happened to be there once in 1936, again in 1946."

"A coincidence once, maybe. But twelve times over a period of ten years, when the accidents occurred as much as three miles from one another, no. Here." He dealt out a dozen photographs. "She's in *all* of these!"

"Maybe she's perverted."

"She's more than that. How does she *happen* to be there so quickly after each accident? And why does she wear the same clothes in pictures taken over a period of a decade?"

"I'll be damned, so she does."

"And, last of all, why was she standing over *me* the night of my accident, two weeks ago!"

They had a drink. Morgan went over the files. "What'd you do, hire a clipping service while you were in the hospital to go back through the newspapers for you?" Spallner nodded. Morgan sipped his drink. It was getting late. The street lights were coming on in the streets below the office. "What does all this add up to?"

"I don't know," said Spallner, "except that there's a universal law about accidents. *Crowds gather.* They always gather. And like you and me, people have wondered year after year, why they gathered so quickly, and how? I know the answer. Here it is!"

He flung the clippings down. "It frightens me."

"These people—mightn't they be thrill-hunters, perverted sensationalists with a carnal lust for blood and morbidity?"

Spallner shrugged. "Does that explain their being at all the accidents? Notice, they stick to certain territories. A Brentwood accident will bring out one group. A Huntington Park another. But there's a norm for faces, a certain percentage appear at each wreck."

Morgan said, "They're not *all* the same faces, are they?"

"Naturally not. Accidents draw normal people, too, in the course of time. But these, I find, are always the *first* ones there."

"Who are they? What do they want? You keep hinting and never telling. Good Lord, you must have some idea. You've scared yourself and now you've got me jumping."

"I've tried getting to them, but someone always trips me up, I'm always too late. They slip into the crowd and vanish. The crowd seems to offer protection to some of its members. They see me coming."

"Sounds like some sort of clique."

"They have one thing in common, they always show up together. At a fire or an explosion or on the sidelines of a war, at any public demonstration of this thing called death. Vultures, hyenas or saints, I don't know which they are, I just don't know. But I'm going to the police with it, this evening. It's gone on long enough. One of them shifted that woman's body today. They shouldn't have touched her. It killed her."

He placed the clippings in a briefcase. Morgan got up and slipped into his coat. Spallner clicked the briefcase shut. "Or, I just happened to think . . ."

"What?"

"Maybe they *wanted* her dead."

"Why?"

"Who knows. Come along?"

"Sorry. It's late. See you tomorrow. Luck." They went out together. "Give my regards to the cops. Think they'll believe you?"

"Oh, they'll believe me all right. Good night."

Spallner took it slow driving downtown.

"I want to get there," he told himself, "alive."

He was rather shocked, but not surprised, somehow, when the truck came rolling out of an alley straight at him. He was just congratulating himself on his keen sense of observation and talking out what he would say to the police in his mind, when the truck smashed into his car. It wasn't really his car, that was the disheartening thing about it. In a preoccupied mood he was tossed first this way and then that way, while he thought, what a shame, Morgan has gone and lent me his extra car for a few days until my other car is fixed, and now here I go again. The windshield hammered back into his face. He was forced back and forth in several lightning jerks. Then all motion stopped and all noise stopped and only pain filled him up.

He heard their feet running and running and running. He fumbled with the car door. It clicked. He fell out upon the pavement drunkenly and lay, ear to the asphalt, listening to them coming. It was like a great rainstorm, with many drops, heavy and light and medium, touching the earth. He waited a few seconds and listened to their coming and their arrival. Then, weakly, expectantly, he rolled his head up and looked.

The crowd was there.

He could smell their breaths, the mingled odors of many people sucking and sucking on the air a man needs to live by. They crowded and jostled and sucked and sucked all the air up from around his gasping face until he tried to tell them to move back, they were making him live in a vacuum. His head was bleeding very badly. He tried to move and he realized something was wrong with his spine. He hadn't felt much at the impact, but his spine was hurt. He didn't dare move.

He couldn't speak. Opening his mouth, nothing came out but a gagging.

Someone said, "Give me a hand. We'll roll him over and lift him into a more comfortable position."

Spallner's brain burst apart.

No! Don't move me!

"We'll move him," said the voice, casually.

You idiots, you'll kill me, don't!

But he could not say any of this out loud. He could only think it.

Hands took hold of him. They started to lift him. He cried out and nausea choked him up. They straightened him out into a ramrod of agony. Two men did it. One of them was thin, bright, pale, alert, a young man. The other man was very old and had a wrinkled upper lip.

He had seen their faces before.

A familiar voice said, "Is—is he dead?"

Another voice, a memorable voice, responded, "No. Not yet. But he will be dead before the ambulance arrives."

It was all a very silly, mad plot. Like every accident. He squealed hysterically at the solid wall of faces. They were all around him, these judges and jurors with the faces he had seen before. Through his pain he counted their faces.

The freckled boy. The old man with the wrinkled upper lip.

The red-haired, red-cheeked woman. An old woman with a mole on her chin.

I know what you're here for, he thought. You're here just as you're at all accidents. To make certain the right ones live and the right ones die. That's why you lifted me. You knew it would kill. You knew I'd live if you left me alone.

And that's the way it's been since time began, when crowds gather. You murder much easier, this way. Your alibi is very simple; you didn't know it was dangerous to move a hurt man. You didn't mean to hurt him.

He looked at them, above him, and he was curious as a man under deep water looking up at people on a bridge. Who are you? Where do you come from and how do you get here so soon? You're the crowd that's always in the way, using up good air that a dying man's lungs are in need of, using up space he should be using to lie in, alone. Tramping on people to make sure they die, that's you. I know *all* of you.

It was like a polite monologue. They said nothing. Faces. The old man. The red-haired woman.

Someone picked up his briefcase. "Whose is this?" they asked.

It's mine! It's evidence against all of you!

Eyes, inverted over him. Shiny eyes under tousled hair or under hats.

Faces.

Somewhere—a siren. The ambulance was coming.

But, looking at the faces, the construction, the cast, the

form of the faces, Spallner saw it was too late. He read it in their faces. They *knew*.

He tried to speak. A little bit got out:

"It—looks like I'll—be joining up with you. I—guess I'll be a member of your—group—now."

He closed his eyes then, and waited for the coroner.

Michael Shea

THE AUTOPSY

Michael Shea's science fiction has twice been nominated for the Nebula Award (once for the story herein)
and he has won the World Fantasy Award for his book,
Nifft the Lean. His strength as a writer is, however, in
the horror mode regardless of genre or category and he
is perhaps the most under-appreciated of the major contemporary talents working in horror—although perhaps
this will be remedied by his forthcoming collection from
Arkham House, at least in part. "The Autopsy" is horror
in the science fiction category, a transformation of the
myth of demonic possession into the realm of objective
science. Shea's cinematic effects compare favorably
with such newer talents as Clive Barker, colorful and
unflinchingly clinical. And this story uses some of Lovecraft's conventions more effectively than any other contemporary horror writer. Shea has been growing in
strength for more than a decade and belongs already to
the company of the best writers of horror today.

Dr. Winters stepped out of the tiny Greyhound station and
into the midnight street that smelt of pines and the river,
though the street was in the heart of the town. But then it
was a town of only five main streets in breadth, and these
extended scarcely a mile and a half along the rim of the

gorge. Deep in that gorge though the river ran, its blurred roar flowed, perfectly distinct, between the banks of dark shop windows. The station's window showed the only light, save for a luminous clock face several doors down and a little neon beer logo two blocks farther on. When he had walked a short distance, Dr. Winters set his suitcase down, pocketed his hands, and looked at the stars—thick as cobblestones in the black gulf.

"A mountain hamlet—a mining town," he said. "Stars. No moon. We are in Bailey."

He was talking to his cancer. It was in his stomach. Since learning of it, he had developed this habit of wry communion with it. He meant to show courtesy to this uninvited guest. Death. It would not find him churlish, for that would make its victory absolute. Except, of course, that its victory would *be* absolute, with or without his ironies.

He picked up his suitcase and walked on. The starlight made faint mirrors of the windows' blackness and showed him the man who passed: lizard-lean, white-haired (at fifty-seven), a man traveling on death's business, carrying his own death in him, and even bearing death's wardrobe in his suitcase. For this was filled—aside from his medical kit and some scant necessities—with mortuary bags. The sheriff had told him on the phone of the improvisations that presently enveloped the corpses, and so the doctor had packed these, laying them in his case with bitter amusement, checking the last one's breadth against his chest before the mirror, as a woman will gauge a dress before donning it, and telling his cancer:

"Oh, yes, that's plenty roomy enough for both of us!"

The case was heavy and he stopped frequently to rest and scan the sky. What a night's work to do, probing soulless filth, eyes earthward, beneath such a ceiling of stars! It had taken five days to dig them out. The autumnal equinox had passed, but the weather here had been uniformly hot. And warmer still, no doubt, so deep in the earth.

He entered the courthouse by a side door. His heels knocked on the linoleum corridor. A door at the end of it, on which was lettered NATE CRAVEN, COUNTY SHERIFF, opened well before he reached it, and his friend stepped out to meet him.

"Damnit, Carl, you're *still* so thin they could use you for a whip. Gimme that. You're in too good a shape already. You don't need the exercise."

The case hung weightless from his hand, imparting no tilt at all to his bull shoulders. Despite his implied self-derogation, he was only moderately paunched for a man his age and size. He had a rough-hewn face and the bulk of brow, nose, and jaw made his greenish eyes look small until one engaged them and felt the snap and penetration of their intelligence. He half-filled two cups from a coffee urn and topped both off with bourbon from a bottle in his desk. When they had finished these, they had finished trading news of mutual friends. The sheriff mixed another round, and sipped from his, in a silence clearly prefatory to the work at hand.

"They talk about rough justice," he said. "I've sure seen it now. One of those . . . patients of yours that you'll be working on? He was a killer. 'Killer' don't even half say it, really. You could say that *he* got justly executed in that blast. That much was justice for damn sure. But rough as hell on those other nine. And the rough don't just stop with their being dead either. That kiss-ass boss of yours! He's breaking his god-damned back touching his toes for Fordham Mutual. How much of the picture did he give you?"

"You refer, I take it, to the estimable Coroner Waddleton of Fordham County." Dr. Winters paused to sip his drink. With a delicate flaring of his nostrils he communicated all the disgust, contempt and amusement he had felt in his four years as Pathologist in Waddleton's office. The sheriff laughed.

"Clear pictures seldom emerge from anything the coroner says," the doctor continued. "He took your name in vain. Vigorously and repeatedly. These expressions formed his opening remarks. He then developed the theme of our office's strict responsibility to the letter of the law, and of the workmen's compensation law in particular. Death benefits accrue only to the dependents of decedents whose deaths arise *out of the course* of their employment, not merely *in* the course of it. Victims of a maniacal assault, though they did die on the job, are by no means necessarily compensable under the law. We then contemplated the tragic injustice of an insurance company—*any* insurance company—having to pay benefits to unentitled persons, solely through the laxity and incompetence of investigating officers. Your name came up again.''

Craven uttered a bark of mirth and fury. ''The impartial public servant! Ha! The impartial brown-nose, flim-flam and bullshit man is what he *is*. Ten to one, Fordham Mutual will slip out of it *without* his help, and those men's families won't see a goddamn nickel.'' Words were an insufficient vent; the sheriff turned and spat into his wastebasket. He drained his cup, and sighed. ''I beg your pardon, Carl. We've been five days digging those men out and the last two days sifting half that mountain for explosive traces, with those insurance investigators hanging on our elbows, and the most they could say was that there was 'strong presumptive evidence' of a bomb. Well, I don't budge for that because I don't have to. Waddleton can shove his 'extraordinary circumstances.' If you don't find anything in those bodies, then that's all the autopsy there is to it, and they get buried right here where their families want 'em.''

The doctor was smiling at his friend. He finished his cup and spoke with his previous wry detachment, as if the sheriff had not interrupted.

''The honorable coroner then spoke with remarkable volubility on the subject of Autopsy Consent forms and the malicious subversion of private citizens by vested officers of the law. He had, as it happened, a sheaf of such forms on his desk, all signed, all with a rider clause typed in above the signatures. A cogent paragraph. It had, among its other qualities, the property of turning the coroner's face purple when he read it aloud. He read it aloud to me three times. It appeared that the survivors' consent was contingent on two conditions: that the autopsy be performed *in locem mortis*, this is to say in Bailey, and that only if the coroner's pathologist found concrete evidence of homicide should the decedents be subject either to removal from Bailey or to further necropsy. It was well written. I remember wondering who wrote it."

The sheriff nodded musingly. He took Dr. Winters' empty cup, set it by his own, filled both two-thirds with bourbon, and added a splash of coffee to the doctor's. The two friends exchanged a level stare, rather like poker players in the clinch. The sheriff regarded his cup, sipped from it.

"*In locem mortis*. What-all does that mean exactly?"

" 'In the place of death.' "

"Oh. Freshen that up for you?"

"I've just started it, thank you."

Both men laughed, paused, and laughed again, some might have said immoderately.

"He all but told me that I *had* to find something to compel a second autopsy," the doctor said at length. "He would have sold his soul—or taken out a second mortgage on it—for a mobile x-ray unit. He's right of course. If those bodies have trapped any bomb fragments, that would be the surest and quickest way of finding them. It still amazes me your Dr. Parsons could let his x-ray go unfixed for so long."

"He sets bones, stitches wounds, writes prescriptions, and sends anything tricky down the mountain. Just barely manages that. Drunks don't get much done."

"He's gotten that bad?"

"He hangs on and no more. Waddleton was right there, not deputizing him pathologist. I doubt he could find a cannonball in a dead rat. I wouldn't say it where it could hurt him, as long as he's still managing, but everyone here knows it. His patients sort of look after *him* half the time. But Waddleton would have sent you, no matter who was here. Nothing but his best for party contributors like Fordham Mutual."

The doctor looked at his hands and shrugged. "So. There's a killer in the batch. *Was* there a bomb?"

Slowly, the sheriff planted his elbows on the desk and pressed his hands against his temples, as if the question had raised a turbulence of memories. For the first time the doctor—half harkening throughout the never-quite-muted stirrings of the death within him—saw his friend's exhaustion: the tremor of hand, the bruised look under the eyes.

"I'm going to give you what I have, Carl. I told you I don't think you'll find a damn thing in those bodies. You're probably going to end up assuming what I do about it, but assuming is as far as anyone's going to get with this one. It is truly one of those Nightmare Specials that the good Lord tortures lawmen with and then hides the answers to forever.

"All right then. About two months ago, we had a man disappear—Ronald Hanley. Mine worker, rock-steady, family man. He didn't come home one night, and we never found a trace of him. OK, that happens sometimes. About a week later, the lady that ran the laundromat, Sharon Starker, *she* disappeared, no trace. We got edgy then. I made an announcement on the local radio about a possible weirdo at large, spelled out special precautions everybody should take. We put both our squadcars on the night beat, and by day we set to work knocking on every door in town collecting alibis for the two times of disappearance.

"No good. Maybe you're fooled by this uniform and think I'm a law officer, protector of the people, and all that? A natural mistake. A lot of people were fooled. In less than seven weeks, six people vanished, just like that. Me and my deputies might as well have stayed in bed round the clock, for all the good we did." The sheriff drained his cup.

"Anyway, at last we got lucky. Don't get me wrong now. We didn't go all hog-wild and actually prevent a crime or anything. But we *did* find a body—except it wasn't the body of any of the seven people that had disappeared. We'd took to combing the woods nearest town, with temporary deputies from the miners to help. Well, one of those boys was out there with us last week. It was hot—like it's been for a while now—and it was real quiet. He heard this buzzing noise and looked around for it, and he saw a bee-swarm up in the crotch of a tree. Except he was smart enough to know that that's not usual around here—bee hives. So it wasn't bees. It was blue-bottle flies, a god-damned big cloud of them, all over a bundle that was wrapped in a tarp.''

The sheriff studied his knuckles. He had, in his eventful life, occasionally met men literate enough to understand his last name and rash enough to be openly amused by it, and the knuckles—scarred knobs—were eloquent of his reactions. He looked back into his old friend's eyes.

''We got that thing down and unwrapped it. Billy Lee Davis, one of my deputies, he was in Viet Nam, been near some bad, bad things and held on. Billy Lee blew his lunch all over the ground when we unwrapped that thing. It was a man. Some of a man. We knew he'd stood six-two because all the bones were there, and he'd probably weighed between two fifteen and two twenty-five, but he folded up no bigger than a big-size laundry package. Still had his face, both shoulders, and the left arm, but all the rest was clean. It wasn't animal work. It was knife work, all the edges neat as butcher cuts. Except butchered meat, even when you drain it all you can, will bleed a good deal afterwards, and there wasn't one god-damned drop of blood on the tarp, nor in that meat. It was just as pale as fish meat.''

Deep in his body's center, the doctor's cancer touched him. Not a ravening attack—it sank one fang of pain, questioningly, into new, untasted flesh, probing the scope for its appetite there. He disguised his tremor with a shake of the head.

''A cache, then.''

The sheriff nodded. ''Like you might keep a potroast in the icebox for making lunches. I took some pictures of his face, then we put him back and erased our traces. Two of the miners I'd deputized did a lot of hunting, were woods-smart. So I left them on the first watch. We worked out positions and cover for them, and drove back.

''We got right on tracing him, sent out descriptions to every town within a hundred miles. He was no one I'd ever seen in Bailey, nor anyone else either, it began to look like, after we'd combed the town all day with the photos. Then, out of the blue, Billy Lee Davis smacks himself on the forehead and says, 'Sheriff, *I* seen this man somewhere in town, and not long ago!'

"He'd been shook all day since throwing up, and then all of a sudden he just snapped to. Was dead sure. Except he couldn't remember where or when. We went over and over it and he tried and tried. It got to where I wanted to grab him by the ankles and hang him upside down and shake him till it dropped out of him. But it was no damn use. Just after dark we went back to that tree—we'd worked out a place to hide the cars and a route to it through the woods. When we were close we walkie-talkied the men we'd left for an all-clear to come up. No answer at all. And when we got there, all that was left of our trap was the tree. No body, no tarp, no Special Assistant Deputies. Nothing."

This time Dr. Winters poured the coffee and bourbon. "Too much coffee," the sheriff muttered, but drank anyway. "Part of me wanted to chew nails and break necks. And part of me was scared shitless. When we got back I got on the radio station again and made an emergency broadcast and then had the man at the station rebroadcast it every hour. Told everyone to do everything in groups of three, to stay together at night in threes at least, to go out little as possible, keep armed and keep checking up on each other. It had such a damn-fool sound to it, but just pairing-up was no protection if half of one of those pairs was the killer. I deputized more men and put them on the streets to beef up the night patrol.

"It was next morning that things broke. The sheriff of Rakehell called—he's over in the next county. He said our corpse sounded a lot like a man named Abel Dougherty, a millhand with Con Wood over there. I left Billy Lee in charge and drove right out.

"This Dougherty had a cripple older sister he always checked back to by phone whenever he left town for long, a habit no one knew about, probably embarrassed him. Sheriff Peck there only found out about it when the woman called him, said her brother'd been four days gone for vacation and not rung her once. Without that Peck might not've thought of Dougherty just from our description, though the photo I showed him clinched it, and one would've reached him by mail soon enough. Well, he'd hardly set it down again when a call came through for me. It was Billy Lee. He'd remembered.

"When he'd seen Dougherty was the Sunday night three days before we found him. Where he'd seen him was the Trucker's Tavern outside the north end of town. The man had made a stir by being jolly drunk and latching onto a miner who was drinking there, man named Joe Allen, who'd started at the mine about two months back. Dougherty kept telling him that he wasn't Joe Allen, but Dougherty's old buddy named Sykes that had worked with him at Con Wood for a coon's age, and what the hell kind of joke was this, come have a beer old buddy and tell me why you took off so sudden and what the hell you been doing with yourself.

"Allen took it laughing. Dougherty'd clap him on the shoulder, Allen'd clap him right back and make every kind of joke about it, say 'Give this man another beer, I'm standing in for a long-lost friend of his.' Dougherty was so big and loud and stubborn, Billy Lee was worried about a fight starting, and he wasn't the only one worried. But this Joe Allen was a natural good ol' boy, handled it perfect. We'd checked him out weeks back along with everyone else, and he was real popular with the other miners. Finally Dougherty swore he was going to take him on to another bar to help celebrate the vacation Dougherty was starting out on. Joe Allen got up grinning, said god damn it, he couldn't accommodate Dougherty by being this fellow Sykes, but he could sure as hell have a glass with any serious drinking man that was treating. He went out with him, and gave everyone a wink as he left, to the general satisfaction of the audience."

Craven paused. Dr. Winters met his eyes and knew his

thought, two images: the jolly wink that roused the room to laughter, and the thing in the tarp aboil with bright blue flies.

"It was plain enough for me." the sheriff said. "I told Billy Lee to search Allen's room at the Skettles' boarding house and then go straight to the mine and take him. We could fine-polish things once we had him. Since I was already in Rakehell, I saw to some of the loose ends before I started back. I went with Sheriff Peck down to Con Wood and we found a picture of Eddie Sykes in the personnel files. I'd seen Joe Allen often enough, and it was his picture in that file.

"We found out Sykes lived alone, was an on-again, off-again worker, private in his comings and goings, and hadn't been around for a while. But one of the sawyers there could be pretty sure of when Sykes left Rakehell because he'd gone to Sykes' cabin the morning after a big meteor shower they had out there about nine weeks back, since some thought the shower might have reached the ground, and not far from Sykes' side of the mountain. He wasn't in that morning, and the sawyer hadn't seen him since.

"It looked sewed up. It *was* sewed up. After all those weeks. I was less than a mile out of Bailey, had the pedal floored. Full of rage and revenge. I felt . . . like a *bullet*, like I was one big thirty-caliber slug that was going to go right through that blood-sucking cannibal, tear the whole truth right out of his heart, enough to hang him a hundred times. That was the closest I got. So close that I *heard* it when it all blew to shit.

"I sound squirrelly. I know I do. Maybe all this gave me something I'll never shake off. We had to put together what happened. Billy Lee didn't have my other deputy with him. Travis was out with some men on the mountain dragnetting around that tree for clues. By luck, he was back at the car when Billy Lee was trying to raise him. He said he'd just been through Allen's room and had got something we could maybe hold him on. It was a sphere, half again big as a basketball, heavy, made of something that wasn't metal or glass but was a little like both. He could half-see into it and it looked to be full of some kind of circuitry and components. If someone tried to spring Allen, we could make a theft rap out of this thing, or say we suspected it was a bomb. Jesus! Anyway, he said it was the only strange thing he found, but it was plenty strange. He told Travis to get up to the mine for back-up. He'd be there first and should already have Allen by the time Travis arrived.

"Tierney, the shift boss up there, had an assistant that told us the rest. Billy Lee parked behind the offices where the men in the yard wouldn't see the car. He went upstairs to arrange the arrest with Tierney. They got half a dozen men together. Just as they came out of the building, they saw Allen take off running from the squadcar with the sphere under his arm.

"The whole compound's fenced in and Tierney'd already phoned to have all the gates shut. Allen zigged and zagged some but caught on quick to the trap. The sphere slowed him, but he still had a good lead. He hesitated a minute and then ran straight for the main shaft. A cage was just going down with a crew, and he risked every bone in him jumping down after it, but he got safe on top. By the time they got to the switches, the cage was down to the second level, and Allen and the crew had got out. Tierney got it back up. Billy Lee ordered the rest back to get weapons and follow, and him and Tierney rode the cage right back down. And about two minutes later half the god-damned mine blew up."

The sheriff stopped as if cut off, his lips parted to say more, his eyes registering for perhaps the hundredth time his amazement that there was no more, that the weeks of death and mystification ended here, with this split-second recapitulation: more death, more answerless dark, sealing all.

"Nate."

"What."

"Wrap it up and go to bed. I don't need your help. You're dead on your feet."

"I'm not on my feet. And I'm coming along."

"Give me a picture of the victims' position relative to the blast. I'm going to work and you're going to bed."

The sheriff shook his head absently. "They're mining in shrinkage stopes. The adits—levels—branch off lateral from the vertical shaft. From one level they hollow out overhand up to the one above. Scoop out big chambers and let most of the broken rock stay inside so they can stand on the heaps to cut the ceilings higher. They leave sections of support wall between stopes, and those men were buried several stopes in from the shaft. The cave-in killed *them*. The mountain just folded them up in their own hill of tailings. No kind of fragments reached them. I'm dead sure. The only ones they *found* were of some standard charges that the main blast set off, and those didn't even get close. The big one blew out where the adit joined the shaft, right where, and right when Billy Lee and Tierney got out of the cage. And there is *nothing* left there, Carl. No sphere, no cage, no Tierney, no Billy Lee Davis. Just rock blown fine as flour."

Dr. Winters nodded and, after a moment, stood up.

"Come on, Nate. I've got to get started. I'll be lucky to have even a few of them done before morning. Drop me off and go to sleep, till then at least. You'll still be there to witness most of the work."

The sheriff rose, took up the doctor's suitcase, and led him out of the office without a word, concession in his silence.

The patrol car was behind the building. The doctor saw a crueller beauty in the stars than he had an hour before. They got in, and Craven swung them out onto the empty street. The doctor opened the window and harkened, but the motor's surge drowned out the river sound. Before the thrust of their headlights, ranks of old-fashioned parking meters sprouted shadows tall across the sidewalks, shadows which shrank and were cut down by the lights' passage. The sheriff said:

"All those extra dead. For nothing! Not even to . . . *feed* him! If it *was* a bomb, and he made it, he'd know how powerful it was. He wouldn't try some stupid escape stunt with it. And how did he even know the thing was there? We worked it out that Allen was just ending a shift, but he wasn't even up out of the ground before Billy Lee'd parked out of sight.''

"Let it rest, Nate. I want to hear more, but after you've slept. I know you. All the photos will be there, and the report complete, all the evidence neatly boxed and carefully described. When I've looked things over I'll know exactly how to proceed by myself.''

Bailey had neither hospital nor morgue, and the bodies were in a defunct ice-plant on the edge of town. A generator had been brought down from the mine, lighting improvised, and the refrigeration system reactivated. Dr. Parsons' office, and the tiny examining room that served the sheriff's station in place of a morgue, had furnished this makeshift with all the equipment that Dr. Winters would need beyond what he carried with him. A quarter-mile outside the main body of the town, they drew up to it. Tree-flanked, unneighbored by any other structure, it was a double building; the smaller half—the office—was illuminated. The bodies would be in the big, windowless refrigerator segment. Craven pulled up beside a second squadcar parked near the office door. A short, rake-thin man wearing a large white Stetson got out of the car and came over. Craven rolled down his window.

"Trav. This here's Dr. Winters.''

"Lo, Nate. Dr. Winters. Everything's shipshape inside. Felt more comfortable out here. Last of those newshounds left two hours ago.''

"They sure do hang on. You take off now, Trav. Get some sleep and be back at sunup. What temperature we getting?''

The pale Stetson, far clearer in the starlight than the shadow-face beneath it, wagged dubiously. "Thirty-six. She won't get lower—some kind of leak.''

"That should be cold enough,'' the doctor said.

Travis drove off and the sheriff unlocked the padlock on the office door. Waiting behind him, Dr. Winters heard the river again—a cold balm, a whisper of freedom—and overlying this, the stutter and soft snarl of the generator behind the building, a gnawing, remorseless sound that somehow fed the obscure anguish which the other soothed. They went in.

The preparations had been thoughtful and complete. "You can wheel 'em out of the fridge on this and do the examining in here," the sheriff said, indicating a table and a gurney. "You should find all the gear you need on this big table here, and you can write up your reports on that desk. The phone's not hooked up—there's a pay phone at the last gas station if you have to call me."

The doctor nodded, checking over the material on the larger table: scalpels, post-mortem and cartilage knives, intestine scissors, rib shears, forceps, probes, mallet and chisels, a blade saw and electric bone saw, scale, jars for specimens, needles and suture, sterilizer, gloves. . . . Beside this array were a few boxes and envelopes with descriptive sheets attached, containing the photographs and such evidentiary objects as had been found associated with the bodies.

"Excellent,"he muttered.

"The overhead light's fluorescent, full spectrum or whatever they call it. Better for colors. There's a pint of decent bourbon in that top desk drawer. Ready to look at 'em?"

"Yes."

The sheriff unbarred and slid back the big metal door to the refrigeration chamber. Icy, tainted air boiled out of the doorway. The light within was dimmer than that provided in the office—a yellow gloom wherein ten oblong heaps lay on trestles.

The two stood silent for a time, their stillness a kind of unpremeditated homage paid the eternal mystery at its threshold. As if the cold room were in fact a shrine, the doctor found a peculiar awe in the row of veiled forms. The awful unison of their dying, the titan's grave that had been made for them, conferred on them a stern authority, Death's chosen Ones. His stomach hurt, and he found he had his hand pressed to his abdomen. He glanced at Craven and was relieved to see that his friend, staring wearily at the bodies, had missed the gesture.

"Nate. Help me uncover them."

Starting at opposite ends of the row, they stripped the tarps off and piled them in a corner. Both were brusque now, not pausing over the revelation of the swelled, pulpy faces—most three-lipped with the gaseous burgeoning of their tongues—and the fat, livid hands sprouting from the filthy sleeves. But at one of the bodies Craven stopped. The doctor saw him look, and his mouth twist. Then he flung the tarp on the heap and moved to the next trestle.

When they came out Dr. Winters took out the bottle and glasses Craven had put in the desk, and they had a drink together. The sheriff made as if he would speak, but shook his head and sighed.

"I *will* get some sleep, Carl. I'm getting crazy thoughts with this thing." The doctor wanted to ask those thoughts. Instead he laid a hand on his friend's shoulder.

"Go home, Sheriff Craven. Take off the badge and lie down. The dead won't run off on you. We'll all still be here in the morning."

When the sound of the patrol car faded, the doctor stood listening to the generator's growl and the silence of the dead, resurgent now. Both the sound and the silence seemed to mock him. The after-echo of his last words made him uneasy. He said to his cancer:

"What about it, dear colleague? We *will* still be here tomorrow? All of us?"

He smiled, but felt an odd discomfort, as if he had ventured a jest in company and roused a hostile silence. He went to the refrigerator door, rolled it back, and viewed the corpses in their ordered rank, with their strange tribunal air. "What, sirs?" he muttered. "Do you judge me? Just who is to examine whom tonight, if I may ask?"

He went back to the office, where his first step was to examine the photographs made by the sheriff, in order to see how the dead had lain at their uncovering. The earth had seized them with terrible suddenness. Some crouched, some partly stood, others sprawled in crazy, free-fall postures. Each successive photo showed more of the jumble as the shovels continued their work between shots. The doctor studied them closely, noting the identifications inked on the bodies as they came completely into view.

One man, Robert Willet, had died some yards from the main cluster. It appeared he had just straggled into the stope from the adit at the moment of the explosion. He should thus have received, more directly than any of the others, the shockwaves of the blast. If bomb fragments were to be found in any of the corpses, Mr. Willet's seemed likeliest to contain them. Dr. Winters pulled on a pair of surgical gloves.

He lay at one end of the line of trestles. He wore a thermal shirt and overalls that were strikingly new beneath the filth of burial. Their tough fabrics jarred with that of his flesh—blue, swollen, seeming easily torn or burst, like ripe fruit. In life Willet had grease-combed hair. Now it was a sculpture of dust, spikes and whorls shaped by the head's last grindings against the mountain that clenched it.

Rigor had come and gone—Willet rolled laxly onto the gurney. As the doctor wheeled him past the others, he felt a slight self-consciousness. The sense of some judgment flowing from the dead assembly—unlike most such vagrant emotional embellishments of experience—had an odd tenacity in him. This stubborn unease began to irritate him with himself, and he moved more briskly.

He put Willet on the examining table and cut the clothes off him with shears, storing the pieces in an evidence box. The overalls were soiled with agonal waste expulsions. The doctor stared a moment with unwilling pity at his naked subject.

"You won't ride down to Fordham in any case," he said to the corpse. "Not unless I find something pretty damned obvious." He pulled his gloves tighter and arranged his implements.

Waddleton had said more to him than he had reported to the sheriff. The doctor was to find, and forcefully to record that he had found, strong "indications" absolutely requiring the decedents' removal to Fordham for x-ray and an exhaustive second post-mortem. The doctor's continued employment with the Coroner's Office depended entirely on his compliance in this. He had received this stipulation with a silence Waddleton had not thought it necessary to break. His present resolution was all but made at that moment. Let the obvious be taken as such. If the others showed as plainly as Willet did the external signs of death by asphyxiation, they would receive no more than a thorough external exam. Willet he would examine internally as well, merely to establish in depth for this one what should appear obvious in all. Otherwise, only when the external exam revealed a clearly anomalous feature—and clear and suggestive it must be—would he look deeper.

He rinsed the caked hair in a basin, poured the sediment into a flask and labeled it. Starting with the scalp, he began a minute scrutiny of the body's surfaces, recording his observations as he went.

The characteristic signs of asphyxial death were evident, despite the complicating effects of autolysis and putrefaction. The eyeballs' bulge and the tongue's protrusion were by now at least partly due to gas pressure as well as the mode of death, but the latter organ was clamped between locked teeth, leaving little doubt as to that mode. The coloration of degenerative change—a greenish-yellow tint, a darkening and mapping-out of superficial veins—was marked, but not sufficient to obscure the blue of cyanosis on the face and neck, or the pinpoint hemorrhages freckling neck, chest, and shoulders. From the mouth and nose the doctor scraped matter he was confident was the blood-tinged mucus typically ejected in the airless agony.

He began to find a kind of comedy in his work. What a buffoon death made of a man! A blue, pop-eyed, three-lipped thing. And there was himself, this curious, solicitous intimacy with this clownish carrion. Excuse me, Mr. Willet, while I probe this laceration. How does it feel when I do

this? Nothing? Nothing at all? Fine, now what about these
nails. Split them clawing at the earth, did you? Yes. A nice
bloodblister under this thumbnail I see—got it on the job a
few days before your accident no doubt? Remarkable calluses
here, still quite tough. . . .

The doctor looked for an unanalytic moment at the hands—
puffed, dark paws, gestureless, having renounced all touch
and grasp. He felt the wastage of the man concentrated in the
hands. The painful futility of the body's fine articulation when
it is seen in death—this poignancy he had long learned not
to acknowledge when he worked. But now he let it move him
a little. This Roger Willet, plodding to his work one afternoon, had suddenly been scrapped, crushed to a nonfunc-
tional heap of perishable materials. It simply happened that
his life had chanced to move too close to the passage of a
more powerful life, one of those inexorable and hungry lives
that leave human wreckage—known or undiscovered—in their
wakes. Bad luck, Mr. Willet. Naturally, we feel very sorry
about this. But this Joe Allen, your co-worker. Apparently he
was some sort of . . . cannibal. It's complicated. We don't
understand it all. But the fact is we have to dismantle you
now to a certain extent. There's really no hope of your using
these parts of yourself again, I'm afraid. Ready now?

The doctor proceeded to the internal exam with a vague
eagerness for Willet's fragmentation, for the disarticulation
of that sadness in his natural form. He grasped Willet by the
jaw and took up the post-mortem knife. He sank its point
beneath the chin and began the long, gently sawing incision
that opened Willet from throat to groin.

In the painstaking separation of the body's laminae Dr.
Winters found absorption and pleasure. And yet throughout
he felt, marginal but insistent, the movement of a stream of
irrelevant images. These were of the building that contained
him, and of the night containing it. As from outside, he saw
the plant—bleached planks, iron roofing—and the trees
crowding it, all in starlight, a ghost-town image. And he saw
the refrigerator vault beyond the wall as from within, feeling

the stillness of murdered men in a cold, yellow light. And at length a question formed itself, darting in and out of the weave of his concentration as the images did: Why did he still feel, like some stir of the air, that sense of mute vigilance surrounding his action, furtively touching his nerves with its inquiry as he worked? He shrugged, overtly angry now. Who else was attending but Death? Wasn't he Death's hireling, and this Death's place? Then let the master look on.

Peeling back Willet's cover of hemorrhage-stippled skin, Dr. Winters read the corpse with an increasing dispassion, a mortuary text. He confined his inspection to the lungs and mediastinum and found there unequivocal testimony to Willet's asphyxial death. The pleurae of the lungs exhibited the expected ecchymoses—bruised spots in the glassy, enveloping membrane. Beneath, the polyhedral surface lobules of the lungs themselves were bubbled and blistered—the expected interstitial emphysema. The lungs, on section, were intensely and bloodily congested. The left half of the heart he found contracted and empty, while the right was over-distended and engorged with dark blood, as were the large veins of the upper mediastinum. It was a classic picture of death by suffocation, and at length the doctor, with needle and suture, closed up the text again.

He returned the corpse to the gurney and draped one of his mortuary bags over it in the manner of a shroud. When he had help in the morning, he would weigh the bodies on a platform scale the office contained and afterwards bag them properly. He came to the refrigerator door, and hesitated. He stared at the door, not moving, not understanding why.

Run. Get out, now.

The thought was his own, but it came to him so urgently he turned around as if someone behind him had spoken. Across the room a thin man in smock and gloves, his eyes shadows, glared at the doctor from the black windows. Behind the man was a shrouded cart; behind that, a wide metal door.

Quietly, wonderingly, the doctor asked, "Run from what?" The eyeless man in the glass was still half-crouched, afraid.

Then, a moment later, the man straightened, threw back his head, and laughed. The doctor walked to the desk and sat down shoulder to shoulder with him. He pulled out the bottle and they had a drink together, regarding each other with identical bemused smiles. Then the doctor said, "Let me pour you another. You need it, old fellow. It makes a man himself again."

Nevertheless his re-entry of the vault was difficult, toilsome, each step seeming to require a new summoning of the will to move. In the freezing half-light all movement felt like defiance. His body lagged behind his craving to be quick, to be done with this molestation of the gathered dead. He returned Willet to his pallet and took his neighbor. The name on the tag wired to his boot was Ed Moses. Dr. Winters wheeled him back to the office and closed the big door behind him.

With Moses his work gained momentum. He expected to perform no further internal necropsies. He thought of his employer, rejoicing now in his seeming-submission to Waddleton's ultimatum. The impact would be dire. He pictured the coroner in shock, a sheaf of Pathologist's Reports in one hand, and smiled.

Waddleton could probably make a plausible case for incomplete examination. Still, a pathologist's discretionary powers were not well-defined. Many good ones would approve the adequacy of the doctor's method, given his working conditions. The inevitable litigation with a coalition of compensation claimants would be strenuous and protracted. Win or lose, Waddleton's venal devotion to the insurance company's interest would be abundantly displayed. Further, immediately on his dismissal the doctor would formally disclose its occult cause to the press. A libel action would ensue which he would have as little cause to fear as he had to fear his firing. Both his savings and the lawsuit would long outlast his life.

Externally, Ed Moses exhibited a condition as typically asphyxial as Willet's had been, with no slightest mark of fragment entry. The doctor finished his report and returned Moses to the vault, his movements brisk and precise. His unease was all but gone. That queasy stirring of the air—had he really felt it? It had been, perhaps, some new reverberation of the death at work in him, a psychic shudder of response to the cancer's stealthy probing for his life. He brought out the body next to Moses in the line.

Walter Lou Jackson was big, 6' 2" from heel to crown, and would surely weigh out at more than two hundred pounds. He had writhed mightily against his million-ton coffin with an agonal strength that had torn his face and hands. Death had mauled him like a lion. The doctor set to work.

His hands were fully themselves now—fleet, exact, intricately testing the corpse's character as other fingers might explore a keyboard for its latent melodies. And the doctor watched them with an old pleasure, one of the few that had never failed him, his mind at one remove from their busy intelligence. All the hard deaths! A worldful of them, time without end. Lives wrenched kicking from their snug meatframes. Walter Lou Jackson had died very hard. Joe Allen brought this on you, Mr. Jackson. We think it was part of his attempt to escape the law.

But what a botched flight! The unreason of it—more than baffling—was eerie in its colossal futility. Beyond question, Allen had been cunning. A ghoul with a psychopath's social finesse. A good old boy who could make a tavernful of men laugh with delight while he cut his victim from their midst, make them applaud his exit with the prey, who stepped jovially into the darkness with murder at his side clapping him on the shoulder. Intelligent, certainly, with a strange technical sophistication as well, suggested by the sphere. Then what of the lunacy yet more strongly suggested by the same object? In the sphere was concentrated all the lethal mystery of Bailey's long nightmare.

Why the explosion? Its location implied an ambush for

Allen's pursuers, a purposeful detonation. Had he aimed at a limited cave-in from which he schemed some inconceivable escape? Folly enough in this—far more if, as seemed sure, Allen had made the bomb himself, for then he would have to know its power was grossly inordinate to the need.

But if it was not a bomb, had a different function and only incidentally an explosive potential, Allen might underestimate the blast. It appeared the object was somehow remotely monitored by him, for the timing of events showed he had gone straight for it the instant he emerged from the shaft—shunned the bus waiting to take his shift back to town and made a beeline across the compound for a patrol car that was hidden from his view by the office building. This suggested something more complex than a mere explosive device, something, perhaps, whose destruction was itself more Allen's aim than the explosion produced thereby.

The fact that he risked the sphere's retrieval at all pointed to this interpretation. For the moment he sensed its presence at the mine, he must have guessed that the murder investigation had led to its discovery and removal from his room. But then, knowing himself already liable to the extreme penalty, why should Allen go to such lengths to recapture evidence incriminatory of a lesser offense, possession of an explosive device?

Then grant that the sphere was something more, something instrumental to his murders that could guarantee a conviction he might otherwise evade. Still, his gambit made no sense. Since the sphere—and thus the lawmen he could assume to have taken it—were already at the mine office, he must expect the compound to be sealed at any moment. Meanwhile, the gate was open, escape into the mountains a strong possibility for a man capable of stalking and destroying two experienced and well-armed woodsmen lying in ambush for him. Why had he all but insured his capture to weaken a case against himself that his escape would have rendered irrelevant? Dr. Winters saw his fingers, like a hunting pack round a covert, converge on a small puncture wound below Walter Lou Jackson's xiphoid process, between the eighth ribs.

His left hand touched its borders, the fingers' inquiry quick and tender. The right hand introduced a probe, and both together eased it into the wound. It inched unobstructed deep into the body, curving upwards through the diaphragm towards the heart. The doctor's own heart accelerated. He watched his hands move to record the observation, watched them pause, watched them return to their survey of the corpse, leaving pen and page untouched.

Inspection revealed no further anomaly. All else he observed the doctor recorded faithfully, wondering throughout at the distress he felt. When he had finished, he understood it. Its cause was not the discovery of an entry wound that might bolster Waddleton's case. For the find had, within moments, revealed to him that, should he encounter anything he thought to be a mark of fragment penetration, he was going to ignore it. The damage Joe Allen had done was going to end here, with this last grand slaughter, and would not extend to the impoverishment of his victims' survivors. No more internals. The externals will-they nill-they, would from now on explicitly contraindicate the need for them.

The problem was that he did not believe the puncture in Jackson's thorax *was* a mark of fragment entry. Why? And, finding no answer to this question, why was he, once again, afraid? Slowly, he signed the report on Jackson, set it aside, and took up the post-mortem knife.

First the long, sawing slice, unzippering the mortal overcoat. Next, two great, square flaps of flesh reflected, scrolled laterally to the armpits' line, disrobing the chest: one hand grasping the flap's skirt, the other sweeping beneath it with the knife, flensing through the glassy tissue that joined it to the chest-wall, and shaving all muscles from their anchorages to bone and cartilage beneath. Then the dismantling of the strong-box within. Rib-shears—so frank and forward a tool, like a gardener's. The steel beak bit through each rib's gristle anchor to the sternum's centerplate. At the sternum's crown-piece the collarbones' ends were knifed, pried, and sprung free from their sockets. The coffer unhasped, unhinged, a knife teased beneath the lid and levered it off.

Some minutes later the doctor straightened up and stepped back from his subject. He moved almost drunkenly, and his age seemed scored more deeply in his face. With loathing haste he stripped his gloves off. He went to the desk, sat down, and poured another drink. If there was something like horror in his face, there was also a hardening in his mouth's line, and the muscles of his jaw. He spoke to his glass: "So be it, your Excellency. Something new for your humble servant. Testing my nerve?"

Jackson's pericardium, the shapely capsule containing his heart, should have been all but hidden between the big, blood-fat loaves of his lungs. The doctor had found it fully exposed, the lungs flanking it wrinkled lumps less than a third their natural bulk. Not only they, but the left heart and the superior mediastinal veins—all the regions that should have been grossly engorged with blood—were utterly drained of it.

The doctor swallowed his drink and got out the photographs again. He found that Jackson had died on his stomach across the body of another worker, with the upper part of a third trapped between them. Neither these two subjacent corpses nor the surrounding earth showed any stain of a blood loss that must have amounted to two liters.

Possibly the pictures, by some trick of shadow, had failed to pick it up. He turned to the Investigator's Report, where Craven would surely have mentioned any significant amounts of bloody earth uncovered during the disinterment. The sheriff recorded nothing of the kind. Dr. Winters returned to the pictures.

Ronald Pollock, Jackson's most intimate associate in the grave, had died on his back, beneath and slightly askew of Jackson, placing most of their torsos in contact, save where the head and shoulder of the third interposed. It seemed inconceivable Pollock's clothing should lack any trace of such massive drainage from a death mate thus embraced.

The doctor rose abruptly, pulled on fresh gloves, and returned to Jackson. His hands showed a more brutal speed now, closing the great incision temporarily with a few widely spaced sutures. He replaced him in the vault and brought out Pollock, striding, heaving hard at the dead shapes in the shifting of them, thrusting always—so it seemed to him—just a step ahead of urgent thoughts he did not want to have, deformities that whispered at his back, emitting faint, chill gusts of putrid breath. He shook his head—denying, delaying—and pushed the new corpse onto the worktable. The scissors undressed Pollock in greedy bites.

But at length, when he had scanned each scrap of fabric and found nothing like the stain of blood, he came to rest again, relinquishing that simplest, desired resolution he had made such haste to reach. He stood at the instrument table, not seeing it, submitting to the approach of the half-formed things at his mind's periphery.

The revelation of Jackson's shriveled lungs had been more than a shock. He felt a stab of panic too, in fact that same curiously explicit terror of this place that had urged him to flee earlier. He acknowledged now that the germ of that quickly suppressed terror had been a premonition of this failure to find any trace of the missing blood. Whence the premonition? It had to do with a problem he had steadfastly refused to consider: the mechanics of so complete a drainage of the lungs' densely reticulated vascular structure. Could the earth's crude pressure by itself work so thoroughly, given only a single vent both slender and strangely curved? And then the photograph he had studied. It frightened him now to recall the image—some covert meaning stirred within it, struggling to be seen. Dr. Winters picked the probe up from the table and turned again to the corpse. As surely and exactly as if he had already ascertained the wound's presence, he leaned forward and touched it: a small, neat puncture, just beneath the xiphoid process. He introduced the probe. The wound received it deeply, in a familiar direction.

The doctor went to the desk, and took up the photograph

again. Pollock's and Jackson's wounded areas were not in contact. The third man's head was sandwiched between their bodies at just that point. He searched out another picture, in which this third man was more central, and found his name inked in below his image: Joe Allen.

Dreamingly, Dr. Winters went to the wide metal door, shoved it aside, entered the vault. He did not search, but went straight to the trestle where his friend had paused some hours before, and found the same name on its tag.

The body, beneath decay's spurious obesity, was trim and well-muscled. The face was square-cut, shelf-browed, with a vulpine nose skewed by an old fracture. The swollen tongue lay behind the teeth, and the bulge of decomposition did not obscure what the man's initial impact must have been—handsome and open, his now-waxen black eyes sly and convivial. Say, good buddy, got a minute? I see you comin' on the swing shift every day, don't I? Yeah, Joe Allen. Look I know it's late, you want to get home, tell the wife you ain't been in there drinkin' since you got off, right? Oh, yeah, I heard that. But this damn disappearance thing's got me so edgy, and I'd swear to God just as I was coming here I seen someone moving around back of that frame house up the street. See how the trees thin out a little down back of the yard, where the moonlight gets in? That's right. Well, I got me this little popper here. Oh, yeah, that's a beauty, we'll have it covered between us. I knew I could spot a man ready for some trouble—couldn't find a patrol car anywhere on the street. Yeah, just down in here now, to that clump of pine. Step careful, you can barely see. That's right. . . .

The doctor's face ran with sweat. He turned on his heel and walked out of the vault, heaving the door shut behind him. In the office's greater warmth he felt the perspiration soaking his shirt under the smock. His stomach rasped with steady oscillations of pain, but he scarcely attended it. He went to Pollock and seized up the post-mortem knife.

The work was done with surreal speed, the laminae of flesh and bone recoiling smoothly beneath his desperate but unerring hands, until the thoracic cavity lay exposed, and in it, the vampire-stricken lungs, two gnarled lumps of grey tissue.

He searched no deeper, knowing what the heart and veins would show. He returned to sit at the desk, weakly drooping, the knife, forgotten, still in his left hand. He looked at the window, and it seemed his thoughts originated with that fainter, more tenuous Dr. Winters hanging like a ghost outside.

What was this world he lived in? Surely, in a lifetime, he had not begun to guess. To feed in such a way! There was horror enough in this alone. But to feed thus *in his own grave*. How had he accomplished it—leaving aside how he had fought suffocation long enough to do anything at all? How was it to be comprehended, a greed that raged so hotly it would glut itself at the very threshold of its own destruction? That last feast was surely in his stomach still.

Dr. Winters looked at the photograph, at Allen's head snugged into the others' middles like a hungry suckling nuzzling to the sow. Then he looked at the knife in his hand. The hand left empty of all technique. Its one impulse was to slash, cleave, obliterate the remains of this gluttonous thing, this Joe Allen. He must do this, or flee it utterly. There was no course between. He did not move.

"I *will* examine him," said the ghost in the glass, and did not move. Inside the refrigerator vault, there was a slight noise.

No. It had been some hitch in the generator's murmur. Nothing in there could move. There was another noise, a brief friction against the vault's inner wall. The two old men shook their heads at one another. A catch clicked and the metal door slid open. Behind the staring image of his own amazement, the doctor saw that a filthy shape stood in the doorway and raised its arms towards him in a gesture of supplication. The doctor turned in his chair. From the shape came a whistling groan, the decayed fragment of a human voice.

Pleadingly, Joe Allen worked his jaw and spread his purple

hands. As if speech were a maggot struggling to emerge from his mouth, the blue, tumescent face toiled, the huge tongue wallowed helplessly between the viscid lips.

The doctor reached for the telephone, lifted the receiver. Its deadness to his ear meant nothing—he could not have spoken. The thing confronting him, with each least movement that it made, destroyed the very frame of sanity in which words might have meaning, reduced the world itself around him to a waste of dark and silence, a starlit ruin where already, everywhere, the alien and unimaginable was awakening to its new dominion. The corpse raised and reached out one hand as if to stay him—turned, and walked towards the instrument table. Its legs were leaden, it rocked its shoulders like a swimmer, fighting to make its passage through gravity's dense medium. It reached the table and grasped it exhaustedly. The doctor found himself on his feet, crouched slightly, weightlessly still. The knife in his hand was the only part of himself he clearly felt, and it was like a tongue of fire, a crematory flame. Joe Allen's corpse thrust one hand among the instruments. The thick fingers, with a queer, simian ineptitude, brought up a scalpel. Both hands clasped the little handle and plunged the blade between the lips, as a thirsty child might a popsicle, then jerked it out again, slashing the tongue. Turbid fluid splashed down to the floor. The jaw worked stiffly, the mouth brought out words in a wet, ragged hiss:

"Please. Help me. Trapped in *this*." One dead hand struck the dead chest. "Starving."

"What are you?"

"Traveler. Not of earth."

"An eater of human flesh. A drinker of human blood."

"No. No. Hiding only. Am small. Shape hideous to you. Feared death."

"You brought death." The doctor spoke with the calm of perfect disbelief, himself as incredible to him as the thing he spoke with. It shook its head, the dull, popped eyes glaring with an agony of thwarted expression.

"Killed none. Hid in this. Hid in this not to be killed. Five days now. Drowning in decay. Free me. Please."

"No. You have come to feed on us, you are not hiding in fear. We are your food, your meat and drink. You fed on those two men within your grave. *Their* grave. For you, a delay. In fact, a diversion that has ended the hunt for you."

"No! No! Used men already dead. For me, five days, starvation. Even less. Fed only from necessity. Horrible necessity!"

The spoiled vocal instrument made a mangled gasp of the last word—an inhuman, snakepit noise the doctor felt as a cold flicker of ophidian tongues within his ears—while the dead arms moved in a sodden approximation of the body language that swears truth.

"No," the doctor said. "You killed them all. Including your . . . tool—this man. *What are you?*" Panic erupted in the question which he tried to bury by answering himself instantly. "Resolute, yes. That surely. You used death for an escape route. You need no oxygen perhaps."

"Extracted more than my need from gasses of decay. A lesser component of our metabolism."

The voice was gaining distinctness, developing makeshifts for tones lost in the agonal rupturing of the valves and stops of speech, more effectively wrestling vowel and consonant from the putrid tongue and lips. At the same time the body's crudity of movement did not quite obscure a subtle, incessant experimentation. Fingers flexed and stirred, testing the give of tendons, groping the palm for the old points of purchase and counter-pressure there. The knees, with cautious repetitions, assessed the new limits of their articulation.

"What was the sphere?"

"My ship. Its destruction our first duty facing discovery." (Fear touched the doctor, like a slug climbing his neck; he had seen, as it spoke, a sharp, spastic activity of the tongue, a pleating and shrinkage of its bulk as at the tug of some inward adjustment.) "No chance to re-enter. Leaving this take far too long. Not even time to set for destruct—must extrude a cilium, chemical key to broach hull shield. In shaft my only chance to halt host.''

The right arm tested the wrist, and the scalpel the hand still held cut white sparks from the air, while the word "host" seemed itself a little knife-prick, a teasing abandonment of fiction—though the dead mask showed no irony—preliminary to attack.

But he found that fear had gone from him. The impossibility with which he conversed, and was about to struggle, was working in him an overwhelming amplification of his life's long helpless rage at death. He found his parochial pity for earth alone stretched to the trans-stellar scope this traveler commanded, to the whole cosmic trashyard with its bulldozed multitudes of corpses; galactic wheels of carnage—stars, planets with their most majestic generations—all trash, cracked bones and foul rags that pooled, settled, reconcatenated in futile symmetries gravid with new multitudes of briefly animate trash.

And this, standing before him now, was the death it was given him particularly to deal—his mite was being called in by the universal Treasury of death, and Dr. Winters found himself, an old healer, on fire to pay. His own, more lethal, blade tugged at his hand with its own sharp appetite. He felt entirely the Examiner once more, knew the precise cuts he would make, swiftly and without error. *Very soon now,* he thought and cooly probed for some further insight before its onslaught:

"Why must your ship be destroyed, even at the cost of your host's life?"

"We must not be understood."

"The livestock must not understand what is devouring them."

"Yes, doctor. Not all at once. But one by one. You will understand what is devouring you. That is essential to my feast."

The doctor shook his head. "You are in your grave already,

Traveler. That body will be your coffin. You will be buried
in it a second time, for all time.''

The thing came one step nearer and opened its mouth. The
flabby throat wrestled as with speech, but what sprang out
was a slender white filament, more than whip-fast. Dr. Winters saw only the first flicker of its eruption, and then his
brain nova-ed, thinning out at light-speed to a white nullity.

When the doctor came to himself, it was in fact to a part
of himself only. Before he had opened his eyes he found that
his wakened mind had repossessed proprioceptively only a
bizarre truncation of his body. His head, neck, left shoulder,
arm and hand declared themselves—the rest was silence.

When he opened his eyes, he found that he lay supine on
the gurney, and naked. Something propped his head. A strap
bound his left elbow to the gurney's edge, a strap he could
feel. His chest was also anchored by a strap, and this he
could not feel. Indeed, save for its active remnant, his entire
body might have been bound in a block of ice, so numb was
it, and so powerless was he to compel the slightest movement
from the least part of it.

The room was empty, but from the open door of the vault
there came slight sounds: the creak and soft frictions of heavy
tarpaulin shifted to accommodate some business involving
small clicking and kissing noises.

Tears of fury filled the doctor's eyes. Clenching his one
fist at the starry engine of creation that he could not see, he
ground his teeth and whispered in the hot breath of strangled
weeping:

"Take it back, this dirty little shred of life! I throw it off
gladly like the filth it is.'' The slow knock of bootsoles loud-
ened from within the vault, and he turned his head. From the
vault door Joe Allen's corpse approached him.

It moved with new energy, though its gait was grotesque,
a ducking, hitching progress, jerky with circumventions of
decayed muscle, while above this galvanized, struggling
frame, the bruise-colored face hung inanimate, an image of

detachment. With terrible clarity it revealed the thing for what it was—a damaged hand-puppet vigorously worked from within. And when that frozen face was brought to hang above the doctor, the reeking hands, with the light, solicitous touch of friends at sickbeds, rested on his naked thigh.

The absence of sensation made the touch more dreadful than it felt. It showed him that the nightmare he still desperately denied at heart had annexed his body while he—holding head and arm free—had already more than half-drowned in its mortal paralysis. There lay his nightmare part, a nothingness freely possessed by an unspeakability. The corpse said:

"Rotten blood. Thin nourishment. Only one hour alone before you came. Fed from neighbor to my left—barely had strength to extend siphon. Fed from the right while you worked. Tricky going—you are alert. Expected Dr. Parsons. Energy needs of animating this"—one hand left the doctor's thigh and smote the dusty overalls—"and a host-transfer, very high. Once I have you synapsed, will be near starvation again."

A sequence of unbearable images unfolded in the doctor's mind, even as the robot carrion turned from the gurney and walked to the instrument table: the sheriff's arrival just after dawn, alone of course, since Craven always took thought for his deputies' rest and because on this errand he would want privacy to consider any indiscretion on behalf of the miners' survivors that the situation might call for; his finding his old friend, supine and alarmingly weak; his hurrying over, his leaning near. Then, somewhat later, a police car containing a rack of still wet bones might plunge off the highway above some deep spot in the gorge.

The corpse took an evidence box from the table and put the scalpel in it. Then it turned and retrieved the mortuary knife from the floor and put that in as well, saying as it did so, without turning, "The sheriff will come in the morning. You spoke like close friends. He will probably come alone."

The coincidence with his thoughts had to be accident, but the intent to terrify and appall him was clear. The tone and timing of that patched-up voice were unmistakably deliberate—sly probes that sought his anguish specifically, sought his mind's personal center. He watched the corpse—back at the table—dipping an apish but accurate hand and plucking up rib shears, scissors, clamps, adding all to the box. He stared, momentarily emptied by shock of all but the will to know finally the full extent of the horror that had appropriated his life. Joe Allen's body carried the box to the worktable beside the gurney, and the expressionless eyes met the doctor's.

"I have gambled. A grave gamble. But now I have won. At risk of personal discovery we are obliged to disconnect, contract, hide as well as possible in host body. Suicide in effect. I disregarded situational imperatives, despite starvation before disinterment and subsequent autopsy all but certain. I caught up with crew, tackled Pollock and Jackson microseconds before blast. Computed five days survival from this cache, could disconnect at limit of strength to do so, but otherwise would chance autopsy, knowing doctor was alcoholic imcompetent. And now see my gain. You are a prize host, can feed with near impunity even when killing too dangerous. Safe meals delivered to you still warm."

The corpse had painstakingly aligned the gurney parallel to the worktable but offset, the table's foot extending past the gurney's, and separated from it by a distance somewhat less than the reach of Joe Allen's right arm. Now the dead hands distributed the implements along the right edge of the table, save for the scissors and the box. These the corpse took to the table's foot, where it set down the box and slid the scissors' jaws round one strap of its overalls. It began to speak again, and as it did, the scissors dismembered its cerements in unhesitating strokes.

"The cut must be medical, forensically right, though a smaller one easier. Must be careful of the pectoral muscles or arms will not convey me. I am no larva anymore—over fifteen hundred grams."

To ease the nightmare's suffocating pressure, to thrust out

some flicker of his own will against its engulfment, the doctor flung a question, his voice more cracked than the other's now was:

"Why is my arm free?"

"The last, fine neural splicing needs a sensory-motor standard, to perfect my brain's fit to yours. Lacking this eye-hand coordinating check, much coarser motor control of host. This done, I flush out the paralytic, unbind us, and we are free together."

The grave-clothes had fallen in a puzzle of fragments, and the cadaver stood naked, its dark, gas-rounded contours making it seem some sleek marine creature, ruddered with the black-veined, gas-distended sex. Again the voice had teased for his fear, had uttered the last word with a savoring protraction, and now the doctor's cup of anguish brimmed over; horror and outrage wrenched his spirit in brutal alternation as if trying to tear it naked from its captive frame. He rolled his head in this deadlock, his mouth beginning to split with the slow birth of a mind-emptying outcry.

The corpse watched this, giving a single nod that might have been approbation. Then it mounted the worktable and, with the concentrated caution of some practiced convalescent reentering his bed, lay on its back. The dead eyes again sought the living and found the doctor staring back, grinning insanely.

"Clever corpse!" the doctor cried. "Clever, carnivorous corpse! Able alien! Please don't think I'm criticizing. Whom am I to criticize? A mere arm and shoulder, a talking head, just a small piece of a pathologist. But I'm confused." He paused, savoring the monster's attentive silence and his own buoyancy in the hysterical levity that had unexpectedly liberated him. "You're going to use your puppet there to pluck you out of itself and put you on me. But once he's pulled you from your driver's seat, won't he go dead, so to speak, and drop you? You could get a nasty knock. Why not set a plank between the tables—the puppet opens the door, and you scuttle, ooze, lurch, flop, slither, as the case may be, across the bridge. No messy spills. And in any case, isn't this an odd, rather clumsy way to get around among your cattle? Shouldn't you at least carry your own scalpels when you travel? There's always the risk you'll run across that one host in a million that isn't carrying one with him.''

He knew his gibes would be answered to his own despair. He exulted, but solely in the momentary bafflement of the predator—in having, for just a moment, mocked its gloating assurance to silence and marred its feast.

Its right hand picked up the post-mortem knife beside it, and the left wedged a roll of gauze beneath Allen's neck, lifting the throat to a more prominent arch. The mouth told the ceiling:

''We retain larval form till entry of the host. As larvae we have locomotor structures, and sense-buds usable outside our ships' sensory amplifiers. I waited coiled round Ed Sykes' bed leg till night, entered by his mouth as he slept.'' Allen's hand lifted the knife, held it high above the dull, quick eyes, turning it in the light. ''Once lodged, we have three instars to adult form,'' the voice continued absently—the knife might have been a mirror from which the corpse read its features. ''Larvally we have only a sketch of our full neural tap. Our metamorphosis is cued and determined by the host's endo-somatic ecology. I matured in three days.'' Allen's wrist flexed, tipping the knife's point downmost. ''Most supreme adaptations are purchased at the cost of the inessential capacities.'' The elbow pronated and slowly flexed, hooking the knife body-wards. ''Our hosts are all sentients, eco-dominants, are already carrying the baggage of coping structures for the planetary environment. Limbs, sensory portals''—the fist planted the fang of its tool under the chin, tilted it and rode it smoothly down the throat, the voice proceeding unmarred from under the furrow that the steel ploughed—''somatic envelopes, instrumentalities''—down the sternum, diaphragm, abdomen the stainless blade painted its stripe of gaping, muddy tissue—''with a host's brain we inherit all these, the mastery of any planet, netted in its dominant's cerebral nexus. Thus our genetic codings are now all but disencumbered of such provisions.''

So swiftly the doctor flinched, Joe Allen's hand slashed four lateral cuts from the great wound's axis. The seeming butchery left two flawlessly drawn thoracic flaps cleanly outlined. The left hand raised the left flap's hem, and the right coaxed the knife into the aperture, deepening it with small stabs and slices. The posture was a man's who searches a breast pocket, with the dead eyes studying the slow recoil of flesh. The voice, when it resumed, had geared up to an intenser pitch:

''Galactically, the chordate nerve/brain paradigm abounds, and the neural labyrinth is our dominion. Are we to make plank bridges and worm across them to our food? Are cockroaches greater than we for having legs to run up walls and antennae to grope their way! All the quaint, hinged crutches that life sports! The stilts, fins, fans, springs, stalks, flippers and feathers, all in turn so variously terminating in hooks, clamps, suckers, scissors, forks or little cages of digits! And besides all the gadgets it concocts for wrestling through its worlds, it is all knobbed, whiskered, crested, plumed, vented, spiked or measeled over with perceptual gear for combing pittances of noise or color from the environing plentitude.''

Invincibly calm and sure, the hands traded tool and tasks. The right flap eased back, revealing ropes of ingeniously spared muscle while promising a genuine appearance once sutured back in place. Helplessly the doctor felt his delirious defiance bleed away and a bleak fascination rebind him.

''We are the taps and relays that share the host's aggregate of afferent nerve-impulse precisely at its nodes of integration. We are the brains that peruse these integrations, integrate them with our existing banks of host-specific data, and, lastly, let their consequences flow down the motor pathway—either the consequences they seek spontaneously, or those we wish to graft upon them. We are besides a streamlined alimentary/circulatory system and a reproductive apparatus. And more than this we need not be.''

The corpse had spread its bloody vest, and the feculent hands now took up the rib shears. The voice's sinister coloration of pitch and stress grew yet more marked—the phrases slid from the tongue with a cobra's seeking sway, winding their liquid rhythms round the doctor till a gap in his resistance should let them pour through to slaughter the little courage left him.

"For in this form we have inhabited the densest brainweb of three hundred races, lain intricately snug within them like thriving vine on trelliswork. We've looked out from too many variously windowed masks to regret our own vestigial senses. None read their worlds definitely. Far better then, our nomad's range and choice, than an unvarying tenancy of one poor set of structures. Far better to slip on as we do whole living beings and wear at once all of their limbs and organs, memories and powers—wear all as tightly congruent to our wills as a glove is to the hand that fills it."

The shears clipped through the gristle, stolid, bloody jaws monotonously feeding, stopping short of the sterno-clavicular joint in the manubrium where the muscles of the pectoral girdle have an important anchorage.

"No consciousness of the chordate type that we have found has been impermeable to our finesse—no dendritic pattern so elaborate we could not read its stitchwork and thread ourselves to match, precisely map its each synaptic seam till we could loosen it and re-tailor all to suit ourselves. We have strutted costumed in the bodies of planetary autarchs, venerable manikins of moral fashion, but cut of the universal cloth: the weave of fleet electric filaments of experience which we easily re-shuttled to the warp of our wishes. Whereafter— newly hemmed and gathered—their living fabric hung obedient to our bias, investing us with honor and influence unlimited."

The tricky verbal melody, through the corpse's deft, unfaltering self-dismemberment—the sheer neuromuscular orchestration of the compound activity—struck Dr. Winters with the detached enthrallment great keyboard performers could bring him. He glimpsed the alien's perspective—a Gulliver waiting in a brobdingnagian grave, then marshaling a dead giant against a living, like a dwarf in a huge mechanical crane, feverishly programming combat on a battery of levers and pedals, waiting for the robot arms' enactments, the remote, titanic impact of the foes—and he marveled, filled with a bleak wonder at life's infinite strategy and plasticity. Joe Allen's hands reached into his half-opened abdominal cavity, reached deep below the uncut anterior muscle that was exposed by the shallow, spurious incision of the epidermis, till by external measure they were extended far enough to be touching his thighs. The voice was still as the forearms advertised a delicate rummaging with the buried fingers. The shoulders drew back. As the steady withdrawal brought the wrists into view, the dead legs tremored and quaked with diffuse spasms.

"You called your kind our food and drink, doctor. If you were merely that, an elementary usurpation of your motor tracts alone would satisfy us, give us perfect cattle-control—for what rarest word or subtlest behavior is more than a flurry of varied muscles? That trifling skill was ours long ago. It is not mere blood that feeds this lust I feel now to tenant you, this craving for an intimacy that years will not stale. My truest feast lies in compelling you to feed in that way and in the utter deformation of your will this will involve. Had gross nourishment been my prime need, then my gravemates—Pollock and Jackson—could have eked out two weeks of life for me or more. But I scorned a cowardly parsimony in the face of death. I reinvested more than half the energy that their blood gave me in fabricating chemicals to keep their brains alive, and fluid-bathed with oxygenated nutriment."

Out of the chasmed midriff the smeared hands dragged two long tresses of silvery filament that writhed and sparkled with a million simultaneous coilings and contractions. The legs jittered with faint, chaotic pulses throughout their musculature, until the bright, vermiculate tresses had gathered into two spheric masses which the hands laid carefully within the incision. Then the legs lay still as death.

"I had accessory neural taps only to spare, but I could access much memory, and all of their cognitive responses, and having in my banks all the organ of Corti's electrochemical conversions of English words, I could whisper anything to them directly into the eighth cranial nerve. Those are our true feast, doctor, such bodiless electric storms of impotent cognition as I tickled up in those two little bone globes. I was forced to drain them yesterday, just before disinterment. They lived till then and understood everything—*everything* I did to them."

When the voice paused, the dead and living eyes were locked together. They remained so a moment, and then the dead face smiled.

It recapitulated all the horror of Allen's first resurrection—this waking of expressive soul from those grave-mound contours. And it was a demon-soul the doctor saw awaken: the smile was barbed with fine, sharp hooks of cruelty at the corners of the mouth, while the barbed eyes beamed fond, languorous anticipation of his pain. Remotely, Dr. Winters heard the flat sound of his own voice asking:

"And Eddie Sykes?"

"Oh, yes, doctor. He is with us now, has been throughout. I grieve to abandon so rare a host! He is a true hermit-philosopher, well-read in four languages. He is writing a translation of Marcus Aurelius—he was, I mean, in his free time. . . ."

Long minutes succeeded of the voice accompanying the surreal self-autopsy, but the doctor lay stilled, emptied of reactive power. Still, the full understanding of his fate reverberated in his mind—an empty room through which the voice, not heard exactly but somehow implanted directly as in the subterranean torture it had just described, sent aftershocks of realization, amplification of the Unspeakable.

The parasite had traced and trapped the complex interface between cortical integration of input and the consequent neu-

ral output shaping response. It had interposed its brain between, sharing consciousness while solely commanding the
pathways of reaction. The host, the bottled personality, was
mute and limbless for any least expression of its own will,
while hellishly articulate and agile in the service of the parasite's. It was the host's own hands that bound and wrenched
the life half out of his prey, his own loins that experienced
the repeated orgasms crowning his other despoliations of their
bodies. And when they lay, bound and shrieking still, ready
for the consummation, it was his own strength that hauled
the smoking entrails from them, and his own intimate tongue
and guzzling mouth he plunged into the rank, palpitating
feast.

And the doctor had glimpses of the history behind this
predation, that of a race so far advanced in the essential-
izing, the inexorable abstraction of their own mental fabric
that through scientific commitment and genetic self-
cultivation they had come to embody their own model of
perfected consciousness, streamlined to permit the entry of
other beings and the direct acquisition of their experiential
worlds. All strictest scholarship at first, until there matured
in the disembodied scholars their long-germinal and now
blazing, jealous hatred for all "lesser" minds rooted and
clothed in the soil and sunlight of solid, particular worlds.
The parasite spoke of the "cerebral music," the "sympho-
nies of agonized paradox" that were its invasions' chief plun-
der. The doctor felt the truth behind this grandiloquence: its
actual harvest from the systematic violation of encoffined per-
sonalities was the experience of a barren supremacy of means
over lives more primitive, perhaps, but vastly wealthier in the
vividness and passionate concern with which life for them
was imbued.

Joe Allen's hands had scooped up the bunched skeins of
alien nerve, with the wrinkled brain-node couched admidst
them, and for some time had waited the slow retraction of a
last major trunkline which seemingly had followed the spine's
axis. At last, when only a slender subfiber of this remained

implanted, the corpse, smiling once more, held up for him to view its reconcatenated master. The doctor looked into its eyes then and spoke—not to their controller, but to the captive who shared them with it, and who now, the doctor knew, neared his final death.

"Goodbye, Joe Allen. Eddie Sykes. You are guiltless. Peace be with you at last."

The demon smile remained fixed, the right hand reached its viscid cargo across the gap and over the doctor's groin. He watched the hand set the glittering medusa's head—his new self—upon his flesh, return to the table, take up the scalpel, and reach back to cut in his groin a four-inch incision—all in eerie absence of tactile stimulus. The line that had remained plunged into the corpse suddenly whipped free of the mediastinal crevice, retracted across the gap and shortened to a taut stub on the seething organism atop the doctor.

Joe Allen's body collapsed, emptied, all slack. He was a corpse again entirely, but with one anomalous feature to his posture. His right arm had not dropped to the nearly vertical hang that would have been natural. At the instant of the alien's unplugging, the shoulder had given a fierce shrug and wrenching of its angle, flinging the arm upward as it died so that it now lay in the orientation of an arm that reaches up for a ladder's next rung. The slightest tremor would unfix the joints and dump the arm back into the gravitational bias; it would also serve to dump the scalpel from the proferred, upturned palm that implement still precariously occupied.

The man had repossessed himself one microsecond before his end. The doctor's heart stirred, woke, and sang within him, for he saw that the scalpel was just in reach of his fingers at his forearm's fullest stretch from the bound elbow. The horror crouched on him and, even now slowly feeding its trunkline into his groin incision, at first stopped the doctor's hand with a pang of terror. Then he reminded himself that, until implanted, the enemy was a senseless mass, bristling with plugs, with input jacks for senses, but, until installed in the physical amplifiers of eyes and ears, an utterly deaf, blind monad that waited in a perfect solipsism between two captive sensory envelopes.

He saw his straining fingers above the bright tool of freedom, thought with an insane smile of God and Adam on the Sistine ceiling, and then, with a lifespan of surgeon's fine control, plucked up the scalpel. The arm fell and hung.

"Sleep," the doctor said. "Sleep revenged."

But he found his retaliation harshly reined-in by the alien's careful provisions. His elbow had been fixed with his upper arm almost at right angles to his body's long axis; his forearm could reach his hand inward and present it closely to the face, suiting the parasite's need of an eye-hand coordinative check, but could not, even with the scalpel's added reach, bring its point within four inches of his groin. Steadily the parasite fed in its tapline. It would usurp motor control in three or four minutes at most, to judge by the time its extrication from Allen had taken.

Frantically the doctor bent his wrist inwards to its limit, trying to pick through the strap where it crossed his inner elbow. Sufficient pressure was impossible, and the hold so awkward that even feeble attempts threatened the loss of the scalpel. Smoothly the root of alien control sank into him. It was a defenseless thing of jelly against which he lay lethally armed, and he was still doomed—a preview of all his thrall's impotence-to-be.

But of course there was a way. Not to survive. But to escape, and to have vengeance. For a moment he stared at his captor, hardening his mettle in the blaze of hate it lit in him. Then, swiftly, he determined the order of his moves, and began.

He reached the scalpel to his neck and opened his superior thyroid vein—his inkwell. He laid the scalpel by his ear, dipped his finger in his blood, and began to write on the metal surface of the gurney, beginning by his thigh and moving towards his armpit. Oddly, the incision of his neck, though this was muscularly awake, had been painless, which gave him hopes that raised his courage for what remained to do. His neat, sparing strokes scribed with ghastly legibility. When he had done the message read:

MIND PARASITE
FM ALLEN IN ME
CUT *all* TILL FIND
1500 GM MASS
NERVE FIBRE

He wanted to write goodbye to his friend, but the alien had begun to pay out smaller, auxiliary filaments collaterally with the main one, and all now lay in speed.

He took up the scalpel, rolled his head to the left, and plunged the blade deep in his ear.

Miracle! Last, accidental mercy! It was painless. Some procedural, highly specific anesthetic was in effect. With careful plunges, he obliterated the right inner ear and then thrust silence, with equal thoroughness, into the left. The slashing of the vocal cords followed, then the tendons in the back of the neck that hold it erect. He wished he were free to unstring knees and elbows too, but it could not be. But blinded, with centers of balance lost, with only rough motor control—all these conditions should fetter the alien's escape, should it in the first place manage the reanimation of a bloodless corpse in which it had not yet achieved a fine-tuned interweave. Before he extinguished his eyes, he paused, the scalpel poised above his face, and blinked them to clear his aim of tears. The right, then the left, both retinas meticulously carved away, the yolk of vision quite scooped out of them. The scalpel's last task, once it had tilted the head sideways to guide the bloodflow absolutely clear of possible effacement of the message, was to slash the external carotid artery.

When this was done the old man sighed with relief and laid his scalpel down. Even as he did so, he felt the deep, inward prickle of an alien energy—something that flared, crackled, flared, *groped for* but did not quite find its purchase. And inwardly, as the doctor sank towards sleep—cerebrally, as a voiceless man must speak—he spoke to the parasite these carefully chosen words:

"Welcome to your new house. I'm afraid there's been some vandalism—the lights don't work, and the plumbing has a very bad leak. There are some other things wrong as well—the neighborhood is perhaps a little *too* quiet, and you may find it hard to get around very easily. But it's been a lovely home for me for fifty-seven years, and somehow I think you'll stay. . . ."

The face, turned towards the body of Joe Allen, seemed to weep scarlet tears, but its last movement before death was to smile.

E. Nesbit

JOHN CHARRINGTON'S WEDDING

Edith Nesbit is a dominant figure in children's literature, but her horror and supernatural fiction is less well known. "John Charrington's Wedding" seems at first just a little romantic fantasy about love conquering all, but there is more than a touch of Le Fanu's "Schalken the Painter" and Ivan Turgenev's "Clara Militch" in this short piece by a woman who was at the center of the intellectual movements of her era.

No one ever thought that May Forster would marry John Charrington; but he thought differently, and things which John Charrington intended had a queer way of coming to pass. He asked her to marry him before he went up to Oxford. She laughed and refused him. He asked her again next time he came home. Again she laughed, tossed her dainty blonde head, and again refused. A third time he asked her; she said it was becoming a confirmed bad habit, and laughed at him more than ever.

John was not the only man who wanted to marry her. She was the belle of our village coterie, and we were all in love with her more or less; it was a sort of fashion, like heliotrope ties or Inverness capes. Therefore we were as much annoyed as surprised when John Charrington walked into our little local Club—we held it in a loft over the saddler's, I remember—and invited us all to his wedding.

"Your wedding?"

"You don't mean it?"

"Who's the happy fair? When's it to be?"

John Charrington filled his pipe and lighted it before he replied. Then he said, "I'm sorry to deprive you fellows of your only joke—but Miss Forster and I are to be married in September."

"You don't meant it?"

"He's got the boot again, and it's turned his head."

"No," I said, rising, "I see it's true. Lend me a pistol someone—or a first-class fare to the other end of Nowhere. Charrington has bewitched the only pretty girl in our twenty-mile radius. Was it mesmerism, or a love potion, Jack?"

"Neither, sir, but a gift you'll never have—perseverance—and the best luck a man ever had in this world."

There was something in his voice that silenced me, and all the chaff of the other fellows failed to draw him further.

The queer thing about it was that when we congratulated Miss Forster, she blushed and smiled and dimpled, for all the world as though she were in love with him, and had been in love with him all the time. Upon my word, I think she had. Women are strange creatures.

We were all asked to the wedding. In Brixham everyone who was anybody knew everybody else who was anyone. My sisters were, I truly believe, more interested in the trousseau than the bride herself, and I was to be best man. The coming marriage was much canvassed at afternoon tea-tables, and at our little Club over the saddler's, and the question was always asked: "Does she care for him?"

I used to ask that question myself in the early days of their engagement, but after a certain evening in August I never asked it again. I was coming home from the Club through the churchyard. Our church is on a thyme-grown hill, and the turf about it is so thick and soft that one's footsteps are noiseless.

I made no sound as I vaulted the low lichened wall and threaded my way between the tombstones. It was at the same instant that I heard John Charrington's voice, and saw her. May was sitting on a low flat gravestone, her face turned towards the full splendor of the western sun. Its expression ended, at once and for ever, any question of love for him; it was transfigured to a beauty I should not have believed possible, even to that beautiful little face.

John lay at her feet, and it was his voice that broke the stillness of the golden August evening. "My dear, my dear, I believe I should come back from the dead if you wanted me!"

I coughed at once to indicate my presence, and passed on into the shadow, fully enlightened.

The wedding was to be early in September. Two days before I had to run up to town on business. The train was late, of course, for we are on the South-eastern, and as I stood grumbling with my watch in my hand, whom should I see but John Charrington and May Forster. They were walking up and down the unfrequented end of the platform, arm in arm, looking into each other's eyes, careless of the sympathetic interest of the porters.

Of course I knew better than to hesitate a moment before burying myself in the booking-office, and it was not till the train drew up at the platform, that I obtrusively passed the pair with my suitcase and took the corner in a first-class smoking-carriage. I did this with as good an air of not seeing them as I could assume. I pride myself on my discretion, but if John was travelling alone I wanted his company. I had it.

"Hullo, old man," came his cheery voice as he swung his bag into my carriage. "Here's luck; I was expecting a dull journey!"

"Where are you off to?" I asked, discretion still bidding me turn my eyes away, though I felt, without looking, that hers were red-rimmed.

"To old Branbridge's," he answered, shutting the door and leaning out for a last word with his sweetheart.

"Oh, I wish you wouldn't go, John," she was saying in a low, earnest voice. "I feel certain something will happen."

"Do you think I should let anything happen to keep me, and the day after tomorrow our wedding-day?"

"Don't go," she answered, with a pleading intensity which would have sent my suitcase onto the platform and me after it. But she wasn't speaking to me. John Charrington was made differently; he rarely changed his opinions, never his resolutions.

He only stroked the little ungloved hands that lay on the carriage door.

"I must, May. The old boy's been awfully good to me, and now he's dying I must go and see him, but I shall come home in time for—" The rest of the parting was lost in a whisper and in the rattling lurch of the starting train.

She spoke as the train moved: "You're sure to come?"

"Nothing shall keep me," he answered; and we steamed out. After he had seen the last of the little figure on the platform, he leaned back in his corner and kept silence for a minute.

When he spoke it was to explain to me that his godfather, whose heir he was, lay dying at Peasmarsh Place, some fifty miles away, and had sent for John, and John had felt bound to go.

"I shall surely be back tomorrow," he said, "or, if not, the day after, in heaps of time. Thank Heaven, one hasn't to get up in the middle of the night to get married nowadays!"

"And suppose Mr. Branbridge dies?"

"Alive or dead I mean to be married on Thursday!" John answered, lighting a cigar and unfolding *The Times*.

At Peasmarsh station we said good-bye, and he got out, and I saw him ride off; I went on to London, where I stayed the night.

When I got home the next afternoon, a very wet one, by the way, my sister Fanny greeted me with: "Where's Mr. Charrington?"

"Goodness knows," I answered testily. Every man, since Cain, has resented that kind of question.

"I thought you might have heard from him," she went on, "as you're to give him away tomorrow."

"Isn't he back?" I asked, for I had confidently expected to find him at home.

"No, Geoffrey"—my sister Fanny always had a way of jumping to conclusions, especially such conclusions as were least favorable to her fellow-creatures—"he has not returned, and, what is more, you may depend upon it he won't. You mark my words, there'll be no wedding tomorrow."

My sister Fanny has a power of annoying me which no other human being possesses.

"*You* mark *my* words," I retorted with asperity, "you had better give up making such a thundering idiot of yourself. There'll be more wedding tomorrow than ever you'll take the first part in." A prophecy which, by the way, came true.

But though I could snarl confidently to my sister, I did not feel so comfortable when late that night, I, standing on the doorstep of John's house, heard that he had not returned. I went home gloomily through the rain. Next morning brought a brilliant blue sky, gold sun, and all such softness of air and beauty of cloud as go to make up a perfect day. I woke with a vague feeling of having gone to bed anxious, and of being rather averse to facing that anxiety in the light of full wakefulness.

But with my shaving-water came a note from John which relieved my mind and sent me up to the Forsters' with a light heart.

May was in the garden. I saw her blue gown through the hollyhocks as the lodge gates swung to behind me. So I did not go up to the house, but turned aside down the turfed path.

"He's written to you too," she said, without preliminary greeting, when I reached her side.

"Yes, I'm to meet him at the station at three and come straight on to the church."

Her face looked pale, but there was a brightness in her

eyes, and a tender quiver about the mouth that spoke of renewed happiness.

"Mr. Branbridge begged him so to stay another night that
he had not the heart to refuse," she went on. "He is so kind,
but I wish he hadn't stayed."

I was at the station at half past two. I felt rather annoyed
with John. It seemed a sort of slight to the beautiful girl who
loved him that he should come, as it were, out of breath, and
with the dust of travel upon him, to take her hand, which
some of us would have given the best years of our lives to
take.

But when the three o'clock train glided in, and glided out
again having brought no passengers to our little station, I was
more than annoyed. There was no other train for thirty-five
minutes; I calculated that, with much hurry, we might just
get to the church in time for the ceremony; but, oh, what a
fool to have missed that first train! What other man could
have done it?

That thirty-five minutes seemed a year as I wandered
around the station reading the advertisements and the time-
tables, and the company's by-laws, and getting more and more
angry with John Charrington. This confidence in his own
power of getting everything he wanted the minute he wanted
it was leading him too far. I hate waiting. Everyone does,
but I believe I hate it more than anyone else. The three thirty-
five was late, of course.

I ground my pipe between my teeth and stamped with impatience as I watched the signals. *Click.* The signal went
down. Five minutes later I flung myself into the carriage that
I had brought for John.

"Drive to the church!" I said as someone shut the door.
"Mr. Charrington hasn't come by this train."

Anxiety now replaced anger. What had become of the man?
Could he have been taken ill suddenly? I had never known
him have a day's illness in his life. And even so he might
have telegraphed. Some awful accident must have happened
to him. The thought that he had played her false never—no,

not for a moment—entered my head. Yes, something terrible had happened to him, and on me lay the task of telling his bride. I almost wished the carriage would upset and break my head so that someone else might tell her, not I, who— But that's nothing to do with this story.

It was five minutes to four as we drew up to the churchyard gate. A double row of eager onlookers lined the path from lych-gate to porch. I sprang from the carriage and passed up between them. Our gardener had a good place near the front door. I stopped.

"Are they waiting still, Byles?" I asked simply to gain time, for of course I knew they were by the waiting crowd's attentive attitude.

"Waiting, sir? No, no, sir; why, it must be over by now."

"Over! Then Mr. Charrington's come?"

"To the minute, sir, must have missed you somehow, and I say, sir," lowering his voice, "I never seen Mr. John the least bit so afore, but my opinion is he's been drinking pretty free. His clothes was all dusty and his face like a sheet. I tell you I didn't like the looks of him at all, and the folks inside are saying all sorts of things. You'll see, something's gone very wrong with Mr. John, and he's tried liquor. He looked like a ghost, and in he went with his eyes straight before him, with never a look or a word for none of us, him that was always such a gentleman!"

I had never heard Byles make so long a speech. The crowd in the churchyard were talking in whispers and getting ready rice and slippers to throw at the bride and bridegroom. The ringers were ready with their hands on the ropes to ring out the merry peal as the bride and bridegroom should come out.

A murmur from the church announced them; out they came. Byles was right. John Charrington did not look himself. There was dust on his coat, his hair was disarranged. He seemed to have been in some row, for there was a black mark above his eyebrow. He was deathly pale. But his pallor was not greater than that of the bride, who might have been carved in ivory—dress, veil, orange blossoms, face and all.

As they passed, the ringers stopped—there were six of them—and then, on the ears expecting the gay wedding peal, came the slow tolling of the passing bell.

A thrill of horror at so foolish a jest from the ringers passed through us all. But the ringers themselves dropped the ropes and fled like rabbits out of the church into the sunlight. The bride shuddered, and grey shadows came about her mouth, but the bridegroom led her on down the path where the people stood with the handfuls of rice; but the handfuls were never thrown, and the wedding-bells never rang. In vain the ringers were urged to remedy their mistake: They protested with many whispered expletives that they would see themselves further first.

In a hush like the hush in the chamber of death, the bridal pair passed into their carriage and its door slammed behind them.

Then the tongues were loosed. A babel of anger, wonder, and conjecture from the guests and the spectators.

"If I'd seen his condition, sir," said old Forster to me as we drove off, "I would have stretched him on the floor of the church, sir, by Heaven I would, before I'd have let him marry my daughter!"

Then he put his head out of the window.

"Drive like hell," he cried to the coachman. "Don't spare the horses."

He was obeyed. We passed the bride's carriage. I forbore to look at it, and old Forster turned his head away and swore. We reached home before it.

We stood in the hall doorway, in the blazing afternoon sun, and in about half a minute we heard wheels crunching the gravel. When the carriage stopped in front of the steps, old Forster and I ran down.

"Great Heaven, the carriage is empty! And yet—"

I had the door opened in a minute, and this is what I saw— no sign of John Charrington; only May, his wife, a huddled heap of white satin lying half on the floor of the carriage and half on the seat.

"I drove straight here, sir," said the coachman, as the bride's father lifted her out; "and I'll swear no one got out of the carriage."

We carried her into the house in her bridal dress and drew back her veil. I saw her face. Shall I ever forget it? White, white and drawn with agony and horror, bearing such a look of terror as I have never seen since except in dreams. And her hair, her radiant blonde hair, I tell you it was white as snow.

As we stood, her father and I, half mad with the horror and mystery of it, a boy came up the avenue—a telegraph boy. He brought the orange envelope to me. I tore it open.

Mr. Charrington was thrown from the dog-cart on his way to the station at half past one. Killed on the spot!

And he was married to May Forster in our parish church at *half past three*, in the presence of half the parish.

"Alive or dead I mean to be married!"

What had passed in that carriage on the homeward drive? No one knows—no one will ever know. Oh, May! Oh, my dear!

Before a week was over, they laid her beside her husband in our little churchyard on the thyme-covered hill—the churchyard where they had kept their love-trysts.

Thus was accomplished John Charrington's wedding.

Karl Edward Wagner

STICKS

Karl Edward Wagner is a young writer committed to the tradition of modern horror and dark fantasy. His mentor was Manly Wade Wellman but his influences range throughout contemporary horror. "Sticks" is generally regarded as his finest work to date. It is based upon an anecdote of the great horror artist, Lee Brown Coye, who told of strange, weird artifacts and drawings found in an abandoned farmhouse in upstate New York and around it. Although Wagner's story is overtly a Lovecraftian story of historical and cosmic evil, a forbidden knowledge piece, it is also structured to awaken in the reader imaginative possibilities deeply embedded in the human subconscious. Wagner is a forceful personality in the contemporary field and editor of the annual volume, *The Year's Best Horror Stories*, as well as the small-press publisher of Carcosa House books.

1

The lashed-together framework of sticks jutted from a small cairn alongside the stream. Colin Leverett studied it in perplexment—half a dozen odd lengths of branch, wired together at cross angles for no fathomable purpose. It reminded him unpleasantly of some bizarre crucifix, and he wondered what might lie beneath the cairn.

It was the spring of 1942—the kind of day to make the war seem distant and unreal, although the draft notice waited on his desk. In a few days Leverett would lock his rural studio, wonder if he would see it again—be able to use its pens and brushes and carving tools when he did return. It was good-by to the woods and streams of upstate New York, too. No fly rods, no tramps through the countryside in Hitler's Europe. No point in putting off fishing that troutstream he had driven past once, exploring back roads of the Otselic Valley.

Mann Book—so it was marked on the old Geological Survey map—ran southeast of DeRuyter. The unfrequented country road crossed over a stone bridge old before the first horseless carriage, but Leverett's Ford eased across and onto the shoulder. Taking fly rod and tackle, he included pocket flask and tied an iron skillet to his belt. He'd work his way downstream a few miles. By afternoon he'd lunch on fresh trout, maybe some bullfrog-legs.

It was a fine clear stream, though difficult to fish as dense bushes hung out from the bank, broken with stretches of open water hard to work without being seen. But the trout rose boldly to his fly, and Leverett was in fine spirits.

From the bridge the valley along Mann Brook began as fairly open pasture, but half a mile downstream the land had fallen into disuse and was thick with second growth evergreens and scrub-apple trees. Another mile, and the scrub merged with dense forest, which continued unbroken. The land here, he had learned, had been taken over by the state many years back.

As Leverett followed the stream he noted the remains of an old railroad embankment. No vestige of tracks or ties—only the embankment itself, overgrown with large trees. The artist rejoiced in the beautiful dry-wall culverts spanning the stream as it wound through the valley. To his mind it seemed eerie, this forgotten railroad running straight and true through virtual wilderness.

He could imagine an old wood-burner with its conical stack, steaming along through the valley dragging two or three wooden coaches. It must be a branch of the old Oswego Midland Rail Road, he decided, abandoned rather suddenly in the 1870's. Leverett, who had a memory for detail, knew of it from a story his grandfather told of riding the line in 1871 from Otselic to DeRuyter on his honeymoon. The engine had so labored up the steep grade over Crumb Hill that he got off to walk alongside. Probably that sharp grade was the reason for the line's abandonment.

When he came across a scrap of board nailed to several sticks set into a stone wall, his darkest thought was that it might read "No Trespassing." Curiously, though the board was weathered featureless, the nails seemed quite new. Leverett scarcely gave it much thought, until a short distance beyond he came upon another such contrivance. And another.

Now he scratched at the day's stubble on his long jaw. This didn't make sense. A prank? But on whom? A child's game? No, the arrangement was far too sophisticated. As an artist, Leverett appreciated the craftsmanship of the work—the calculated angles and lengths, the designed intricacy of the maddeningly inexplicable devices. There was something distinctly uncomfortable about their effect.

Leverett reminded himself that he had come here to fish and continued downstream. But as he worked around a thicket he again stopped in puzzlement.

Here was a small open space with more of the stick lattices and an arrangement of flat stones laid out on the ground. The stones—likely taken from one of the many dry-wall culverts—made a pattern maybe twenty by fifteen feet, that at first glance resembled a ground plan for a house. Intrigued, Leverett quickly saw that this was not so. If the ground plan were for anything, it would have to be for a small maze.

The bizarre lattice structures were all around. Sticks from trees and bits of board nailed together in fantastic array. They defied description; no two seemed alike. Some were only one or two sticks lashed together in parallel or at angles. Others were worked into complicated lattices of dozens of sticks and

boards. One could have been a child's tree house—it was built
in three planes, but was so abstract and useless that it could
be nothing more than an insane conglomeration of sticks and
wire. Sometimes the contrivances were stuck in a pile of
stones or a wall, maybe thrust into the railroad embankment
or nailed to a tree.

It should have been ridiculous. It wasn't. Instead it seemed
somehow sinister—these utterly inexplicable, meticulously
constructed stick lattices spread through a wilderness where
only a tree-grown embankment or a forgotten stone wall gave
evidence that man had ever passed through. Leverett forgot
about trout and frog-legs, instead dug into his pockets for a
notebook and stub of pencil. Busily he began to sketch the
more intricate structures. Perhaps someone could explain
them; perhaps there was something to their insane complexity
that warranted closer study for his own work.

Leverett was roughly two miles from the bridge when he
came upon the ruins of a house. It was an unlovely colonial
farmhouse, box-shaped and gambrel-roofed, fast falling into
the ground. Windows were dark and empty; the chimneys on
either end looked ready to topple. Rafters showed through
open spaces in the room, and the weathered boards of the
walls had in places rotted away to reveal hewn timber beams.
The foundation was stone and disproportionately massive.
From the size of the unmortared stone blocks, its builder had
intended the foundation to stand forever.

The house was nearly swallowed up by undergrowth and
rampant lilac bushes, but Leverett could distinguish what had
been a lawn with imposing shade trees. Farther back were
gnarled and sickly apple trees and an overgrown garden where
a few lost flowers still bloomed—wan and serpentine from
years in the wild. The stick lattices were everywhere—the
lawn, the trees, even the house were covered with the uncanny structures. They reminded Leverett of a hundred mis-
shapen spider webs—grouped so closely together as to almost
ensnare the entire house and clearing. Wondering, he

sketched page on page of them, as he cautiously approached the abandoned house.

He wasn't certain just what he expected to find inside. The aspect of the farmhouse was frankly menacing, standing as it did in gloomy desolation where the forest had devoured the works of man—where the only sign that man had been here in this century were these insanely wrought latticeworks of sticks and board. Some might have turned back at this point. Leverett, whose fascination for the macabre was evident in his art, instead was intrigued. He drew a rough sketch of the farmhouse and the grounds, overrun with the enigmatic devices, with thickets of hedges and distorted flowers. He regretted that it might be years before he could capture the eeriness of this place on scratchboard or canvas.

The door was off its hinges, and Leverett gingerly stepped within, hoping that the flooring remained sound enough to bear even his sparse frame. The afternoon sun pierced the empty windows, mottling the decaying floorboards with great blotches of light. Dust drifted in the sunlight. The house was empty—stripped of furnishings other than indistinct tangles of rubble mounded over with decay and the drifted leaves of many seasons.

Someone had been here, and recently. Someone who had literally covered the mildewed walls with diagrams of the mysterious lattice structures. The drawings were applied directly to the walls, crisscrossing the rotting wallpaper and crumbling plaster in bold black lines. Some of the vertiginous complexity covered an entire wall like a mad mural. Others were small, only a few crossed lines, and reminded Leverett of cuneiform glyphics.

His pencil hurried over the pages of his notebook. Leverett noted with fascination that a number of the drawings were recognizable as schematics of lattices he had earlier sketched. Was this then the planning room for the madman or educated idiot who had built these structures? The gouges etched by the charcoal into the soft plaster appeared fresh—done days or months ago, perhaps.

A darkened doorway opened into the cellar. Were these drawings there as well? And what else? Leverett wondered if he should dare it. Except for streamers of light that crept through cracks in the flooring, the cellar was in darkness.

"Hello?" he called. "Anyone here?" It didn't seem silly just then. These stick lattices hardly seemed the work of a rational mind. Leverett wasn't enthusiastic with the prospect of encountering such a person in this dark cellar. It occurred to him that virtually anything might transpire here, and no one in the world of 1942 would ever know.

And that in itself was too great a fascination for one of Leverett's temperament. Carefully he started down the cellar stairs. They were stone and thus solid, but treacherous with moss and debris.

The cellar was enormous—even more so in the darkness. Leverett reached the foot of the steps and paused for his eyes to adjust to the damp gloom. An earlier impression recurred to him. The cellar was too big for the house. Had another dwelling stood here originally—perhaps destroyed and rebuilt by one of lesser fortune? He examined the stonework. Here were great blocks of gneiss that might support a castle. On closer look they reminded him of a fortress—for the dry-wall technique was startlingly Mycenaean.

Like the house above, the cellar appeared to be empty, although without light Leverett could not be certain what the shadows hid. There seemed to be darker areas of shadow along sections of the foundation wall, suggesting openings to chambers beyond. Leverett began to feel uneasy in spite of himself.

There was something here—a large tablelike bulk in the center of the cellar. Where a few ghosts of sunlight drifted down to touch its edges, it seemed to be of stone. Cautiously he crossed the stone paving to where it loomed—waist-high, maybe eight feet long and less wide. A roughly shaped slab of gneiss, he judged, and supported by pillars of unmortared stone. In the darkness he could only get a vague conception of the object. He ran his hand along the slab. It seemed to have a groove along its edge.

His groping fingers encountered fabric, something cold and leathery and yielding. Mildewed harness, he guessed in distaste.

Something closed on his wrist, set icy nails into his flesh.

Leverett screamed and lunged away with frantic strength. He was held fast, but the object on the stone slab pulled upward.

A sickly beam of sunlight came down to touch one end of the slab. It was enough. As Leverett struggled backward and the thing that held him heaved up from the stone table, its face passed through the beam of light.

It was a lich's face—desiccated flesh tight over its skull. Filthy strands of hair were matted over its scalp, tattered lips were drawn away from broken yellowed teeth, and, sunken in their sockets, eyes that should be dead were bright with hideous life.

Leverett screamed again, desperate with fear. His free hand clawed the iron skillet tied to his belt. Ripping it loose, he smashed at the nightmarish face with all his strength.

For one frozen instant of horror the sunlight let him see the skillet crush through the mould-eaten forehead like an axe—cleaving the dry flesh and brittle bone. The grip on his wrist failed. The cadaverous face fell away, and the sight of its caved-in forehead and unblinking eyes from between which thick blood had begun to ooze would awaken Leverett from nightmare on countless nights.

But now Leverett tore free and fled. And when his aching legs faltered as he plunged headlong through the scrub-growth, he was spurred to desperate energy by the memory of the footsteps that had stumbled up the cellar stairs behind him.

2 _____

When Colin Leverett returned from the war, his friends marked him a changed man. He had aged. There were streaks of gray in his hair; his springy step had slowed. The athletic leanness of his body had withered to an unhealthy gauntness. There were indelible lines to his face, and his eyes were haunted.

More disturbing was an alteration of temperament. A mordant cynicism had eroded his earlier air of whimsical asceticism. His fascination with the macabre had assumed a darker mood, a morbid obsession that his old acquaintances found disquieting. But it had been that kind of a war, especially for those who had fought through the Apennines.

Leverett might have told them otherwise, had he cared to discuss his nightmarish experience on Mann Brook. But Leverett kept his own counsel, and when he grimly recalled that creature he had struggled with in the abandoned cellar, he usually convinced himself it had only been a derelict—a crazy hermit whose appearance had been distorted by the poor light and his own imagination. Nor had his blow more than glanced off the man's forehead, he reasoned, since the other had recovered quickly enough to give chase. It was best not to dwell upon such matters, and this rational explanation helped restore sanity when he awoke from nightmares of that face.

This Colin Leverett returned to his studio, and once more plied his pens and brushes and carving knives. The pulp magazines, where fans had acclaimed his work before the war, welcomed him back with long lists of assignments. There were commissions from galleries and collectors, unfinished sculptures and wooden models. Leverett busied himself.

There were problems now. *Short Stories* returned a cover painting as "too grotesque." The publishers of a new anthology of horror stories sent back a pair of his interior drawings—"too gruesome, especially the rotted, bloated faces of those hanged men.'' A customer returned a silver figurine, complaining that the martyred saint was too thoroughly martyred. Even *Weird Tales*, after heralding his return to his ghoul-haunted pages, began returning illustrations they considered ''too strong, even for our readers.''

Leveret tried half-heartedly to tone things down, found the results vapid and uninspired. Eventually the assignments stopped trickling in. Leverett, becoming more the recluse as years went by, dismissed the pulp days from his mind. Working quietly in his isolated studio, he found a living doing occasional commissioned pieces and gallery work, from time to time selling a painting or sculpture to major museums. Critics had much praise for his bizarre abstract sculptures.

3

The war was twenty-five years history when Colin Leverett received a letter from a good friend of the pulp days—Prescott Brandon, now editor-publisher of Gothic House, a small press that specialized in books of the weird-fantasy genre. Despite a lapse in correspondence of many years, Brandon's letter began in his typically direct style:

> *The Eyrie/Salem, Mass./Aug. 2*
> *To the Macabre Hermit of the Midlands:*
> *Colin, I'm putting together a deluxe three-volume collection of H. Kenneth Allard's horror stories. I well recall that Kent's stories were personal favorites of yours. How about shambling forth from retirement and illustrating these for me? Will need two-color jackets and a dozen line interiors each. Would hope that you can startle fandom with some especially ghastly drawings for these—something different from the hackneyed skulls and bats and werewolves carting off half-dressed ladies.*

Interested? I'll send you the materials and details, and you can have a free hand. Let us hear—Scotty.

Leverett was delighted. He felt some nostalgia for the pulp days, and he had always admired Allard's genius in transforming visions of cosmic horror into convincing prose. He wrote Brandon an enthusiastic reply.

He spent hours rereading the stories for inclusion, making notes and preliminary sketches. No squeamish subeditors to offend here; Scotty meant what he said. Leverett bent to his task with maniacal relish.

Something different, Scotty had asked. A free hand. Leverett studied his pencil sketches critically. The figures seemed headed in the right direction, but the drawings needed something more—something that would inject the mood of sinister evil that pervaded Allard's work. Grinning skulls and leathery bats? Trite. Allard demanded more.

The idea had inexorably taken hold of him. Perhaps because Allard's tales evoked that same sense of horror; perhaps because Allard's vision of crumbling Yankee farmhouses and their depraved secrets so reminded him of that spring afternoon at Mann Brook . . .

Although he had refused to look at it since the day he had staggered in, half-dead from terror and exhaustion, Leverett perfectly recalled where he had flung his notebook. He retrieved it from the back of a seldom used file, thumbed through the wrinkled pages thoughtfully. These hasty sketches reawakened the sense of forboding evil, the charnel horror of that day. Studying the bizarre lattice patterns, it seemed impossible to Leverett that others would not share his feeling of horror that the stick structures evoked in him.

He began to sketch bits of stick latticework into his pencil roughs. The sneering faces of Allard's degenerate creatures took on an added shadow of menace. Leverett nodded, pleased with the effect.

4

Some months afterward a letter from Brandon informed Leverett he had received the last of the Allard drawings and was enormously pleased with the work. Brandon added a postscript:

> *For God's sake Colin—What is it with these insane sticks you've got poking up everywhere in the illos! The damn things get really creepy after awhile. How on earth did you get onto this?*

Leverett supposed he owed Brandon some explanation. Dutifully he wrote a lengthy letter, setting down the circumstances of his experience at Mann Brook—omitting only the horror that had seized his wrist in the cellar. Let Brandon think him eccentric, but not madman and murderer.

Brandon's reply was immediate:

> *Colin—Your account of the Mann Brook episode is fascinating—and incredible! It reads like the start of one of Allard's stories! I have taken the liberty of forwarding your letter to Alexander Stefroi in Pelham. Dr. Stefroi is an earnest scholar of this region's history—as you may already know. I'm certain your account will interest him, and he may have some light to shed on the uncanny affair.*
>
> *Expect 1st volume, Voices from the Shadow, to be ready from the binder next month. The proofs looked great. Best—Scotty.*

The following week brought a letter postmarked Pelham, Massachusetts:

> *A mutual friend, Prescott Brandon, forwarded your fascinating account of discovering curious sticks and*

stone artifacts on an abandoned farm in upstate New York. I found this most intriguing, and wonder if you recall further details? Can you relocate the exact site after thirty years? If possible, I'd like to examine the foundations this spring, as they call to mind similar megalithic sites of this region. Several of us are interested in locating what we believe are remains of megalithic constructions dating back to the Bronze Age, and to determine their possible use in rituals of black magic in colonial days.

Present archaeological evidence indicates that ca. 1700–2000 B.C. there was an influx of Bronze Age peoples into the Northeast from Europe. We know that the Bronze Age saw the rise of an extremely advanced culture, and that as seafarers, they were to have no peers until the Vikings. Remains of a megalithic culture originating in the Mediterranean can be seen in the Lion Gate in Mycenae, in the Stonehenge, and in dolmens, passage graves and barrow mounds throughout Europe. Moreover, this seems to have represented far more than a style of architecture peculiar to the era. Rather, it appears to have been a religious cult whose adherents worshipped a sort of Earth-mother, served her with fertility rituals and sacrifices, and believed that immortality of the soul could be secured through interment in megalithic tombs.

That this culture came to America cannot be doubted from the hundreds of megalithic remnants found—and now recognized—in our region. The most important site to date is Mystery Hill in N.H., comprising a great many walls and dolmens of megalithic construction— most notably the Y Cavern barrow mound and the Sacrificial Table (see postcard). Less spectacular megalithic sites include a group of cairns and carved stones at Mineral Mt., subterranean chambers with stone passageways such as at Petersham and Shutesbury, and uncounted shaped megaliths and buried "monks' cells" throughout this region.

Of further interest, these sites seem to have retained their mystic aura for the early colonials, and numerous megalithic sites show evidence of having been used for sinister purposes by colonial sorcerers and alchemists. This became particularly true after the witchcraft persecutions drove many practitioners into the western wilderness—explaining why upstate New York and western Mass. have seen the emergence of so many cultist groups in later years.

Of particular interest here is Shadrach Ireland's "Brethren of the New Light," who believed that the world was soon to be destroyed by sinister "Powers from Outside" and that they, the elect, would then attain physical immortality. The elect who died beforehand were to have their bodies preserved on tables of stone until the "Old Ones" came forth to return them to life. We have definitely linked the megalithic sites at Shutesbury to later unwholesome practices of the New Light cult. They were absorbed in 1781 by Mother Ann Lee's Shakers, and Ireland's putrescent corpse was hauled from the stone table in his cellar and buried.

Thus I think it probable that your farmhouse may have figured in similar hidden practices. At Mystery Hill a farmhouse was built in 1826 that incorporated one dolmen in its foundations. The house burned down ca. 1848–55, and there were some unsavory local stories as to what took place there. My guess is that your farmhouse had been built over or incorporated a similar megalithic site—and that your "sticks" indicate some unknown cult still survived there. I can recall certain vague references to lattice devices figuring in secret ceremonies, but can pinpoint nothing definite. Possibly they represent a development of occult symbols to be used in certain conjurations, but this is just a guess. I sug-

gest you consult Waite's Ceremonial Magic *or such to see if you can recognize similar magical symbols.*

Hope this is of some use to you. Please let me hear back.

Sincerely, Alexander Stefroi.

There was a postcard enclosed—a photograph of a four-and-a-half-ton slab, ringed by a deep groove with a spout, identified as the Sacrificial Table at Mystery Hill. On the back Stefroi had written:

You must have found something similar to this. They are not rare—we have one in Pelham removed from a site now beneath Quabbin Reservoir. They were used for sacrifice—animal and human—and the groove is to channel blood into a bowl, presumably.

Leverett dropped the card and shuddered. Stefroi's letter re-awakened the old horror, and he wished now he had let the matter lie forgotten in his files. Of course, it couldn't be forgotten—even after thirty years.

He wrote Stefroi a careful letter, thanking him for his information and adding a few minor details to his account. This spring, he promised, wondering if he would keep that promise, he would try to relocate the farmhouse on Mann Brook.

5

Spring was late that year, and it was not until early June that Colin Leverett found time to return to Mann Brook. On the surface, very little had changed in three decades. The ancient stone bridge yet stood, nor had the country lane been paved. Leverett wondered whether anyone had driven past since his terror-sped flight.

He found the old railroad grade easily as he started downstream. Thirty years, he told himself—but the chill inside him only tightened. The going was far more difficult than before. The day was unbearably hot and humid. Wading through the rank underbrush raised clouds of black flies that savagely bit him.

Evidently the stream had seen severe flooding in the past years, judging from piled logs and debris that blocked his path. Stretches were scooped out to barren rocks and gravel. Elsewhere gigantic barriers of uprooted trees and debris looked like ancient and mouldering fortifications. As he worked his way down the valley, he realized that his search would yield nothing. So intense had been the force of the long-ago flood that even the course of the stream had changed. Many of the dry-wall culverts no longer spanned the brook, but sat lost and alone far back from its present banks. Others had been knocked flat and swept away, or were buried beneath tons of rotting logs.

At one point Leverett found remnants of an apple orchard groping through weeds and bushes. He thought that the house must be close by, but here the flooding had been particularly severe, and evidently even those ponderous stone foundations had been toppled over and buried beneath debris.

Leverett finally turned back to his car. His step was lighter.

A few weeks later he received a response from Stefroi to his reported failure:

Forgive my tardy reply to your letter of 13 June. I have recently been pursuing inquiries which may, I hope, lead to the discovery of a previously unreported megalithic site of major significance. Naturally I am disappointed that no traces remained of the Mann Brook site. While I tried not to get my hopes up, it did seem likely that the foundations would have survived. In searching through regional data, I note that there were particularly severe flashfloods in the Otselic area in July 1942 and again in May 1946. Very probably your old

farmhouse with its enigmatic devices was utterly de-
stroyed not very long after your discovery of the site.
This is weird and wild country, and doubtless there is
much we shall never know.

I write this with a profound sense of personal loss of
the death two nights ago of Prescott Brandon. This was
a severe blow to me—as I am sure it was to you and to
all who knew him. I only hope the police will catch the
vicious killers who did this senseless act—evidently
thieves surprised while ransacking his office. Police be-
lieve the killers were high on drugs from the mindless
brutality of their crime.

I had just received a copy of the third Allard volume,
Unhallowed Places. *A superbly designed book, and this*
tragedy becomes all the more insuperable with the re-
alization that Scotty will give the world no more such
treasures. In Sorrow, Alexander Stefroi.

Leverett stared at the letter in shock. He had not received
news of Brandon's death—had only a few days before opened
a parcel from the publisher containing a first copy of *Unhal-*
lowed Places. A line in Brandon's last letter recurred to him—
a line that seemed amusing to him at the time:

Your sticks have bewildered a good many fans, Colin,
and I've worn out a ribbon answering inquiries. One
fellow in particular—a Major George Leonard—has
pressed me for details, and I'm afraid that I told him
too much. He has written several times for your ad-
dress, but knowing how you value your privacy I told
him simply to permit me to forward any correspon-
dence. He wants to see your original sketches, I gather,
but these overbearing occult types give me a pain.
Frankly, I wouldn't care to meet the man myself.

6

"Mr. Colin Leverett?"

Leverett studied the tall lean man who stood smiling at the doorway of his studio. The sports car he had driven up in was black and looked expensive. The same held for the turtleneck and leather slacks he wore, and the sleek briefcase he carried. The blackness made his thin face deathly pale. Leverett guessed his age to be late forty by the thinning of his hair. Dark glasses hid his eyes, black driving gloves his hands.

"Scotty Brandon told me where to find you," the stranger said.

"Scotty?" Leverett's voice was wary.

"Yes, we lost a mutual friend, I regret to say. I'd been talking with him just before. . . . But I see by your expression that Scotty never had time to write."

He fumbled awkwardly. "I'm Dana Allard."

"Allard?"

His visitor seemed embarrassed. "Yes—H. Kenneth Allard was my uncle."

"I hadn't realized Allard left a family," mused Leverett, shaking the extended hand. He had never met the writer personally, but there was a strong resemblance to the few photographs he had seen. And Scotty had been paying royalty checks to an estate of some sort, he recalled.

"My father was Kent's half-brother. He later took his father's name, but there was no marriage, if you follow."

"Of course." Leverett was abashed. "Please find a place to sit down. And what brings you here?"

Dana Allard tapped his briefcase. "Something I'd been discussing with Scotty. Just recently I turned up a stack of my uncle's unpublished manuscripts." He unlatched the briefcase and handed Leverett a sheaf of yellowed paper. "Father collected Kent's personal effects from the state hospital as next-of-kin. He never thought much of my uncle, or his writing. He stuffed this away in our attic and forgot about it. Scotty was quite excited when I told him of my discovery."

Leverett was glancing through the manuscript—page on page of cramped handwriting, with revisions pieced throughout like an indecipherable puzzle. He had seen photographs of Allard manuscripts. There was no mistaking this.

Or the prose. Leverett read a few passages with rapt absorption. It was authentic—and brilliant.

"Uncle's mind seems to have taken an especially morbid turn as his illness drew on," Dana hazarded. "I admire his work very greatly but I find these last few pieces . . . well a bit *too* horrible. Especially his translation of his mythical *Book of Elders*."

It appealed to Leverett perfectly. He barely noticed his guest as he pored over the brittle pages. Allard was describing a megalithic structure his doomed narrator had encountered in the crypts beneath an ancient churchyard. There were references to "elder glyphics" that resembled his lattice devices.

"Look here," pointed Dana. "These incantations he records here from Alorri-Zrokros's forbidden tome: 'Yogth-Yugth-Sut-Hyrath-Yogng'—hell, I can't pronounce them. And he has pages of them."

"This is incredible!" Leverett protested. He tried to mouth the alien syllables. It could be done. He even detected a rhythm.

"Well, I'm relieved that you approve. I'd feared these last few stories and fragments might prove a little too much for Kent's fans."

"Then you're going to have them published?"

Dana nodded. "Scotty was going to. I just hope those thieves weren't searching for this—a collector would pay a fortune. But Scotty said he was going to keep this secret until he was ready for announcement." His thin face was sad.

"So now I'm going to publish it myself—in a deluxe edition. And I want you to illustrate it."

"I'd feel honored!" vowed Leverett, unable to believe it.

"I really liked those drawings you did for the trilogy. I'd like to see more like those—as many as you feel like doing. I mean to spare no expense in publishing this. And those stick things . . ."

"Yes?"

"Scotty told me the story on those. Fascinating! And you have a whole notebook of them? May I see it?"

Leverett hurriedly dug the notebook from his file, returned to the manuscript.

Dana paged through the book in awe. "These things are totally bizarre—and there are references to such things in the manuscript, to make it even more fantastic. Can you reproduce them all for the book?"

"All I can remember," Leverett assured him. "And I have a good memory. But won't that be overdoing it?"

"Not at all! They fit into the book. And they're utterly unique. No, put everything you've got into this book. I'm going to entitle it *Dwellers in the Earth*, after the longest piece. I've already arranged for its printing, so we begin as soon as you can have the art ready. And I know you'll give it your all."

7

He was floating in space. Objects drifted past him. Stars, he first thought. The objects drifted closer.

Sticks. Stick lattices of all configurations. And then he was drifting among them, and he saw that they were not sticks—not of wood. The lattice designs were of dead-pale substance, like streaks of frozen starlight. They reminded him of glyphics of some unearthly alphabet—complex, enigmatic symbols arranged to spell . . . what? And there *was* an arrangement—a three-dimensional pattern. A maze of utterly baffling intricacy . . .

Then somehow he was in a tunnel. A cramped, stone-lined

tunnel through which he must crawl on his belly. The dank, moss-slimed stones pressed close about his wriggling form, evoking shrill whispers of claustrophobic dread.

And after an indefinite space of crawling through this and other stone-lined burrows, and sometimes through passages whose angles hurt his eyes, he would creep forth into a subterranean chamber. Great slabs of granite a dozen feet across formed the walls and ceiling of this buried chamber, and between the slabs other burrows pierced the earth. Altarlike, a gigantic slab of gneiss waited in the center of the chamber. A spring welled darkly between the stone pillars that supported the table. Its outer edge was encircled by a groove, sickeningly stained by the substance that clotted in the stone bowl beneath its collecting spout.

Others were emerging from the darkened burrows that ringed the chamber—slouched figures only dimly glimpsed and vaguely human. And a figure in a tattered cloak came toward him from the shadow—stretched out a clawlike hand to seize his wrist and draw him toward the sacrificial table. He followed unresistingly, knowing that something was expected of him.

They reached the altar and in the glow from the cuneiform lattices chiseled into the gneiss slab he could see the guide's face. A mouldering corpse-face, the rotten bone of his forehead smashed inward upon the foulness that oozed forth . . .

And Leveret would awaken to the echo of his screams . . .

He'd been working too hard, he told himself, stumbling about in the darkness, getting dressed because he was too shaken to return to sleep. The nightmares had been coming every night. No wonder he was exhausted.

But in his studio his work awaited him. Almost fifty drawings finished now, and he planned another score. No wonder the nightmares.

It was a grueling pace, but Dana Allard was ecstatic with the work he had done. And *Dwellers in the Earth* was waiting. Despite problems with typesetting, with getting the special paper Dana wanted—the book only waited on him.

Though his bones ached with fatigue, Leverett determinedly trudged through the graying night. Certain features of the nightmare would be interesting to portray.

8

The last of the drawings had gone off to Dana Allard in Petersham, and Leverett, fifteen pounds lighter and gutweary, converted part of the bonus check into a case of good whiskey. Dana had the offset presses rolling as soon as the plates were shot from the drawings. Despite his precise planning, presses had broken down, one printer quit for reasons not stated, there had been a bad accident at the new printer—seemingly innumerable problems, and Dana had been furious at each delay. But the production pushed along quickly for all that. Leverett wrote that the book was cursed, but Dana responded that a week would see it ready.

Leverett amused himself in his studio constructing stick lattices and trying to catch up on his sleep. He was expecting a copy of the book when he received a letter from Stefroi:

> *Have tried to reach you by phone last few days, but no answer at your house. I'm pushed for time just now, so must be brief. I have indeed uncovered an unsuspected megalithic site of enormous importance. It's located on the estate of a long-prominent Mass. family—and as I cannot receive authorization to visit it, I will not say where. Have investigated secretly (and quite illegally) for a short time one night and was nearly caught. Came across reference to the place in collection of seventeenth century letters and papers in a divinity school library. Writer denouncing the family as a brood of sorcerers and witches, references to alchemical activities and other less savory rumors—and describes underground stone chambers, megalithic artifacts, etc. which are put to "foul usage and diabolic praktise."*

Just got a quick glimpse but his description was not exaggerated. And Colin—in creeping through the woods to get to the site, I came across dozens of your mysterious "sticks"! Brought a small one back and have it here to show you. Recently constructed and exactly like your drawings. With luck, I'll gain admittance and find out their significance—undoubtedly they have significance—though these cultists can be stubborn about sharing their secrets. Will explain my interest is scientific, no exposure to ridicule—and see what they say. Will get a closer look one way or another. And so—I'm off! Sincerely, Alexander Stefroi.

Leverett's bushy brows rose. Allard had intimated certain dark rituals in which the stick lattices figured. But Allard had written over thirty years ago, and Leverett assumed the writer had stumbled onto something similar to the Mann Brook site. Stefroi was writing about something current.

He rather hoped Stefroi would discover nothing more than an inane hoax.

The nightmares haunted him still—familiar now, for all that its scenes and phantasms were visited by him only in dream. Familiar. The terror that they evoked was undiminished.

Now he was walking through forest—a section of hills that seemed to be close by. A huge slab of granite had been dragged aside, and a pit yawned where it had lain. He entered the pit without hesitation, and the rounded steps that led downward were known to his tread. A buried stone chamber, and leading from it stone-lined burrows. He knew which one to crawl into.

And again the underground room with its sacrificial altar and its dark spring beneath, and the gathering circle of poorly glimpsed figures. A knot of them clustered about the stone table, and as he stepped toward them he saw they pinned a frantically writhing man.

It was a stoutly built man, white hair disheveled, flesh gouged and filthy. Recognition seemed to burst over the contorted features, and he wondered if he should know the man. But now the lich with the caved-in skull was whispering in his ear, and he tried not to think of the unclean things that peered from that cloven brow, and instead took the bronze knife from the skeletal hand, and raised the knife high, and because he could not scream and awaken, did with the knife as the tattered priest had whispered . . .

And when after an interval of unholy madness, he at last did awaken, the stickiness that covered him was not cold sweat, nor was it nightmare the half-devoured heart he clutched in one fist.

9

Leverett somehow found sanity enough to dispose of the shredded lump of flesh. He stood under the shower all morning, scrubbing his skin raw. He wished he could vomit.

There was a news item on the radio. The crushed body of noted archaeologist, Dr. Alexander Stefroi, had been discovered beneath a fallen granite slab near Whately. Police speculated the gigantic slab had shifted with the scientist's excavations at its base. Identification was made through personal effects.

When his hands stopped shaking enough to drive, Leverett fled to Petersham—reaching Dana Allard's old stone house about dark. Allard was slow to answer his frantic knock.

"Why, good evening, Colin! What a coincidence your coming here just now! The books are ready. The bindery just delivered them."

Leverett brushed past him. "We've got to destroy them!" he blurted. He'd thought a lot since morning.

"Destroy them?"

"There's something none of us figured on. Those stick lattices—there's a cult, some damnable cult. The lattices have some significance in their rituals. Stefroi hinted once they might be glyphics of some sort, I don't know. But the cult is still alive. They killed Scotty . . . they killed Stefroi. They're onto me—I don't know what they intend. They'll kill you to stop you from releasing this book!''

Dana's frown was worried, but Leverett knew he hadn't impressed him the right way. ''Colin, this sounds insane. You really have been overextending yourself, you know. Look, I'll show you the books. They're in the cellar.''

Leverett let his host lead him downstairs. The cellar was quite large, flagstoned and dry. A mountain of brown-wrapped bundles awaited them.

''Put them down here where they wouldn't knock the floor out,'' Dana explained. ''They start going out to distributors tomorrow. Here, I'll sign your copy.''

Distractedly Leverett opened a copy of *Dwellers in the Earth*. He gazed at his lovingly rendered drawings of rotting creatures and buried stone chambers and stained altars—and everywhere the enigmatic latticework structures. He shuddered.

''Here.'' Dana Allard handed Leverett the book he had signed. ''And to answer your question, they *are* elder glyphics.''

But Leverett was staring at the inscription in its unmistakable handwriting: ''For Colin Leverett, Without whom this work could not have seen completion—H. Kenneth Allard.''

Allard was speaking. Leverett saw places where the hastily applied flesh-toned make-up didn't quite conceal what lay beneath. ''Glyphics symbolic of alien dimensions—inexplicable to the human mind, but essential fragments of an evocation so unthinkably vast that the 'pentagram' (if you will) is miles across. Once before we tried—but your iron weapon destroyed part of Althol's brain. He erred at the last instant—almost annihilating us all. Althol had been formulating the evocation since he fled the advance of iron four millennia past.

''Then you reappeared, Colin Leverett—you with your artist's knowledge and diagrams of Althol's symbols. And now a thousand new minds will read the evocation you have returned to us, unite with our minds as we stand in the Hidden Places. And the Great Old Ones will come forth from the earth, and we, the dead who have steadfastly served them, shall be masters of the living.''

Leverett turned to run, but now they were creeping forth from the shadows of the cellar, as massive flagstones slid back to reveal the tunnels beyond. He began to scream as Althol came to lead him away, but he could not awaken, could only follow.

Robert Aickman

LARGER THAN ONESELF

Robert Aickman was the great English master of the ghost story of the second half of this century. Editor, theoretician and writer, he never attained the recognition or popularity his immense contributions deserved, although he did win a World Fantasy Award in the decade before his death. A significant portion of his fiction remained unpublished in the U.S. at the time of his death. "Larger Than Oneself" is an ironic reinterpretation of the moral tale for our era. Mrs. Iblis spends the weekend at a convention of people interested in the supernatural, the metaphysical and the occult, and finds it uniquely disturbing. One might compare the story of Joyce Carol Oates' treatment of similar matter in "Nightside." "Larger Than Oneself" is an interesting example of the blend of all three major streams of horror fiction.

Upon the death of his father, Vincent Coner got out of mine owning, which had always been the family business, and invested heavily in popular journalism with himself as editor in chief. It is hard to believe that in any other place or time, past or future, his publications would have found many readers; but as it was, the thing most needed by his generation seemed to be the recipe he offered: the sweet things of life (the more obvious of them) smeared and contaminated with envious guilt.

A typical man of his time, Coner throve exceedingly. While at Cambridge, he edited a symposium of modern philosophy, which attracted considerable attention; and he soon became known for his advocacy of a synthesis between the best of this world and the best of the next. Already he was giving parties: his thin figure, precociously bald, wove in and out pouring gin while others talked. Occasionally he would bring the uproar back to the point as he conceived it. He developed an exceptional eye for the view which would prevail.

With increasing popular success, easily acquired, Coner's main business in life became more and more an almost paranoiac pursuit of self-integration. He read Berdyaev, Maritain, and C. S. Lewis, and even the first thirty pages of Ouspensky. Almost he believed what he read. Kierkegaard and Leopardi, rebound by a refugee craftsman, always attended his bedside (he had married a nightclub singer named Eileen); and Pascal he constantly rediscovered with new understanding, gorging on the insane root as he passed class-conscious photographs for the press. At the time Mrs. Iblis entered his life, he was greatly interested in several of the newer spiritual movements competing to offer a deadbeat world metaphysical immunization against its own shadow. He had decided to ask the different leaders to Bunhill for the weekend in order that they might have the chance to exchange views on neutral ground. A symposium for *Roundabout* might emerge, a real chance to give a lead.

Mrs. Iblis entered Coner's life in the usual way through the front door. While waiting for the bell to be answered, she was joined on the large white step by two other visitors, who introduced themselves as David Stillman and Ruth. Ruth was not Mr. Stillman's daughter, but Mrs. Iblis was unable to catch her other name, nor did she ever learn it. Mr. Stillman appeared to be a prosperous businessman. He arrived in a large car, which, when he had alighted, immediately drove away. He was well preserved and had excellent manners, but Mrs. Iblis had had little contact with Jews. Ruth was a highly strung voluble creature, little more than a girl in appearance, small and thin, with tousled hair, a round face, and restless hands. She wore red corduroy trousers, a shapeless jumper, and sandals. Mrs. Iblis had been speaking to Mr. Stillman when she appeared, presumably from the dense bushes which closely lined the drive, but carrying a bulging reticule with two handles. Mrs. Iblis had a suitcase; Mr. Stillman a dressing case of a type which Mrs. Iblis had thought obsolete.

Presumably the din inside the house made it difficult for the servant to hear the bell, so, at Mr. Stillman's suggestion, Mrs. Iblis rang again. Ruth maintained an intermittent flow of observations about the difficulty of reaching Bunhill (or indeed anywhere) by train and her own trials with the timetable.

"I do hope you've not been kept waiting." The door had been opened by Mrs. Coner, wearing a long tight dress of blue-bottle green and smoking a cigarette from which the ash needed removing. "My husband's sent all the servants to a Domestic Science Congress at Littlehampton, and we're entirely in the hands of the caterers this weekend. Do come in."

Immediately inside stood a large figure in evening dress, with drink written all over him.

"Your names, please." He prepared to tick them off on a list with an indelible pencil.

"Mrs. Iblis."

He crawled slowly through the list, stopping at each name with the pencil. Three raw youths in dinner jackets had seized the visitors' luggage and were standing at the ready.

"Could you spell it?"

"I-B-L-I-S."

He repeated the search, then turned with irritation to Mrs. Coner.

In the meantime, the masterful figure of Coner had appeared from the crowd within. "Ruth, my darling. How lovely to see you." He kissed her mouth violently but dispassionately. "Did we ask you this weekend, or have you just dropped from heaven?"

"Surely you asked me, Vincent."

"It's wonderful to see you anyhow. Do come and join in right away. It will be really valuable to have the orthodox point of view."

"Could I have a sandwich first?"

"Have everything there is. Haven't you lunched?"

"I left London at half past ten."

"If we'd known, we'd have sent a car. It only takes half an hour by road. But come on and eat." Gripping her round the waist, he dragged her towards the hubbub.

"Vincent." His wife had clutched him by the other sleeve of his beautifully made gray suit. He stopped.

"What is it, Eileen?"

"Why do we have to have that damned list?"

"I've told you more than once. The people we've asked this weekend have all been carefully picked by me for the contribution they can make. As I've hardly met any of them before, we must have a list and keep to it. What's gone wrong?"

"Two people have arrived. They are not on the list. They both say they were told to arrive at three. I can hardly send them away."

"All the people this weekend were told to arrive for breakfast if they could. Who are they?"

"Mrs. Iblis and Mr. Stillman. They don't seem like the others." The suspect guests could be seen in the still open door miserably awaiting their fate.

"Mavis!" Coner bawled at the top of his voice. "Forgive me a moment, Ruth." With a violent squeeze, he released her.

A tall, bony, off-blonde, ageless woman strode forward. Coner succinctly outlined the crisis.

"I'll have a look in the invitations book, Mr. Coner." She departed.

Coner addressed his wife. "I leave it to you, my dear. But

whoever they are, we don't want them unless they harmonize. Come on, Ruth.'' Resuming his python hold round Ruth's narrow waist, he propelled her forward.

Mavis returned with a huge folio volume of the minute book type. It must have contained five hundred pages. It was ruled into dates and packed with thousands of names in Mavis's small clear writing.

Almost at once Mavis had the answer. ''They're left over from the lot we asked before Mr. Coner decided on the Forum. Haven't they had their postponement letters?''

''I'd better let them in. They'll have to share rooms with someone.''

''Everyone's doing that this weekend, Mrs. Coner.''

''Can you take over, Mavis?''

Explaining the situation about the rooms in a few courteous but emotionless words, Mavis was simultaneously scanning the hired butler's list of guests and their accommodation. ''So I do hope you don't mind sharing,'' she concluded. ''This weekend is rather a special occasion.''

Mr. Stillman smiled acquiescence, though he did not look too happy. Mrs. Iblis said: ''Please do not go to any trouble about me.''

''No trouble at all.'' Then Mavis decided. ''Mr. Stillman can have the Louise Room. I doubt Rabbi Morocco will come at all now. And perhaps Mrs. Iblis won't mind sleeping with Sister Nuper? Our House Sister, you know.''

''Is part of the house used as a hospital?''

''Oh no. It's just in case of sudden or serious illness. And Sister Nuper advises us on our diet and on questions of personal hygiene as well. You'll find her a delightful person. Really, you couldn't find anyone better to room with.''

The youth who had seized Ruth's piece of luggage had long ago departed with it, presumably to her room. Now the other two youths constituted themselves escorts to Mr. Stillman and Mrs. Iblis.

''The lift's through 'ere.'' They held back heavy, dark brown velvet curtains.

The lift, a Waywood-Otis installation capacious enough for twelve at a hoist, was descending. When it reached the ground floor, there emerged two apparently identical Negroes in clerical dress. Small, compact, and beautifully polished, they looked like marionettes. They smiled and bowed in unison to the new arrivals, then walked off in step, conversing enthusiastically in some African tongue.

At the first-floor landing (Mrs. Iblis felt that it would have been quicker to have walked it), Mr. Stillman was at once shown into an enormous room which even through the door Mrs. Iblis could see contained at least two canopied beds. Mrs. Iblis was led away down a long passage, not too well proportioned, decorated in goose gray and lined with modern religious paintings, ascending on occasion as high in the scale as Vanessa Bell, and even Rouault. (Mrs. Iblis could not be sure, however, that they were not merely good reproductions.) From the opposite direction advanced an extremely good-looking woman of bold proportions; she was wearing a heavy black brassière, black-and-white striped knickers, and huge furry slippers. She made no acknowledgment of Mrs. Iblis's presence, still less of the luggage carrier's, and in the end, having passed the lift, vanished round the corner beyond the Louise Room, as Mrs. Iblis was unable to resist turning to see.

Sister Nuper's room was beautifully light and filled with built-in cupboards. There was a large, double divan-bed with silk sheets. Above the bed was a ghastly and lurid cartoon of the Crucifixion by Edward Burra. Mrs. Iblis was unable to make up her mind whether the artist was in favor of religion or against it. A satinwood bookcase, which had been scraped and painted white like the other furniture, proved to contain mainly volumes of the more popular nursing and home medical journals (bound by Coner's refugee craftsman). A French window and small balcony overlooked a garden of about an acre, from which rose a smell of intensive composting. A figure in a boiler suit could be seen at the dark work now.

Mrs. Iblis peered into one of the built-in cupboards. It was stuffed with evening dresses, depending from a thick chromium-plated rail and each in a transparent envelope made of plastic.

Not caring to unpack without consulting Sister Nuper, Mrs. Iblis nonetheless changed into the other dress she had brought. Looking for an ashtray, she noticed the Sister's bedside book: entitled *Bowel Discipline*, it was a lesser work by a well-known member of the Labor party. A realistic colored drawing on the jacket depicted the alimentary system surrounded by a luminous radiation.

For some time after Mrs. Iblis had descended (by the stairs) into the mêlée below, no one took any notice of her. The Forum, about fifty strong, were surging and wheeling between the drawing room, the dining room, and the large hall. Most of them, of course, were shouting at the tops of their voices, or reasoning at the full stretch of their intellects; but some, Mrs. Iblis noticed, sat or even stood perfectly silent and ignored. She had read an article in the *Evening News* of the previous night upon the value in a bustling noisy life of regular periods of meditation, and gazed at these mute figures with interest and awe. Press photographers moved about the throng. In the end Mrs. Iblis's eye lighted upon Ruth eating a strawberry ice cream. This being the only person present to whom she had ever spoken (there was no sign of Mr. Stillman), Mrs. Iblis advanced.

"Hullo. I'm afraid I know no one else here but you. Can you tell me who some of these people are?"

"Don't know. I'm strictly orthodox."

"How interesting! In what way?"

"Full Anglican. I accept the Thirty-Nine Articles. Unconditionally." Ruth looked round for somewhere to deposit the ice cream glass.

"Well, so do I, I suppose."

"What's Article Thirty-three?"

"I can hardly recall the exact words."

"Then you're not an Anglican, are you?" Ruth was reduced to laying the receptacle in much jeopardy on the floor.

"Can *you* recite Article Thirty-three?" This feeble rejoinder was the best Mrs. Iblis could muster. It was so long since one had been at school.

"That person which by open denunciation of the Church is rightly cut off from the unity of the Church and excommunicated ought to be taken of the whole multitude of the faithful as a Heathen and Publican until he be openly reconciled by penance and received into the Church by a Judge that hath authority there-unto."

"Not a very Christian sentiment surely?" Mrs. Iblis inquired almost involuntarily.

"Why not?"

"More like the Church of Rome. Excommunication and penance, you know."

"I do penance daily." Ruth's voice was dreamy, her eyes blank.

"You can hardly be as wicked as that!" But Mrs. Iblis's mind recalled the alarming figure she had seen upstairs in the passage, and was instantly less sure.

"Not wicked. Sinful."

"Is there any difference?"

"Sin is a sense of something larger than oneself."

"Ah, now I understand you." Mrs. Iblis began to glance about for some sign of tea, surely overdue. "I think that is something we all feel."

But Ruth ignored her. "To merge," she cried in her soft, light voice. "To break through the barrier and become One. For a single infinitely small person to meet the infinitely vast. The end of every pilgrimage must be orthodoxy." Her eye lighted upon a fellow guest the other side of the room. "You see that man to the left of the big 'Annunciation'?"

"The red-haired one in tweeds?"

"He's a Lewisite. He's misplaced, like me."

"I thought lewisite was a kind of explosive."

Ruth merely said in the most casual way, "Have you read *Arrival and Departure*?"

"No."

"I'm going to look for another ice.'

Before she had disappeared, Mrs. Iblis had time to ask: "Do you know what time we get tea?"

Ruth replied: "Any time you like. Ask at the buffet in the billiard room." And she was gone before Mrs. Iblis had completed the horrifying realization that at Bunhill there were no regular meals.

The better to face the situation, Mrs. Iblis opened her handbag and produced a compact. Peering into the little mirror, she failed to notice that two strange men now stood before her.

"Permit me to introduce my friend, Professor Dr. Borgia, principal of the Demokratischereligion Gesellschaft of Zürich." The speaker was a rotund young man of highly educated accent and masterful demeanor.

"How do you do? I suppose you must be used to people asking whether you are really one of the Borgias?"

"But *natürlich* I am one of the Borgias." The professor had the strongest of Teutonic accents. He was a slight, worn, Semitic-looking figure, with large fanatical eyes. "The Borgias were a great *aristocratische* family of old Spain. My family."

The rotund young man said: "I am sure you will both have much to say. Will you excuse me if I seek a word with Dr. Spade?" He was gone.

Professor Borgia rolled his eyes. "Have you found spiritual proficiency, *gnädige Frau*? You see I come straight from the point."

Mrs. Iblis considered carefully. "Well, actually, not yet, I think."

"Mine is the shortest way to truth." His diction had much of the charm of the German classical actor, the aptitude for making the most commonplace words profound and stirring. "I am in a sense a commercial traveler for God." This was uttered in a tone which recalled Manfred confronting the abyss. "You have first to sign your name only." He was holding out a quite fat booklet closely printed in a way which reminded Mrs. Iblis of Dutch seed catalogues.

"Thank you very much. I shall look forward to reading it."

"Reading alone will not avail. Words reach only the mind. It is the spirit, the *Geist*, we grope for, *nicht wahr*?"

"I suppose so." Mrs. Iblis was beginning to feel cowed and upset, unequal to life.

"Do you come much to Switzerland?" He pronounced the English name so elaborately that Mrs. Iblis had difficulty in following him.

"Only for the winter sports, I'm afraid. And that not for some years now."

"*Ach, so?* But no matter. We are starting an *Enfiedelei* in London this very winter. There will be your rebirth."

At this point it dawned on Mrs. Iblis that quite possibly the rotund young man had merely intended to unload upon her a bigger than ordinary bore, a person recognized to be such even in this company.

Excusing herself, she began firmly to look for the billiard room. The professor stood quite still, smiling after her retreating figure.

En route she passed a particularly frenzied group, at the center of which a man was saying, "Now can't we reduce our differences to a few simple points which we could talk over?" This, though Mrs. Iblis did not know it, was her host.

"What is the use of words if the spirit is wrong?" screamed out a woman whose style of looks Mrs. Iblis considered obsolete, and who wore a complex, black tea gown. For people who set so little store by words, they seemed to Mrs. Iblis remarkably dependent on them.

There were only ten or eleven people at the buffet, eating and drinking not being primary interests of the present gathering (unlike some at Bunhill). The billiard room also contained two tables, on one of which a couple of young waiters were playing half-hearted snooker. Above the dark brown mantelpiece was a huge vague-colored drawing of a Universal

City designed by Patrick Geddes. A new strip-lighting system had been installed; but something had gone wrong with it and instead of giving better than daylight, it emitted a depressing yellow red glare as dusk descended outside.

As Mrs. Iblis stood drinking Indian tea and nibbling a maid of honor, a massive figure approached her, wearing enormous highly polished shoes.

"And what do *you* make of it all?" The accent was transatlantic.

"I'm afraid I know very little about it. I'm not really a member of the Forum."

"Nor I, ma'am. I just dropped in to see that Coner's on the right lines."

"And is he?" There seemed nothing else to say.

"Well now, I'm a Canadian. I'm also a businessman and editor, like Coner. But that doesn't mean I'm impervious to spiritual values. Quite the contrary. The one thing the whole world needs, the one thing every man's heart is sighing for—*and* every woman's—is a big spiritual revival. And what I say is, it's up to us servants of the public to get things rolling."

"I always think the press could be such an influence for good," said Mrs. Iblis, selecting an éclair. "After all, it's foolish not to take things as we find them."

"Sure, sure. Those are wise words, ma'am. I swear to you that not a copy goes out of a single journal in my group without it contains both a passage from the good book and some words of cheer by one of a panel of leading ministers."

"That must be very nice for your readers." Mrs. Iblis wished she had a larger handkerchief on which to deposit some of the sticky chocolate now coating her fingers. Nonetheless, she took a second éclair.

"You should see the thankful letters. Never less than sixty a day and often above the century. I tell you they make me a humble man. But I'm not a narrow man either, and I tell you something more is needed."

"Yes?" said Mrs. Iblis.

"After all, what are sects? What are denominations,

creeds, dogmas, rituals? Aren't we all the same where it really matters—in our hearts? What are the little orthodoxies besides the great universal need, man's eternal quest for something larger than his puny self? That's what I'm doing here this very afternoon. Watching Coner pull the old country's socks up.'' His somewhat inflexible features almost beamed upon Mrs. Iblis.

"You think all this will really lead to something useful?" She turned to the buffet. The waiter was at the other end, and Mrs. Iblis raised her voice: "Could I have another cup of tea, please?"

"Sure, sure. There's just nothing that can't be had if you'll give your soul for it." Mrs. Iblis turned back to him with some surprise; but now he had seized the sleeve of a cadaverous, academic-looking young man with an enormous Wellingtonian nose. "And you, sir. What do you think?"

The young man merely snatched away his sleeve without a word or even a glance. He was like a preoccupied child. In ardent tones, he addressed his friend: "You know, Neville, I've found that much of the best modern thought, the really deep stuff, now comes from inside the Salvation Army."

"I still remain faithful to the dear old Hibbert Journal. That and my Karma Research Group. Let's have a cup of char, then I'll tell you about a new technique we're working on to accelerate the ecstasy." His voice had hushed almost to inaudibility. They glanced at one another, conscious of secrets shared.

The Canadian was now conversing with an enormously fat woman in a cassock. About her neck, on the end of a brass chain, hung an object which Mrs. Iblis fancied was called an *ankh*. Or was it a *crux ansata*?

At this point an exceedingly attractive woman entered the billiard room accompanied by a positive throng of unusually handsome young men. She wore a gray nurse's uniform made of silk, like the nurse's uniforms worn by film stars in the early silent days, and a high white collar. Mrs. Iblis had been about to leave the billiard room but, supposing that this might be Sister Nuper, remained for a moment.

The posse advanced upon the buffet, laughing and calling loudly for refreshments, which seemed to be brought to them with more alacrity than had attended the service of the other guests. They stood in a group exchanging merry commonplaces, carefree, exuberant. They were totally unlike the rest of the Forum, but no one other than Mrs. Iblis and the waiter seemed to be taking any particular notice of them. To Mrs. Iblis, however, they seemed in the end even to be engaged in parodying the transactions around them.

"And what faith are you, my pretty maid?" cried out an Apollo-like young man.

And Sister Nuper (if she it was) instantly replied in a cooing, but perfectly clear, voice: "I worship St. Nicholas, sir," she said.

At this all the young men laughed very loudly. The group made Mrs. Iblis feel a wild girl again. But the billiard room was emptying and the waiter beginning to assemble supper dishes and bottles of beer. Mrs. Iblis felt she could not stay longer without becoming conspicuous, possibly a butt, not for any sort of unkindness (the group did not seem unkind), but simply for witty remarks calling for witty answers which she had never been able to provide, even long after the need. Before she left, she noticed through the line of long windows that the lurid light in the billiard room seemed to have its counterpart in a livid autumnal glare outside. Was it something to do with the equinox, she wondered.

"Shall I find you a chair?" The speaker was a shaggy, elderly, paternal figure.

"That would be very kind of you. Such tiring weather."

He guided her gently forward by the arm. They reached a small sofa. He seated himself beside her. This was not exactly what she wanted.

"Permit me to introduce myself. O'Rorke: founder of the New Vision Movement, small for the present, it is true, but a veritable seed of mustard, if I may quote from an anachronistic scripture.''

"How do you do? My name is Iblis. Mrs. Iblis.''

"Ah yes.'' He seemed abstracted. "I think I have convinced Mr. Coner. I think I have moved his heart to see that a new world demands a new faith and will not be put off.'' The speaker appeared to be at least seventy-five.

"There have indeed been many changes.''

"But still we worship the old false gods! Still we prostrate ourselves before the concepts of medieval anthropomorphism.'' He looked exactly like a cathedral figure of St. Peter.

"Life is not easy,'' said Mrs. Iblis.

"But need we therefore rend ourselves like vultures? Can we not seek the truth each in his own way? Or, of course, hers? After all, in every heart is an unimaginable arcana: must we sell out to the money changers of the temple? Evil is, after all, so very small.''

Mrs. Iblis looked up. "Is it?''

"Indeed it is. In how many mythologies the Devil is represented as a little fellow, as Mannikin or Peterkin, and how rightly! It is only the sophisticated theologians who make him vast and roaring and terrible: in order that we may be afraid of him and in their power. But pluck up your heart, Mrs.—er—'' He stumbled for the name. "Only God is vast and great: that is to say, Good; for they are one and the same.''

"How convincingly you put it!'' Mrs. Iblis said this without the slightest irony. It was merely that the lowering weather was giving her a headache. Even as she passed her hand across her brow, there was a distant roll of thunder, too faint to be generally heard above the many voices, the diversities of business.

"It is God who speaks through me,'' said the patriarch modestly. "Or rather Good, the life spirit of the universe, to which it is within all of us to hearken.''

Mrs. Iblis wondered whether Sister Nuper could produce

some aspirin. Somehow it seemed improbable. It also seemed almost impossible to ask her.

Suddenly, however, the chic but world-worn figure of Mrs. Coner leaned over the back of the sofa and spoke in Mrs. Iblis's ear.

"Mavis tells me that you are unfortunately not feeling too good." Mrs. Iblis had not consciously set eyes on Mavis since her arrival.

"I *have* a slight headache, I'm afraid. It is foolish of me. The weather, I think."

"Take my advice and have a rest on your bed. Mavis is mixing you a draught."

With relief, Mrs. Iblis rose to her feet. "You are very kind." She addressed the patriarch: "Please excuse me. I'm not feeling very well, I'm afraid. I am going to rest for a little. I expect we shall meet again later."

He grasped her hand and held it. "Hold on to the spirit, Mrs.—er—I shall confidently await your return—purged and splendid." It was not quite what was usually said in such circumstances.

Mrs. Coner came with her upstairs. As they passed the door to the Louise Room, Mrs. Coner said: "We've been having some trouble there, I'm afraid. Mavis thought that Rabbi Morocco and your friend Mr. Stillman would have a lot in common. Anyway, she didn't expect Rabbi Morocco to turn up at all. But he has. And he and Mr. Stillman seem to be somehow different *kinds* of Jews. I don't really get it. They always seem to cause some sort of trouble, don't they?" She and Mrs. Iblis exchanged glances.

Lying on Sister Nuper's double bed was a girl in her underclothes and black silk stockings. Her thick black hair was drawn into a ballet dancer's bun, and she was reading a tome by Karl Barth.

"Sorry, Mrs. Coner. I thought Sister Nuper wouldn't mind." She sat up, staring at Mrs. Iblis.

"I am sure she won't, Patacake. But haven't we given you a room?"

"Can't stop. Have to get back to the Shelter."

"Oh." Mrs. Coner didn't seem to like her very much. But she did her duty as hostess. "This is Mrs. Iblis. Lady Cecilia Capulet."

"How do you do?" said Mrs. Iblis. "Please don't move." But her head was splitting, and she very much hoped that Lady Cecilia would move.

"I must go anyway." With great elegance she crossed to the window and looked out between the bright Gordon Russel curtains. "Oh God, it's raining."

Mavis appeared, bearing a large graduated glass filled to the brim with a blue green liquor, seething and opaque.

"Vincent's special," said Mrs. Coner. "Drink it down."

"You're really very kind," said Mrs. Iblis weakly. She sipped. Mavis, she noticed, had changed her dress and now wore a flame-colored model, very out of key with her apparent general temperament. Lady Cecilia was washing her hands and forearms with great thoroughness.

"It's almost pure peptomycin," said Mavis encouragingly.

The beverage tasted of liquid candle-grease gone flat with the years.

"Down the hatch," said Mrs. Coner, displaying for the first time the slightest hint of impatience.

There was a terrific crash of thunder. The four women looked at one another momentarily. Mrs. Iblis felt quite frightened.

"Christ!" ejaculated Lady Cecilia. "Can you lend me a mack, Mavis?"

"Of course, Patacake—if you'll give me five minutes." Mavis collected the now empty glass (a sticky bright yellow sediment occupied the last inch of it), said "Thank you" to Mrs. Iblis, and departed. It was now thundering briskly.

"Well now," said Mrs. Coner, once more sensibly sympathetic. "Lie down with your feet up so that the vapors can rise, and get some sleep. When you're better, come down again. The Forum will carry on most of the night, I expect, so you needn't rush things." She dragged out the bolster from the head of the bed and put it under Mrs. Iblis's feet. Mrs. Iblis had cast off her shoes but did not care to remove her dress, being conscious that her underclothes compared unfavorably with Lady Cecilia's. Lady Cecilia was now carefully rubbing under her arms with (presumably) Sister Nuper's Arrid.

"Bye-bye," said Mrs. Coner in the idiom of her former avocation. She went, shutting the door which Mavis had left open.

"These clothes do make one stink." Lady Cecilia was putting on a plain navy blue skirt. Mrs. Iblis only wished she would go. Then Lady Cecilia put on a matching tunic, and Mrs. Iblis realized.

"I've never actually met a Salvation Army lassie before."

"It gives one a standing," said Lady Cecilia. "At places like this and times like the present. Major Barbara was on to something." She had buttoned the tunic to the neck. "It's a damned fetching outfit, you know." She extended one black silk leg. "The number it fetches might surprise you."

"Are you making it your career?"

"Until they chuck me out." There was a tap on the door. It was Mavis with an emerald-colored silk mackintosh. "How frightfully sweet of you! I'll be back immediately the Shelter shuts."

"Hurry. The Forum will give out if you don't keep their glands working."

"Your book!" cried Mrs. Iblis. It had obviously been forgotten.

"You read it," said Lady Cecilia. *"Auf Wiedersehen."*

Mrs. Iblis had hoped to see Patacake put on her bonnet; but she was gone with no sign of the object.

"Shall I lock you in?" inquired Mavis. "It might be quieter for you, and there's a bell."

"Thank you very much," said Mrs. Iblis. "But no."

When Mrs. Iblis awoke, she felt extremely hungry. Used to four reasonable meals a day, she had had nothing of the kind since an early and rushed luncheon at the London railway terminus. She had turned out the light but could see by the illuminated dial of her wristwatch that it was half past eleven. Despite Mrs. Coner's words, surely the party below might be over? Panic seized Mrs. Iblis, confronted with a foodless night. Switching on the bedside light, she rose, tried to smooth her dress, and put on her shoes. If the party were over, then Sister Nuper would have been with her by now. The thunder and rain seemed to have stopped, though Mrs. Iblis did not give the time to making sure. She felt once more in vigorous health, considering the hour. Mrs. Iblis did what she could with her hair and hastened downstairs.

There was still a great crowd, but the atmosphere had changed. There was very little light (Bunhill was supplied by two separate circuits, one of which had been affected by the thunderstorm) and astonishingly little noise. People were sitting about in small groups, often on the floor: and the general conversational level rose little above a mutter. Mrs. Iblis recalled a number of the faces, but none in the hall (to her relief) belonged to anyone with whom she had spoken.

To reach the billiard room, it was necessary to pass through the drawing room and take a passage leading off between the drawing room and the dining room. In the murky drawing room (decorated with neutral-colored abstractions screwed in pale frames to the walls) Mrs. Iblis noticed the unmistakable figure of Ruth. She was lying on the antique-shop chaise-lounge, with an entirely blank expression on her round face and clasped frankly and ruthlessly in the arms of a man whose back was turned to Mrs. Iblis, but who was wearing a black suit. Ruth's moplike hair was in worse disarray than ever. Mrs. Iblis could not help wondering if Ruth were happy.

From off the passage led an apartment known as the music room, which Mrs. Iblis had not so far entered. The door of this room was open, and from it came a loud and cheerful noise, contrasting with the subdued, almost dead tone which ruled elsewhere. When Mrs. Iblis reached the door, she could not but look in. Seated on top of a vast black concert grand was the woman she had supposed to be Sister Nuper, in her silken nurse's dress and tall stiff collar. She appeared to be administering some kind of light-hearted "quiz" to her group of young men, now apparently increased in number, who were gathered round her on the floor. They had mostly placed themselves very close to her. The prevailing attitude among them was far from one of relaxation; on the contrary, most of them were kneeling and leaning eagerly forward. Though the distance from the door was not great, Mrs. Iblis was unable to hear the question asked in Sister Nuper's soft cooing voice; but a number of the young men appeared to answer in unison. Sister Nuper's position, dangling her beautifully shaped legs in gray silk stockings from the piano, enabled Mrs. Iblis to see that, unlike most tenders of the sick, she was wearing shoes with enormously high heels. In the back row of the cluster of men, one figure, Mrs. Iblis noticed, seemed almost hysterically eager to answer the question or to answer it first. As Sister Nuper asked another question, Mrs. Iblis passed on. She was far from sure that she agreed with Mavis's view that no better person than Sister Nuper could be found with whom to share her bedroom.

The billiard room, still illuminated from the defective strip, looked exactly as before, except that there was now only one surviving waiter, the toiler behind the buffet, the other two having cut the cloth to bits and then gone back to London together, leaving the damaged table littered with colored balls and cubes of chalk. As before, there were about a dozen guests eating and drinking. The tone of their hushed conversations suggested that they were complaining of one another to confidential friends.

Mrs. Iblis asked what there was to eat. Little seemed visible on the buffet but débris.

"There's only lobster salad." The waiter had had enough.

It was not at all what Mrs. Iblis wanted. "That will be delicious." She recognized that it was late.

The waiter shoved up from under the buffet a plateful assembled many hours earlier.

"Cider? No beer."

"I'd love a glass of cider."

It was drawn from a plywood cask and was a product of a local industries group which Coner fostered. The smell and flavor were unusual, but Mrs. Iblis almost at once recognized that the brew was potent.

She was so hungry that the lobster salad was soon gone, though normally she avoided tinned shellfish.

"There's some cake."

"Thank you. I'd love some cake." Again, however, she felt that there were at the moment more desirable foods.

The waiter gave her two large pieces, as the buffet was soon to close. The plate was too small for its load, but the cake was cake, not good, not bad, not indifferent.

This time no one came near Mrs. Iblis, or enforced conversation. This time she would almost have been glad for someone to do so (though not, for choice, any single one of the day's previous new acquaintances).

"Could I possibly have some coffee if there's any left?" She had not yet finished the cider.

The waiter glared at her, then went to the other end of the buffet, produced a full cup from under it, and returned to her without a word. He had slopped much of the contents into the saucer. The coffee was far from hot and contained insufficient sugar. When it was finished, Mrs. Iblis was unsure what to do next. She stood sipping the remains of the peculiar amateur cider. To the waiter she might not have existed. To her fellow guests, as they finished their scraps of food and drink, she might have been a hostile object.

In the end she was almost alone and contemplating a return to bed, when Coner entered. Mrs. Iblis identified him at once as the overanxious figure in the back row round Sister Nuper. He advanced upon the buffet. His face was strained and his gait slightly shambling.

"Got any Scotch?"

"Only cider left, Mr. Coner."

Encountering her host thus for the first time, Mrs. Iblis

wondered whether good manners enjoined that she should speak to him. On the whole, she thought it would be simpler to do nothing. Coner, however, took the initiative. Glancing round the room before departing to unlock his spirit store, his eye lighted upon her isolated figure, still holding the glass. He stared at her for several moments, then advanced.

"Who are *you*?"

"I'm Mrs. Iblis. I've no business here, really. My invitation was postponed on account of the Forum. But your wife asked me to stay as I didn't get the letter of postponement."

"I'm glad she did." Coner was still staring hard. The flesh on his face was like a loose mask covering another face beneath. "I hope they're looking after you properly."

"Perfectly, thank you. I'm having a lovely time."

"What d'you think of the Forum? We've got pretty well everyone who carries weight, don't you think?"

"I'm afraid some of it's rather above my head."

Though continuing to stare at her in a way which Mrs. Iblis was beginning to find odd, Coner seemed hardly to be attending.

"No real synthesis has emerged," he said. "Nothing beyond the separate individual arguments and experiences." He spoke like a defeated general referring to reinforcements. "Pity about Rabbi Morocco having to go home. He could have helped a lot."

"How?" Mrs. Iblis wanted to enter into the spirit of it.

"The A. G. S. is making headway all the time, you know."

"I'm sure I've no business not to know, but what is the A. G. S.?"

"The Avant Garde Synagogue. Something entirely new. It's a great mistake to ignore what the Jews are doing."

"I am told that the Salvation Army are doing a lot too," said Mrs. Iblis, greatly venturing.

"Of course Patacake's utterly irreplaceable. One just wouldn't try." His eyes were now wandering up and down her body in a way to which she was unaccustomed; but he sank into silence.

"Will you be writing about the Forum in your papers?" inquired Mrs. Iblis, in order to say something.

"The whole of the next issue in each case except for a slaughterhouse feature in *Roundabout*. But I doubt whether we really reach them." He seemed in the last stages of gloom.

"Oh, I'm sure you do," said Mrs. Iblis comfortingly. "All those millions of copies. Power like that over people's minds must be a rather terrible thing." She was conscious that the very strong cider had reached her very weak head from her very empty stomach.

The pupils of Coner's eyes seemed to perform a complete halfcircle. Then he said: "You should wear nothing but black. Cut rather low. The sort of style young girls can't manage." He had placed his hand firmly on Mrs. Iblis's thorax to indicate precisely how low. Mrs. Iblis withdrew slightly with a distinct shudder.

"Thank you for the advice."

He stepped toward her again. "I find something quite remarkably charming about you. Even in pale blue."

Without the cider, Mrs. Iblis would probably have blushed and felt flattered. As it was, she answered: "Nonsense, Mr. Coner. I'm not quite to silly as that."

The waiter had just drawn a greasy overcoat from the hidden recess which had earlier evicted lobster salad. He departed, worming his way into the garment.

"Shall I leave the lights, Mr. Coner?"

"Yes. I'll put them out."

The last guests having also withdrawn, Mrs. Iblis was alone in the billiard room with her host and a dish filled with sliced cake.

"What's your name?"

"Iblis. I-B-L-I-S."

"How much do you know about me?"

"Very little more than I've read in the papers and so forth. Only what everyone knows."

"Shall we sit down?"

Mrs. Iblis wanted few things less. However, they sat in the

depressing yellow glare on blue basketwork chairs brought in for use by frequenters of the buffet. It was not even very warm.

"It's close." Coner passed his handkerchief round the inside of his collar. "But never mind that. Now where shall I begin?" This question was for answer by the speaker himself. Clearly he was about to tell his life story.

"I expect you'll soon have to join your other guests, so I mustn't keep you too long."

"Oh God," said Coner, "the world's weight! The terror of one's own littleness." He was even whiter and had begun to weep profusely. His head dropped onto his hands, so that they covered his face. A cataract of tears fell through his fingers onto his gray trousers, which became as if spattered with ink.

Mrs. Iblis, who had never seen a man behave like this before (and hardly even a woman), was completely at a loss. After all the events of that day, Coner's demonstration was too much for her. Her body was insufficiently nourished, her mind awash in homemade cider. She too began gaspingly to weep. The scene in the billiard room was as if the two of them had just forsaken the last childhood's illusions.

Coner seemed quite lost to the world. Tears flooded his clothing. His body shook. His mind might have ceased to function.

Mrs. Iblis was less collapsed. The tears raced down her face, but she scrabbled through her handbag for a handkerchief and after a few minutes had somewhat pulled herself together.

"Please forgive me, Mr. Coner," she said. "Is there anything I can do to help?"

Coner went on sobbing and shivering like a man whose heart was long since broken and for whom such episodes as this were regular occurrences.

"Please, Mr. Coner." She extended her own rather unsteady hand and touched his shoulder. "What can I do?"

Afraid, like most women, to go too far in sympathy lest the sympathy be misinterpreted, she had never in her life gone further than this.

Coner began to babble distressingly of his littleness and inadequacy; his responsibilities; his uncertainties; his health troubles. "The human mind is such a minnow," he sputtered out. "If only one could find some all-embracing pattern to guide one."

"The human mind is a whale." The speaker was Mr. Stillman, who had entered the large murky room unnoticed. It was the first time Mrs. Iblis had seen him since her arrival. He looked businesslike and prosperous in his well-cut dark suit. He carried a copy of the *Jewish Monthly*.

"The human mind is a whale," said Mr. Stillman again. "It's all there inside you, enormous unknown things, difficult to reach. And woe betide the man who looks outside himself for what he can only find inside. That is surely one thing which modern psychology has made clearer than ever. The subconscious mind, you know. So much larger than the conscious. The sublimal self." He paused. His eye was traveling along the buffet. "Ah, cake. There are hungry people in the house. Do you mind if I take the cake?"

Coner was staring at him, his face like an idiot's.

Mrs. Iblis replied: "I am sure that will be all right."

"Thank you," said Mr. Stillman, picked up the large white dish in his free hand, and left.

Coner now partially came to. "That's what we're all trying to do," he said. "To find ourselves."

"I gather not," rejoined Mrs. Iblis, with what might almost have been acerbity. "You're all trying to find something larger than yourselves."

She rose and left the billiard room, leaving Coner recumbent like a drenched tea cloth.

Everybody was eating cake and seemed more cheerful. It was like the miracle of the loaves, until Mrs. Iblis realized that volunteers had scoured the house for food and had stumbled upon a cache in the little pantry allotted to the caterers for their supplies. Also in the pantry were traces of protein-ous foodstuffs which the hired staff had withheld and taken home to sell. The discovery had diverted much of the conversation to questions of supply and then rapidly to politics. Altogether, though disagreeing with many of the views expressed, Mrs. Iblis had never felt so much at home at Bunhill as now. Even Professor Borgia made comparatively agreeable company when discoursing upon the complexities of Swiss dietetics. Mrs. Iblis took another piece of cake herself, though it was long past her hour. After the last crumb went down, Sister Nuper emerged from the music room at the head of her young men. Idly curious, Mrs. Iblis counted them. They numbered no less than twelve, each as radiantly good-looking as the rest. Would Sister Nuper, her pleasant evening over, now proceed to bed? Apparently not: Sister Nuper went directly to the front door, opened it, and led the way out into the chilly night, closely attended as ever by her faithful followers. The door banged loudly behind the last of them, shaking the house.

Mrs. Iblis now dared to ask questions. "Where are they going at this hour?"

Her neighbor, a metaphysical daredevil who had recently been the youngest Ph.D. of his year, became suddenly reserved, almost aggressive. "They've gone for a walk," he replied rudely, as if it were no business of hers.

Mrs. Iblis did not care to invite another snub from these strange people by pursuing the matter further. Despite the welcome loosening up of the talk, she had the irritating feeling that she alone (or almost alone) was excluded from a general and advantageous secret. Of course, she reflected, she had not been really intended to be present that weekend.

Nonetheless, she felt piqued. She decided to go to bed and went. One or two of her fellow guests to whom she said good night (there was no sign of Coner or Mrs. Coner, or even Mr. Stillman) seemed surprised, but only faintly.

* * *

Mrs. Iblis turned out the light and drew back the curtains, glad to stand for a moment in the cool darkness. Though the storm was long since over, the sky was not clear. There appeared, on the contrary, to be a dense ceiling of low cloud obscuring the stars but tinged with a radiance towards the east, which Mrs. Iblis supposed to come from the moon.

In the comfortable bed Mrs. Iblis soon fell asleep once more, despite the uncertainties relating to Sister Nuper's movements. After a dreamless span of uncertain length, she was awakened by a knocking on the door, at once purposeful and agitated.

"Come in, come in," said Mrs. Iblis rather peevishly. She switched on the bedside light.

She supposed it to be Sister Nuper (in who knows what condition?); but, in fact, it was Mavis. She wore saffron silk pajamas and no dressing gown. Her face was covered with unpleasing traces of what Mrs. Iblis presumed to be a "pack."

"I'm sorry, but there's something wrong. I'm frightened." Mavis was shivering noticeably.

Mrs. Iblis felt none too helpful. "You should have put something on."

"Yes. I suppose I should." Mavis vaguely clasped her pajamas about her.

"Have my dressing gown?"

"Thank you." Rather halfheartedly, she donned it. "Forgive my coming to you. Mrs. Coner's right out."

"Out?"

"Stuff she takes to make her sleep. She's never *compos mentis* till midday."

"What about the other guests? Not that I don't want to help," Mrs. Iblis added. Still, she did feel that this was the last straw.

"That's just it. They're not in their rooms. I'm frightened," repeated Mavis. "It's bloody awful."

Mrs. Iblis was now sitting up in bed and herself feeling none too warm. "Tell me exactly what's the matter."

"There's a queer light." Mavis crossed to the window and slightly drew back one of the curtains. "Look!"

"It's the moon."

"There's no moon."

"How do you know?"

"We compost the garden. You need to know for that. It's left to me, like most other things. I do know."

"Do you think it's a fire?"

"No." Mavis further withdrew the curtain. "Do you?"

A white radiance filled the air.

"It was beginning when I went to bed. I thought it was the moon. Are you quite sure?"

"Quite sure. It comes from the other side of the house."

"Searchlights?"

"It's not in beams. It's everywhere."

Mrs. Iblis felt no particular eagerness to leave her bed and investigate further.

"Have you *looked* on the other side of the house?"

"No. I wanted some moral support. Things go on here, you know." Mavis looked around the room so as to seem in part to localize her reference in a way which Mrs. Iblis found rather unpleasant. "I went to Ruth's room and it was empty. Then I went to several other rooms. They are all empty."

"So then you thought of Sister Nuper?"

"No. I thought of you. Will you come down with me?"

"Yes, of course, if you wish it." Mrs. Iblis got out of bed. "But why do we have to go down? Is that the first thing?"

"They're all in the hall. I can hear them."

Mrs. Iblis was reduced to putting on her overcoat. "Well now, let's see."

In what was precisely a half-light, the house did seem to Mrs. Iblis somewhat eerie. A life-sized figure of Buddha stood on the half landing, serenely menacing.

Through the thick brown curtains below and up the stair-well ascended a wavering hubbub. Then, just as Mrs. Iblis and her companion reached the bottom, a woman screamed sharply. She controlled herself almost at once.

The scene in the hall was certainly the strangest Mrs. Iblis had yet seen. The entire Forum (or so it seemed) were packed in, like refugees from some catastrophe. All appeared to be in their nightclothes, and there were the usual contrasts, comic and revealing. Professor Borgia's friend, the rotund young man, Mrs. Iblis noticed, was wearing a rich Oriental dressing gown. The leader of the New Vision Movement was wearing a nightshirt. Mrs. Iblis looked at once for Coner but could not see him.

In the poor light the throng appeared all to be gazing at the front door. They were now quite silent. Ruth, in the loose sweater and trousers she had worn by day, was elbowing her way forward, her face like that of St. Joan en route to the stake. Mrs. Iblis realized that she was going to open the door and deduced that someone had screamed when Ruth had made clear this intention.

All their faces were wrung in a conflict between a dreadful curiosity and the instinct to flee. A grim figure of the Kingsley Martin type collapsed upon his knees and, sinking his tortured face in his hands, began to pray. The rotund young man glanced at him and smiled faintly. A tall woman in an ulsterlike garment began to emit crooning sounds. Her face was stony with dread. Mrs. Iblis suspected that it had been she who had screamed.

Ruth had now struggled through to the door. With a final self-dedicatory gesture she lugged it open.

The strange luminosity fell upon her martyr's face. The doorway was filled with light. Behind could be seen a huge luminous shape. The light filled this shape and seemed to go towering upwards. The shape recalled in Mrs. Iblis's mind some common quotation: something about the feet of the gods on the mountains.

The Forum began to creep out into the garden, silently like snails under the moon.

"Come away," said a voice quietly to Mrs. Iblis. "Come upstairs." Mr. Stillman, in white silk pajamas and a black dressing gown, had gently touched her arm. He still carried a copy of the *Jewish Monthly*, his finger between the pages. Round his neck was a scarf with the colors of some good club.

Mrs. Iblis glanced at Mavis.

"You come too," said Mr. Stillman.

"I wonder what's become of Mr. Coner?"

"He's in good hands," said Mr. Stillman; and Mavis seemed willing to leave it at that.

The trio ascended to the first floor. There Mrs. Iblis had expected them to stop. But Mr. Stillman said: "We're going on the roof."

They went up two more stories; then by a Slingsby ladder to the roof, which Coner had laid out for sunbathing and deck games. Inflatable rubber objects lay about, once bright and crude, now discolored. Every now and then one stumbled over a quoit. The house was L-shaped, so that, by looking over the rail, Mrs. Iblis could see the Forum still issuing slowly from the front door. The light kept burning all night in Mrs. Coner's bedroom could also be seen.

Once outside, members of the Forum seemed to lose initiative and to accumulate in a mass against the wall of the house. The entire atmosphere was filled with the strange light, but Mrs. Iblis began to realize that the light nonetheless had a distinct source, a source independent of the general air. It was like the concentration and narrowing of the perceptions which often follow emergence from an anesthetic. The cause of the confusion was simply the vastness of the source. Up here it looked as if the air was alight: but in fact it was a vast shining figure which filled the entire visible earth and sky. As each member of the Forum realized this fact, he or she drew back into the company of the other members against the wall.

Although the members of the Forum might have been frightened, Mrs. Iblis found the scale of the occurrence simply too large for fright. She quite consciously rehearsed this fact over to herself in her mind. Mavis, however, was shaking more than ever and looked about to faint. Mrs. Iblis drew forward a striped deck chair and seated Mavis upon it, whispering some comforting words to her. She noticed that the strange light drew all the strong color from Mavis's pajamas. Mr. Stillman was looking on at these particular workings of the universe with apparently complete equipoise. The paper in his hand might have been a program of events.

The light suddenly increased around and upon the Forum huddled against the wall to the left of the front door. It was as if an immense spotlight picked out a group of the opposition about to be laid low with machine-gun fire. But in fact it was that the vast figure was looking downwards from the empyrean.

Mr. Stillman had placed his forearms on the railing round the roof. Mavis had sunk her head between her knees. It was only Mrs. Iblis who looked upwards, and what she saw nearly finished her.

When Mrs. Iblis came round, the radiance in the air was much diminished. Mavis and Mr. Stillman had lifted her into Mavis's deck chair. It was cold.

Mrs. Iblis peered through the railings. There was no one in sight. Only the light in Mrs. Coner's bedroom burned reddish through the glimmer.

"Where are they?"

"They have merged," said Mr. Stillman. "They are at one." He was rubbing her left wrist. Mavis, now apparently much recovered, was rubbing her right.

"Where have they gone to?"

Mavis made a slight gesture away from the house. "We shan't see *them* any more."

Mrs. Iblis hardly dared to follow with her eyes. Then she saw that the radiance had entirely faded. It was a starry, moonless night without a cloud in the sky.

"I no longer feel frightened."

"Nor I," said Mavis. "Only cold. Why don't we?"

"Why should you?" said Mr. Stillman. "They've got what

they wanted. As everyone does.'' He retied the cord of his dressing gown. ''Shall we go down?'' He led the way.

''I must look for Mr. Coner,'' said Mavis as they descended. Mrs. Iblis realized that she had not noticed her host among the group in the garden.

They found him sitting in the empty hall. He was drunk and still drinking. The key of his private spirit store was gripped tightly in his hand. The hall looked as if recently swept by a cyclone.

Mr. Stillman shut the open front door.

''Please God,'' said Coner in weak and sozzled accents, ''please God give me something larger than myself.''

He dropped into stupor, knocking a full glass to the floor. The disordered room began to reek of whiskey.

''Let me give you a hand,'' said Mr. Stillman to Mavis. They began to ease Coner toward the lift. ''I think *you'd* better get some sleep,'' said Mr. Stillman to Mrs. Iblis. ''Good night. See you in the morning.'' Mavis merely smiled at her.

Just as the cortège had passed through the brown curtains, the front door burst open once more. It was Sister Nuper and her friends. Their clothes seemed much damaged and covered with mud. It was as if they had been riding to hounds. But they all seemed as cheerful and gay as ever.

Mrs. Iblis had withdrawn into the shadows. She rather gathered that the revelers were contemplating final drinks.

Sister Nuper, graceful even in fatigue, dropped into the armchair just vacated by her employer. The bad light fell upon her beautiful features. Her face was glistening in a way Mrs. Iblis did not like. Her eyes were filled with such happiness that Mrs. Iblis was thoroughly scared all over again.

Unnoticed by the group of companions, Mrs. Iblis slipped away. Rather than pass what was left of the night with such a happy woman, she hastened to that room with the painted Crucifixion in it, she stuffed her possessions into her suitcase, and she left the house by a window at the back which had been carelessly left open by the hired staff.

Fritz Leiber

BELSEN EXPRESS

Fritz Leiber was a correspondent of H. P. Lovecraft and an admirer of Robert E. Howard, the great dark fantasist of the pulps and inventor of the "heroic fantasy" genre (typified in his Conan the Barbarian stories). Leiber's first stories appeared in *Unknown* magazine and *Astounding*—he was a Campbell writer who later became the standard bearer of 1950s SF with revolutionary stories in *Galaxy* magazine. But his early triumphs were in the horror mode: the classic novel *Conjure Wife*, and the stories collected in his first book, *Night's Black Agents* (Arkham House, 1949). His stories of urban horrors were a key factor in establishing the new horror mode of *Unknown* magazine. Now an elder statesman of his field, he continues to produce a tale or two a year over the past decade, including this World Fantasy Award–winner, "Belsen Express," a classic examination of the most egregious of horrors of the century, an understated contrast to the city horrors of Ellison or Bradbury.

George Simister watched the blue flames writhe beautifully in the grate, like dancing girls drenched with alcohol and set afire, and congratulated himself on having survived well through the middle of the Twentieth Century without getting involved in military service, world-saving, or any activities that interfered with the earning and enjoyment of money.

Outside rain dripped, a storm snarled at the city from the outskirts, and sudden gusts of wind produced in the chimney a sound like the mourning of doves. Simister shimmied himself a fraction of an inch deeper in his easy chair and took a slow sip of diluted scotch—he was sensitive to most cheaper liquors. Simister's physiology was on the delicate side; during his childhood certain tastes and odors, playing on an elusive heart weakness, had been known to make him faint.

The outspread newspaper started to slip from his knee. He detained it, let his glance rove across the next page, noted a headline about an uprising in Prague like that in Hungary in 1956 and murmured, "Damn Slavs," noted another about border fighting around Israel and muttered, "Damn Jews," and let the paper go. He took another sip of his drink, yawned, and watched a virginal blue flame flutter frightenedly the length of the log before it turned to a white smoke ghost. There was a sharp *knock-knock*.

Simister jumped and then got up and hurried tight-lipped to the front door. Lately some of the neighborhood children had been trying to annoy him probably because his was the most respectable and best-kept house on the block. Doorbell ringing, obscene sprayed scrawls, that sort of thing. And hardly children—young rowdies rather, who needed rough handling and a trip to the police station. He was really angry by the time he reached the door and swung it wide. There was nothing but a big wet empty darkness. A chilly draft spattered a couple of cold drops on him. Maybe the noise had come from the fire. He shut the door and started back to the living room, but a small pile of books untidily nested in wrapping paper on the hall table caught his eye and he grimaced.

They constituted a blotchily addressed parcel which the postman had delivered by mistake a few mornings ago. Simister could probably have deciphered the address, for it was clearly on this street, and rectified the postman's error, but he did not choose to abet the activities of illiterates with leaky pens. And the delivery must have been a mistake for the top book was titled *The Scourge of the Swastika* and the other two had similar titles, and Simister had an acute distaste for books that insisted on digging up that satisfactorily buried historical incident known as Nazi Germany.

The reason for this distaste was a deeply hidden fear that George Simister shared with millions, but that he had never revealed even to his wife. It was a quite unrealistic and now completely anachronistic fear of the Gestapo.

It had begun years before the Second World War, with the first small reports from Germany of minority persecutions and organized hoodlumism—the sense of something reaching out across the dark Atlantic to threaten his life, his security, and his confidence that he would never have to suffer pain except in a hospital.

Of course it had never got at all close to Simister, but it had exercised an evil tyranny over his imagination. There was one nightmarish series of scenes that had slowly grown in his mind and then had kept bothering him for a long time. It began with a thunderous knocking, of boots and rifle butts rather than fists, and a shouted demand: "Open up! It's the Gestapo." Next he would find himself in a stream of frantic people being driven toward a portal where a division was made between those reprieved and those slated for immediate extinction. Last he would be inside a closed motor van jammed so tightly with people that it was impossible to move. After a long time the van would stop, but the motor would keep running, and from the floor, leisurely seeking the crevices between the packed bodies, the entrapped exhaust fumes would begin to mount.

Now in the shadowy hall the same horrid movie had a belated showing. Simister shook his head sharply, as if he could shake the scenes out, reminding himself that the Gestapo was dead and done with for more than ten years. He felt the angry impulse to throw in the fire the books responsible for the return of his waking nightmare. But he remembered that books are hard to burn. He stared at them uneasily, excited by thoughts of torture and confinement, concentration and death camps, but knowing the nasty aftermath they left in his mind. Again he felt a sudden impulse, this time to bundle the books together and throw them in the trash can. But that would mean getting wet, it could wait until tomorrow. He put the screen in front of the fire, which had died and was smoking like a crematory, and went up to bed.

Some hours later he waked with the memory of a thunderous knocking.

He started up, exclaiming, "Those damned kids!" The drawn shades seemed abnormally dark—probably they'd thrown a stone through the street lamp.

He put one foot on the chilly floor. It was now profoundly still. The storm had gone off like a roving cat. Simister strained his ears. Beside him his wife breathed with irritating evenness. He wanted to wake her and explain about the young delinquents. It was criminal that they were permitted to roam the streets at this hour. Girls with them too, likely as not.

The knocking was not repeated. Simister listened for footsteps going away, or for the creaking of boards that would betray a lurking presence on the porch.

After awhile he began to wonder if the knocking might not have been part of a dream, or perhaps a final rumble of actual thunder. He lay down and pulled the blankets up to his neck. Eventually his muscles relaxed and he got to sleep.

At breakfast he told his wife about it.

"George, it may have been burglars," she said.

"Don't be stupid, Joan. Burglars don't knock. If it was anything it was those damned kids."

"Whatever it was, I wish you'd put a bigger bolt on the front door."

"Nonsense. If I'd known you were going to act this way I wouldn't have said anything. I told you it was probably just the thunder."

But next night at about the same hour it happened again.

This time there could be little question of dreaming. The

knocking still reverberated in his ears. And there had been words mixed with it, some sort of yapping in a foreign language. Probably the children of some of those European refugees who had settled in the neighborhood.

Last night they'd fooled him by keeping perfectly still after banging on the door, but tonight he knew what to do. He tiptoed across the bedroom and went down the stairs rapidly, but quietly because of his bare feet. In the hall he snatched up something to hit them with, then in one motion unlocked and jerked open the door.

There was no one.

He stood looking at the darkness. He was puzzled as to how they could have got away so quickly and silently. He shut the door and switched on the light. Then he felt the thing in his hand. It was one of the books. With a feeling of disgust he dropped it on the others. He must remember to throw them out first thing tomorrow.

But he overslept and had to rush. The feeling of disgust or annoyance, or something akin, must have lingered, however, for he found himself sensitive to things he wouldn't ordinarily have noticed. People especially. The swollen-handed man seemed deliberately surly as he counted Simister's pennies and handed him the paper. The tight-lipped woman at the gate hesitated suspiciously, as if he were trying to pass off a last month's ticket.

And when he was hurrying up the stairs in response to an approaching rumble, he brushed against a little man in an oversize coat and received in return a glance that gave him a positive shock.

Simister vaguely remembered having seen the little man several times before. He had the thin nose, narrow-set eyes and receding chin that is by a stretch of the imagination described as "rat-faced." In the movies he'd have played a stool pigeon. The flapping overcoat was rather comic.

But there seemed to be something at once so venomous and sly, so time-bidingly vindictive, in the glance he gave

Simister that the latter was taken aback and almost missed the train.

He just managed to squeeze through the automatically closing door of the smoker after the barest squint at the sign to assure himself that the train was an express. His heart was pounding in a way that another time would have worried him, but now he was immersed in a savage pleasure at having thwarted the man in the oversize coat. The latter hadn't hurried fast enough and Simister had made no effort to hold open the door for him.

As a smooth surge of electric power sent them sliding away from the station Simister pushed his way from the vestibule into the car and snagged a strap. From the next one already swayed his chief commuting acquaintance, a beefy, suspiciously red-nosed, irritating man named Holstrom, now reading a folded newspaper one-handed. He shoved a headline in Simister's face. The latter knew what to expect.

"Atomic Weapons for West Germany," he read tonelessly. Holstrom was always trying to get him into outworn arguments about totalitarianism, Nazi Germany, racial prejudice and the like. "Well, what about it?"

Holstrom shrugged. "It's a natural enough step, I suppose, but it started me thinking about the top Nazis and whether we really got all of them."

"Of course," Simister snapped.

"I'm not so sure," Holstrom said. "I imagine quite a few of them got away and are still hiding out somewhere."

But Simister refused the bait. The question bored him. Who talked about the Nazis any more? For that matter, the whole trip this morning was boring; the smoker was overcrowded; and when they finally piled out at the downtown terminus, the rude jostling increased his irritation.

The crowd was approaching an iron fence that arbitrarily split the stream of hurrying people into two sections which reunited a few steps farther on. Beside the fence a new guard was standing, or perhaps Simister hadn't noticed him before.

A cocky-looking young fellow with close-cropped blond hair and cold blue eyes.

Suddenly it occurred to Simister that he habitually passed to the right of the fence, but that this morning he was being edged over toward the left. This trifling circumstance, coming on top of everything else, made him boil. He deliberately pushed across the stream, despite angry murmurs and the hard stare of the guard.

He had intended to walk the rest of the way, but his anger made him forgetful and before he realized it he had climbed aboard a bus. He soon regretted it. The bus was even more crowded than the smoker and the standees were morose and lumpy in their heavy overcoats. He was tempted to get off and waste his fare, but he was trapped in the extreme rear and moreover shrank from giving the impression of a man who didn't know his own mind.

Soon another annoyance was added to the ones already plaguing him—a trace of exhaust fumes was seeping up from the motor at the rear. He immediately began to feel ill. He looked around indignantly, but the others did not seem to notice the odor, or else accepted it fatalistically.

In a couple of blocks the fumes had become so bad that Simister decided he must get off at the next stop. But as he started to push past her, a fat woman beside him gave him such a strangely apathetic stare that Simister, whose mind was perhaps a little clouded by nausea, felt almost hypnotized by it, so that it was several seconds before he recalled and carried out his intention.

Ridiculous, but the woman's face stuck in his mind all day. In the evening he stopped at a hardware store. After supper his wife noticed him working in the front hall.

"Oh, you're putting on a bolt," she said.

"Well, you asked me to, didn't you?"

"Yes, but I didn't think you'd do it."

"I decided I might as well." He gave the screw a final turn and stepped back to survey the job. "Anything to give you a feeling of security."

Then he remembered the stuff he had been meaning to throw out that morning. The hall table was bare.

"What did you do with them?" he asked.

"What?"

"Those fool books."

"Oh, those. I wrapped them up again and gave them to the postman."

"Now why did you do that? There wasn't any return address and I might have wanted to look at them."

"But you said they weren't addressed to us and you hate all that war stuff."

"I know, but—" he said and then stopped, hopeless of making her understand why he particularly wanted to feel he had got rid of that package himself, and by throwing it in the trash can. For that matter, he didn't quite understand his feelings himself. He began to poke around the hall.

"I did return the package," his wife said sharply. "I'm not losing my memory."

"Oh, all right!" he said and started for bed.

That night no knocking awakened him, but rather a loud crashing and rending of wood along with a harsh metallic *ping* like a lock giving.

In a moment he was out of bed, his sleep-sodden nerves jangling with anger. Those hoodlums! Rowdy pranks were perhaps one thing, deliberate destruction of property certainly another. He was halfway down the stairs before it occurred to him that the sound he had heard had a distinctly menacing aspect. Juvenile delinquents who broke down doors would hardly panic at the appearance of an unarmed householder.

But just then he saw that the front door was intact.

Considerably puzzled and apprehensive, he searched the first floor and even ventured into the basement, racking his brains as to just what could have caused such a noise. The water heater? Weight of the coal bursting a side of the bin? Those objects were intact. But perhaps the porch trellis giving way?

That last notion kept him peering out of the front window several moments. When he turned around there was someone behind him.

"I didn't mean to startle you," his wife said. "What's the matter, George?"

"I don't know. I thought I heard a sound. Something being smashed."

He expected that would send her into one of her burglar panics, but instead she kept looking at him.

"Don't stand there all night," he said. "Come on to bed."

"George, is something worrying you? Something you haven't told me about?"

"Of course not. Come on."

Next morning Holstrom was on the platform when Simister got there and they exchanged guesses as to whether the dark rainclouds would burst before they got downtown. Simister noticed the man in the oversize coat loitering about, but he paid no attention to him.

Since it was a bank holiday there were empty seats in the smoker and he and Holstrom secured one. As usual the latter had his newspaper. Simister waited for him to start his ideological sniping—a little uneasily for once; usually he was secure in his prejudices, but this morning he felt strangely vulnerable.

It came. Holstrom shook his head. "That's a bad business in Czechoslovakia. Maybe we were a little too hard on the Nazis."

To his surprise Simister found himself replying with both nervous hypocrisy and uncharacteristic vehemence. "Don't be ridiculous! Those rats deserved a lot worse than they got!"

As Holstrom turned toward him saying, "Oh, so you've changed your mind about the Nazis," Simister thought he heard someone just behind him say at the same time in a low, distinct, pitiless voice: "I heard you."

He glanced around quickly. Leaning forward a little, but with his face turned sharply away as if he had just become interested in something passing the window, was the man in the oversize coat.

"What's wrong?" Holstrom asked.

"What do you mean?"

"You've turned pale. You look sick."

"I don't feel that way."

"Sure? You know, at our age we've got to begin to watch out. Didn't you once tell me something about your heart?"

Simister managed to laugh that off, but when they parted just outside the train he was conscious that Holstrom was still eying him rather closely.

As he slowly walked through the terminus his face began to assume an abstracted look. In fact he was lost in thought to such a degree that when he approached the iron fence, he started to pass it on the left. Luckily the crowd was thin and he was able to cut across to the right without difficulty. The blond young guard looked at him closely—perhaps he re-membered yesterday morning.

Simister had told himself that he wouldn't again under any circumstances take the bus, but when he got outside it was raining torrents. After a moment's hesitation he climbed aboard. It seemed even more crowded than yesterday, if that were possible, with more of the same miserable people, and the damp air made the exhaust odor particularly offensive.

The abstracted look clung to his face all day long. His secretary noticed, but did not comment. His wife did, how-ever, when she found him poking around in the hall after supper.

"Are you still looking for that package, George?" Her tone was flat.

"Of course not," he said quickly, shutting the table drawer he'd opened.

She waited. "Are you sure you didn't order those books?"

"What gave you that idea?" he demanded. "You know I didn't."

"I'm glad," she said. "I looked through them. There were pictures. They were nasty."

"You think I'm the sort of person who'd buy books for the sake of nasty pictures?"

"Of course not, dear, but I thought you might have seen them and they were what had depressed you."

"Have I been depressed?"

"Yes. Your heart hasn't been bothering you, has it?"

"No."

"Well, what is it then?"

"I don't know." Then with considerable effort he said, "I've been thinking about war and things."

"War! No wonder you're depressed. You shouldn't think about things you don't like, especially when they aren't happening. What started you?"

"Oh, Holstrom keeps talking to me on the train."

"Well, don't listen to him."

"I won't."

"Well, cheer up then."

"I will."

"And don't let anyone make you look at morbid pictures. There was one of some people who had been gassed in a motor van and then laid out—"

"Please, Joan! Is it any better to tell me about them than to have me look at them?"

"Of course not, dear. That was silly of me. But do cheer up."

"Yes."

The puzzled, uneasy look was still in her eyes as she watched him go down the front walk next morning. It was foolish, but she had the feeling that his gray suit was really black—and he had whimpered in his sleep. With a shiver at her fancy she stepped inside.

That morning George Simister created a minor disturbance in the smoker, it was remembered afterwards, though Holstrom did not witness the beginning of it. It seems that Simister had run to catch the express and had almost missed it, due to a collision with a small man in a large overcoat. Someone recalled that trifling prelude because of the amusing circumstance that the small man, although he had been thrown to his knees and the collision was chiefly Simister's fault, was still anxiously begging Simister's pardon after the latter had dashed on.

Simister just managed to squeeze through the closing door while taking a quick squint at the sign. It was then that his queer behavior started. He instantly turned around and unsuccessfully tried to force his way out again, even inserting his hands in the crevice between the door frame and the rubber edge of the sliding door and yanking violently.

Apparently as soon as he noticed the train was in motion, he turned away from the door, his face pale and set, and roughly pushed his way into the interior of the car.

There he made a beeline for the little box in the wall containing the identifying signs of the train and the miniature window which showed in reverse the one now in use, which read simply EXPRESS. He stared at it as if he couldn't believe his eyes and then started to turn the crank, exposing in turn all the other white signs on the roll of black cloth. He scanned each one intently, oblivious to the puzzled or outraged looks of those around him.

He had been through all the signs once and was starting through them again before the conductor noticed what was happening and came hurrying. Ignoring his expostulations, Simister asked him loudly if this was really the express. Upon receiving a curt affirmative, Simister went on to assert that he had in the moment of squeezing aboard glimpsed another sign in the window—and he mentioned a strange name. He seemed both very positive and very agitated about it, the conductor said. The latter asked Simister to spell the name. Simister haltingly complied: "B . . . E . . . L . . . S . . . E . . . N . . . ." The conductor shook his head, then his eyes widened and he demanded, "Say, are you trying to kid me? That was one of those Nazi death camps." Simister slunk toward the other end of the car.

It was there that Holstrom saw him, looking "as if he'd just got a terrible shock." Holstrom was alarmed—and as it happened felt a special private guilt—but could hardly get a word out of him, though he made several attempts to start a conversation, choosing uncharacteristically neutral topics. Once, he remembered, Simister looked up and said, "Do you suppose there are some things a man simply can't escape, no matter how quietly he lives or how carefully he plans?" But his face immediately showed he had realized there was at least one very obvious answer to this question, and Holstrom didn't know what to say. Another time he suddenly remarked, "I wish we were like the British and didn't have standing in buses," but he subsided as quickly. As they neared the downtown terminus Simister seemed to brace up a little, but Holstrom was still worried about him to such a degree that he went out of his way to follow him through the terminus. "I was afraid something would happen to him, I don't know what," Holstrom said. "I would have stayed right beside him except he seemed to resent my presence."

Holstrom's private guilt, which intensified his anxiety and doubtless accounted for his feeling that Simister resented him, was due to the fact that ten days ago, cumulatively irritated by Simister's smug prejudices and blinkered narrow-mindedness, he had anonymously mailed him three books recounting with uncompromising realism and documentation some of the least pleasant aspects of the Nazi tyranny. Now he couldn't but feel they might have helped to shake Simister up in a way he hadn't intended, and he was ashamedly glad that he had been in such a condition when he sent the package that it had been addressed in a drunken scrawl. He never discussed this matter afterwards, except occasionally to make strangely feelingful remarks about "what little things can un-seat a spring in a man's clockworks!"

So, continuing Holstrom's story, he followed Simister at a distance as the latter dejectedly shuffled across the busy ter-minus. "Terminus?" Holstrom once interrupted his story to remark. "He's a god of endings, isn't he?—and of human rights. Does that mean anything?"

When Simister was nearing an iron fence a puzzling episode occurred. He was about to pass it to the right, when someone just ahead of him lurched or stumbled. Simister almost fell himself, veering toward the fence. A nearby guard reached out and in steadying him pulled him around the fence to the left.

Then, Holstrom maintains, Simister turned for a moment and Holstrom caught a glimpse of his face. There must have been something peculiarly frightening about that backward look, something perhaps that Holstrom cannot adequately describe, for he instantly forgot any idea of surveillance at a distance and made every effort to catch up.

But the crowd from another commuters' express enveloped Holstrom. When he got outside the terminus it was some moments before he spotted Simister in the midst of a group jamming their way aboard an already crowded bus across the street. This perplexed Holstrom, for he knew Simister didn't have to take the bus and he recalled his recent complaint.

Heavy traffic kept Holstrom from crossing. He says he shouted, but Simister did not seem to hear him. He got the impression that Simister was making feeble efforts to get out of the crowd that was forcing him onto the bus, but, "They were all jammed together like cattle."

The best testimony to Holstrom's anxiety about Simister is that as soon as the traffic thinned a trifle he darted across the street, skipping between the cars. But by then the bus had started. He was in time only for a whiff of particularly obnoxious exhaust fumes.

As soon as he got to his office he phoned Simister. He got Simister's secretary and what she had to say relieved his worries, which is ironic in view of what happened a little later.

What happened a little later is best described by the same girl. She said, "I never saw him come in looking so cheerful, the old grouch—excuse me. But anyway he came in all smiles, like he'd just got some bad news about somebody else, and right away he started to talk and kid with everyone, so that it was awfully funny when that man called up worried about him. I guess maybe, now I think back, he did seem a bit shaken underneath, like a person who's just had a narrow squeak and is very thankful to be alive.

"Well, he kept it up all morning. Then just as he was throwing his head back to laugh at one of his own jokes, he grabbed his chest, let out an awful scream, doubled up and fell on the floor. Afterwards I couldn't believe he was dead, because his lips stayed so red and there were bright spots of color on his cheeks, like rouge. Of course it was his heart, though you can't believe what a scare that stupid first doctor gave us when he came in and looked at him."

Of course, as she said, it must have been Simister's heart, one way or the other. And it is undeniable that the doctor in question was an ancient, possibly incompetent dispenser of penicillin, morphine and snap diagnoses swifter than Charcot's. They only called him because his office was in the same building. When Simister's own doctor arrived and pronounced it heart failure, which was what they'd thought all along, everyone was much relieved and inclined to be severely critical of the first doctor for having said something that sent them all scurrying to open the windows.

For when the first doctor had come in, he had taken one look at Simister and rasped, "Heart failure? Nonsense! Look at the color of his face. Cherry red. That man died of carbon monoxide poisoning."

Robert Bloch

YOURS TRULY, JACK THE RIPPER

Robert Bloch was a correspondent of Lovecraft and became a supernatural horror writer for *Weird Tales*, a science fiction writer, a mystery writer, then a film writer. "Bloch epitomizes the horror dimension of today's pop culture," says one major reference book. His novel, *Psycho*, appeared on Stephen King's ten-best list and the film made by Alfred Hitchcock is a classic. He has published more than a dozen story collections principally horrific. His earliest stories, such as "The Shambler From the Stars," are Lovecraftian but his characteristic work has as its hallmark abnormal psychology and absurd irony. He is a master of the pun. "Yours Truly, Jack the Ripper" is arguably his best story, an ironic blend of psychology and the supernatural, a monster story, a story that reinforces our belief in supernatural evil and connects it cleverly to evil in the real world. While later Bloch is often psychological horror (some of his best effects occur in mystery novels such as *The Scarf*), this story suggests the same moral universe as Harlan Ellison's "The Whimper of Whipped Dogs." Bloch was the first winner of the Grand Master Award for Life Achievement at the first World Fantasy Convention in 1975.

1

I looked at the strange Englishman. He looked at me.

"Sir Guy Hollis?" I asked.

"Indeed. Have I the pleasure of addressing John Carmody, the psychiatrist?"

I nodded. My eyes swept over the figure of my distinguished visitor. Tall, lean, sandy-haired—with the traditional tufted moustache. And the tweeds. I suspected a monocle concealed in a vest pocket, and wondered if he'd left his umbrella in the outer office.

But more than that, I wondered what the devil had impelled Sir Guy Hollis of the British Embassy to seek out a total stranger here in Chicago.

Sir Guy didn't help matters any as he sat down. He cleared his throat, glanced around nervously, tapping his pipe against the side of the desk. Then he opened his mouth.

"Mr. Carmody," he said, "have you ever heard of—Jack the Ripper?"

"The murderer?" I asked.

"Exactly. The greatest monster of them all Worse than Springheel Jack or Crippen. Jack the Ripper. Red Jack."

"I've heard of him," I said.

"Do you know his history?"

"I don't think we'll get any place swapping old wives' tales about famous crimes of history."

He took a deep breath.

"This is no old wives' tale. It's a matter of life or death."

He was so wrapped up in his obsession he even talked that way. Well—I was willing to listen. We psychiatrists get paid for listening.

"Go ahead," I told him. "Let's have the story."

Sir Guy lit a cigarette and began to talk.

"London, 1888," he began. "Late summer and early fall. That was the time. Out of nowhere came the shadowy figure of Jack the Ripper—a stalking shadow with a knife, prowling through London's East End. Haunting the squalid dives of Whitechapel, Spitalfields. Where he came from no one knew. But he brought death. Death in a knife.

"Six times that knife descended to slash the throats and bodies of London's women. Drabs and alley sluts. August 7th was the date of the first butchery. They found her lying there with thirty-nine stab wounds. A ghastly murder. On August 31st, another victim. The press became interested. The slum inhabitants were more deeply interested still.

"Who was this unknown killer who prowled in their midst and struck at will in the deserted alleyways of nighttown? And what was more important—when would he strike again?

"September 8th was the date. Scotland Yard assigned special deputies. Rumors ran rampant. The atrocious nature of the slayings was the subject for shocking speculation.

"The killer used a knife—expertly. He cut throats and removed—certain portions—of the bodies after death. He chose victims and settings with a fiendish deliberation. No one saw him or heard him. But watchmen making their gray rounds in the dawn would stumble across the hacked and horrid thing that was the Ripper's handiwork.

"Who was he? What was he? A mad surgeon? A butcher? An insane scientist? A pathological degenerate escaped from an asylum? A deranged nobleman? A member of the London police?

"Then the poem appeared in the newspapers. The anonymous poem, designed to put a stop to speculations—but which only aroused public interest to a further frenzy. A mocking little stanza:

> I'm not a butcher, I'm not a Yid
> Nor yet a foreign skipper,
> But I'm your own true loving friend,
> Yours truly—Jack the Ripper.

"And on September 30th, two more throats were slashed open. There was silence, then, in London for a time. Silence, and a nameless fear. When would Red Jack strike again? They waited through October. Every figment of fog concealed his phantom presence. Concealed it well—for nothing was learned of the Ripper's identity, or his purpose. The drabs of London shivered in the raw wind of early November. Shivered, and were thankful for the coming of each morning's sun.

"November 9th. They found her in her room. She lay there very quietly, limbs neatly arranged. And beside her, with equal neatness, were laid her breasts and heart. The Ripper had outdone himself in execution.

"Then, panic. But needless panic. For though press, police, and populace alike waited in sick dread, Jack the Ripper did not strike again.

"Months passed. A year. The immediate interest died, but not the memory. They said Jack had skipped to America. That he had committed suicide. They said—and they wrote. They've written ever since. But to this day no one knows who Jack the Ripper was. Or why he killed. Or why he stopped killing."

Sir Guy was silent. Obviously he expected some comment from me.

"You tell the story well," I remarked. "Though with slight emotional bias."

"I suppose you want to know why I'm interested?" he snapped.

"Yes. That's exactly what I'd like to know."

"Because," said Sir Guy Hollis. "I am on the trail of Jack the Ripper now. I think he's here—in Chicago!"

"Say that again."

"Jack the Ripper is alive, in Chicago, and I'm out to find him."

He wasn't smiling. It wasn't a joke.

"See here," I said. "What was the date of these murders?"

"August to November, 1888."

"1888? But if Jack the Ripper was an able-bodied man in

1988, he'd surely be dead today! Why look, man—if he were merely born in that year, he'd be fifty-seven years old today!"

"Would he?" smiled Sir Guy Hollis. "Or should I say, 'Would she?' Because Jack the Ripper may have been a woman. Or any number of things."

"Sir Guy," I said. "You came to the right person when you looked me up. You definitely need the services of a psychiatrist."

"Perhaps. Tell me, Mr. Carmody, do you think I'm crazy?"

I looked at him and shrugged. But I had to give him a truthful answer.

"Frankly—no."

"Then you might listen to the reasons I believe Jack the Ripper is alive today."

"I might."

"I've studied these cases for thirty years. Been over the actual ground. Talked to officials. Talked to friends and acquaintances of the poor drabs who were killed. Visited with men and women in the neighborhood. Collected an entire library of material touching on Jack the Ripper. Studied all the wild theories or crazy notions.

"I learned a little. Not much, but a little. I won't bore you with my conclusions. But there was another branch of inquiry that yielded more fruitful return. I have studied unsolved crimes. Murders.

"I could show you clippings from the papers of half the world's greatest cities. San Francisco. Shanghai. Calcutta. Omsk. Paris. Berlin. Pretoria. Cairo. Milan. Adelaide.

"The trail is there, the pattern. Unsolved crimes. Slashed throats of women. With the peculiar disfigurations and removals. Yes, I've followed a trail of blood. From New York westward across the continent. Then to the Pacific. From there to Africa. During the World War of 1914-18 it was Europe. After that, South America. And since 1930, the United States again. Eighty-seven such murders—and to the trained criminologist, all bear the stigma of the Ripper's handiwork.

"Recently there were the so-called Cleveland torso slayings. Remember? A shocking series. And finally, two recent deaths in Chicago. Within the past six months. One out on South Dearborn. The other somewhere up on Halsted. Same type of crime, same technique. I tell you, there are unmistakable indications in all these affairs—indications of the work of Jack the Ripper!"

"A very tight theory," I said. "I'll not question your evidence at all, or the deductions you draw. You're the criminologist, and I'll take your word for it. Just one thing remains to be explained. A minor point, perhaps, but worth mentioning."

"And what is that?" asked Sir Guy.

"Just how could a man of, let us say, eight-five years commit these crimes? For if Jack the Ripper was around thirty in 1888 and lived, he'd be eighty-five today."

"Suppose he didn't get any older?" whispered Sir Guy.

"What's that?"

"Suppose Jack the Ripper didn't grow old? Suppose he is still a young man today?

"It's a crazy theory, I grant you," he said. "All the theories about the Ripper are crazy. The idea that he was a doctor. Or a maniac. Or a woman. The reasons advanced for such beliefs are flimsy enough. There's nothing to go by. So why should my notion be any worse?"

"Because people grow older," I reasoned with him. "Doctors, maniacs and women alike."

"What about—*sorcerers*?"

"Sorcerers?"

"Necromancers. Wizards. Practicers of Black Magic."

"What's the point?"

"I studied," said Sir Guy. "I studied everything. After a while I began to study the dates of the murders. The pattern those dates formed. The rhythm. The solar, lunar, stellar rhythm. The sidereal aspect. The astrological significance.

"Suppose Jack the Ripper didn't murder for murder's sake alone? Suppose he wanted to make—a sacrifice?"

"What kind of sacrifice?"

Sir Guy shrugged. "It is said that if you offer blood to the dark gods they grant boons. Yes, if a blood offering is made at the proper time—when the moon and the stars are right—and with the proper ceremonies—they grant boons. Boons of youth. Eternal youth."

"But that's nonsense!"

"No. That's—Jack the Ripper."

I stood up. "A most interesting theory," I told him. "But why do you come here and tell it to me? I'm not an authority on witchcraft. I'm not a police official or criminologist. I'm a practicing psychiatrist. What's the connection?"

Sir Guy smiled.

"You are interested, then?"

"Well, yes. There must be some point."

"There is. But I wished to be assured of your interest first. Now I can tell you my plan."

"And just what is that plan?"

Sir Guy gave me a long look.

"John Carmody," he said, "you and I are going to capture Jack the Ripper."

2

That's the way it happened. I've given the gist of that first interview in all its intricate and somewhat boring detail, because I think it's important. It helps to throw some light on Sir Guy's character and attitude. And in view of what happened after that—

But I'm coming to those matters.

Sir Guy's thought was simple. It wasn't even a thought. Just a hunch.

"You know the people here," he told me. "I've inquired. That's why I came to you as the ideal man for my purpose. You number amongst your acquaintances many writers, painters, poets. The so-called intelligentsia. The lunatic fringe from the near north side.

"For certain reasons—never mind what they are—my clues lead me to infer that Jack the Ripper is a member of that element. He chooses to pose as an eccentric. I've a feeling that with you to take me around and introduce me to your set, I might hit upon the right person."

"It's all right with me," I said. "But just how are you going to look for him? As you say, he might be anybody, anywhere. And you have no idea what he looks like. He might be young or old. Jack the Ripper—a Jack of all trades? Rich man, poor man, beggar man, thief, doctor, lawyer—how will you know?"

"We shall see." Sir Guy sighed heavily. "But I must find him. At once."

"Why the hurry?"

Sir Guy sighed again. "Because in two days he will kill again."

"Are you sure?"

"Sure as the stars. I've plotted this chart, you see. All of the murders correspond to certain astrological rhythm patterns. If, as I suspect, he makes a blood sacrifice to renew his youth, he must murder within two days. Notice the pattern of his first crimes in London. August 7th. Then August 31st. September 8th. September 30th. November 9th. Intervals of twenty-four days, nine days, twenty-two days—he killed two this time—and then forty days. Of course there were crimes in between. There had to be. But they weren't discovered and pinned on him.

"At any rate, I've worked out a pattern for him, based on all my data. And I say that within the next two days he kills. So I must seek him out, somehow, before then."

"And I'm still asking you what you want me to do."

"Take me out," said Sir Guy. "Introduce me to your friends. Take me to parties."

"But where do I begin? As far as I know, my artistic friends, despite their eccentricities, are all normal people."

"So is the Ripper. Perfectly normal. Except on certain nights." Again that faraway look in Sir. Guy's eyes. "Then he becomes an ageless pathological monster, crouching to kill."

"All right," I said. "All right, I'll take you."

We made our plans. And that evening I took him over to Lester Baston's studio.

As we ascended to the penthouse roof in the elevator I took the opportunity to warn Sir Guy.

"Baston's a real screwball," I cautioned him. "So are his guests. Be prepared for anything and everything."

"I am." Sir Guy Hollis was perfectly serious. He put his hand in his trousers pocket and pulled out a gun.

"What the—" I began.

"If I see him I'll be ready," Sir Guy said. He didn't smile, either.

"But you can't go running around at a party with a loaded revolver in your pocket, man!"

"Don't worry, I won't behave foolishly."

I wondered. Sir Guy Hollis was not, to my way of thinking, a normal man.

We stepped out of the elevator, went toward Baston's apartment door.

"By the way," I murmured, "just how do you wish to be introduced? Shall I tell them who you are and what you are looking for?"

"I don't care. Perhaps it would be best to be frank."

"But don't you think that the Ripper—if by some miracle he or she is present—will immediately get the wind up and take cover?"

"I think the shock of the announcement that I am hunting the Ripper would provoke some kind of betraying gesture on his part," said Sir Guy.

"It's a fine theory. But I warn you, you're going to be in for a lot of ribbing. This is a wild bunch."

Sir Guy smiled.

"I'm ready," he announced. "I have a little plan of my own. Don't be shocked at anything I do."

I nodded and knocked on the door.

Baston opened it and poured out into the hall. His eyes were as red as the maraschino cherries in his Manhattan. He teetered back and forth regarding us very gravely. He squinted at my square-cut homburg hat and Sir Guy's moustache.

"Aha," he intoned. "The Walrus and the Carpenter."

I introduced Sir Guy.

"Welcome," said Baston, gesturing us inside with over-elaborate courtesy. He stumbled after us into the garish parlor.

I stared at the crowd that moved restlessly through the fog of cigarette smoke.

It was the shank of the evening for this mob. Every hand held a drink. Every face held a slightly hectic flush. Over in one corner the piano was going full blast, but the imperious strains of the *March* from *The Love for Three Oranges* couldn't drown out the profanity from the crap game in the other corner.

Prokofieff had no chance against African polo, and one set of ivories rattled louder than the other.

Sir Guy got a monocle-full right away. He saw LaVerne Gonnister, the poetess, hit Hymie Kralik in the eye. He saw Hymie sit down on the floor and cry until Dick Pool accidentally stepped on his stomach as he walked through to the dining room for a drink.

He heard Nadia Vilinoff, the commercial artist, tell Johnny Odcutt that she thought his tattooing was in dreadful taste, and he saw Barclay Melton crawl under the dining room table with Johnny Odcutt's wife.

His zoological observations might have continued indefinitely if Lester Baston hadn't stepped to the center of the room and called for silence by dropping a vase on the floor.

"We have distinguished visitors in our midst," bawled Lester, waving his empty glass in our direction. "None other than the Walrus and the Carpenter. The Walrus is Sir Guy Hollis, a something-or-other from the British Embassy. The Carpenter, as you all know, is our own John Carmody, the prominent dispenser of libido liniment.''

He turned and grabbed Sir Guy by the arm, dragging him to the middle of the carpet. For a moment I thought Hollis might object, but a quick wink reassured me. He was prepared for this.

''It is our custom, Sir Guy,'' said Baston, loudly, ''to subject our new friends to a little cross-examination. Just a little formality at these very formal gatherings, you understand. Are your prepared to answer questions?''

Sir Guy nodded and grinned.

''Very well,'' Baston muttered. ''Friends—I give you this bundle from Britain. Your witness.''

Then the ribbing started. I meant to listen, but at that moment Lydia Dare saw me and dragged me off into the vestibule for one of those Darling-I-waited-for-your-call-all-day routines.

By the time I got rid of her and went back, the impromptu quiz session was in full swing. From the attitude of the crowd, I gathered that Sir Guy was doing all right for himself.

Then Baston himself interjected a question that upset the apple-cart.

''And what, may I ask, brings you to our midst tonight? What is your mission, oh Walrus?''

''I'm looking for Jack the Ripper.''

Nobody laughed.

Perhaps it struck them all the way it did me. I glanced at my neighbors and began to *wonder*.

LaVerne Gonnister. Hymie Kralik. Harmless. Dick Pool. Nadia Vilinoff. Johnny Odcutt and his wife. Barclay Melton. Lydia Dare. All harmless.

But what a forced smile on Dick Pool's face! And that sly, self-conscious smirk that Barclay Melton wore!

Oh, it was absurd, I grant you. But for the first time I saw

these people in a new light. I wondered about their lives—
their secret lives beyond the scenes of parties.

How many of them were playing a part, concealing something?

Who here would worship Hecate and grant that horrid
goddess the dark boon of blood?

Even Lester Baston might be masquerading.

The mood was upon us all, for a moment. I saw questions
flicker in the circle of eyes around the room.

Sir Guy stood there, and I could swear he was fully conscious of the situation he'd created, and enjoyed it.

I wondered idly just what was *really* wrong with him. Why
he had this odd fixation concerning Jack the Ripper. Maybe
he was hiding secrets, too. . . .

Baston, as usual, broke the mood. He burlesqued it.

"The Walrus isn't kidding, friends," he said. He slapped
Sir Guy on the back and put his arm around him as he orated.
"Our English cousin is really on the trail of the fabulous Jack
the Ripper. You all remember Jack the Ripper, I presume?
Quite a cut-up in the old days, as I recall. Really had some
ripping good times when he went out on a tear.

"The Walrus has some idea that the Ripper is still alive,
probably prowling around Chicago with a Boy Scout knife.
In fact"—Baston paused impressively and shot it out in a
rasping stage whisper—"in fact, he has reason to believe that
Jack the Ripper might even be right here in our midst tonight."

There was the expected reaction of giggles and grins. Baston eyed Lydia Dare reprovingly. "You girls needn't laugh,"
he smirked. "Jack the Ripper might be a woman, too, you
know. Sort of a Jill the Ripper."

"You mean you actually suspect one of us?" shrieked
LaVerne Gonnister, simpering up to Sir Guy. "But that Jack
the Ripper person disappeared ages ago, didn't he? In 1888?"

"Aha!" interrupted Baston. "How do you know so much
about it, young lady? Sounds suspicious! Watch her, Sir

Guy—she may not be as young as she appears. These lady poets have dark pasts.''

The tension was gone, the mood was shattered, and the whole thing was beginning to degenerate into a trivial party joke. The man who had played the *March* was eyeing the piano with a *scherzo* gleam in his eye that augured ill for Prokofieff. Lydia Dare was glancing at the kitchen, waiting to make a break for another drink.

Then Baston caught it.

"Guess what?" he yelled. "The Walrus has a gun."

His embracing arm had slipped and encountered a hard outline of the gun in Sir Guy's pocket. He snatched it out before Hollis had the opportunity to protest.

I stared hard at Sir Guy, wondering if this thing had carried far enough. But he flicked a wink my way and I remembered he had told me not to be alarmed.

So I waited as Baston broached a drunken inspiration.

"Let's play fair with our friend the Walrus," he cried. "He came all the way from England to our party on this mission. If none of you is willing to confess, I suggest we give him a chance to find out—the hard way."

"What's up?" asked Johnny Odcutt.

"I'll turn out the lights for one minute. Sir Guy can stand here with his gun. If anyone in this room is the Ripper he can either run for it or take the opportunity to—well, eradicate his pursuer. Fair enough?"

It was even sillier than it sounds, but it caught the popular fancy. Sir Guy's protests went unheard in the ensuing babble. And before I could stride over and put in my two cents' worth, Lester Baston had reached the light switch.

"Don't anybody move," he announced, with fake solemnity. "For one minute we will remain in darkness—perhaps at the mercy of a killer. At the end of that time, I'll turn up the lights again and look for bodies. Choose your partners, ladies and gentlemen."

The lights went out.

Somebody giggled.

I heard footsteps in the darkness. Mutterings.

A hand brushed my face.

The watch on my wrist ticked violently. But even louder, rising above it, I heard another thumping. The beating of my heart.

Absurd. Standing in the dark with a group of tipsy fools. And yet there was real terror lurking here, rustling through the velvet blackness.

Jack the Ripper prowled in darkness like this. And Jack the Ripper had a knife. Jack the Ripper had a madman's brain and a madman's purpose.

But Jack the Ripper was dead, dead and dust these many years—by every human law.

Only there are no human laws when you feel yourself in the darkness, when the darkness hides and protects and the outer mask slips off your face and you feel something welling up within you, a brooding shapeless purpose that is brother to the blackness.

Sir Guy Hollis shrieked.

There was a grisly thud.

Baston put the lights on.

Everybody screamed.

Sir Guy Hollis lay sprawled on the floor in the center of the room. The gun was still clutched in his hand.

I glanced at the faces, marveling at the variety of expressions human beings can assume when confronting horror.

All the faces were present in the circle. Nobody had fled. And yet Sir Guy Hollis lay there.

LaVerne Gonnister was wailing and hiding her face.

"All right."

Sir Guy rolled over and jumped to his feet. He was smiling.

"Just an experiment, eh? If Jack the Ripper *were* among those present, and thought I had been murdered, he would have betrayed himself in some way when the lights went on and he saw me lying there.

"I am convinced of your individual and collective innocence. Just a gentle spoof, my friends."

Hollis stared at the goggling Baston and the rest of them
crowding in behind him.

"Shall we leave, John?" he called to me. "It's getting late,
I think."

Turning, he headed for the closet. I followed him. Nobody
said a word.

It was a pretty dull party after that.

3

I met Sir Guy the following evening as we agreed, on the
corner of Twenty-Ninth and South Halsted.

After what had happened the night before, I was prepared
for almost anything. But Sir Guy seemed matter-of-fact
enough as he stood huddled against a grimy doorway and
waited for me to appear.

"Boo!" I said, jumping out suddenly. He smiled. Only the
betraying gesture of his left hand indicated that he'd instinctively reached for his gun when I startled him.

"All ready for our wild-goose chase?" I asked.

"Yes." He nodded. "I'm glad that you agreed to meet me
without asking questions," he told me. "It shows you trust
my judgment." He took my arm and edged me along the
street slowly.

"It's foggy tonight, John," said Sir Guy Hollis. "Like
London."

I nodded.

"Cold, too, for November."

I nodded again and half-shivered my agreement.

"Curious," mused Sir Guy. "London fog and November.
The place and the time of the Ripper murders."

I grinned through darkness. "Let me remind you, Sir Guy,
that this isn't London, but Chicago. And it isn't November,
1888. It's over fifty years later."

Sir Guy returned my grin, but without mirth. "I'm not so sure, at that," he murmured. "Look about you. Those tangled alleys and twisted streets. They're like the East End. Mitre Square. And surely they are as ancient as fifty years, at least."

"You're in the black neighborhood of South Clark Street," I said shortly. "And why you dragged me down here I still don't know."

"It's a hunch," Sir Guy admitted. "Just a hunch on my part, John. I want to wander around down here. There's the same geographical conformation in these streets as in those courts where the Ripper roamed and slew. That's where we'll find him, John. Not in the bright lights, but down here in the darkness. The darkness where he waits and crouches."

"Isn't that why you brought a gun?" I asked. I was unable to keep a trace of sarcastic nervousness from my voice. All this talk, this incessant obsession with Jack the Ripper, got on my nerves more than I cared to admit.

"We may need a gun," said Sir Guy, gravely. "After all, tonight is the appointed night."

I sighed. We wandered on through the foggy, deserted streets. Here and there a dim light burned above a gin-mill doorway. Otherwise, all was darkness and shadow. Deep, gaping alleyways loomed as we proceeded down a slanting side street.

We crawled through that fog, alone and silent, like two tiny maggots floundering within a shroud.

"Can't you see there's not a soul around these streets?" I said.

"He's bound to come," said Sir Guy. "He'll be drawn here. This is what I've been looking for. A *genius loci*. An evil spot that attracts evil. Always, when he slays, it's in the slums.

"You see, that must be one of his weaknesses. He has a fascination for squalor. Besides, the women he needs for sacrifice are more easily found in the dives and stewpots of a great city."

"Well, let's go into one of the dives or stewpots," I suggested. "I'm cold. Need a drink. This damned fog gets into your bones. You Britishers can stand it, but I like warmth and dry heat."

We emerged from our sidestreet and stood upon the threshold of an alley.

Through the white clouds of mist ahead, I discerned a dim blue light, a naked bulb dangling from a beer sign above an alley tavern.

"Let's take a chance," I said. "I'm beginning to shiver."

"Lead the way," said Sir Guy. I led him down the alley passage. We halted before the door of the dive.

"What are you waiting for?" he asked.

"Just looking in," I told him. "This is a rough neighborhood, Sir Guy. Never know what you're liable to run into. And I'd prefer we didn't get into the wrong company. Some of these places resent white customers."

"Good idea, John."

I finished my inspection through the doorway. "Looks deserted," I murmured. "Let's try it."

We entered a dingy bar. A feeble light flickered above the counter and railing, but failed to penetrate the further gloom of the back booths.

A gigantic black lolled across the bar. He scarcely stirred as we came in, but his eyes flicked open quite suddenly and I knew he noted our presence and was judging us.

"Evening," I said.

He took his time before replying. Still sizing us up. Then, he grinned.

"Evening, gents. What's your pleasure?"

"Gin," I said. "Two gins. It's a cold night."

"That's right, gents."

He poured, I paid, and took the glasses over to one of the booths. We wasted no time in emptying them.

I went over to the bar and got the bottle. Sir Guy and I poured ourselves another drink. The big man went into his doze, with one wary eye half-open against any sudden activity.

The clock over the bar ticked on. The wind was rising outside, tearing the shroud of fog to ragged shreds. Sir Guy and I sat in the warm booth and drank our gin.

He began to talk, and the shadows crept up about us to listen.

He rambled a great deal. He went over everything he'd said in the office when I met him, just as though I hadn't heard it before. The poor devils with obsessions are like that.

I listened very patiently. I poured Sir Guy another drink. And another.

But the liquor only made him more talkative. How he did run on! About ritual killings and prolonging the life unnaturally—the whole fantastic tale came out again. And of course, he maintained his unyielding conviction that the Ripper was abroad tonight.

I suppose I was guilty of goading him.

"Very well," I said, unable to keep the impatience from my voice. "Let us say that your theory is correct—even though we must overlook every natural law and swallow a lot of superstition to give it any credence.

"But let us say, for the sake of argument, that you are right. Jack the Ripper was a man who discovered how to prolong his own life through making human sacrifices. He did travel around the world as you believe. He is in Chicago now and is planning to kill. In other words, let us suppose that everything you claim is gospel truth. So what?"

"What do you mean, 'so what'?" said Sir Guy.

"I mean—so what?" I answered him. "If all this is true, it still doesn't prove that by sitting down in a dingy gin-mill on the South Side, Jack the Ripper is going to walk in here and let you kill him, or turn him over to the police. And come to think of it, I don't even know now just what you intend to *do* with him if you ever did find him.

Sir Guy gulped his gin. "I'd capture the bloody swine," he said. "Capture him and turn him over to the government, together with all the papers and documentary evidence I've collected against him over a period of many years. I've spent a fortune investigating this affair, I tell you, a fortune! His capture will mean the solution of hundreds of unsolved crimes, of that I am convinced.''

In vino veritas. Or was all this babbling the result of too much gin? It didn't matter. Sir Guy Hollis had another. I sat there and wondered what to do with him. The man was rapidly working up to a climax of hysterical drunkenness.

''That's enough,'' I said, putting out my hand as Sir Guy reached for the half-emptied bottle again. ''Let's call a cab and get out of here. It's getting late and it doesn't look as though your elusive friend is going to put in his appearance. Tomorrow, if I were you, I'd plan to turn all those papers and documents over to the FBI. If you're so convinced of the truth of your theory, they are competent to make a very thorough investigation, and find your man.''

''No.'' Sir Guy was drunkenly obstinate. ''No cab.''

''But let's get out of here anyway,'' I said, glancing at my watch. ''It's past midnight.''

He sighed, shrugged, and rose unsteadily. As he started for the door, he tugged the gun free from his pocket.

''Here, give me that!'' I whispered. ''You can't walk around the street brandishing that thing.''

I took the gun and slipped it inside my coat. Then I got hold of his right arm and steered him out of the door. The black man didn't look up as we departed.

We stood shivering in the alleyway. The fog had increased. I couldn't see either end of the alley from where we stood. It was cold. Damp. Dark. Fog or no fog, a little wind was whispering secrets to the shadows at our backs.

Sir Guy, despite his incapacity, still stared apprehensively at the alley, as though he expected to see a figure approaching.

Disgust got the better of me.

''Childish foolishness,'' I snorted. ''Jack the Ripper, indeed! I call this carrying a hobby too far.''

"Hobby?" He faced me. Through the fog I could see his distorted face. "You call this a hobby?"

"Well, what is it?" I grumbled. "Just why else are you so interested in tracking down this mythical killer?"

My arm held his. But his stare held me.

"In London," he whispered. "In 1888 . . . one of those nameless drabs the Ripper slew . . . was my mother."

"What?"

"Later I was recognized by my father, and legitimatized. We swore to give our lives to find the Ripper. My father was the first to search. He died in Hollywood in 1926—on the trail of the Ripper. They said he was stabbed by an unknown assailant in a brawl. But I knew who that assailant was.

"So I've taken up his work, do you see, John? I've carried on. And I will carry on until I do find him and kill him with my own hands."

I believed him then. He wouldn't give up. He wasn't just a drunken babbler any more. He was as fanatical, as determined, as relentless as the Ripper himself.

Tomorrow he'd be sober. He'd continue the search. Perhaps he'd turn those papers over to the FBI. Sooner or later, with such persistence—and with his motive—he'd be successful. I'd always known he had a motive.

"Let's go," I said, steering him down the alley.

"Wait a minute," said Sir Guy. "Give me back my gun." He lurched a little. "I'd feel better with the gun on me."

He pressed me into the dark shadows of a little recess.

I tried to shrug him off, but he was insistent.

"Let me carry the gun, now, John," he mumbled.

"All right," I said.

I reached into my coat, brought my hand out.

"But that's not a gun," he protested. "That's a knife."

"I know."

I bore down on him swiftly.

"John!" he screamed.

"Never mind the 'John,' " I whispered, raising the knife. "Just call me . . . Jack."

Charles L. Grant

If Damon Comes

Charles L. Grant is the most important anthologist of horror fiction since August Derleth in the U.S., principally for his reprint works and for his original series, *Shadows*, annually nominated for the World Fantasy Award as best collection of the year (and often the winner, or the source of the short fiction winner). Grant is a prolific novelist and short story writer of the company of Ramsey Campbell and Stephen King and a popular figure among fans of horror fiction for his novels and stories of Oxrun Station, an imaginary Connecticut town (based to a certain extent upon Lovecraft's Dunwich and Arkham, from the Cthulhu mythos stories). ''If Damon Comes'' is one of the finest Oxrun stories. Grant is at his best in the short form, as here, and is a salient example of the traditional horror writer of his generation, initially influenced by Bradbury (primarily . . . then Bloch and Leiber and Matheson—all short fiction writers), then in the mid-seventies breaking into the novel form during the great commercial boom in horror.

Fog, nightbreath of the river, luring without whispering in the thick crown of an elm, huddling without creaking around the base of a chimney; it drifted past porch lights, and in passing blurred them, dropped over the streetlights, and in dropping grayed them. It crept in with midnight to stay until dawn, and there was no wind to bring the light out of hiding.

Frank shivered and drew his raincoat's collar closer around his neck, held it closed with one hand while the other wiped at the pricks of moisture that clung to his cheeks, his short dark hair. He whistled once, loudly, but in listening heard nothing, not even an echo. He stamped his feet against the November cold and moved to the nearest corner, squinted and saw nothing. He knew the cat was gone, had known it from the moment he had seen the saucer still brimming with milk on the back porch. Damon had been sitting beside it, hands folded, knees pressed tightly together, elbows tucked into his sides. He was cold, but refused to acknowledge it, and Frank had only tousled his son's softly brown hair, squeezed his shoulder once and went inside to say good-bye to his wife.

And now . . . now he walked, through the streets of Oxrun Station, looking for an animal he had seen only once—a half-breed Siamese with a milk white face—whistling like a fool afraid of the dark, searching for the note that would bring the animal running.

And in walking, he was unpleasantly reminded of a night the year before, when he had had one drink too many at someone's party, made one amorous boast too many in someone's ear, and had ended up on a street corner with a woman he knew only vaguely. They had kissed once and long, and once broken, he had turned around to see Damon staring up at him. The boy had turned, had fled, and Frank had stayed away most of the night, not knowing what Susan had heard, fearing more what Damon had thought.

It had been worse than horrid facing the boy again, but Damon had acted as though nothing had happened; and the guilt passed as the months passed, and the wondering why his son had been out in the first place.

He whistled. Crouched and snapped his fingers at the dark of some shrubbery. Then he straightened and blew out a deeply held breath. There was no cat, there were no cars, and he finally gave in to his aching feet and sore back and headed for home. Quickly. Watching the fog tease the road before him, cut it sharply off behind.

It wasn't fair, he thought, his hands shoved in his pockets, his shoulders hunched as though expecting a blow. Damon, in his short eight years, had lost two dogs already to speeders, a canary to some disease he couldn't even pronounce, and two brothers stillborn—it was getting to be a problem. *He* was getting to be a problem, fighting each day that he had to go to school, whining and weeping whenever vacations came around and trips were planned.

He'd asked Doc Simpson about it when Damon turned seven. Dependency, he was told; clinging to the only three things left in his life—his short, short life—that he still believed to be constant: his home, his mother . . . and Frank.

And Frank had kissed a woman on a corner and Damon had seen him.

Frank shuddered and shook his head quickly, remembering how the boy had come to the office at least once a day for the next three weeks, saying nothing, just standing on the sidewalk looking in through the window. Just for a moment. Long enough to be sure that his father was still there.

Once home, then, Frank shed his coat and hung it on the rack by the front door. A call, a muffled reply, and he took the stairs two at a time and trotted down the hall to Damon's room set over the kitchen.

"Sorry, old pal," he said with a shrug as he made himself a place on the edge of the mattress. "I guess he went home."

Damon, small beneath the flowered quilt, innocent from behind long curling lashes, shook his head sharply. "No," he said. "This is home. It is, Dad, it really is."

Frank scratched at the back of his neck. "Well, I guess he didn't think of it quite that way."

"Maybe he got lost, huh? It's awfully spooky out there. Maybe he's afraid to come out of where he's hiding."

"A cat's never—" He stopped as soon as he saw the expression on the boy's thin face. Then he nodded and broke out a rueful smile, "Well, maybe you're right, pal. Maybe the fog messed him up a little." Damon's hand crept into his, and he squeezed it while thinking that the boy was too thin by far; it made his head look ungainly. "In the morning," he promised. "In the morning. If he's not back by then, I'll take the day off and we'll hunt him together."

Damon nodded solemnly, withdrew the hand and pulled the quilt up to his chin. "When's mom coming home?"

"In a while. It's Friday, you know. She's always late on Fridays. And Saturdays." And, he thought, Wednesdays and Thursdays, too.

Damon nodded again. And, as Frank reached the door and switched off the light: "Dad, does she sing pretty?"

"Like a bird, pal," he said, grinning. "Like a bird."

The voice was small in the dark: "I love you, dad."

Frank swallowed hard, and nodded before he realized the boy couldn't see him. "Well, pal, it seems I love you, too. Now you'd better get some rest."

"I thought you were going to get lost in the fog."

Frank stopped the move to close the door. He'd better get some rest himself, he thought; that sounded like a threat.

"Not me," he finally said. "You'd always come for me, right?"

"Right, dad."

Frank grinned, closed the door, and wandered through the small house for nearly half an hour before finding himself in the kitchen, his hands waving at his sides for something to do. Coffee. No. He'd already had too much of that today. But the walk had chilled him, made his bones seem brittle. Warm milk, maybe, and he opened the refrigerator, stared, then took out a container and poured half its contents into a pot. He stood by the stove, every few seconds stirring a finger through the milk to check its progress. Stupid cat, he thought; there ought to be a law against doing something like that to a small boy that never hurt anyone, never had anyone to hurt.

He poured himself a glass, smiling when he didn't spill a

drop, but he refused to turn around and look up at the clock; instead, he stared at the flames as he finished the second glass, wondering what it would be like to stick his finger into the fires. He read somewhere . . . he thought he'd read somewhere that the blue near the center was the hottest part and it wasn't so bad elsewhere. His hand wavered, but he changed his mind, not wanting to risk a burn on something he only thought he had read; besides, he decided as he headed into the living room, the way things were going these days, he probably had it backward.

He sat in an armchair flanking the television, took out a magazine from the rack at his side and had just found the table of contents when he heard a car door slam in the drive. He waited, looked up and smiled when the front door swung open and Susan rushed in. She blew him a distant kiss, mouthed *I'll be back in a second*, and ran up the stairs. She was much shorter than he, her hair waist-long black and left free to fan in the wind of her own making. She'd been taking vocal lessons for several years now, and when they'd moved to the Station when Damon was five, she had landed a job singing at the Chancellor Inn. Torch songs, love songs, slow songs, sinner songs; she was liked well enough to be asked to stay on after the first night, but she began so late that Damon had never heard her. And for the last six months, the two-nights-a-week became four, and Frank became adept at cooking supper.

When she returned, her make-up was gone and she was in a shimmering green robe. She flopped on the sofa opposite him and rubbed her knees, her thighs, her upper arms. "If that creep drummer tries to pinch me again, so help me I'll castrate him."

"That is hardly the way for a lady to talk," he said, smiling. "If you're not careful, I'll have to punish you. Whips at thirty paces."

In the old days—the very old days, he thought—she would have laughed and entered a game that would last for nearly an hour. Lately, however, and tonight, she only frowned at him as though she were dealing with a dense, unlettered child. He ignored it, and listened politely as she detailed her evening, the customers, the compliments, the raise she was looking for so she could buy her own car.

"You don't need a car," he said without thinking.

"But aren't you tired of walking home every night?"

He closed the magazine and dropped it on the floor. "Lawyers, my dear, are a sedentary breed. I could use the exercise."

"If you didn't work so late on those damned briefs," she said without looking at him, "and came to bed on time, I'd give you all the exercise you need."

He looked at his watch. It was going on two.

"The cat's gone."

"Oh no," she said. "No wonder you look so tired. You go out after him?"

He nodded, and she rolled herself suddenly into a sitting position. "Not with Damon."

"No. He was in bed when I came home."

She said nothing more, only examined her nails. He watched her closely, the play of her hair falling over her face, the squint that told him her contact lenses were still on her dresser. And he knew she meant: *did you take Damon with you?* She was asking if Damon had followed him. Like the night in the fog, with the woman; like the times at the office; like the dozens of other instances when the boy just happened to show up at the courthouse, in the park while Frank was eating lunch under a tree, at a nearby friend's house late one evening, claiming to have had a nightmare and the sitter wouldn't help him.

Like a shadow.

Like a conscience.

"Are you going to replace it?" He blinked. "The cat, stupid. Are you going to get him a new cat?"

He shook his head. "We've had too much bad luck with animals. I don't think he could take it again."

She swung herself off the sofa and stood in front of him,

her hands on her hips, her lips taut, her eyes narrowed. "You don't care about him, do you?"

"What?"

"He follows you around like a goddamn pet because he's afraid of losing you, and you won't even buy him a lousy puppy or something. You're something else again, Frank, you really are. I work my tail trying to help—"

"My salary is plenty good enough," he said quickly.

"—this family and you're even trying to get me to stop that, too."

He shoved himself to his feet, his chest brushing against hers and forcing her back. "Listen," he said tightly. "I don't care if you sing your heart out a million times a week, lady, but when it starts to interfere with your duties here—"

"My *duties*?"

"—then yes, I'll do everything I can to make sure you stay home when you're supposed to."

"You're raising your voice. You'll wake Damon."

The argument was familiar, and old, and so was the rage he felt stiffening his muscles. But this time she wouldn't stop when she saw his anger. She kept on, and on, and he didn't even realize it when his hand lifted and struck her across the cheek. She stumbled back a step, whirled to run out of the room, and stopped.

Damon was standing at the foot of the stairs.

He was sucking his thumb.

He was staring at his father.

"Go to bed, son," Frank said quietly. "Everything's all right."

For the next week the tension in the house was proverbially knife-cutting thick. Damon stayed up as late as he could, sitting by his father as they watched television together or read from the boy's favorite books. Susan remained close, but not touching, humming to herself and playing with her son whenever he left—for the moment—his father's side; each time, however, her smile was more forced, her laughter more strained, and it was apparent to Frank that Damon was merely tolerating her, nothing more. That puzzled him. It was he who had struck her, not the other way around, and the boy's loyalty should have been thrown into his mother's camp. Yet it hadn't. And it was apparent that Susan was growing more resentful of the fact each day. Each hour. Each time Damon walked silently to Frank's side and slid his hand around the man's waist, or into his palm, or into his hip pocket.

He began showing up at the office again, until one afternoon when Susan skidded the car to a halt at the curb and ran out, grabbed the boy and practically threw him, arms and legs thrashing, into the front seat. Frank raced from his desk and out the front door, leaned over and rapped at the window until Susan lowered it.

"What the hell are you doing?" he whispered, with a glance to the boy.

"You hit me, or had you forgotten," she whispered back. "And there's my son's alienation of affection."

He almost straightened. "That's lawyer talk, Susan," he said.

"Not here," she answered. "Not in front of the boy."

He stepped back quickly as the car growled away from the curb, walked in a daze to his desk and sat there, chin in one palm, staring out the window as the afternoon darkened and a faint drizzle began to fall. His secretary muttered something about a court case the following morning, and Frank nodded until she stared at him, gathered her purse and raincoat and left hurriedly. He continued to nod, not knowing the movement, trying to understand what he had done, what both of them had done to bring themselves to this moment. Ambition, surely. A conflict of generations where women were homebodies and women had careers; where men tried to adjust when they couldn't have both. But he had tried, he told himself . . . or he thought he had, until the dishes began to pile up and the dust stayed on the furniture and Damon said *does she sing pretty*?

It's always the children who get hurt, he thought angrily. Held that idea in early December when the separation papers had been prepared and he stood on the front porch watching his car, his wife, and his son drive away from Oxrun Station south toward the city. Damon's face was in the rear window, nose flat, palms flat, hair pressed down over his forehead. He waved, and Frank answered.

I love you, dad.

Frank wiped a hand under his nose and went back inside, searched the house for some liquor and, in failing, went straight to bed where he watched the moonshadows make monsters of the curtains.

"Dad," the boy said, "do I have to go with mommy?"

"I'm afraid so. The judge . . . well, he knows better, believe it or not, what's best right now. Don't worry, pal. I'll see you at Christmas. It won't be forever."

"I don't like it, dad. I'll run away."

"No! You'll do what your mother tells you, you hear me? You behave yourself and go to school every day, and I'll . . . call you whenever I can."

"The city doesn't like me, dad. I want to stay at the Station."

Frank said nothing.

"It's because of the lady, isn't it?"

He had stared, but Susan's back was turned, bent over a suitcase that would not close once it had sprung open again by the front door.

"What are you talking about?" he'd said harshly.

"I told," Damon said as though it were nothing. "You weren't supposed to do that."

When Susan straightened, her smile was grotesque.

And when they had driven away, Damon had said *I love you, dad.*

Frank woke early, made himself breakfast and stood at the back door, looking out into the yard. There was a fog again, nothing unusual as the Connecticut weather fought to stabilize into winter. But as he sipped at his coffee, thinking how large the house had become, how large and how empty, he saw a movement beside the cherry tree in the middle of the yard. The fog swirled, but he was sure . . .

He yanked open the door and shouted: "Damon!"

The fog closed, and he shook his head. Easy, pal, he told himself; you're not cracking up yet.

Days.

Nights.

He called Susan regularly, twice a week at preappointed times. But as Christmas came and Christmas went, she became more terse, and his son more sullen.

"He's getting fine grades, Frank, I'm seeing to that."

"He sounds terrible."

"He's losing a little weight, that's all. Picks up colds easily. It takes a while, Frank, to get used to the city."

"He doesn't like the city."

"It's his home. He will."

In mid-January Susan did not answer the phone and finally, in desperation, he called the school, was told that Damon had been in the hospital for nearly a week. The nurse thought it was something like pneumonia.

When he arrived that night, the waiting room was crowded with drab bundles of scarves and overcoats, whispers and moans and a few muffled sobs. Susan was standing by the window, looking out at the lights far colder than stars. She didn't turn when she heard him, didn't answer when he demanded to know why she had not contacted him. He grabbed her shoulder and spun her around; her eyes were dull, her face pinched with red hints of cold.

"All right," she said. "All right, Frank, it's because I didn't want you to upset him."

"What the hell are you talking about?"

"He would have seen you and he would have wanted to go back to Oxrun." Her eyes narrowed. "This is his home, Frank! He's got to learn to live with it."

"I'll get a lawyer."

She smiled. "Do that. You do that, Frank."

He didn't have to. He saw Damon a few minutes later and

could not stay more than a moment. The boy was in dim light and almost invisible, too thin to be real beneath the clear plastic tent and the tubes and the monitors . . . too frail, the doctor said in professional conciliation, too frail for too long, and Frank remembered the day on the porch with the saucer of milk when he had thought the same thing and had thought nothing of it.

He returned after the funeral, all anger gone. He had accused Susan of murder, knowing at the time how foolish it had been, but feeling better for it in his own absolution. He had apologized. Had been, for the moment, forgiven.

Had stepped off the train, had wept, had taken a deep breath and decided to live on.

Returned to the office the following day, piled folders onto his desk and hid behind them for most of the morning. He looked up only once, when his secretary tried to explain about a new client's interest, and saw around her waist the indistinct form of his son peering through the window.

"Damon," he muttered, brushed the woman to one side and ran out to the sidewalk. A fog encased the road whitely, but he could see nothing, not even a car, not even the blinking amber light at the nearest intersection.

Immediately after lunch he dialed Susan's number, stared at the receiver when there was no answer and returned it to the cradle. Wondering.

"You look pale," his secretary said softly. She pointed with a pencil at his desk. "You've already done a full day's work. Why don't you go home and lie down? I can lock up. I don't mind."

He smiled, turned as she held his coat for him, touched her cheek . . . and froze.

Damon was in the window.

No, he told himself . . . and Damon was gone.

He rested for two days, returned to work and lost himself in a battle over a will probated by a judge he thought nothing less than senile, to be charitable. He tried calling Susan again, and again received no answer.

And Damon would not leave him alone.

When there was fog, rain, clouds, wind . . . he would be there by the window, there by the cherry tree, there in the darkest corner of the porch.

He knew it was guilt, for not fighting hard enough to keep his son with him, thinking that if he had the boy might still be alive; seeing his face everywhere and the accusations that if the boy loved him, why wasn't he loved just as much in return?

By February's end he decided it was time to make a friendly call on a fellow professional, a doctor who shared the office building with him. It wasn't so much the faces that he saw— he had grown somewhat accustomed to them and assumed they would vanish in time—but that morning there had been snow on the ground; and in the snow by the cherry tree the footprints of a small boy. When he brought the doctor to the yard to show him, they were gone.

"You're quite right, Frank. You're feeling guilty. But not because of the boy in and of himself. The law and the leanings of most judges are quite clear—you couldn't be expected to keep him at his age. You're still worrying yourself about that woman you kissed and the fact that Damon saw you; and the fact that you think you could have saved his life somehow, even if the doctors couldn't; and lastly, the fact that you weren't able to give him things like pets, like that cat. None of it is your fault, really. It's merely something unpleasant you'll have to face up to. Now."

Though he didn't feel all that much better, Frank appreciated the calm that swept over him when the talk was done and they had parted. He worked hard for the rest of the day, for the rest of the week, but he knew that it was not guilt and it was not his imagination and it was not anything the doctor would be able to explain away when he opened his door on Saturday morning and found, lying carefully atop his newspaper, the white-faced Siamese. Dead. Its neck broken.

He stumbled back over the threshold, whirled around and raced into the downstairs bathroom where he fell onto his knees beside the bowl and lost his breakfast. The tears were acid, the sobs like blows to his lungs and stomach, and by the time he had pulled himself together, he knew what was happening.

The doctor, the secretary, even his wife . . . they were all wrong.

There was no guilt.

There was only . . . Damon.

A little boy with large brown eyes who loved his father. Who loved his father so much that he would never leave him. Who loved his father so much that he was going to make sure, absolutely sure, that he would never be alone.

You've been a bad boy, Daddy.

Frank stumbled to his feet, into the kitchen, leaned against the back door. There was a figure by the cherry tree dark and formless; but he knew there was no use running outside. The figure would vanish.

You never did like that cat, daddy. Or the dogs. Or mommy.

The telephone rang. He took his time getting to it, stared at it dumbly for several moments before lifting the receiver. He could see straight down the hall and into the kitchen. He had not turned on the overhead light and, as a consequence, could see through the small panes of the back door to the yard beyond. The air outside was heavy with impending snow. Gray. Almost lifeless.

"Frank? Frank, it's Susan. Frank, I've been thinking . . . about you and me . . . and what happened."

He kept his eyes on the door. "It's done, Sue. Done."

"Frank, I don't know what happened. Honest to God, I was trying, really I was. He was getting the best grades in school, had lots of friends . . . I even bought him a little dog, a poodle, two weeks before he . . . I don't know what happened, Frank! I woke up this morning and all of a sudden I was so damned *alone*. Frank, I'm frightened. Can . . . can I come home?"

The gray darkened. There was a shadow on the porch, much longer now than the shadow in the yard.

''No,'' he said.

''He thought about you all the damned time,'' she said, her voice rising into hysteria. ''He tried to run away once, to get back to you.''

The shadow filled the panes, the windows on either side, and suddenly there was static on the line and Susan's voice vanished. He dropped the receiver and turned around.

In the front.

Shadows.

He heard the furnace humming, but the house was growing cold.

The lamp in the living room flickered, died, shone brightly for a moment before the bulb shattered.

He was . . . wrong.

God, he was wrong!

Damon . . . Damon didn't love him.

Not since the night on the corner in the fog; not since the night he had not really tried to locate a cat with a milk white face.

Damon knew.

And Damon didn't love him.

He dropped to his hands and knees and searched in the darkness for the receiver, found it and nearly threw it away when the bitterly cold plastic threatened to burn through his fingers.

''Susan!'' he shouted. ''Susan, dammit, can you hear me?''

A bad boy, daddy.

There was static, but he thought he could hear her crying into the wind.

''Susan . . . Susan, this is crazy, I've no time to explain, but you've got to help me. You've got to do something for me.''

Daddy.

''Susan, please . . . he'll be back, I know he will. Don't ask me how, but I know! Listen, you've got to do something for me. Susan, dammit, can you hear me?''

Daddy, I'm—

''For God's sake, Susan, if Damon comes, tell him I'm sorry!''

home.

Manly Wade Wellman

VANDY, VANDY

Manly Wade Wellman was a prolific writer for the pulp magazines in the 1930s and 1940s whose work appeared in many genres. Today he is remembered for that portion of his work, principally from *Weird Tales* magazine, that is horror fiction, and for a series of regional horror tales published in the 1950s in *The Magazine of Fantasy and Science Fiction* (alongside Shirley Jackson's stories and the works of Matheson, Sturgeon and most of the other masters of that decade). Now called the "Silver John" stories and novels, these supernatural tales of an itinerant, John, whose guitar is strung with silver strings, are rich in Southern U.S. folklore and settings. John meets a variety of supernatural evils but perhaps the most typical, and one of Wellman's finest achievements, is the historic warlock of "Vandy, Vandy." Wellman's best stories are collected in *Worse Things Waiting* (1973) and *Who Fears the Devil?* (1963).

Nary name that valley had. Such outside folks as knew about it just said, "Back in yonder," and folks inside said, "Here." The mail truck would drop a few letters in a hollow tree next to a ridge where the trail went up and over and down. Three-four times a year bearded men in homemade clothes and shoes fetched out their makings—clay dishes and pots, mostly—for dealers to sell to the touristers. They toted back coffee, salt, gunpowder, a few nails. Stuff like that.

It was a day's scramble along that ridge trail. I vow, even with my long legs and no load but my silver-strung guitar. The thick, big old trees had never been cut, for lumber nor yet for cleared land. I found a stream, quenched my thirst, and followed it down. Near sunset time, I heard music a-jangling, and headed for that.

Fire shone out through an open cabin door, to where folks sat on a stoop log and front-yard rocks. One had a banjo, another fiddled, and the rest slapped hands so a boy about ten or twelve could jig. Then they spied me and fell quiet. They looked at me, but they didn't know me.

"That was right pretty, ladies and gentlemen," I said, walking in, but nobody remarked.

A long-bearded old man with one suspender and no shoes held the fiddle on his knee. I reckoned he was the grandsire. A younger, shorter-bearded man with the banjo might could be his son. There was a dry old mother, there was the son's plump wife, there was a young yellow-haired girl, and there was that dancing little grandboy.

"What can we do for you, young sir?" the old man asked. Not that he sounded like doing aught—mountain folks say that even to the government man who comes hunting a still on their place.

"Why," I said, "I sort of want a place to sleep."

"Right much land to stretch out on down the hollow a piece," said the banjo man.

I tried again. "I was hearing you folks play first part of *Fire in the Mountains*."

"Is they two parts?" That was the boy, before anyone could silence him.

"Sure enough, son," I said. "I'll play you the second part."

The old man opened his beard, like enough to say wait till I was asked, but I strummed my guitar into second part, best

I knew how. Then I played the first part through, and, "You sure God can pick that," said the short-bearded one. "Do it again."

I did it again. When I reached the second part, the fiddle and banjo joined me in. We went round *Fire in the Mountains* one time more, and the lady-folks clapped hands and the boy jigged. When we stopped, the old man made me a nod.

"Sit on that there rock," he said. "What might we call you?"

"My name's John."

"I'm Tewk Millen. Mother, I reckon John's a-tired, coming from outside. Might be he'd relish a gourd of cold water."

"We're just before having a bite," the old lady said to me. "Ain't but just smoke meat and beans, but you're welcome."

"I'm sure enough honored, Mrs. Millen," I said. "But I don't wish to be a trouble to you."

"No trouble," said Mr. Tewk Millen. "Let me make you known to my son Heber and his wife Jill, and this here is their boy Calder."

"Proud to know you, John," they said.

"And my girl Vandy," said Mr. Tewk.

I looked on her hair like yellow corn silk and her eyes like purple violets. "Miss Vandy," I said.

Shy, she dimpled at me. "I know that's a scarce name, Mr. John. I never heard it anywhere but among my kinfolks."

"I have," I said. "It's what brought me here."

Mr. Tewk Millen looked funny above his whiskers. "Thought you was a young stranger-man."

"I heard the name outside, in a song, sir. Somebody allowed the song's known here. I'm a singer, I go a far piece after a good song." I looked around. "Do you folks know that Vandy song?"

"Yes, sir," said little Calder, but the others studied a minute. Mr. Tewk rubbed up a leaf of tobacco into his pipe.

"Calder," he said, "go in and fetch me a chunk of fire to light up with. John, you certain sure you never met my girl Vandy?"

"Sure as can be," I replied him. "Only I can figure how any young fellow might come long miles to meet her."

She stared down at her hands in her lap. "We learnt the song from papa," she half-whispered, "and he learnt it from his papa."

"And my papa learnt it from his," finished Mr. Tewk for her. "I reckon that song goes long years back."

"I'd relish hearing it," I said.

"After you learnt it yourself," said Mr. Tewk, "what would you do then?"

"Go back outside," I said, "and sing it some."

He enjoyed to hear me say that. "Heber," he told his son, "you pick out and I'll scrape this fiddle, and Calder and Vandy can sing it for John."

They played the tune through once without words. The notes came together lonesomely, in what schooled folks call minors. But other folks, better schooled yet, say such tunes come out strange and lonesome because in the ancient times folks had another note-scale from our do-re-mi-fa today. Little Calder piped up, high and young but strong:

"Vandy, Vandy, I've come to court you,
   Be you rich or be you poor,
   And if you'll kindly entertain me,
   I will love you forever more.

"Vandy, Vandy, I've gold and silver,
   Vandy, Vandy, I've a house and land,
   Vandy, Vandy, I've a world of pleasure,
   I would make you a handsome man. . . ."

He sang that far for the fellow come courting, and Vandy sang back the reply, sweet as a bird:

"I love a man who's in the army,
    He's been there for seven long years,
    And if he's there for seven years longer,
    I won't court no other dear.

"What care I for your gold and silver,
    What care I for—"

She stopped, and the fiddle and banjo stopped, and it was
like the sudden death of sound. The leaves didn't rustle in
the trees, nor the fire didn't stir on the hearth inside. They
all looked with their mouths half open, where somebody
stood with his hands crossed on the gold knob of a black
cane and grinned all on one side of his toothy mouth.

Maybe he'd come down the stream trail, maybe he'd
dropped from a tree like a possum. He was built slim and
spry, with a long coat buttoned to his pointed chin, and brown
pants tucked into elastic-sided boots, like what your grandsire wore. His hands on the cane looked slim and strong. His
face, bar its crooked smile, might could be called handsome.
His dark brown hair curled like buffalo wool, and his eyes
were as shiny pale gray as a new knife. Their gaze crawled
all over us, and he laughed a slow, soft laugh.

"I thought I'd stop by," he crooned out, "if I haven't worn
out my welcome."

"Oh, *no*, sir!" said Mr. Tewk, quick standing up on his
two bare feet, fiddle in hand. "No, sir, Mr. Loden, we're
right proud to have you," he jabber-squawked, like a rooster
caught by the leg. "You sit down, sir, make yourself easy."

Mr. Loden sat down on the rock Mr. Tewk had got up
from, and Mr. Tewk found a place on the stoop log by his
wife, nervous as a boy caught stealing apples.

"Your servant, Mrs. Millen," said Mr. Loden. "Heber,
you look well, and your good wife. Calder, I brought you
candy."

His slim hand offered a bright striped stick, red and yellow. You'd think a country child would snatch it. But Calder

took it slow and scared, as he'd take a poison snake. You'd know he'd decline if only he dared, but he didn't dare.

"For you, Mr. Tewk," went on Mr. Loden, "I fetched some of my tobacco, an excellent weed." He handed out a soft brown leather pouch. "Empty your pipe and fill it with this."

"Thank you kindly," said Mr. Tewk, and sighed, and began to do as he'd been ordered.

"Miss Vandy." Mr. Loden's crooning voice petted her name. "I wouldn't venture here without hoping you'd receive a trifle at my hands."

He dangled it from a chain, a gold thing the size of his pink thumbnail. In it shone a white jewel that grabbed the firelight and twinkled red.

"Do me the honor, Miss Vandy, to let it rest on your heart, that I may envy it."

She took the thing and sat with it between her soft little hands. Mr. Loden's eye-knives turned on me.

"Now," he said, "we come round to the stranger within your gates."

"We come around to me," I agreed him, hugging my guitar on my knees. "My name's John, sir."

"Where are you from, John?" It was sudden, almost fierce, like a lawyer in court.

"From nowhere," I said.

"Meaning, from everywhere," he supplied me. "What do you do?"

"I wander," I said. "I sing songs. I mind my business and watch my manners."

"*Touché!*" he cried out in a foreign tongue, and smiled on that one side of his mouth. "My duties and apologies, John, if my country ways seem rude to a world traveler. No offense meant."

"None taken," I said, and didn't add that country ways are most times polite ways.

"Mr. Loden," put in Mr. Tewk again, "I make bold to offer you what poor rations my old woman's made for us—"

"They're good enough for the best man living," Mr. Loden broke him off. "I'll help Mrs. Millen prepare them. After you, ma'am."

She walked in, and he followed. What he said there was what happened.

"Miss Vandy," he said over his shoulder, "you might help."

She went in, too. Dishes clattered. Through the doorway I saw Mr. Loden fling a tweak of powder in the skillet. The menfolks sat outside and said naught. They might have been nailed down, with stones in their mouths. I studied what might could make a proud, honorable mountain family so scared of a guest, and knew it wouldn't be a natural thing. It would be a thing beyond nature or the world.

Finally little Calder said, "Maybe we'll finish the singing after while," and his voice was a weak young voice now.

"I recollect another song from around here," I said. "About the fair and blooming wife."

Those closed mouths all snapped open, then shut again. Touching the silver strings, I began:

> "There was a fair and blooming wife
> And of children she had three,
> She sent them to Northern school
> To study gramarie.
>
> "But the King's men came upon that school,
> And when sword and rope had done,
> Of the children three she sent away,
> Returned to her but one. . . ."

"Supper's made," said Mrs. Millen from inside.

We went in to where there was a trestle table and a clean home-woven cloth and clay dishes set out. Mr. Loden, by the pots at the fire, waved for Mrs. Millen and Vandy to dish up the food.

It wasn't smoke meat and beans I saw on my plate. Whatever it might be, it wasn't that. They all looked at their helps of food, but not even Calder took any till Mr. Loden sat down.

"Why," said Mr. Loden, "one would think you feared poison."

Then Mr. Tewk forked up a bit and put it into his beard. Calder did likewise, and the others. I took a mouthful; sure enough, it tasted good.

"Let me honor your cooking, sir," I told Mr. Loden. "It's like witch magic."

His eyes came on me, and he laughed, short and sharp.

"John, you were singing about the blooming wife," he said. "She had three children who went North to study gramarie. Do you know what gramarie means?"

"Grammar," spoke up Calder. "The right way to talk."

"Hush," whispered his father, and he hushed.

"Why," I replied. "Mr. Loden, I've heard that gramarie is witch stuff, witch knowledge and power. That Northern school could have been at only one place."

"What place, John?" he almost sang under his breath.

"A Massachusetts Yankee town called Salem. Around three hundred years back—"

"Not by so much," said Mr. Loden. "In 1692, John."

Everybody was staring above those steaming plates.

"A preacher-man named Cotton Mather found them teaching the witch stuff to children," I said. "I hear tell they killed twenty folks, mostly the wrong ones, but two-three were sure enough witches."

"George Burroughs," said Mr. Loden, half to himself. "Martha Carrier. And Bridget Bishop. They were real. But others got safe away, and one young child of the three. Somebody owed that child the two young lost lives of his brothers, John."

"I call something else to mind," I said. "They scare young folks with the tale. The one child lived to be a hundred, and his son likewise and a hundred years of life, and his son's son a hundred more. Maybe that's why I thought the witch school at Salem was three hundred years back.''

"Not by so much, John," he said again. "Even give that child that got away the age of Calder there, it would be only about two hundred and eighty years, or thereabouts.''

He was daring any of Mr. Tewk Millen's family to speak or even breathe heavy, and none took the dare.

"From three hundred, that would leave twenty," I reckoned. "A lot can be done in twenty years, Mr. Loden."

"That's the naked truth," he said, the knives of his eyes on Vandy's young face, and he got up and bowed all round. "I thank you all for your hospitality. I'll come again if I may."

"Yes, sir," said Mr. Tewk in a hurry, but Mr. Loden looked at Vandy and waited.

"Yes, sir," she told him, as if it would choke her.

He took his gold-headed cane, and gazed a hard gaze at me. Then I did a rude thing, but it was all I could think of.

"I don't feel right, Mrs. Millen, not paying for what you gave me," I allowed, getting up myself. From my dungaree pocket I took a silver quarter and dropped it on the table, right in front of Mr. Loden.

"Take it away!" he squeaked, high as a bat, and out of the house he was gone, bat-quick and bat-sudden.

The others gopped after him. Outside the night had fallen, thick as black wool round the cabin. Mr. Tewk cleared his throat.

"John, I hope you're better raised than that," he said. "We don't take money from nobody we bid to our table. Pick it up."

"Yes, sir, I ask pardon."

Putting away the quarter, I felt a mite better. I'd done that one other time with a silver quarter, I'd scared Mr. Onselm almost out of the black art. So Mr. Loden was a witch man, too, and could be scared the same way. I reckon I was foolish for the lack of sense to think it would be as easy as that.

I walked outside, leaving Mrs. Millen and Vandy to do the

dishes. The firelight showed me the stoop log to sit on. I touched my guitar strings and began to pick out the *Vandy, Vandy* tune, soft and gentle. After while, Calder came out and sat beside me and sang the words. I liked the best the last verse:

"Wake up, wake up! The dawn is breaking.
Wake up, wake up! It's almost day.
"Open up your doors and your divers windows,
See my true love march away. . . ."

"Mr. John," said Calder, "I never made sure what divers windows is."

"That's an old-timey word," I said. "It means different kinds of windows. Another thing proves it's a right old song. A man seven years in the army must have gone to the first war with the English. It lasted longer here in the South than other places—from 1775 to 1782. How old are you, Calder?"

"Rising onto ten."

"Big for your age. A boy your years in 1692 would be a hundred if he lived to 1782, when the English war was near done and somebody or other had been seven years in the army."

"Washington's army," said Calder. "King Washington."

"King who?" I asked.

"Mr. Loden calls him King Washington—the man that hell-drove the English soldiers and rules in his own name town."

So that's what they thought in that valley. I never said that Washington was no king but a president, and that he'd died and gone to his rest when his work was done and his country safe. I kept thinking about somebody a hundred years old in 1782, trying to court a girl whose true love was seven years marched off in the army.

"Calder," I said, "does the *Vandy, Vandy* song tell about your own folks?"

He looked into the cabin. Nobody listened. I struck a chord on the silver strings. He said, "I've heard tell so, Mr. John."

I hushed the strings with my hand, and he talked on:

"I reckon you've heard some about it. That witch child that lived to be a hundred—he come courting a girl named Vandy, but she was a good girl."

"Bad folks sometimes try to court good ones," I said.

"She wouldn't have him, not with all his land and money. And when he pressed her, her soldier man come home, and in his hand was his discharge-writing, and on it King Washington's name. He was free from the war. He was Hosea Tewk, my grandsire some few times removed. And my own grandsire's mother was Vandy Tewk, and my sister is Vandy Millen."

"What about the hundred-year-old witch man?"

Calder looked round again. Then he said, "I reckon he got him some other girl to birth him a son, and we think that son married at another hundred years, and his son is Mr. Loden, the grandson of the first witch man."

"Your grandsire's mother, Vandy Tewk—how old would she be, Calder?"

"She's dead and gone, but she was born the first year her pa was off fighting the Yankees."

Eighteen sixty-one, then. In 1882, end of the second hundred years, she'd have been ripe for courting. "And she married a Millen," I said.

"Yes, sir. Even when the Mr. Loden that lived then tried to court her. But she married Mr. Washington Millen. That was my great grandsire. He wasn't feared of aught. He was like King Washington."

I picked a silver string. "No witch man got the first Vandy," I reminded him. "Nor yet the second Vandy."

"A witch man wants the Vandy that's here now," said Calder. "Mr. John, I wish you'd steal her away from him."

I got up. "Tell your folks I've gone for a night walk."

"Not to Mr. Loden's." His face was pale beside me. "He won't let you come."

The night was more than black then, it was solid. No sound in it. No life. I won't say I couldn't have stepped off into it, but I didn't. I sat down again. Mr. Tewk spoke my name, then Vandy.

We sat in front of the cabin and spoke about weather and crops. Vandy was at my one side, Calder at the other. We sang—*Dream True*, I recollect, and *The Rebel Soldier*. Vandy sang the sweetest I'd ever heard, but while I played I felt that somebody harked in the blackness. If it was on Yandro Mountain and not in the valley, I'd have feared the Behinder sneaking close, or the Flat under our feet. But Vandy's violet eyes looked happy at me, her rose lips smiled.

Finally Vandy and Mrs. Millen said good night and went into a back room. Heber and his wife and Calder laddered up into the loft. Mr. Tewk offered to make me a pallet bed by the fire.

"I'll sleep at the door," I told him.

He looked at me, at the door. And: "Have it your way," he said.

I pulled off my shoes. I said a prayer and stretched out on the quilt he gave me. But long after the others must have been sleeping, I lay and listened.

Hours afterward, the sound came. The fire was just only a coal ember, red light was soft in the cabin when I heard the snicker. Mr. Loden stooped over me at the door sill.

"I won't let you come in," I said to him.

"Oh, you're awake," he said. "The others are asleep, by my doing. And you can't move, any more than they can."

It was true. I couldn't sit up. I might have been dried into clay, like a frog or a lizard that must wait for the rain.

"Bind," he said above me. "Bind, bind. Unless you can count the stars or the ocean drops, be bound."

It was a spell saying. "From the *Long-Lost Friend*?" I asked.

"Albertus Magnus. The book they say he wrote."

"I've seen the book."

"You'll lie where you are till sunrise. Then—"

I tried to get up. It was no use.

"See this?" He held it to my face. It was my picture,

drawn true to how I looked. He had the drawing gift. "At sunrise I'll strike it with this."

He laid the picture on the ground. Then he brought forward his gold-headed cane. He twisted the handle, and out of the cane's inside he drew a blade of pale iron, thin and mean as a snake. There was writing on it, but I couldn't read in that darkness.

"I'll touch my point to your picture," he said. "Then you'll bother Vandy and me no more. I should have done that to Hosea Tewk."

"Hosea Tewk," I said after him, "or Washington Millen."

The tip of his blade stirred in front of my eyes. "Don't say that name, John."

"Washington Millen," I said it again. "Named for George Washington. Did you hate Washington when you knew him?"

He took a long, mean breath, as if cold rain fell on him. "You've guessed what these folks haven't guessed, John."

"I've guessed you're not a witch man's grandson, but a witch woman's son," I said. "You got free from that Salem school in 1692. You've lived near three hundred years, and when they're over, you know where you'll go and burn, forever amen."

His blade hung over my throat, like a wasp over a ripe peach. Then he drew it back. "No," he told himself. "The Millens would know I'd stabbed you. Let them think you died in your sleep."

"You knew Washington," I said again. "Maybe—"

"Maybe I offered him help, and he was foolish enough to refuse it. Maybe—"

"Maybe Washington scared you off from him," I broke in the way he had, "and won his war without your witch magic. And maybe that was bad for you, because the one who'd given you three hundred years expected pay—good hearts turned into bad ones. Then you tried to win Vandy for yourself, the first Vandy."

"A little for myself," he half sang, "but mostly for—"

"Mostly for who gave you three hundred years," I finished for him.

I was tightening and swelling my muscles, trying to pull a-loose from what held me down. I might as well have tried to wear my way through solid rock.

"Vandy," Mr. Loden's voice touched her name. "The third Vandy, the sweetest and the best. She's like a spring day and like a summer night. When I see her with a bucket at the spring or a basket in the garden, my eyes swim, John. It's as if I see a spirit walking past."

"A good spirit," I said. "Your time's short. You want to win her from good ways to bad ways."

"Her voice is like a lark's," he crooned, the blade low in his hand. "It's like wind over a bank of roses and violets. It's like the light of stars turned into music."

"And you want to lead her down into hell," I said.

"Maybe we won't go to hell, or to heaven either. Maybe we'll live and live. Why don't you say something about that, John?"

"I'm thinking," I made answer, and I was. I was trying to remember what I had to remember.

It's in the third part of the Albertus Magnus book Mr. Loden had mentioned, the third part full of holy names he sure enough would never read. I'd seen it, as I'd told him. If the words would come back to me—

Something sent part of them.

"The cross in my right hand," I said, too soft for him to hear, "that I may travel the open land . . . ."

"Maybe three hundred years more," said Mr. Loden, "without anyone like Hosea Tewk, or Washington Millen, or you, John, to stop us. Three hundred years with Vandy, and she'll know the things I know, do the things I do."

I'd been able to twist my right forefinger over my middle one, for the cross in my right hand. I said more words as I remembered:

". . . So must I be loosed and blessed, as the cup and the holy bread. . . ."

Now my left hand could creep along my side, as far as my belt. But it couldn't lift up just yet, because I couldn't think of the rest of the charm.

"The night's black just before dawn," Mr. Loden was saying. "I'll make my fire. When I've done what I'll do, I can step over your dead body, and Vandy's mine."

"Don't you fear Washington?" I asked him, and my left fingertips were in my dungaree pocket.

"Can he come from the place to which he's gone? Washington has forgotten me and our old falling-out."

"Where he is, he remembers you," I said.

Mr. Loden was on his knee. His blade point scratched a circle round him on the ground. The circle held him and the paper with my picture. Then he took a sack from inside his coat, and poured powder along the scratched circle. He stood up, and golden-brown fire jumped up around him.

"Now we begin," he said.

He sketched in the air with his blade. He put his boot toe on my picture. He looked into the golden-brown fire.

"I made my wish before this," he spaced out the words. "I make it now. There was no day when I have not seen my wish fulfilled."

Paler than the fire shone his eyes.

"No son to follow John. No daughter to mourn him."

My fingers in my pocket touched something round and thin. The quarter he'd been scared by, that Mr. Tewk Millen had made me take back.

Mr. Loden spoke names I didn't like to hear. "Haade," he said. "Mikaded. Rakeben. Rika. Tasarith. Modeka."

My hand worried out, and in it the quarter.

"Truth," said Mr. Loden. "Tumch. Here with this image I slay—"

I lifted my left hand three inches and flung the quarter. My heart went rotten with sick sorrow, for it didn't hit Mr. Loden—it fell into the fire—

Then in one place up there shot white smoke, like a steam puff from an engine, and the fire died down everywhere else.

Mr. Loden stopped his spell-speaking and wavered back. I saw the glow of his goggling eyes and of his open mouth.

Where the steamy smoke had puffed, it was making a shape.

Taller than a man. Taller than Mr. Loden or me. Wide-shouldered, long-legged, with a dark tail coat and high boots and hair tied back behind the head. It turned, and I saw the brave face, the big, big nose—

"King Washington!" screamed out Mr. Loden, and tried to stab.

But a long hand like a tongs caught his wrist, and I heard the bones break like dry sticks, and Mr. Loden whinnied like a horse that's been bad hurt. That was the grip of the man who'd been America's strongest, who could jump twenty-four feet broad or throw a dollar across the Rappahannock River or wrestle down his biggest soldier.

The other hand came across, flat and stiff, to strike. It sounded like a door a-slamming in a high wind, and Mr. Loden never needed to be struck the second time. His head sagged over widewise. When the grip left his broken wrist, he fell at the booted feet.

I sat up, and stood up. The big nose turned to me, just a second. The head nodded. Friendly. Then it was gone back into steam, into nothing.

I'd said the truth. Where George Washington had been, he'd remembered Mr. Loden. And the silver quarter, with his picture on it, had struck the fire just when Mr. Loden was conjuring with a picture he was making real. And then there had happened what had happened.

A pale streak went up the back sky for the first dawn. There was no fire left, and of the quarter was just a spatter of melted silver. And there was no Mr. Loden, only a mouldy little heap like a rotted-out stump or a hammock or loam or what might could be left of a man that death had caught up with after two hundred years. I picked up the iron blade and broke it on my knee and flung it away into the trees. Then I picked up the paper with my drawn picture. It wasn't hurt a bit, and it looked a right much like me.

Inside the door I put that picture, on the quilt where I'd lain. Maybe the Millens would keep it to remember me by, after they found I was gone and that Mr. Loden came round no more to try to court Vandy. Then I started away, carrying my guitar. If I made good time, I'd be out of the valley by high noon.

As I went, pots started to rattle. Somebody was awake in the cabin. And it was hard, hard, not to turn back when Vandy sang to herself, not thinking what she sang:

> "Wake up, wake up! The dawn is breaking.
> Wake up, wake up! It's almost day.
> Open up your doors and your divers windows,
> See my true love march away. . . ."